THEME SONG FOR AN OLD SHOW

THEME SONG FOR AN OLD SHOW

A Novel by

JEFFREY LEWIS

Other Press • New York

Production Editor: Mira S. Park
Text design: Natalya Balnova
This book was set in 11.5 pt. ACaslon Regular by Alpha Graphics of Pittsfield, NH.

10 9 8 7 6 5 4 3 2 1

Library of Congress Cataloging-in-Publication Data

Lewis, Jeffrey.
  Theme song for an old show : a novel / by Jeffrey Lewis.
    p. cm.
  ISBN-13: 978-1-59051-233-3 (acid-free paper)
  ISBN-10: 1-59051-233-2 (acid-free paper)   1. Fathers and sons–
Fiction.   2. Hollywood (Los Angeles, Calif.)–Fiction.   I. Title.
  PS3612.E965T47 2007
  813'.6–dc22

                                        2006024583

To my parents

In a cavern, in a canyon,
Excavating for a mine,
Dwelt a miner, forty-niner,
And his daughter Clementine.

Refrain:
Oh my darling, oh my darling,
Oh my darling Clementine,
You are lost and gone forever,
Dreadful sorry, Clementine.

CALIFORNIA

MY FATHER HAD A FRIEND named Gene Lang who went to California in the forties and became a composer for the movies. He lived in a house that had orange trees. You could walk outside and pick oranges off your own tree. I heard about this when I was young. Maybe my father told me about it or maybe he showed me a photograph that he had received. Either way, I formed a sunlit image of these trees with their large orange fruit within easy reach, in the backyard of a house. They were, I suppose, like the trees you might see in a Persian or Indian miniature, in pleasure gardens or gardens meant to represent perfection. Many years later I would put into a TV script that one of our show's main characters, a scruffy former police snitch from the East who's come to California to start over, buys an orange tree in a five-gallon pot on the street and then spends a majority of his time watering it and feeding it and pruning it and fretting when its leaves turn yellow, as though this tree embodied all his hopes for a sunny new beginning. A few years after Gene Lang, my father left my mother and our family and went to California with another woman to become a producer for television, and a little bit also, the movies. I was nine years old then. He moved almost three thousand miles away, which in those days seemed as far as I don't even know what would seem today. The gallery where I stored my dream images of California expanded to include a kidney-shaped pool in Bel Air, surrounded by the sorts of vegetation I'd only ever seen possibly in the bird house at the zoo, tall and weeping, dense and dark, guardians of an exotic life. The fact that the pool was kidney-shaped was particularly important. I wasn't sure what a kidney was shaped like, nor even what a kidney was exactly. If you'd asked me, from my photograph of my father's swimming pool, I might have called it peanut-shaped. But I knew, from magazines, from my mother's talk, that kidney-shaped pools were particularly precious and rare, as if the effort to make the pool's sides other than straight required expense a little beyond reason. No one in our neighborhood in Rochester, where my mother moved us after my father left, had a pool at all, except for the DeKovens and theirs wasn't even sunk in the ground. My father was also in the photograph, placed a little to the side of the pool, the way they place the owners of racehorses in photos of the horse in the winner's circle. He stared through thick-framed sunglasses at the camera, looking proprietary and self-confident. His striped swimming trunks appeared to be dry. He had a short-sleeve shirt on that looked to be made of the same stuff they made towels from—I'd never seen such a thing. But his hairy arms stuck out from the shirt, and these seemed familiar and friendly enough. His hairy arms and legs: when I saw these, I had the feeling of almost claiming him back. Beside him were Irene and her son. The new happy family. My mother didn't even know I had this photograph. I kept it between pages of my stamp album. The only other things I knew about California were from television. The white picket fences and white clapboard houses of the sitcoms, the priapic city hall on *Dragnet*, the Hollywood-and-Vine signs on some early variety show, oversized and preposterously cheerful, as if they deserved an exclamation point at the end of each of them. And somehow I also imagined: a convertible in every driveway. My father was a convertible man. We had convertibles even in New York. An Olds, then a Buick. The convertibles had names. Esmeralda. Esmeralda was lost in the divorce. Really lost, the registration papers got lost in some exchange of documents and nobody seemed able to find them or get them replaced and the car sat in a garage until it was towed for scrap. Or that was the story I was told anyway. Looking back, I'm not sure it makes sense. I didn't know what car my father drove in California, but I was sure it was a convertible, while we in Rochester drove the used '52 Chevy four door that my mother's father sometimes loaned us.

*

One song, too. "Oh My Darling Clementine." Where it entered my brain I never knew, never asked. I suppose everybody knew that song. The miner, the lost daughter, the mournful, sentimental, sappy emblem of the West. But it wasn't sappy to me then. It filled my mind. It was there when I took out the photograph of my father by his pool. It was there when I went to sleep at night dreaming of convertibles and driveways. It was a companion of my solitude.

*

Irene. Made-up name. Maybe not even a good made-up name. What about Phoebe? What about Liz? So many to choose from but I said Irene and I'll stick to it. Irene, so much like Eileen. Or is the "r" in it a little angrier? Irene had her moments of anger. She was rich, she was from New York, so my mother used to say as if that would explain pretty much all of it. "Park Avenue, no less." Irene's father, I would learn one day, made his fortune in war profiteering. I'm not sure in which war, and I suppose it's not the polite way to put it. He supplied socks for the boys overseas. A Park Avenue apartment resulted, and a country place in Connecticut on a lake, and private schools for the girls. Irene went to Sweet Briar College in Virginia. I don't know how many Jewish girls from New York went to Sweet Briar in the late thirties but I imagine not too many. At Sweet Briar Irene played golf and tennis and rode a horse. She was tall enough to be athletic in a lanky way, she looked good in clothes, her face was long and her blue eyes pierced and pleaded as though to say I'm a complicated one and she may have had a nose job along the way. Or anyway her nose was as pretty and complicated as she was. She was "best friends" with my mother in Scarsdale, where we lived before the divorce. How this came about I was never sure, but my father and Irene's husband had been in college together, so it must have had to do with that. The four of them played bridge and golf and tennis. I struggle now to imagine my mother keeping up with all of this. She was a small woman who left home to go to nursing school in New York and met my father while a nurse at a camp in the Poconos and he was a counselor there. He had just finished his third year at Yale, young because he'd skipped grades in school. He rowed her on the lake. They were each other's first lover. My mother joined the Book-of-the-Month Club so she'd know what to say and think. And she acquired golf clubs and a tennis racquet and learned how to drive. And in truth she liked all of these things, but especially the books. She liked books more than my father did, who had gone to Yale but took things more for granted. But how to compete with Irene? I try to imagine my mother, four or five inches shorter than Irene and shy and socially uncertain, trying to drive a ball down the center of a Scarsdale fairway. She was left-handed too, but owned right-handed clubs, because she wanted to do things the way other people did them. After my father left with Irene, she hated them both with a hatred I'd never seen in anyone.

*

I made up an imaginary city from the name of my father's departed friend Gene Lang. The city was Langden and it was on the border of California and Oregon, across from its rival city of Jansen, against which it played in all sports in a thousand foot long stadium. Each was a city of two million. Patrup Langden was Langden's police chief and star pitcher. He won thousands of games each year. Everything in Langden was bigger than it was elsewhere, and more modern, and Langden nearly always beat Jansen. Though Jansen also had its virtues. It was named after a pitcher who won twenty-three games for the New York Giants in 1951. Then the Giants left too, for San Francisco. Everything good seemed to be in California, and for this opinion of mine, or perhaps it was more a feeling, I felt guilty. When Irene was still my mother's best friend, I had found her pretty. One day she came over with her son, who wasn't my friend, and for some reason, in the front yard of our house, she lifted him up and started shaking him and kissing him at the same time. I must have walked into this. I wasn't there when it started. I couldn't tell whether she was angry or happy with him, but I wished she would do that to me too. For this I also later felt guilty. My mother did not have an easy time of it, all of us living with her parents again. She got a modest job in a doctor's office. She made us breakfast and dinner. Privately she must have cursed herself and her trustfulness and the presumption of her leaving home to start with, to go to someplace like New York to nursing school. Who did she think she was? But she didn't say these things to my sister and me. Instead she cursed men.

And how could I really disagree with her? The facts looked pretty bad. Here we were with not enough money living in her parents' house and there he was out in California with her "best friend" and a kidney-shaped swimming pool. Even if all men weren't like this, wasn't I likely to be? Who was she training me up to be, the anti-*him*? I never thought things through quite that way. But I knew I didn't want to be against my father. It wasn't long before his name started appearing on television, at the ends of mysteries or westerns. Though, if she could, my mother would shut the set off before his name came on. But I knew it was there. I'd seen it a few times. And it was actually better, I thought, that she shut it off, because if she left it on it would give her another chance to curse him. When his check was late, which it often was, she cursed him. When it was too small, which it always was, she cursed him. Or she would be silent and bitter. And who was I to blame her, who had liked Irene when she tossed her son up and down and wished it were me being tossed and kissed? Where was my backbone, what sort of boy/man was I? There was a time for a person to take sides and say what was right. Which I would then do. I wrote him letters of reasoned complaint. We could use this, we could use that, surely he could see the reasonableness of my mother's position. He told me my mother was putting me up to things. He explained everything from his own point of view, and then that would seem reasonable too.

This would take place in phone conversations. The phone in my grandparents' house was on the stairs, in the middle of the house. The phone would ring and someone would call out "long distance," and life in the house would freeze, as if it were one of the games of red light/green light that my sister and I played outside and the person who was it had just shouted "red light." I felt every word I said on the phone was being heard by several sets of ears. And surely it was. I could barely get words out on the phone. I never said what I meant. I wondered what it was like at the other end of the line, in California.

Then, after a long enough time had passed, my chance. My father asked me if I would like to come to Los Angeles over my summer vacation. This, too, was said on the phone. I said I'd have to ask my mother. But I didn't know how to ask her. I didn't know how not to hurt her feelings. How could I explain to her that I *wanted* to go there? In my bed at night I would get clever about this. I would tell her that I would bring back things for everybody. I would tell her that I would argue with him on our behalf. I would tell her that I just wanted to see a Giants game. Yes, the Giants were in San Francisco, but they'd come down to Los Angeles some time, and that's the time I would choose to go, and come home right after. But I never said any of these things. I could hear what she would say back, or not say.

Time passed and my father called to say that I would have to decide. But still I couldn't, the whole question having become like a record needle stuck in a groove. I went around and around. I bicycled up to the drugstore and took my paper route change and called him from the pay phone so that I could talk without fear. But that was ridiculous because I was always afraid, of one thing or the other, one side of me or the other. My father said I shouldn't have to ask my mother, because this was something I could decide myself. I had never thought my father was unreasoning but I thought he was unreasoning then. Of course I *could* decide. But how could I say to him that I didn't want to hurt my mother's feelings because he had hurt them enough already and I didn't want to hurt them any more?

Or how could I say what I didn't quite understand, that I was doing part of his job for him? Not that it was his job anymore. He'd quit that job. This too I didn't quite understand. Especially since he seemed to think he was taking care of things as well as he ought to, given all the circumstances. Did he not call, did he not write, did he not send checks? I could protest, pick all these apart, but I would never win. Not when he was out by the kidney-shaped pool and I was not.

Three days before the day my father said I would have to decide, I told my mother whatever I could tell her. That I wanted to do this, that I would not be gone long, that another year my sister could go. Not about the Giants or any of that. I had this weird hope that if I was simply honest she would see there was nothing to fear and how much I loved her and wasn't deserting her and would reward me. She didn't seem surprised. Maybe she had read my mail, or things had been said on the phone on the stairs. Whatever. She said of course I could go; but if I went I shouldn't come back. I remember not being afraid of this. I remember thinking that I could do it, that is, go, and if she really meant it, not come back. I remember how small and undefended my mother seemed then. What made it impossible is that I knew she couldn't bully me, and what made it sad is that she knew this too. It was in the way she turned away, busily, busying herself with something, putting the dishes away. She had to busy herself, so that she wouldn't say more, so that the speech she had carefully prepared for herself, her position, the best she could do, as against absolutely everything, *him*, the whole world, wouldn't be lost. Later I bicycled up to the drugstore and put more of my paper route change in the pay phone and told my father thank you very much for the invitation but I couldn't this year, but maybe next year?

*

Instead of going to California, I started writing him stories, set in the cities of Langden and Jansen. In Langden, this. In Jansen, that. They were often stories of calamities; shipwrecks, floods, big dams breaking. Though Patrup Langden, mayor, chief of police, announcer, pitcher, captain of all Langden teams, would occasionally come up with something to save the day. There were a couple my father seemed to like, where the quotient of catastrophe was less. Once he wrote me, "Keep it up." A boy writes stories to his father. Evidence that writers aren't really born, that something happens and then they are?

*

Polio. A year or two before Dr. Salk produced his vaccine, I came down with a mild case. This was just before my father went away.

9

In fact I may have caught it on a two-week visit to my grand-parents upstate, going to the Rochester beach every day with my mother, while my father was in New York putting the finishing touches on his affair with Irene. Returning to Scarsdale, I fell off my bicycle one day and went into a long sleep. I stayed in bed for six weeks. Only when I was recovered enough to be walking around did my parents tell me that I had had polio. A few weeks after that my father said he was leaving. My being sick must have delayed his plans. He said the usual things about how they'd not been get-ting along and so he would be staying in the city for awhile and would call every night. The fact of Irene only came out days or weeks later, in my mother's screams and her collapsing on her bed. Later I came to believe, with a rare, even odd, certainty, as if the only thing I could ever truly trust again was my own intuition, that my contracting polio had to do with my father's affair, that it was my own desperate effort to save my parents' marriage, or a confession of guilt for the collapse that was coming. How could I have known? But on the other hand, how could I not have known, who was my father's son, and who had wanted Irene to shake and kiss me? When, fifty years later, the tsunami struck in Asia, it was easy for me to believe that the animals had sensed it in advance and sought higher ground.

Irene was the one, I decided. Without Irene none of this would have happened. Even if he'd left, which he wouldn't have, he would have called every night like he said he would, if it wasn't for Irene. He would have visited every weekend, if it wasn't for Irene, and on the phone he would have sounded like he cared more, like it was more important to him. He would maybe not even have left New York, if not for her. Though this last idea produced in me more complicated feelings. I couldn't quite begrudge my father California. It seemed too great for that. And the thought of us all going out there, packing up Esmeralda, making a trek like the pioneers, my parents sharing the driving, didn't quite seem real to me. I could imagine Irene out in California, driving my father's convertible, her golf clubs in the backseat, in a way that I could not imagine my mother doing the same.

I imagined Irene in beautiful clothes, the sun always shining, the convertible always washed, going here and there in a daytime that never quite ended. My father, in the strain of our now-rarer conversations, would tell me things about her as if catching me up on the news. Probably he didn't know what else to say, after the baseball and how I was doing in school and whether he was busy or not. "Irene's working at the museum." "Irene's taken up gardening." "Irene sends her love." But she never got on the phone herself. I was left to imagine a person who my father thought to be more or less perfect. Meanwhile my own life went along. I learned how to play tennis in the high school gym. I started playing golf on the public course with my mother's old clubs. My paper route gave me money to spend. Girls grew breasts in Rochester, as elsewhere, and boys' voices broke. And I began to see that I was a smart kid and that smart kids, even from Rochester, could begin to chart their own paths. Staking out some future position for myself, I began to buy Ivy League clothes. I could tell Gant shirts from others. And the roll of the collar of a Brooks Brothers shirt and how the Brooks shirts came without pockets. As if, with such knowledge as this, the world could be conquered. I must have told my father somewhere along the way that I had taken up tennis. He played tennis himself. I imagined him in white Lacoste shirts with alligators playing every weekend with Irene. His white socks, his white sneaks, his white shorts, all new and the best, and Irene playing with a visor. The kind of tennis that was advertised, tennis as it was meant to be, with something of the upper-class purity of a dream.

I am trying to get to something here. I am trying to lay the foundation. Gifts from California were another sort of tension in our house. My father was not great with gifts. He would be late with Christmas, late with birthdays, or he would forget altogether. Or perhaps he didn't forget. Perhaps I only assumed this. Perhaps, for some reason, he simply didn't want to. But if a box did come, it was best not to make a big deal of it. It was best not to open it with other things. I would take my box to my room and open it there and whatever was in the box I would leave there. A book about art. Probably there were others but I can't remember what they were, things that if they were brought out of my room would revive my mother's bitterness and spoil whatever else was out there. Until one day a box came with no reason. It came in July and my birthday was in March. So it was a surprise in a way, and I treated it as a surprise, I didn't take it at once to my room. My mother walked into the living room as I opened it, and I didn't walk away with it, I'm not sure why. I suppose it was too late for me just to walk away. I suppose I could still not imagine that my father was sending me a gift in July. Or maybe I had decided to take some sort of stand, full of goodwill and understanding, but nevertheless a stand, which I could even back up if necessary, by saying, here, you see, he's not so bad, he sent a gift for no reason at all. Anyway I opened it. It was a rectangular box, not deep, and about two feet long, the sort of box you might send a suit jacket in. My sister walked in as well, three years younger than me, whom I always meant to protect and sometimes did. I sliced the wrapping tape with a steak knife. I popped the corners of the box. There was a note from my father. I read it quickly, refolded it, and put it under the tissue. "Irene thought you would like these." Wrapped in the tissue were four cream-colored Banlon tennis shirts. They gave me a queasy feeling at once, as if I'd suddenly realized that something I was looking forward to had actually been meant for somebody else, the sender had accidentally put my name on the package instead of the right person. I lifted them up to show to the others. The smooth synthetic fabric clung to my open hand and draped over it, as if it had no life of its own. My mother said, "Well wasn't *that* nice and thoughtful," and went off. I expected her to add more, because she wasn't always pithy with her sarcasm, but this time she was.

As I took them to my room, it was as if I were trying to question these shirts. Who sent you and what do you want? They had no tags on them and I began to think that they were actually used shirts, or shirts that somebody had given them and they didn't want them. Because I could not imagine Irene having such bad taste in shirts. How could you play tennis in *Banlon? Cream-colored Banlon?* Even I, in Rochester, had a few old Lacoste shirts that a friend of mine had outgrown and his mother who was friends with my mother had passed along. And they were white and cotton and had alligators on them, or hanging half-off them by then, and they didn't cling to you as if they were dead. Is this how life was really lived in California? *Cream-colored Banlon?* I couldn't believe it. And yet I did, somehow. In a way, it was the beginning of my education. I never knew for sure whether Irene was sending me some things she thought were wonderful or passing off on me things she didn't really want. In a way, the second would have been better. It would have preserved something pristine in my mind. I duly sent a polite thank-you. I put the shirts in the bottom of my bottom drawer, underneath pants that were too small for me, and never wore them once.

*

In a sense, I walked into my grandmother's death. I went to New York on some sort of scholarship sponsored by the Lions Club to study the United Nations and when I went to visit my grandparents on Eightieth Street she was in bed dying. Nobody had told me that she had breast cancer and was dying, just as no one had told me that ten years before she had had a first bout with breast cancer. She was my beloved grandmother, generous and vital, the sort of person my sister later became, and I could scarcely believe it when I saw her in bed, shriveled and weak-voiced and without makeup, her teeth not even in her mouth. As I understood it, she managed to stay alive an extra three days until my father could break free from work and arrive from California. I had not seen my father in eight years. He and Irene were staying at the Carlyle, which until then I had never heard of. The three of us, my father and Irene and I, were eating in the Schraffts on Seventy-ninth Street when word came that my grandmother had died. Until then we had been conversing easily enough. I had found out from Irene, though I don't recollect precisely how, that the Carlyle was the best of hotels, and perhaps from my father that this was where executives of his company stayed. I felt buoyed by this, as if vicariously I was staying there too. The two of them seemed happy to see me then. They even felt like family, a special, seldom-heard-from branch of the family where life went on easily and people spoke politely and about things like art and stayed at the Carlyle when they came in from California; but family nonetheless. For a little while I lost the sense that it was us against them. I had never been on a family vacation, but this was like one, until the Schraffts waitress came over and said there was a call for my father from the doctor.

They didn't want me to go to the "viewing." The Mets were new to New York that year and they sent me to the Polo Grounds to see a game. It wasn't like seeing the Giants but it was the next best thing. I got to see the Polo Grounds one last time, before they tore it down. Again, I felt that my father and Irene were being kind. I didn't know why I shouldn't attend the "viewing," but I liked it that they were thinking about me, and thinking about getting me out of something even if it wasn't clear what their reasoning was. And I liked it that they sent me to the Polo Grounds, as if they had to know that the very words of the place, "Polo Grounds," had a magical aura for me, a mixture of the gigantic and happier times and polar bears and Willie Mays. Though one thing was odd: my father had become a Dodgers fan. I asked him why and he said it was because he was living in Los Angeles now. And something also about the company getting tickets to the games. This still didn't seem to me sufficient. I felt that I had inherited from him the Giants blood that was in my veins. I finally decided sports weren't as important to him as they were to me. Or loyalty? But I scarcely dared think this. Things were going too nicely now. It was as if my grandmother in her death had placed a blessing over us.

Before they left town, my father asked me what I was thinking about for college. We were in a car going up to Irene's place in Connecticut on the lake. My father said that Berkeley was a good school. I said I had been thinking about Yale. If I could get in, that is. I didn't know if I could get in. My father said one or two more good things about Berkeley, it was in California and I could be a California resident and go almost for free. I got fearful because this sounded to me somehow like my father becoming a Dodgers fan, and like the Banlon tennis shirts. I didn't want to go to a public school. I wanted to go to the best. Why had he brought up the idea of almost going for free, when I felt that Yale blood flowed in my veins just like Giants blood, intermingled, my inheritance, my chance? I couldn't say all of this or even really think it, consciously anyway. Instead I said almost the same thing I had said already, with the words changed a little so that it wouldn't seem like I was repeating myself and being obnoxious about it. "I don't know, Yale's really good, I'm sure Berkeley is too, but I really like Yale, if I could get in, if it could work out. But my mother couldn't afford to send me," I added. We drove along. The inside of the car, its padded gray upholstery, seemed cosseting and protective. I was not afraid. I could hear my own voice, saying what I thought, the way I thought normal people said their thoughts. I was in the back. My father was driving. I could see his sunglasses in the rearview, and the back of Irene's short, frosted hair. He said if I got into Yale we'd figure out how I could go there, we'd make sure I could go there. Earnest and firm, sincere without being extravagant, it seemed like the most wonderful promise he could make me. He was treating me like a man. It was the happiest time I ever spent with my father and Irene.

*

Before I applied to college, I had another conversation with my father, from the pay phone in the drug store. He hadn't said anything more about paying for Yale and I wanted to be sure.

"I'm applying."

"Great."

"They also sent some financial aid forms. Should I? . . . Do I? . . . I'm not sure if I should fill them out."

"Well won't you need a scholarship?"

"I thought . . . what we talked about . . . in New York . . ."

"What did I say? Tell me. Remind me."

"You said we'd make sure I could go to Yale if I got in."

"I do remember. But let's see if you get in first."

"I just need to know, about these forms."

"Financial aid? Of course. Apply. What I said in New York— I meant, after whatever scholarship you get, then whatever's left, we'll try to make up the difference, so you can go."

"But the financial aid is based on need."

"With your mother's income, you'll probably qualify."

"But it says, there's a line for your name, and they want to know your income."

"You have to explain. I'm sure there's a way to do that. You live with your mother. You put down your mother's income."

My father's voice, in all of this, was calm and friendly, as if he really was on my side of this and if I followed his advice, things would be alright.

I tried to imagine his position. He had a son who was Irene's son and a second young son that he'd had by Irene and then he had me and my sister and the checks he sent to my mother every month and a new life to build in California by the kidney-shaped pool, so why, if he had all this expense, would he not want to take advantage of the possibility of my qualifying for a scholarship by dint of living with my mother whom after all he supported, after a fashion? Especially since I was his Rochester son who wouldn't come visit him in California when invited and wanted to go to Yale instead of Berkeley, which, yes, was a public school but a good school, one of the glories of California, where college would almost be free. Maybe he even thought I was avoiding him again, but I don't think it was that. I think, I thought then, that it was the money.

I got into Yale and got financial aid because it was true they looked to what my mother had and not my father, or more accurately they looked to what *I* had, that is, what I would need if I was going to be able to go, and they got that right. My father filled in the cracks a little with checks twice a year and once in a while I bought clothes on sale at J. Press instead of the Co-op. I became infatuated with the rich, and some of that is in the book I wrote a couple before this one. But it was the old rich that allured me, not the new, not the rich who acted as if they had eaten a lot of money and choked on it. These new rich were in California and wore Banlon shirts. They visited me once in a while when my father was in New York on MCA's dime staying at the Carlyle. We would have dinner and be polite. Soon enough, my stepbrother joined me at Yale. *He* wasn't on scholarship. We still were not friends. And he didn't really get Yale. From time to time in college I felt as if I were participating in a scam, sent out to fleece Yale out of a scholarship like one of Fagin's boys sent out to fleece honest Londoners. I hated that feeling. The only way I could make it go away was to remember that I was not going to Yale as my father's son. I was going as not his son.

*

Meanwhile they were flying around. They went to Europe every year and stayed in the apartment in a mews in Mayfair that MCA owned and my father did a day's business and then they went to museums and restaurants and at night my father gambled and after England they went to the other countries and more museums and restaurants. One summer they asked me along. Irene's son, whom my father had adopted by then, came too, and I got to know him better than I had. The whole time he wanted to be back in California with the girl he was in love with. To judge by Fred, California didn't seem that great a place to grow up. You grew up whiny and discontent and unable to cope with the world outside California, to judge by him. They sent Fred back after two weeks because he was so unhappy, and I traveled with them ten days more, to Munich, then to Paris, and I went with them to more museums and learned more about how things were done in a certain sphere, you had your hotel in Munich (the Vierjahrheitzen) where you always stayed, and your hotel in Paris (the Bristol) where you always stayed, and you commented about the nice things about each specific hotel, for instance, the fantastic venison at the Vier Jahreszeiten, or some exiled prince of Spain in the elevator at the Bristol; and of course I learned how to leave my shoes out at night to be polished, and I learned what "Alte Pinakothek" meant. These things, actually, I loved to learn. Knowing them made me feel less like a bastard. Though I still felt like one sometimes, when I remembered my scholarship and my father's name nowhere on my Yale application.

In those couple of weeks in Munich and Paris, when we spoke, or more particularly when they spoke, it was with greater familiarity. My father confided that his own father had been a weak man, that my grandmother had been the boss and made the money and took a lover. Irene once noticed me clearing my navel of bellybutton lint and told me this was a masturbatory habit. This annoyed me to hear. Where had she heard that, and why was she saying it? I personally could find no connection between my navel and my masturbatory practice, but I've never forgotten it. Did Irene see a shrink, did she read books of pop psychology, did she know sophisticated things that I didn't? I came to see it as part of the whole picture, just as my picture of my father's father, punching an adding machine in the back of my grandparents' shop while my grandmother and her staff sold the dresses out front, now incorporated that he was "weak." My father particularly mentioned how for years in the Depression my grandfather had spent his time gardening in a house they had rented in the country while my grandmother worked for Saks and made important trips for the company to Europe and made a *friend* on one of the ships who eventually paid for part of my father's college. So was this why I was going to Yale as not my father's son, because he had gone as not *his* father's son? At the time, this never occurred to me.

The following winter they were back in New York on his business and took Fred and me both out to dinner. Another meal where their appetites were great, and mine, and Fred's, a little slack, as if we were looking at different movies. Later, in New Haven, Fred and I were walking back from the train when Fred got emotional and shouted that he hated Yale and hated his mother and hated my father. I felt oddly happy to hear this. I would have been happy for him to leave Yale and it reassured me that he had grown up *out there*, and with *them*, by the kidney-shaped pool, and look where he was now and where I was. The next day or the day after, I was never sure which, Fred flew back out to California to see his girl. This was sudden and he told no one. Things may have gone badly with the girl. My father called a couple days later to say that Fred was dead. He had been driv-

ing their Karmann Ghia convertible without sleep and gone off
a mountain road.

I put him, I put all of it, in a distant corner of my mind. I
felt guilty that Fred had sounded so bitter with me, which was
surely a sign of trouble, but what should I have done? Called my
father, snitched, caused trouble? There were other things Fred
had said as well. "Oh, they're fine if you want to have a good time
all the time!" He shouted this across the whole freshman campus
after midnight as though he were a crier reporting the British were
coming, after I had said something tepid in support of them, he
shouldn't hate them, they meant well, something like that. So he
left me with a delicate secret. If I confessed to them that I'd seen
Fred in trouble and done nothing about it, I'd have also to tell
them how, in his last days, he'd screamed that he hated them. Or
maybe they would not have been surprised. When I visited them
in Los Angeles the following Christmas, my first time in California, I summarized that evening by saying that Fred had been
upset. They seemed as content as I was to leave the rest vague.
And anyway the description they seem to have agreed to regarding Fred's death, at least for public consumption—that he had
spent two days with the girl and left "upset"—dovetailed with
mine of the last night I saw him. Upset and sleepless when he
left the girl. Suicide was never mentioned, nor was it assumed.

It's absurd to say that Irene had gotten over it by the time,
ten months later, that I went out there. She never got over Fred's
death. But on the surface it was hard to tell. Maybe she was trying
a little harder to be kind, to hold her tongue; or at other moments
she seemed to be thinking, regarding anything and everything, that
there was no time to waste. My heart warmed to her a little then.
My own mother was far away. I spent my week in California going

out to more restaurants or playing with their young kid Thomas who was shy and seven years old and seemed to need a lot of playing with then or driving their new Dodge convertible around, the substitute for the Karmann Ghia, as if the small, foreign, German car had been somehow to blame for Fred. My father even said this. No more small cars. He never owned one again. In the Dodge I spent most of the time dating the daughters of their friends and trying to make out. In this I had limited success. Either I simply pushed them too hard and too fast and was a little bit uncouth, or they hadn't the sophistication to see what they had here, a cool Yale guy from the East who knew a lot more than they did. I even knew about LSD, which none of them had ever heard of. The beach, the hills, the curves on Sunset, the Strip, the clubs, the studio in the Valley. They gave me money and I spent it. My conclusion after a week was that California was nice but a little bit inferior. Every minute I was there I felt as if I was taking Fred's place.

*

I'm not sure when Irene and my father first moved back to New York. It must have been when I was in law school. But it began a period of their lives when they were unsettled and ping-ponged back and forth from coast to coast, uncertain where they should be. Irene now seemed to blame California, or Los Angeles anyway, for Fred's death. Or maybe it wasn't blame at all, maybe it was more a sense of not wanting to be so near the place of his wreck, his crack-up, her failure, whatever it was. They moved to Darien, then to Santa Barbara, then New York, then Los Angeles again, temporarily, when my father had his last show on, then to someplace out in the country near Chappaqua. At the time they first moved East, my father was near the height of his success in television. He had produced a dozen shows, many of them westerns with huge weekly audiences, *The Dooley Boys*, *The Outpost*, *Canyon Creek*, and could lay a decent claim to having pioneered a whole new form, the TV movie. A dozen other men, I'm sure, have laid claim to the exact same invention, but I believed my father when he told me that he went to the Universal head Lew Wasserman and sold him on the idea. And, oddly, I believe him to this day. What's true for sure is that he produced one of the first ones, a scary take on the Mafia taking over everything. Let others come with their claims.

My father's successes gave me courage in a way. As in: if he did this well, you won't do worse. Something like that, some combination of mythology and pride. Not that I knew what I would be in life. I had ideas to be a writer. But then there was this law school I was dragging myself through and I wasn't sure how being a writer would work. I suppose I assumed I would be a successful writer, because my father was a successful producer, and the word "successful," like a blank check, would cover it all. My father then made a U-turn on himself. It was the late sixties and the notion of self-actualization, of do-it-now, laid claim to him as to so many others. This and the fact that Fred was dead and Irene felt life was short, and the wholesale revulsion against the corporate that was in the culture. Normal run of stuff, but it wasn't everybody who gave up as much money as he did to become an independent film producer. I felt actually kind of flattered by him then, and fearful at the same time, as he reached to grab hold of a *zeitgeist* that was obviously more mine than his. He took an office in midtown Manhattan. I worked for him one summer, reading scripts and being really no help at all. I hadn't a clue as to what something "commercial" meant. My mind was far away from it. I couldn't even say what the "youth" wanted, because my Ivy League slice of the "youth" was pretty well severed from the rest. I believed in art. He, with reservations, did too. We were not a successful couple, and I slept on the rollaway couch in his office and seemed to provoke the resentment of his secretary, who had followed him over from Universal and would come in each morning to find me there. I sometimes wondered whether she had had an affair with my father, or had wanted to, so that my presence was more than an inconvenience, more a roadblock that for some reason he had placed in her way. She had a body that looked to have been pressed into a nice-enough shape.

Irene's troubles didn't end. She had minor abdominal surgery for something and peritonitis developed and she wound up with a catheter that she would have for the rest of her life. Does this make sense medically? It's what I remember, anyway. It came from a time in her life—and I suppose on reflection that was nearly all of it—when I wasn't paying close attention. And one good friend in particular didn't welcome her back to New York as Irene had expected and hoped for, and maybe even needed; instead, the friend seemed to imply that Irene had screwed up out in California and Fred's death was the proof of it. Or this was how Irene understood her friend's coolness, and it didn't help.

Meanwhile my father was headed for success or failure, depending how you chose to look at it, and I imagine he chose the rosy view one day and the dark glass the next. He got two movies made in New York. This was at a time when scarcely any movies were getting made in the city, it was considered impossible, too expensive, the unions, all of that, and to get two movies made without even a major studio in back of you could have been thought a minor miracle. On the other hand, they were both flops. A good review here and there, but no one in the theaters. One of them was for the "youth" market, or the twenty-something market anyway, and it starred a gay guy who was being directed by another gay guy and who was supposed to be playing a horny, mixed-up twenty-something not-gay guy and neither of the gay guys was experienced in film and the thing came off sexless, curdled, and campy. The other was a sci-fi thing about mind control and it was less embarrassing but boring.

Or these were the thoughts anyway, of me, in my twenties with my own hopes and pretensions, who either wanted my father to be king so that he could anoint me the prince or wanted him to stay clear of my turf altogether, leave the "youth" market for me to fail to understand. It lessened my own self-confidence when he failed. I suppose I believed in genes.

It was in these years when we were all living around New York that I noticed a subtle change in my father and Irene. They had always doted on one another, supported one another, shored up one another's jokes and shared their food in restaurants as if it were a daringly informal and intimate thing to do. But now they seemed so polite to one another. Please's and thank you's and taking extra care not to give each other offense, as if they were dancing minuets with their words. Where had that come from, or had it always been there and I'd never noticed? But I noticed it now and it had to have been big enough for me to notice. I brought blinders to them. There's no less shameful way to say it. Though is it half a defense to say that I was in my twenties then, and brought blinders, more or less, to pretty much everyone who was not? The proof that they were extra-polite to each other came from the fact that otherwise I would never have noticed it. But what did it mean? All I sensed really was that my father had reached the apogee of his life and had begun to decline. Or was it my perception of him that had reached its apogee and begun to decline?

It was about this time that my father began writing letters to the editor. So many problems with the country, so much to try and make right. I'd not even known before of his civic inclinations. Maybe it was only that he had a lot more time, as a movie producer in perpetual development rather than a TV producer in actual production, to see how the world was going. Mostly he sent them to the *New York Times*. They published a few. Every time they published one, he called me up to tell me. "They're publishing my Archie Cox." Remember the WIN buttons, Whip Inflation Now? He had one in on those. They titled it "Whip Ford Now." I suppose these could also be thought distractions from his life. But he seemed to believe he was making a difference, and he may have needed that for Irene as well. Her feet on the ground somewhere, however futile. Some response to outrage after outrage, to the dislocations of the times. Dirtying her hands with the world at last.

*

I remember Calvin Trillin saying something like there should be a Dostoevsky Rule for writers and the Dostoevsky Rule should be this, that if you have the talent of Dostoevsky you can write anything you want about people you are close to but if you have less talent than Dostoevsky then you had better not. I like Calvin Trillin a lot, not least for suggesting that the shelf life of a book these days is somewhere between that of milk and yogurt, but I've found myself unable to abide by his rule. When I came back to writing fiction some years ago, I had in mind to write a kind of "meritocracy" series, novels that would chart the progress of my generation, or anyway the narrow slice of it that I knew well. The first book, in retrospect, came easily enough. Nothing ever comes easily, but I had a story to tell that was clear and seemed true enough, and I had feeling to put into it that had never gone away. It was the story of my hero in college, Harry Nolan, who might have been president of the country one day, and his wife Sascha Maclaren on whom I had a crush. My sixties book, so to speak. The sixties. The seventies. The eighties. The nineties. A book for each decade, a neat quartet, about the best and the brightest and what happened to them, or us. Something you weren't going to see on TV or in the movies. Something, I told myself, that you might not even read in somebody else's book. The novel as sociology? A dirty job but somebody's got to do it? Maybe so or maybe not. But also Forster's thing about if you had to choose between your country and your friends, would you have the courage to choose your friends? Not that in my case courage was involved. Rather, more, the imagination of courage: *if* I had to choose, which would it be? I feel even now maybe more loyal to my generation than to a generalized idea of "America," and more loyal still to a class that may never even have existed—it may all have been a fiction, the way some have said that romantic love is a fiction, or anyway a literary convention. In the second book, the characters come at the world from a different angle, seem for a little while to say good-bye to it. Probably that description reduces it too much. They join a group. They're looking for something. A sort of schema, then, in the sixties embracing the world as their natural inheritance and in the seventies feeling disinherited and seeking transcendence. Which was whatever it was, which left them wherever they were left. Still trying to come out on top, you could say that much anyway, and now in the eighties, if the scheme would hold, they would have to return to the world because where else was there to go? Change the world, change yourself, change nothing. Only accept.

But I had a terrible time with this third book, my eighties book. What I knew on the ground in the eighties was the same thing that I knew in dreams when I was young: California. I went out to Los Angeles, ostensibly, because where else would a writer in 1980s America go who wanted only to accept "what is"? I wanted to make a living. I didn't want to be poor anymore. Or things must have seemed that way, to myself, to others. What really was going on would be for the novel, the third book, to explore.

I started the book again and again. I will record for you what some of these beginnings were, the ones that I never got around to trashing.

The way we used to do the show, we'd start every episode with a typewriter-like font in a corner of the screen: NIGHTSHIFT. Then the NIGHTSHIFT would fade out and the date would fade in. Then the show would start.

The idea I had then was that I would use the celebrated television show *Northie* that made my show business fortune and reputation such as they were as the formal basis for the book and the center of its interest. After all, were the eighties not all about business, and what place could be more archetypal of this than the place that made Reagan a star? Moreover it was not unusual in the eighties for pundits to write articles in the Sunday papers or *Vanity Fair* about how television drama would soon be replacing literature as the mirror and conscience of our age. The very form of the screenplay seemed compelling, for its concision, its no-bullshit approach. I intended to call this version of my book, *Notes for an Unproduced Teleplay*.

I never liked Zacky Kurtz much. He wore pressed jeans. I don't care what year it was, can you imagine such a thing, such a style? Can you imagine what went into making a guy who could think such a style was acceptable, who could stand there looking at his pressed jeans piled in his bottom drawer?

Or if they were pressed, would you if you were Zacky Kurtz eschew a drawer and hang them all on hangers? Zacky in his walk-in closet looking at his long row of pressed jeans on hangers, lined up like his equally long row of Houston Astro baseball hats. Two hundred dollar jeans, by the way. No Levi's, no Dockers here. Beverly Hills jeans.

Not that I know anything really about jeans. I haven't worn them since fourth or fifth grade—too tight on my skin or in the crotch or something. A baggy pants guy, all the way. Zacky gave me a pair of Nocona crocodile cowboy boots once, hardly used, right out of his closet. He probably thought he was spiffing me up, and maybe he was, but I hated the high heels, they made me feel phony. And they weren't even so high, they were high heels only compared to what you would find on ratted-out old loafers. But I guess that was me, baggy pants and ratted-out old loafers from Bean's. Incorrigible, in Zacky's view. And someone who'd squeeze a nickel till the buffalo crapped, in one of Zacky's occasional sage Texasisms, thrown off with an ironic flourish, as if to show he hadn't forgotten where he came from.

Thrifty, I liked to think. I who before 1981 had never had more than three thousand dollars in the bank. And I was a grown man then, close to forty years old. Not that Zacky hadn't once been poor, or felt he was poor. That was essential to him, that explained so much about him. Houston, the great, zoneless nowhere, father a Methodist minister who died penniless and young, as if Zacky had been born just too late for a thirties movie of upward mobility. But Zacky had never squeezed a nickel, not as long as I'd known him anyway. Get it and spend it, get it and spend it. That was his joy, or, as Zacky would have had it, who balanced his Texasisms with equally sardonic outbursts of Latin, his *delectatio*. He really wasn't cheap about anything, he was six feet four inches tall with broad shoulders and a long reach and he'd hug you with those great appendages of his if he hardly knew you, and it wasn't, all of it, anyway, a scam. If you were a help to him, he hugged you for real.

He also put an avuncular arm around people and squeezed their shoulder and kissed them, often with a bit of athletic elegance, as if reminding them or reminding himself that Columbia University had once brought him north to be their quarterback. Or maybe he was suggesting that he was somehow the entertainment industry's answer to Lyndon B. Johnston. Texas charm,

Texas power? He presumed, I suppose. But why shouldn't he have? For most people who knew him he was the boss, or they aspired to have him be their boss, they angled to be on his team. He seemed to bring good luck; Zacky was a hit. And when he squeezed my shoulder, I, who had helped him a lot, felt a shiver, a twitch, something I could no more locate than deny.

In this version, as I now read it over, I must have thought to focus on the period when Zacky was my boss on *Northie*. He brought me along, he gave me my start, and later he was my partner. I've included as much of this second false start as I have because on reading it over it rings true, and Zacky remains an important figure in this story I'm telling now. Why write the same thing twice?

And here was a third beginning:

It seemed like a good idea once. Maybe one day it will seem that way again, but today it does not. Today I wish I'd never told anybody that I was going to carry my tale into the eighties.

Speaks for itself, I guess. For the problems I was having, which if I could summarize went something like this: I would write forty, fifty, seventy pages, I would have an outline in hand, and I would begin to lose interest in what I was writing. Something seemed missing. I didn't think the problem was in the story. Enough had happened to me and I'd found my characters and a plot, I jiggled them here and there but mostly they were what they were. And the setting seemed to fit, the land without shadows.

Morning in America, the city on a hill, all that rubbish, or was it? Reagan brought the top tax bracket down to twenty-eight percent. Now wasn't *that* something to write about? The meritocrats were approaching middle age. In eras of less advanced medicine they'd already be old.

I was stymied. My feelings ran cold. And I suppose I could point out something about myself that of course must be true for others too, but that maybe I have a bit of a special gift for: things hiding from me in plain sight. A couple of Christmases ago I was given Amos Oz's wonderful book of growing up in Jerusalem, *A Tale of Love and Darkness*. Later I saw Oz on C-Span and he was joking about how his American publisher said he had to put the word "memoir" on the cover of the book because in America people wanted to know whether they were buying a fish or a chicken, and so Oz let them do it even though he knew that his book, partly about distant ancestors, contained the truths of imagination as well as memory. I loved this man when I saw him on television, his playfully narrowed eyes and the thick, proud emphases of his accented English, as if every sentence he spoke was a definitive affirmation of some hopeless contradiction that he was more than willing to call life. But I digress, maybe. Never mind love, maybe. The man gave me something. Later in his book he wrote about how he got started as a writer. He was stuck in a kibbutz in the middle of nowhere believing that if you were going to be a writer you had to live out in the wide world, "Paris, Madrid, New York, Monte Carlo, the African deserts or the Scandinavian forests," where real things happened. Romantic things, daring things, lonely brave things, scarcely known in the lives of those he lived with then, or in the lives of the people he had grown up with in a lower middle-class neighborhood in Jerusalem. Then one night he read Sherwood Anderson's *Winesburg, Ohio*, about a place he had scarcely ever heard of, where people were as "ordinary" as those he'd always known. And Anderson had found dignity and complexity and of course everything else in Winesburg's citizens, and Oz took this to heart and never after looked back. He realized, he said, that wherever a writer is, *that* is the center of his universe. And eventually he came to be writing about his family in this beautiful tale that I held in my hands until late in my own night in Los Angeles during the last days of the year 2004. What touched me most, really, was how honored he was when, decades later, someone asked him to write a blurb for a new edition of *Winesburg, Ohio*. I imagined someday someone asking me to write a blurb for *A Tale of Love and Darkness* and how dumbfounded I would be. I knew then that what was hiding in plain sight, vis-à-vis this book that I could not write, was my father.

I resisted at first. I was worried that putting my father into a book about my generation in the eighties would pull the book out of shape. I would of course have to start decades before. And what about my scheme, my best and brightest characters first embracing the world as their natural inheritance, then feeling disinherited and seeking transcendence, then in the third book returning to the world because where else was there to go? What had my father, my family, to do with that? Everything, I decided. What is coming back to the world about if it is not about coming back to our fathers? We never really leave our mothers, no matter where or what. And really, when I thought about it, I knew so many people like myself who came back to their fathers in the eighties. "Business." That, too. Going into "business," our fathers' world. It was a book that, finally, I felt I could write.

33

LOS ANGELES

WHEN I ARRIVED IN LOS ANGELES in the spring of 1980, I
found an apartment in a rent-controlled building two blocks from
the beach in Ocean Park. The building had once been an Elks
retirement home. Many of the people living there were on county
assistance. My room had a sliver of an ocean view and my rent
was one hundred seventy-six dollars a month.

On arriving there some guy on the boardwalk could have
painted my picture and put the following caption on it: "Portrait
of a Young Mystic, Recently Returned to the World."

That would be referencing the esoteric group that I had been
a part of in New York and that I had left when my friend jumped
out a window. I arrived in Ocean Park with enough attention
mustered from five years in the group that I felt I could bust open
brick walls. The world seemed bright and endlessly interesting,
as it might to someone released after years in jail. I was broke and
meant to do something about it, but this problem, if it was a problem at all, more often than not lacked immediacy. I ran off a succession of quick affairs. Sometimes I went in the ocean. I spent

hours in the Rose Café, where there always seemed to be sand on the floor, reading the papers and trying to pick up still more girls, between bouts of turning out sample scripts to send around. Yes, I was looking for my chance, but if I didn't get it, then what? The prettiest girl I met the whole time was in the very building where I lived. Her name was Melissa and I met her in the laundry room and she had a bigger apartment than mine. She may have paid three hundred in rent.

The most vivid image I hold of Melissa from that time is not strictly from that time at all—I must have cobbled it together from things she said, places where we happened to be together, photographs. And although I can almost see her within a photograph's borders, and in the slightly hazed-over colors of an aging print, there is to my knowledge no photograph that has it all. A little bit younger than I ever knew her, almost in profile, a breeze scattering her hair across her cheek, in front of her pale green Cadillac. The Cadillac is so long it takes up the whole image, an old car but Melissa has waxed the paint so it shines. She wears a fitted, thin red sweater. A few of her dresses that she sells to shops from the back of her car are cradled over her joined arms. It's impossible to know what she's looking off at. It's possible that she's looking off at nothing, that the entire image is a pose. Her complexion is pale, as if she hadn't been in the sun, but it is a bright California day, the sun glints off her hair and the hood of the car. Her nose is a little long. She has the look of a swan. She's probably a bit too thin and her hair, cut shorter than when I ever knew her, so that one can see her neck's slender elongation, is the honey-est of blond. She seems to be in her late twenties. I would have met her a year or two later. I have no idea why this image stays with me. Maybe the courage of it. She seems to me brave in the picture, with her dresses, her sweater, her car. It's possible there was something like this image in her apartment, in a frame or an album, but I don't remember.

She was having an affair at the time, with someone who turned out to be Zacky Kurtz. I learned this only slowly. Melissa was not free with information. Yet we became friends. Maybe this was because so many of the people in our building were old and on welfare and we must have stood out to each other. We would have coffee once in a while at the Rose. I must have told her about my intentions, how I was here to make some money writing scripts and then when I had a pile of it, say, a hundred thousand dollars, I would leave and rent a place in the Hamptons where rents were cheap in the winter and begin to write my books, or in all events, even if I didn't have a hundred thousand dollars, I would leave before the Olympics came in 1984. The Olympics would be my alarm clock, my last-ditch warning, the way that I could tie my-self to the mast against the sirens. Though I didn't say "sirens" to her. Melissa would more than likely not have known much about where they came from, and I had the feeling even then that she was not somebody you could charm with clever allusions, that you could only hurt her feelings that way. Nor did she seem to have any "intentions" herself. Not the way I had them. Not that she would talk about, anyway. She had come to Los Angeles because she married a musician and when they had no money she made shirts for rock guys. The rock guys thought the shirts were beau-ties; it was said that Melissa could do anything with a sewing machine, that hers would fetch a bone if she wanted it to. Then her marriage to the musician ended and she was even broker than before and an old guy came along who gave her valuable watches and knew people in L.A.'s garment district and he set her up as a maker of dresses. This was before Zacky Kurtz. She designed everything as if she were going to wear it herself. She had reps in a few places, but she sold the dresses better herself, out of the old Cadillac's enormous trunk which she had lined with silk and rayon. Buyers and shop owners liked it when she came around. Her toothy smile, the big old Caddy, and she would be wearing one of her dresses and they looked great on Melissa. She was charming. She never really *sold* anything. She just showed up and the clothes were in her arms, and people would take them. She was too shy to sell—the secret of her success. Though if she was a success, it was a modest one. She paid the rent and bought a few things. People said that Melissa was so beautiful she should be a movie star. Local version of praise, replacing the national hopefulness of "could" with the more expectant and knowing "should," yet Melissa would have been even more shy to act than she was shy to sell. Lord knows her boyfriend Zacky could have made something out of her. But Melissa liked doing what she did, and it was something that no one else did, not the way she did it anyway.

Six or eight months passed from the time I got my apartment and when I got a call from my father that he and Irene were coming out, he had a couple meetings with people and they would stay a few days then go up to Santa Barbara, but when I was in Los Angeles would I like to have dinner? For some years previous I'd been almost out of touch with him, involved with my New York "group," in which it was often said that parents and conditioning and habits were the source of most of our difficulties. I took this lesson as far as it would take me and where it left me off, I imagined, was with my feelings about my father and growing up and my mother and divorce and California and Irene and kidney-shaped swimming pools exposed and worn away, so that I could begin to live my own life now. So that I could come to California aware that this was where my father and Irene had made their lives without me, but not because of it. I had my own reasons. I was a writer and I needed the money and it was some-place I hadn't tried. And in fact my life in Los Angeles after I arrived was nothing like my images of what theirs had been. My life was Venice and the beach and the bungalows of Ocean Park and people who were passing through or just getting by. I never went to Bel Air, nor to a museum. I called up an agent or two who my father suggested might help me, but they didn't and I stopped calling. It was as if our two paths never crossed. In this, Melissa was like an archetype, of a Los Angeles unlike theirs, and when they invited me for dinner it seemed almost natural for me to invite her along.

We went to one of their old places in Beverly Hills. Unlike everything in Venice in those years, it wasn't painted white. And the food was old-fashioned too, veal in this or that. But tasty enough, in a way that reminded me of Europe, of them in Eu-rope with their red guides and concierge tips; they would never go to a restaurant with bad food. As soon as we sat down, as if surprised by an inevitability, I began comparing Melissa to Irene. There were odd similarities, in height, in the blue metallic of their eyes, in their somewhat elongated slender noses and lanky frames. Irene had never been as blond as Melissa but she must have been a little bit blond once. And Melissa looked great in her clothes, and Irene maybe still did too, she who I used to imagine playing sports in just the right thing. Though I don't quite remember what Irene was wearing that night. Something roughly woven, a jacket? I'm not that good at this, remembering her, or clothes. What I do recall is that the politeness of Irene and my father to each other was out in full force. She told a flattering story about him playing chess with Ronnie Reagan in the Universal commissary and having to explain to Ronnie gently how if your pawn got to the end of the board you could get any piece you wanted back. He told a flattering story about her binding books with tactile covers for the blind in Tijuana. They were bragging, really. It's what it came down to when you subtracted out that she was talking about him and he was talking about her. But who were they trying to impress? Surely not me, the unemployed writer. It must have been Melissa, the beauty, my friend. They must have thought she was my girlfriend and were making sure she knew what worldly, accomplished, humane, and well-thought-of parents I had. I was afraid that Melissa would feel hurt by this, as she would have been hurt if they had started quizzing her on the capital of Delaware or South Dakota. What amazed me more than their name-dropping was that, far from retreating into a shell of resentment, Melissa could compete. For every name they dropped, she dropped one of equal or greater value. She didn't mind at all. It was like a contest to her—she wouldn't have started it but now that they'd started it—to see who was best. And younger people, more currently stylish people, were in her armory. I had neglected to calculate that even a clandestine affair with Zacky Kurtz would result in a slurry of celebrity acquaintances. Referred to obliquely, of course, the exact circumstances of each bit of her gossip or observation left nicely obscure. And before Zacky, all those rock guys she made shirts for. Though of course Irene and my father didn't know the rock guys, so mentioning those was like serving outside the lines, in a tennis match where it was two against one. I was the one who knew nobody. Not in person, anyway. Later I told Melissa I didn't know she had it in her. She said she didn't know what I was talking about. She had gone back to being quiet. I thought about it again and decided that Melissa, despite her shyness, and some other things, was a lot like Irene.

*

A short catalog of the kinds of things my father professed to have an opinion about. The show at the Met, the Baryshnikov this or that, the oil situation in the Emirates, the op-ed piece about the secretary of the treasury, the Booker Prize, the best-seller list, new advances in cloning, the Knicks, the Mets, the electric cars, the mayor's temper, the race situation here and in postcolonial Africa, communists, land mines, Academy Awards, Nobel Prizes, the U.N. and American intransigence about it, the decline of statesmanship, steroids in the Olympics, hormones in beef, child labor in developing countries, plundered Nazi art, Klee, Ernst, Pollack, whoever, Warhol, Schnabel, grand pianos.

*

It was Melissa who introduced me to Zacky and Zacky who put me on what seemed like a magic carpet, something out of *The Thief of Baghdad*. Zacky at the time with his partner James Morton had one of the big new hits on television, a cop show set in the nighttime of an absurd ghetto world. Depending who you listened to, *Northie* was realistic, surrealistic, tragic, comic, tragicomic, or way over the top. Certainly it took a lot of chances. It did shows entirely from the criminals' point of view, where you hardly saw the cops at all, and then the same stories entirely from the victims' point of view, where you also hardly saw the cops at all. It did shows that took place in "real time," and shows where one hour covered an entire year. It did a silent movie hour complete with dialogue cards. It did black-and-white hours. It did one hour where the first act was in black-and-white and the second in color and so on. It did an entire hour shot with a stationary camera. It did an hour show entirely inside a police car. It did an hour where the actors switched their parts around.

And it was as energetic as it was risk-taking. There were other shows with bigger casts, *Northie* had only six regulars, but things were always bumping into other things or getting smashed up. Zacky took an interest in me because Melissa told him I was smart and because they wanted writers who hadn't been corrupted by writing for older shows and because I'd put in my time with the D.A.'s office in New York and seemed to know what I was talking about when it came to the mean streets. Then he read my scripts and laughed. He gave me an assignment, then another. My young mystic's training in self-abnegation resulted in scripts that were just like theirs. I had a gift for imitation. Which in a television series was a particularly good gift to have, since of all art forms the one a TV series most resembles is the skyscraper—ornamentation on the first few floors and on the top, but in between, seventy or ninety or a hundred floors that are just windows, as if it were true that a giraffe is just a horse that reached for the highest leaves.

And this was true even in shows that were daring. Within months of my joining the staff, in a year when shows from our rival MTM were favored to sweep the board, *Northie* won enough Emmys to stuff the trunk of Zacky and Morty's limo, and then came a string of other awards, and the magazines and entertainment shows, and the ratings, and more money. Though Morty was tired of it already, and there were rumors that he was angry at Zacky for hogging the publicity. Not that Morty wanted it himself, but he seemed to have contempt for anybody who would. The publicity and the credit: who would want such things? What kind of person? Morty had been a master printer before he was a writer and soon was thinking of going back to Oregon and a letterpress. Which seemed as if it would be fine with Zacky, who in the seventies had often been called the "King of TV," mostly on account of a wildly popular, easy-going detective show called *Darlington* and another called *Billie Rae*, and was hoping to ride *Northie* past those up-and-coming MTM guys to become reigning king once more. Both Zacky and James were soon grooming me to be Morty's successor. Or not a successor precisely, because Zacky didn't want another partner. He simply needed someone who could do the work that Morty did, which in Morty's view was more than his share, of the experimental work anyway, that had come from the fevered brain of a master printer and not been on television before, as opposed to the tropes of a veteran like Zacky. Zacky had been in TV his whole adult life, and he was forty-seven years old, nine years my senior, the year I joined *Northie*. And I was grateful to him.

But sardonic, bleak, and younger James Morton was closer to my style. I had complaints with even *Northie*'s television from the start. Until he left the show, Morty and I would go out to lunch and grouse. How manipulated most of it was, how calculated, a dollop of emotion here, a zinger of a joke there, as if the only point was to please. Yet in truth, I liked such grousing. It was something, for a writer who had been in his room, to come out and have others to grouse with. I liked the company, the free lunches, even the pleasure of reintegration into a society that I'd scarcely known was there. And having people say nice things about you all the time, even if they were lying, agents buttering you up for future commissions, actors buttering you up for better lines. As Zacky would put it, when Texas overcame him, it was like stepping in high cotton. I vaguely knew that I'd been lucky. But I put stock as well in another of Zacky's favorite bits of schoolboy Latin: *Fortuna est fortuna, sed labor omnia vincit.* And then too, the money coming in, like thunderstorms rolling over a desert that had been parched for years.

My father was maybe even prouder of me than he was shocked by my rapid progress, which must have seemed to him like an unexpected September run from a ball club previously struggling in the second division. After my first show was on, he called up of course. It seemed as if everybody I knew called up, as if everybody had seen. Most had just a few kind words. But my father said, "Very professional."

"Thanks."

"I had a little trouble hearing a few lines. I guess I'm getting old."

"All the crosstalk."

"Is that what they call it? When everybody talks at once?"

"I think so. I guess so."

"But *she's* marvelous. The girl."

"She is . . ."

"And the thing about the autistic kid who ran numbers was touching."

"It happens to be true. The kid's at Harvard now."

"Look, could I make one suggestion?"

"Why not?"

"Just a little one. . . . Take the episode, make ten copies, I'll give you a list, you send them to the top ten agents in town."

"But I've got an agent."

"Now's your chance to get a better one."

"I like the one I've got."

"Just making a little suggestion."

"Thanks. Really. I'll consider it."

"This is your chance."

"I think I'm okay."

"It was a *marvelous* show. It really was."

"Thanks."

"Well if there's anything I can do . . . If you want that list of agents . . ."

"Let me think about it."

"Think about it."

"Good-night."

"Good-night."

"Thanks for the call."

"If I can be of any help . . ."

Only a producer, was pretty much my thought; as if the subtlest art of the producer was to noodge tenderly.

*

The odd thing was, he didn't seem to know exactly how far I'd already come. Either that or he couldn't quite acknowledge it. Or couldn't quite believe it. As if it was as much a dream to him as it was to me.

Yet it wasn't a dream to me. It felt more like something natural, or expected, like an inheritance. I could do this because he had done it before me. Stepping into this world that I half-wanted and half-despised felt like stepping into a bath that was exactly my body temperature.

*

One small miracle of *Northie*: that it really did feel like a northern, inner-city show, even though Zacky had Houston in his bones. And his co-creator, Morty, was from Eugene.

Zacky had come north only when Columbia gave him his scholarship. But he made up for lost time. He quit football after his freshman year. He spent the rest of his time, by his own account, "down the hill" in Harlem. Either in Harlem or at Rockefeller Center, where NBC had its headquarters, hoping for his break into show business.

For reasons known only to themselves, Zacky and Morty set their show in Boston, in what felt like Roxbury or Dorchester, but it never lost the rhythms and rhymes of Zacky's years spent close to that other great institution of learning called UCLA, the University on the Corner of Lenox Avenue.

*

Another small miracle, not only of *Northie* but of all the break-through TV dramas of the eighties, in my opinion anyway: their zest. There was little about the demented, confused, heroic, pre-posterous, greedy, scatological, contemporary fairy tale of urban life in America in the eighties, in other words the life so many of us lived or would have lived if we could, that couldn't fit some-how into their maws. In many respects, we who were doing them just took our own lives and plastered them onto whatever world our show was set in. What a wrong thing to do, bad, bad, bad, except it worked. Maybe because everyone in the eighties had middle-class hopes.

Yet they were never entirely realistic shows, nor as far as I knew were they meant to be. That's where the critics, I thought, had it wrong. They thought what was good about *Northie*, or for that matter the MTM shows or even *Cagney & Lacey* or *China Beach*, was their "realism," and whenever a new one came along where the toilets flushed louder they thought that was more realistic and better. I can only speak for *Northie*, but in our case the "realism" was only a tease. There were all our formal experiments, for one thing. And then there was that huge appetite, as if that night we were eternally playing in might gobble up the world. Surreal, vain, a little nuts, a little wrong. But the heart of it never broke. It had pity. It had mercy. It took its share of cheap shots and believed in everybody. When it was good, anyway. It had the bitter exuberance of the end of our youth.

*

The next time the Emmys came around, I took my mother. Invited her out, put her up in a hotel, took her out shopping for a dress. I've heard the TV and movie stars have made mom night kind of a fashion recently, but she was the only one, or close to it, that year. People doted on her. Hagle, the star of our show who played the unflappable Lieutenant Donald D. O'Brien, kissed her hand, hugged her, and bored her for twenty minutes talking about his hiking experiences in the Carpathian Alps. Or "bored" is strictly my interpretation. I'd heard about his hiking experiences in the Carpathian Alps so many times and I felt she should be bored, but actually she was the ideal listener. Everything interested her, and as soon as she had the chance she returned his conversational favor, telling him all about her varied experience volunteering at the library back home. I had wondered how she would feel coming to the place where the one whose name she wouldn't even say unless it was absolutely necessary ran off with her best friend. But it didn't seem to faze her. It was as if she had waited a very long time to make her entrance, but when she made it, she made it in triumph. I was her triumph. In the limo back to Santa Monica she went through the goodies bag they give you at the dinner like a child with a Christmas stocking. It's weird how even the rich like these things, but my mother seemed not so much greedy as surprised. As in: how could they afford to give out all this for free? The companies must be going broke! It was my year that year and I placed the ungainly statue they'd given me in her lap. The statue had electric-like wings that were kind of sharp, and she rubbed her fingers over them. "A person could get cut," she said.

"So be careful."

"They should sand them down at least. This is terrible."

"They leave them that way so the envious can keep stabbing one another."

"Your father never won one of these."

She said it in such a way that I could imagine malice in her voice when it wasn't really there. No echo, no disappointment, nothing. As if she could have added: "Just an observation." But she got quiet, picked up some of the Revlon stuff they'd given her, the cleanser, the moisturizer, the whatever else, and looked at it all with a curiosity not so different from a child's.

It was at moments such as these that I least felt like I was living my own life, or rather that I had my own life but was loaning it out, to others' purposes and feelings. If it was me, I told myself, I'd have gotten right out of this limo. But I was happy enough for her to be in it and she wouldn't have been in it if I wasn't in it too. We drove along through rain-dampened streets with the dark windows making everything darker and the statue still in her lap and I took a kind of spiritual siesta. It's what it felt like, slipping off to a pied-à-terre of the mind where everything was more or less at rest. A pied-à-terre I kept just in case all of the rest of this didn't work out.

As I understand, or understood, what Krishna once told Arjuna, it is proper for people to spend their lives living out the societal roles that fate has given them. Then when those roles are fulfilled, a man may wander off. To the forest, wherever, in search of his soul.

*

Now I read over what I wrote previously, and I ask myself: would I really have gotten right out of the limo?

Second thoughts. A book of second thoughts.

*

My father became more collegial with me. One measure of which that I happened to notice was that he began to swear in my presence. Nothing terribly daring, no motherfucking motherfucker fucking cocksucking bitch whore cunts, just a smattering of shits and damns. But they were there, in the natural rhythms of his speech. As if we were both in the same business now, we both knew the same jokes.

He was still in New York and was trying to get shows on again because his movies had been flops. He knew he was getting older and he may have needed the money. I don't know how much money they had spent, on moving back and forth, on Europe, on art, on restaurants, on her catheter or whatever it was and the aftermath of Fred and on bringing up Thomas, whom after our few days together in Bel Air I hardly knew at all. I didn't seek him out. He went to private schools and then he went to Yale. We were seldom in the same city. I heard, from my father, from Irene, that he was a nice kid.

It was much harder for my father to get shows on now. He no longer had a big studio behind him. Then as now, television was not receptive to the old guys, unless the old guys were so rich they could hire the young guys to do their work for them. Instead he hired Irene. They were partners, after a fashion. They had an office on Thirty-eighth Street and tried to tap, as my father said, the tremendous talent of the Broadway playwrights for television. This was what he now had to sell, this and his track record, but his track record was from a ways back. And why Irene? Because she needed to work? Because it was keeping it all in the family, a mom-and-pop shop, no outside salaries to pay? Because of Fred and her bad dreams? Because it was a way of holding it all together, just as their politeness and their ping-ponging back and forth across the country and his letters to the editor and sharing their food in restaurants was a way of holding it all together? A sentence in which the "all" must refer to their marriage, their bet together—but anything else?

They would take the Broadway playwrights out to lunch. The fun part of the job. Irene learning what my father really did. And my father doing his determined best to be a man of his times, liberal and forward-thinking, making his wife his equal in all he did.

I'm not sure whether Irene had ever held a job in her life before. That must have been part of it too.

Irene reading scripts and answering the phone and having opinions, like a D-girl almost sixty. And why not? Brave enough.

Yet the odds seemed long. And being in New York didn't help, when most of the business wasn't. A quixotic thing in a way, a way of saying, to yourself or others, that you were keeping your hand in. He began to call me more frequently. To catch me up on what he was doing or tell me what I should be doing. Always polite, almost deferential, as if he wouldn't presume to tell me whatever it was he was about to tell me, but what the hell, he'd take a chance, he was my dad after all, and so what about this or what about that. I loved this. I think I loved it. I loved being treated like a colleague, which was different from being treated like an equal because with a colleague you didn't have to measure so precisely, who was up, who was down. It reminded me, a little, of when my father had told me at my grandmother's funeral that he would make sure I could go to Yale if I got in.

And so I was also wary, as if on the lookout for something unsaid. Was my father just buttering me up? Did he want something from me? And yet, if so, why not? Wasn't that what colleagues were for, to commiserate with each other and want things from each other? One day my father asked me if he could send me a script. He said it was something that he and Irene were both quite proud of, it was by E_____, the well-known, highly regarded Broadway playwright, and they were going to turn it in soon to CBS, but if I had any thoughts before they turned it in, that would be great. There were ways that I felt flattered by this. He was asking me to critique this well-known, highly regarded Broadway playwright, or to put my two cents in anyway. Or even more flattering: he seemed to be asking me for a pat on the back. Was I now someone he would like a pat on the back from? I was terrified that I would hate the script.

It was set in some future world where there was a pioneering civilization and then there were marauders and it was going to be an updated western, a sci-fi western, or that's how they pitched it anyway. Always make the pitch simple. Of course there'd not been a successful western on television in fifteen years, but that was exactly the point, bring 'em back, the classic formula for success, take an old, worn-out genre and give it a new lease on life. Wasn't that how shows like *Northie* succeeded? I remember my father asking me this, telling me most of this, when we were on the phone and he asked me if he could send out the script. He seemed to be trying out the point that his script and *Northie* were similar types of projects, revolutionary yet with a memory of hits past in their bones.

I did hate that script. I hated it so much that I wondered if I was fated to hate it, if no matter it had been written by Mark Twain and named *The Adventures of Huckleberry Finn* I would have hated it. It was sentimental and trite and labored and well-meaning and pathetically, falsely optimistic and the characters speechified and postured and each one was better than the last, except for the "baddies," of course, and the women were all gems and strong and the future didn't look so bad. Mostly I hated the well-known highly regarded Broadway playwright's patronization, as if he was going to use television to teach everybody something, as if people needed to be taught. Since I wasn't aware that such patronization was in his work on Broadway, I was afraid that my father and Irene in the do-gooding spirit that was taping them together had put him up to it, or at least had let him get away with it, get away with not understanding the medium at all. It was as if the well-known, highly regarded Broadway playwright had decided that he could only rationalize taking such big, easy bucks as these and stooping so low as to *do television* if he was being uplifting. Old-fashioned? Anyway, without nuance or laughs-in-the-middle-of-tragedy or sarcasm or absurdity or doubt. As if the broad American demographic wouldn't get such things. But I was in the process of making a small fortune precisely because America would, did, get such things.

Or was I wrong about it? It's what I feared. The arising of my unconscious, bopping my father over the head at the first opportunity? And the fact that I was doing one of these lucky, advanced, sophisticated shows. Wasn't most of television still not like this, didn't you have to be sentimental and trite, especially on CBS, with its audience in the "C" towns and "D" towns of middle America? I wasn't sure. I didn't watch the stuff. I was less of an expert than a hundred million Americans. And everybody else was telling him the script was great. It's what he told me, anyway. But wasn't that what people did? You tell your friend, your colleague, your whatever the script is great and wait for the network, or whoever's up the food chain, to shoot it down.

"Hi, Dad."

"Hi."

"I read the script."

"Oh?"

"Actually, I read it twice."

"Great."

"Have you turned it in yet?"

"Not yet. Friday. Unless, of course, you have things to suggest. I told E_____ my son was reading it."

"You did?"

"He knows your show."

"Oh. Good."

"I don't know if he actually *watches* it every week . . ."

"Well, whatever. Look, I don't have too much to say. A couple of things."

"Did I tell you, Mike Landrum called. He thought the script was *marvelous*."

"Great."

"People seem to like that it has, I don't know how else to put it, an old-fashioned feel, I guess. They feel like they're on solid ground. With a twist, of course."

"The future."

"The whole universe, that E_____ created, the whole *Star Trek* thing."

"But there isn't really too much science fiction in it, I mean, you know, special effects."

"It's not a special effects show. It's a character show. It's all about people, that's all. Just people."

"I think that's great. I mean, it's the right place to start."

"So tell me. . . . You said you had a couple things."

"Nothing much. Just general. If there was one thing, I'd mess up the characters a little."

"Make them *quirkier*?"

"Not quirkier, necessarily. Quirky's a little creepy. To me, anyway. Just mess 'em up a little."

"I'm not sure what you mean, 'mess 'em up a little.'"

"Just . . . some of them . . . I guess I mean less one-dimensional."

"The characters are one-dimensional?"

"It's not that they *are*. It's they could be . . . *less so*? Am I making any sense? Less good guys and bad guys."

"There's always been good guys and bad guys."

"Of course. Of course."

"Look at *Star Trek.*"

"Right. You're right. . . . Though actually, I don't know you're right. I never saw *Star Trek.*"

"You never saw *Star Trek?*"

"Bits. I've seen bits of one or two."

And so I guess I'd found my excuse. I didn't know television.

"Anything else?" my father asked.

"I don't know."

"You said you had a couple things."

"I guess I'd wait, I'd see what they say, the network. I mean, if they love it . . ."

"They love E_____. They couldn't have been more complimentary."

"I'd just wait then. When they have notes, I mean, if they even have any, maybe it'll be exactly what they want just the way it is right now, and I wouldn't want to say something, and E_____ changes it, and that's what they don't like . . . so if they have notes, then, if you want, we can talk some more."

"Sounds good. But basically you liked it?"

"I did."

"Great."

But CBS never gave him notes. They must have hated it so much, they didn't bother.

What my father and I never talked about was doing a project together. The assumption was always that I was busy with *Northie*, or busy with Zacky, or busy with something. I imagined he didn't want to presume on my success. I imagine he was being kind in not asking. But I think he would have liked to do a show with me then. I could add, "especially after the debacle with E_____."

But even if that hadn't been a disaster, I think he would have. For the pride of it, if nothing else. Though, if I could generalize, with a producer there's always something else. The enhanced chances for success, the fresh stories to tell your friends, the competition of it, ha ha, beat you at last, beat you with my own son. All of those and more. I would have liked to do a project with my father for the roundedness of it, and the warm bath of generosity I would swim in, but I feared it. Why work with him and have to argue against the sentimental and old and tell him that Irene would have to butt out of it because I couldn't listen to her as well as everybody else? I was on a roll. I had Zacky Kurtz or he had me. I was part of one of TV's big hits. I kept telling myself maybe. Time passed and we said nothing.

*

And now a sort of forward movement of the plot. While my father got older, Zacky's wife, Maryanna, a black-haired Italian girl from South San Francisco who had some street fighter instincts in her, got an inkling about Zacky's affair with Melissa. Or maybe she didn't get an inkling, maybe Zacky only imagined she got an inkling, or maybe it wasn't even that, maybe he simply wanted to distract her so that she would never get an inkling. Or maybe he just felt guilty. In all events, Maryanna was an actress and she had a small, recurring role on *Northie* from the start of it, playing a police department nutritionist who would come around and complain about the food in the vending machines and try with little success to improve the cops' diets. Maryanna was brilliant in the role, funny and sharp, wistful and wry, and we liked having her come around. But now Zacky began to build up the part, so that soon there was a "Maryanna" plot in nearly every episode. The problem was that on *Northie*, a show about cops, Maryanna wasn't playing a cop. Over at the network, there were grumblings that the show was losing its masculine edge, or more importantly, its male viewers. Which was fine by Zacky, who was content to explain it by saying that he was exploring his feminine side and who would add that people with paired X chromosomes watched television too. But it was really, I thought, about Melissa.

I would tactfully suggest to Zacky that even though I really loved Maryanna, we were beginning to overuse her. My reward was that when the network called to complain, Zacky would tell them the problem wasn't Maryanna or his desire to explore his feminine side, the problem was me. Time for recourse to one of the entertainment industry's most eternal clichés: no good deed goes unpunished. Then Maryanna found out about Melissa for sure and Zacky dropped Melissa and I was angry with him then, for the way he did it, over a weekend and not looking back, and even for the way he set Melissa up with an old shrink of his, as though mental health benefits were part of her severance package, or he was afraid she would kill herself and make a scene. I said something to him once. Innocuous enough, but it was something. I said, "Melissa doesn't need a shrink, she needs someone to take care of her." Taken out of context the words may seem harsh, but they were hedged when I said them, with "I don't know's" and "maybe's," and they were in answer to his question whether I knew how she was doing. But he hated me for saying it. He hated me for knowing. I felt like when I was little, writing my father or riding my bicycle to the drug store pay phone, in defense or explanation of my mother. Which I suppose, if we're talking about me, got close to the heart of it all. Zacky as another father figure. I'd had one in college, my friend Harry Nolan, who might have been president of the whole country one day and who I wrote about. Then I'd had another in Joe, the "group" leader who I also wrote about. Always looking for a father. As if: my own father was back, yet I still didn't quite believe that he was back, or it was too late for it now, even if my own father was kinder than Zacky, which he was. But Zacky was stronger than my father, depending on what you thought "strong" was. "Strong" in the way my father meant it when he said his own father was "weak"? All of this confused me. Zacky told me the shrink he set her up with had fallen in love with Melissa. So she would have someone to "take care of her," if that's what I meant. He said it with cold eyes.

And he would have gotten rid of me. My contract was coming up and he would have done something. I was pretty sure of it and my agent Sterner was pretty sure of it, he'd heard it at the network, and anyway it fit what Zacky did, according to Sterner anyway. There were lines you could cross with him and lines you couldn't. As there should be with men who would be king. Stifled finally, exhausted possibly, Morty had escaped by simply leaving. But what about me, who wasn't ready to leave?

I found an answer that had a name. Adam Bloch. If I were writing a script now, I would capitalize his name, so that the actor playing him would wake up and start reading. I had known Bloch at university. He played the most tragic part of all in the events I wrote about before. He was the one who drove us all, figuratively and all but literally, off a cliff. And I had never forgiven him. To paraphrase something I heard in a movie once, he was the kind of Jew you boiled down ten Jews in order to get. The adjectives I might apply won't barely cover him. Awkward, sincere, quiet, observant of a vast range of things and unobservant of a vast range of others. How he bore the guilt of the accident I'd never known, we'd never talked about it. What could I have said if I had been unwilling to forgive and what could he have said if he had been unable to forget? Or not "forget." "Forget" isn't right. If he'd been unable *not to obsess*? Adam went on from Yale to get his Ph.D. from Chicago in economics, taught someplace a couple of years, and, as if furtively, as if all his decisions were made at night, decided to chuck the academy and go into business. He never told anybody why. It must have seemed—to his parents, to whomever else, though there may have been nobody else, he was an only child—a more than small step backward on the ladder of assimilation when he took the output of a hippie cousin's barn in the hills of Pennsylvania, where the hippie cousin was dyeing old shirts in fresh colors, and opened a storefront in downtown New York to sell them by the armload. But this was the start for Adam in purveying stonewashed everything. He became the Ralph Lauren of stonewashed. He made a mint. He became, after Fred Smith who founded Federal Express, the most successful entrepreneur that our class at Yale produced. And with his winnings he went to Hollywood, in time to be my savior. Adam wanted to buy something, wanted to live in the sunshine at last. He called me and I took him around and introduced him to people, at my agency, at

the network, wherever. The time came for my contract to be renewed and Zacky blocked it; or he didn't block it precisely, guys
in Zacky's position seldom left their fingerprints on anything if
they could help it, but he made sure conditions were attached that
I would never accept. The way it was done. I felt a sort of dull
dread, ubiquitous and clammy, what you might feel for something long awaited as inevitable that nevertheless, when time
passed and it didn't happen, you finally dared believe it might
not. But shmuck me once, shame on you; shmuck me twice,
shame on me. Another of the industry's sagest clichés. I'd been
left by one producer in my life and was damned if I'd be left by
another. I went to Bloch. I told him of a company he could buy,
if the money was really burning a hole. He did a short course in
figures, he made the kind of offer that even a cliché couldn't
refuse, and I am making a long business story much shorter in
the interests of concision but anyway in a matter of months if not
weeks he owned Cangaroo, the company that made *Northie*. It
was Zacky who got fired and not me. Bloch didn't know enough
about the business to know he couldn't do that, so he did. Or he
didn't actually do it, he was about to do it, and the network was
said to be backing him and I would become the boss. But then I
myself intervened, out of loyalty and guilt. Not much of a scene.
I just did it, made a few calls and it was done. Told Bloch, when
all was said and done, he'd be making a mistake. Made out Zacky
to be something like a designated hitter in the American League,
an aging slugger who could still give you a big year. Zacky said,
"Thanks, guy." We didn't talk about it more. We were partners
after that.

*

I suppose a boy whose father left is later a man who is easily led. Or could almost the opposite be true, will he pick men to lead him who themselves will leave, and he knows it, and he will leave first if he can? Is betrayal his fate and his action? Is loyalty his curse?

*

Despite the money coming in, I had never quite moved out of the Ocean Park Apartments. I liked the idea of a guy making big bucks keeping his rent-controlled apartment. Ed Koch, when he was mayor of New York and got Gracie Mansion to live in, had done the same. Everyone in New York seemed to know this at the time and it may have won him some votes, as it tended to prove what a true-blue New Yorker he was. Kept you in touch with your roots, anyway. Or maybe it was this that Zacky was referring to when he said I'd squeeze a nickel till the buffalo crapped. I just didn't want to be suburban, I didn't want to be like Zacky, who by the way had settled in Hancock Park instead of the Westside, as if to remind his cohorts in TV's upper echelons that he remained a Protestant in their midst. The big Spanish job with eighteen rooms on South Muirfield, the expanse of granite countertop in the kitchen, the stove that could roast whole babies, the three thousand dollar heated Japanese toilet that adjusted to your every contour like a seat in an expensive car and did many other wonderful things. To all of this I continued to say no. I continued to chat up the welfare cases in the lobby and use the coin-ops in the laundry room to wash my clothes and when I felt like it I'd go down to the second floor and see if Melissa was around. Or sometimes I would know that she was around because I could look out and see her big green gleaming Caddy in the parking lot.

One day I knocked on her door and there was no answer when I'd seen the big green Caddy and I touched the knob and was able to turn it, and the door came open in my hand. Stupid thing for me to do, she could have been in there fucking somebody, fucking the psychiatrist who'd fallen in love with her, or sleeping or anything else that was none of my business, though I was her friend. Anyway, the door fell open in my hand and I called her name, Melissa, Melissa, and when there was no answer I took a couple steps in. A beautiful place, by the way. One of those places where there were flowers on the windowsills and the lamplight had a pink cast and the refrigerator was mostly empty. I guess I'd had some sort of instinct. It wasn't anything I'd ever done before, go into some girl's place without a key. She was on the couch passed out and there were bottles of pills on the floor.

Sounds like a scene that enough guys have written but it was real enough then. She wasn't quite passed out, because when I sat beside her and said her name and shook her, she whispered my name back. I did this, we did this, a number of times. Her eyes slid almost open, then slid back again, and her breathing was soft. She was in a white bathrobe that made her look like a ghost and her hair was damp, so that I imagined she must have taken a shower and come out here to read the *People* magazine that was by the pills. There was also the core of an apple on a plate. The pills, whatever they were, were prescribed by Zacky's psychiatrist and I called his number that was on one of the bottles. He came over in twenty minutes, which is as fast as anybody gets any-place in Los Angeles, and we got her to a sitting position so that she could swallow some other pills he gave her, and he did a few probes and tests and said a hospital wasn't necessary, so we waited. The psychiatrist was a short man with twinkly eyes and a pudgy face like a clown. A kindly man, by the look of it, formerly married to someone well-known in the business and for a long time a shrink to the stars. I asked him what had done this to Melissa and he said her medication for her "unstable condition." I said I didn't know Melissa had an unstable condition, and I'd never seen her unstable until now, but the psychiatrist—whom we may as well call Candleman, Kenneth Candleman, another name to put in capital letters for the script—assured me that he knew this. I began to feel contempt for him then. What was he doing telling me anything about her, when he'd fallen in love with his own damn patient and here she was passed out? What were these pills, anyway, I asked, and he said again that they were medication for her unstable condition. I asked him if she'd taken too many of them, and he said he didn't know. But there were still lots of them in each of the bottles. That, and the apple core, and the *People* magazine. So we sort of both of us ruled out a suicide attempt. Candleman made a point of telling me that as soon as he felt a "countertransference" with Melissa, he'd given her up as a patient. But then what was he doing prescribing her these pills? I asked him that. He said he'd prescribed them "before." After that, we were quiet, and after that, we talked about football. He'd gone to Michigan and they were good that fall. As I said, he seemed to be a kindly man, and at one point when he looked at Melissa there seemed to be tears in his eyes. Enough to change them from sparkly to watery, anyway.

Candleman didn't leave until she was awake. That was after three or four hours. Three hours and a half. She was groggy. She got up and took another shower. She said she didn't know what happened. Candleman asked her a few questions, had she been drinking, other medications. Yes, and yes. The night before anyway. And little sleep. He told her don't do any of those things anymore, not for now anyway, and then he left. I fixed her tea. It was dark by then. I went out to the pizza place and brought back pizza. She ate a little of it and I did too and then put it in the empty refrigerator. I told her I didn't think she should be taking those pills at all and also that if she suffered from anything it wasn't some mental disease *du jour* but rather a spiritual ailment that pills could hide but never cure. I felt full of a kind of certainty that I had seldom felt in my life. We made love for the first time that night.

The next day she went over to Candleman's and threw all her pills at him like they were buckshot and yelled at him that he had made her sick in order to control her and *he* was the sick fuck and why shouldn't she be mad, of course she was mad! She left with tears of righteous anger in her eyes. I imagined Candleman watching her get back in her car as if she were a Greek goddess returning to the woods. Later that day he left three messages on her machine. Melissa was there sewing curtains and never picked up the phone. In the first he was earnest and rational and said he had picked up the pills off the floor and would like to drop them by because as she could see from the rage she flew into, there was a reason for the pills. He was not trying to manipulate her, he was not trying for advantage, he was trying only . . . and there was no finish to that thought. In the second message he was pleading and admitting mistakes and saying again that he would like to come over. His voice was hoarse and he didn't mention pills or helping her or anything but, as she knew, his love of her. In the third he asked where she was and suspected that she was there and if she was there would she please pick up because it was important and he'd called before as she knew and if she didn't call soon he'd be coming over to check on her because he was afraid. She listened as if to lies, picking them out like nits, and made her curtains because she could do nothing else. I came back to her apartment after work. She told me about her day and about Candleman's messages and I felt less certain than I had been. But I still felt like I could take over for the pills.

We made love that night and the next night. I stopped going to my apartment. On the fourth night she told me how Candleman had given her magazines to make her smarter like the *New Republic* that she didn't care about but she felt she should. Even though she hated him for it, I thought better about Candleman for that. Why shouldn't Melissa read such things and see what worthless gab was in them? Why shouldn't she have the chance not to feel bad about herself over nothing? I could imagine her quoting the *New Republic* about this and that, Reagan or the East Germans, I could imagine her getting away with it, as if sometimes a scam's the best thing for you. But I knew she didn't want to hear it, and she knew what I was thinking. The next day was a weekend and we took a walk in a park in Malibu, overlooking the ocean on a cloudy day. On the walk Melissa began to cry. She asked me to tell her the truth, was she too stupid for me? I could have given her the easy answer, because of course she wasn't stupid at all, but I knew what she was talking about. And that she was giving me a chance then to walk away. Every single thing that I could ever hate about her was right there asking to be hated. I could take my stand against self-pity, passive-aggression, lack of irony, humorlessness, narcissism, the need to control, latent hysteria, and ignorance. I felt a thousand miles away from her. She could have jumped off the nearest cliff and I wouldn't have seen. Or to put it another way, everything human about her that I had rejected and left in enough other women I could have rejected and left in Melissa just then, and yet for no reason at all, or what seemed like no reason at all, I didn't. I suppose it was because I had already saved her. Or imagined that I had, hoped that I had. The cruelest seduction of all or the cleverest anyway, you save someone and you're the one seduced. I told her she wasn't stupid at all, because of course she wasn't stupid at all, but I didn't add that she shouldn't have to be told. "Really?" Melissa asked, turning her head back from the ocean. It seemed as if she were trying to believe something, but I wasn't sure if it was what I'd said. Her eyes were as dark as the ocean was that day. Confusion in them, then something tentative, as if asking, or telling, *look where my life has brought me.* We kissed as if each was kissing the other's tender weakness, we walked out of the park, and we stayed with each other again.

*

After that, the closest I ever came to leaving Melissa was when we went to see her parents in Seattle. Nothing against her parents. They were good, decent people, her father had worked at Boeing on the shop floor and worked his way up and her mother had religious faith. Artistic people, too, her mother beautified and her father could do or make anything. Their clapboard house in the far suburbs with the screened-in porch was filled with everything he had carved or painted, some of it kitsch but some of it not, some of it, like the hordes of World War I lead doughboys he'd painted all white so that they looked like an army of ghosts, you wondered, as you might wonder occasionally about artists in museums of the new, how he thought to do that. We went up there the Easter after we started being together. The evangelical church was fine, the relatives were fine, the rampant Republicanism was fine. What got me was going out to dinner at the Applebee's restaurant. Applebee's is a chain, as maybe you know. They had them in Rochester, they had them outside Seattle. Big pictures of the food on the menu. Dinners at six or seven ninety-nine, or those were the prices then, and I ordered the ribs and Melissa a salad and her parents the surf-and-turf. And I felt so at home. Gentiles or no, across the country or no. I could have been out to dinner with my mother and my sister the way we'd go to the HoJo's on Saturday nights for fried clams, the big treat of the week, which was beautiful and sweet and sad, seeing my mother paying for anything at all, or remembering her paying for anything at all. It was as if the restaurant and her parents and the surf-and-turf and the pictures of the food on the menu had all conspired to betray Melissa, to reveal her as from my mother's world and not Irene's. The four of us sitting in the vinyl booth and Melissa with her iceberg lettuce salad so happy to be home with her parents or maybe even happy to have brought one home to her parents, and me thinking: she is happy now like my mother must have been once, and when she was happy was that not a sign for my father's betrayal to start? I felt starved and nourished by the Applebee's ribs and corn on the cob, that I could hardly eat, and then in a panic wolfed down, as if desperate not to reveal my mind. The others saying the sweet-enough, middle-of-the-country things you say when you're going out to dinner and it's a treat. How is it, delicious, they do a nice job in these places. And from Gil, her father: "Get enough to eat?"

Could I live my whole life at Applebee's and not run away? Or to put it otherwise, if I was going to betray Melissa someday, wouldn't it be best to leave now, before the dessert came? But because I'd saved her life once or imagined that I had, I decided to wait this one out. The chocolate pudding with the swirl of Reddi-wip was fantastic.

It wasn't until we had flown south to Los Angeles and were again in her rent-controlled apartment with the flowers on the sills and her mannequin pinned up with jagged shards of raw silk that soon enough would be something surprising and the soft light of her lamps, that I recalled fully, which is to say with a full heart, that Melissa was as self-made as I was, that we'd both run away and started over, and that it was this running away and starting over that had brought us both to the Ocean Park Apartments. She was my mother and she was not. She was Irene and she was not. And I was just plain lucky. To be able finally to be a sentimental slob once in a while.

*

In Melissa's austerity, the erotic seemed to flow most excessively. Another of her paradoxes. She seemed to live by her paradoxes, as if jumping from puddle to puddle. Or do I mean jumping over the puddles, from one bit of dry land to the next? I'm not even sure, not even now. Her diets, the periods she went through when she wore only white, her susceptibility to every banal new fad, like Proust's maid and the *pneu*. Or you could say also, her embrace of the new, she wasn't afraid of the new. The erotic all bottled up in her, headaches, confusions, explosions. The erotic as a great engine of her being.

And another interesting fact about her: Melissa didn't like me all that much. Not after we became lovers, not after, as it were or as she thought, she could see me up close. And how could I disagree? There was so much that she observed. My holding back, my failure to speak my mind, my speaking my mind, my weird opinions, my obscure intuitions, my old "group" and whatever that was all about, my snobbery, my disbelief in fashions, gyms, and health, my grumpy dogmas about such things, my cocksureness, my doubting all the time, my doubting her, my saving whatever I was saving in order to write it down somewhere, my tendency to look at other women's tits if I could get away with it which I could but not quite with her, my laziness, my so-called Jewishness, my working all the time and ambition and need to get someplace that always remained obscure, my father and Irene, my irony, my ironic critiques of her, sneaking them in there as if she wouldn't notice, my own passive-aggression, my evident desire for money, my contempt for those who desired money, my trying to keep one step ahead of everybody which in practical terms meant trying to keep one step ahead of her and her opinions and beliefs with the result that she could hustle and bustle all day to keep up with me about one stupid thing or other that she didn't really care about anyway and as soon as she got there I'd be gone, my sarcasm, my liking for jokes as crude and mean as they come, my eagerness to *épater the bourgeoisie* which she wouldn't even know what it meant but she feared the bourgeoisie meant her, my tolerance for smokers, my cheapness just like Zacky said, my obsessive persistent obnoxious pathetic one-track-mind predictable demand for sex all the time, my fetishizing of her, my objectifying of her, my refusal to buy a new car, my old J. Press clothes, though a few of these she liked a little bit, my hesitation to get in the habit of taking a shower absolutely every day, my not caring that much if I got food on my clothes, my refusal to lose my temper unless goaded beyond all reason, the anger in my eyes, the stiffness in my neck which wasn't all the time but sometimes. It didn't take Melissa so long to accumulate such a list. A couple of months, maybe. On review I wish I could find some points on which she was wrong. But anyway, she didn't leave. Or rather, since we were staying at her place, she didn't kick me out.

And on another, perhaps not entirely unrelated, issue: Melissa's long roster of Jewish boyfriends. She had known no Jews at all when she grew up. There were maybe none in twenty miles, if by "none" you could mean only a few, the owner of the tailor shop or the stationery store. She only started meeting Jews when she was with the rock musician. They, we, must have seemed like part of her brave new world, the world that welcomed her or anyway was receptive to the possibility of her, when she ran away from everything she had known. And by now I was well down a list, of which the only recent exception had been Zacky, but that did include Candleman and the old guy who gave her the watches and a sitcom writer and a computer whiz and there were others before those, I was never certain how many, but at least one had been a so-called Zen rabbi who held forth and/or sat somewhere in Hollywood and who I knew about only because when I told Melissa she didn't have a mental disease *du jour* but rather a spiritual ailment that pills could cover up but never cure, she said this Zen rabbi had once told her the same thing. I eventually called up the Zen rabbi and found we had quite a lot in common. There could have been a couple lawyers, too. And a plastic surgeon, who promised her that if she ever wanted her tits done, he'd do a bang-up job. But there was nothing wrong with Melissa's tits. I was never sure about the plastic surgeon, whether he was a lover or just someone she met somewhere, like me, who became a friend.

Anyway, a good-sized sampling of the Jewish gene pool. Enough to make comparisons, enough to spot trends. And did there come a moment after one of them when she confided to a friend, "Never again. I'm off Jewish men." But she wasn't. Something in her of Portnoy's shikse goddess, who wanted a man who would give her a kid who read Kafka? Maybe. Or more likely, not so much. Melissa would have heard of Kafka but not been sure at first if you meant Kafka the dress designer or Kafka the writer. Yet she was surely looking for something she felt was missing in herself.

*

More plot, more business. After the third season of *Northie,* James Morton had taken his winnings and enough of his printing apparatus as he needed and gone to France, St. Paul de Vence having won out over the backwoods of the American northwest in the contest for who would get his discontented soul. But after a year and a half he'd come back, on account of either being pissed off at the French or pissed off at a French-Italian woman in particular, and Adam Bloch on my advice made my pal a rich deal. It wasn't long before it was in *Daily Variety* that Morty was developing a new police show. This drove Zacky nuts. By now he and Morty were hardly speaking. If anyone was a bridge between them it was me, but even I didn't see Morty much since he disdained the studio and the drive to the Valley and got away with mostly working at home. To Zacky, the fact that Morty was developing a new cop show, even for a different network, suggested that Bloch or somebody somewhere was losing faith in *Northie*. And then the rumors began to flare again that it was Morty's talent and not Zacky's that had made *Northie* fresh to start with. Zacky and I had a shared series commitment with the network to produce a new show for them after *Northie*, but even this failed to mellow Zacky's qualms. It was enough that he had to worry about the younger guys over at MTM, Bochco and Paltrow and the others, but now his own erstwhile partner might be coming up with something to put *Northie* in the shade. On the morning of the debut of Morty's new show, Zacky's envy was so great that he avoided even opening his newspapers, as if it were a good case for mind over matter, if he never looked, then the reviews would not exist. But they did exist and they were glowing. "A genius of the small screen," said the guy in the *LA Times*. Maryanna didn't know about Zacky's approach/avoidance game with the papers and blew it by trying to commiserate, "Morty must have sucked Clarence's dick," she said, in reference to the *LA Times* reviewer, and in a bitter mood Zacky took her revelation as enmity, rubbing the salt of Morty's apotheosis in his wounds: Here, dear, let me be the first to tell you that you're officially second-rate. He who'd done so much yoga and t'ai chi he now confided in people only half-facetiously that he was L.A.'s most centered Gentile felt he knew uncentered aggression when he saw it. Riding over the hill in his beat-up Bronco to the Burbank studio he was still thinking how he ought to divorce the black widow (a reference to Maryanna's first husband, who died in a skiing accident), if it wouldn't be so damn expensive. I met with Zacky every morning to work on *Northie* stories, but we got no work done that day. Neither of us had seen Morty's show. I was waiting for it to air, as I always did with new shows; saw them, if I saw them at all, the way the audience would see them. We tossed the football back and forth. The ritual of all the writing teams in Hollywood, a football, a basketball, a whiffleball. Saying pretty much nothing, supposedly thinking, but thinking about what? And then Zacky said, "What about . . . *bare ass?*" He said it like he'd invented something big. The emphasis of it, the drama. I said I didn't know what he was talking about. "We go for . . . *bare ass.* Not on *Northie.* On the new show." I felt like a straight man in a bad joke.

"Why are we talking about the new show now? I thought we were talking about *Northie.*"

But of course I knew why we were talking about the new show. Zacky's way to recoup, his way to reclaim his crown. It was all he cared about.

"Can we do that?" I asked.

"We don't have to get balls, we don't have to get shaved pussy—but a little cheek? Why not? You know other guys are going for it, you bet they are, it's the fucking Holy Grail if you could get it, if you were the first one to get it . . ."

I could exaggerate this, but I swear Zacky's blue eyes glazed over then. Thinking of being king forever, maybe, thinking of showing them all.

"Has this got to do with Morty?"

"Morty? What's it got to do with Morty?"

"Nothing. Of course. Nothing."

"Hey, in this business, you've got to be a *visionary.*"

But when I got back from lunch that day, Zacky had something entirely else on his mind. I found him in a state. He looked at me with beseeching, puppy dog eyes. Whatever it was, I told myself I was not going to fall for it. Yet my words stumbled over his mooniness and I asked him anyway, "What is it?"

"Maryanna's filed for divorce."

I wasn't sure how I was supposed to take this. No more black widow? But Zacky was morose. And then, could he ask me if I'd do him a favor?

"No. You can't."

"Kind of a big favor."

"Certainly not."

"Would you go to the Sav-On and buy me some underpants?"

"Oh, Zack." I said something like that.

He looked sorry enough and what else was there to say? Remind him how often he'd expressed the wish to divorce her himself? Zacky reached for his wallet. I told him don't bother.

"I didn't shit on the wallet," he said.

So I didn't ask for the details, nor did he offer them. At the Sav-On, I spent a while contemplating whether Zacky would prefer the ones with baseballs and footballs or the ones with cows and cowboy hats. I finally chose the latter, reminded of another of Zacky's Texasisms, about some producer who was all hat and no cattle. I don't know if I hated him or thought he was fantastic then, for sending me on that errand. L.A.'s most centered Gentile, well, maybe. When I got back he was more distraught than when I left. The lawyer had called. Zacky was still behind his desk, his mooniness turned to stone disbelief. The only word that escaped his tongue as I handed him the drugstore bag with the underpants was "half." It was muttered like an oracle. Apparently California laws on divorce were going to apply even to the one-time King of Television. It was going to cost him half of all he had, even his points on *Northie*.

And then. And then. So much happened on this one day that it was why I first started thinking about putting all the action of my book on one day. Not this day, precisely, but this day combined with one or two others, so that the sum of it would be like a jam-packed night on the Roxbury streets. But it was this one day where I started, when Zacky was envious, and came up with "bare ass" as if he were Einstein, and Maryanna left him, and it was going to cost him half. The envy, that was the thing that kind of stuck. How could people so rich and famous still be so envious? How could it drive them, contort them, so? The facility even Zacky the most centered Gentile in Los Angeles had for comparing himself to his peers, as opposed to all the rest of humanity.

Later that day Zacky took a suite at the Bel Air and invited the head of the network over for a drink. I only heard exactly what happened some years later, when the network head, Jaworsky, happened to be passing through the village back east where I had a summer house, and we went out for our own drinks. Zacky had by then gone to a different network, there was some bitterness involved, and Jaworsky was not unhappy to tell me the tale. He'd showed up at the Bel Air and, like myself, found Zacky in a state. Zacky told him about the scene with his three girls where he had to tell them he was moving out, then he told him about coming to the hotel and calling all the escort services then hanging up every time a woman's voice answered, then he told him how he'd hated Maryanna and sworn to leave her this very day but now that she was gone he didn't want to live without her. And he told him how it was going to cost him half. Jaworsky told me how flattered he felt, that Zacky would confide all this to him, that Jaworsky was the man he would turn to in the hour of his distress. Then Zacky said to him, "This life goes fast, you know that, Jaw? You have to make things count. You have to dare and you have to believe.

What's the point of half-measures, when you only go round once? Am I starting to sound like a beer commercial yet?" Zacky looked so droopy that Jaworsky hugged him then. And that's when Zacky proposed bare ass for the new show.

When Jaworsky told me this, we both laughed our asses off. I'd known that Zacky broached the subject that night, but not how. I suppose I was filled with awe for Zacky then, years after I'd last seen him, when I heard the story of him using the pathos of his own divorce to get bare cheeks on network television. Jaworsky told him he'd think about it.

But the day wasn't quite over yet. I went home and watched Morty's new show when it aired. It was so remarkably predictable that I could almost not believe Morty did it. It was like a *Northie* with all the experiments and emotions and absurdity left out, so that what you were left with was most of the production values but a plot structure going back to television's earliest days, to *Dragnet* or maybe even before. Just the facts, ma'am. Jesus, Morty—was this what happens when a guy does something he doesn't really want to do? It felt almost as if Morty was expiating all he had contributed to the rollicking embraces of *Northie*'s nights. I couldn't believe it was going to be a hit, but halfway through I knew I was wrong, or I knew what he was going for anyway: his main cop, his hero, slugged a wobbly prisoner because he didn't like his answers. Morty's hero was a bully. Morty was idealizing the authoritarian. Putting the pig back in the pigs, playing the conservative card, as if to say, haven't you noticed, this is the Reagan era. It felt almost as if he were pushing your face in it. And the critics didn't seem to care about the hero slugging a wobbly prisoner because he didn't like his answers. Unless it was that precisely that they were calling "daring," as if Morty at last was telling it like it is. And ah, the subtle performances, the terse writing, the production values, the *realism*, all in an old-fashioned no-nonsense cop show! However surprised I was at how little joy there was in it, I was more surprised that no one in the papers seemed to notice. Even before the end credits rolled, my mind filled with calculations as if it were a train station full of strangers. Were *Northie* and its kind finished? Had Morty stolen the future, or only seen it? Were all my gut instincts wrong? Was my lucky run over? Where would my next deal come from? Morty had always been my friend, and yet what I felt, actually, was envy.

*

And later I saw him on the interview shows, doing the circuit, getting as complicated and high-flown as he could get about the police role in society, and violence and redemption and Dostoevsky and the criminal's need for punishment, and the interviewers fawning and lapping it up, and all I could see was a guy who didn't really want to be there. Envy. Envy that rubs your heart with salt.

Zacky told me he never watched any of these interviews. The prerequisites, the strategies, of envy and I who recently enough had had contempt for Zacky on account of his envy began to envy him for his excellent management of it. He knew how to avoid what he wanted to avoid.

*

But was envy what I really wanted to write about? Envy or Hollywood or television or the new rich? As well as I can describe it, my self-hatred got wind of what was going on and said, "I thought you were writing about the meritocracy and the best and the brightest. What have *these* to do with that?" Or more particularly, writing so much about myself. "I" "I" "I" "I" "I," like a lament in an old song of the Pale. People talk about self-loathing as if it were the Cracker Jack prize inside the box of suffering souls, but I don't think it's that. In my view it's more like they're all one and the same thing, the box, the candy, the prize. And is that really such a bad thing, a vigorous brushing of the back of self, as in a Russian bath? Doesn't self-hatred keep us honest, doesn't it lead us toward love?

The corollary to this being, perhaps, that if you talk about love all the time the crud accumulates on your skin and pretty soon you're not too healthy at all.

In all events, shortly after I conceived of keying my eighties book on envy and television and the new rich, I had a grave doubt and spun in the opposite direction and felt it should be all about my friend from Yale Teddy Redmond, who was in *Meritocracy: A Love Story* and who came out to Los Angeles in the mid-eighties. Teddy was a WASP if there ever was one, St. Paul's and Greenwich and Yale and for a long time a bit of an attitude that the world, if it didn't exactly owe him a living, was likely to hand him one anyway. But the years stripped a lot of that away. Working for Chase or Cravath and joining the Field Club were not what he had in mind from life. Teddy joined the Peace Corps, came first to believe and then to disbelieve in the Third World, bummed around in Spain, wound up finally in New York, became a writer after all. I didn't see him much in New York. He worked for *Newsday* for awhile. He moved to Brooklyn, lived with a girl, broke up with the girl. He had always been sarcastic, and over time his sarcasm seemed to harden and grow crusty. He became obsessed with the world situation, especially when under Reagan the Cold War resumed full bore. His sense of entitlement increasingly was buoyed by outrage. He felt the wisdom we as a nation had learned the hard way was being tossed heedlessly away. By the early eighties he had moved to New Orleans, lived with and broken up with another girl there, begun and abandoned a novel. He inherited a small amount of money and invested it, badly, in a private school scheme for inner-city kids. He was still good-looking and athletic, in a bony, trim way. He decided he was emotionally isolated and went into therapy. We had become friends, I once told him, either in spite of or because of his inherited anti-Semitism. Or mine, he shot back.

There was more about Teddy, that I'll get to later. All I want to say here is that I was desperate once for him to be the center of my book. I felt he spoke for "us" better than I ever could. "Us" being who, exactly? The meritocrats, the Yale and Harvard guys, the best and the brightest, the captains of a more-or-less liberal America whose ship by the eighties was sailing on a windless sea?

Though there was something else useful about Teddy: his hatred for Los Angeles, that was almost funny it was so comprehensive. You wouldn't want to get Teddy started on Los Angeles. The fake tits, the fake Spanish houses, the clean cars, the roads without potholes, the possibility of getting a ticket for jaywalking, the possibility of getting a ticket for not stopping at a crosswalk, the local news, the ignorance of the world, the bland faces, the bodies as overgrown as the vegetables, the landscapes that didn't belong there, the incessant hum of the boulevards that were too wide to cross, the lack of anyplace to walk to, the guys with their business, the girls who cared about the guys' business, the lack of appreciation of the Eastern type of person, the bland Okie speech, the silly Val girl speech, the moronic Watts guy speech, the perfidious Dodgers, the perfidious Lakers, the lack of decent hamburgers combined with the local conviction that there were good hamburgers there, that it was right for a hamburger to be thin as a pancake and well-done and covered with mustard and mayonnaise instead of ketchup, the lack of ivy-covered towers, the lack of Sunoco stations, the dreamy reasoning, the self-satisfaction, the failure to produce any world-class serial killers lately, the anomie, the lack of family tie, the ease of getting laid that almost took the fun out of it, the surfer clothes, the bland politicians without an ethnic smell to them, the bland cops without an ethnic smell to them, and what the cops wore, those dark ties on dark shirts, even the chief wore one, the chief of police looked like a weenie or a fascist instead of just an ordinary Irish thug, the fact that it was the second biggest city in the country and it had only one newspaper left, the fact that nobody read a newspaper, the contentment with jobs, with capitalism, with status quo, the lack of political consciousness, the lack of literary consciousness, the lack of consciousness at all. No, you didn't want to get Teddy started on L.A.

So with Teddy there would be some jokes and some vestigial high church backbone and some political sense-of-the-world, and to boot a grand project he had in mind for years, a tragic seed, against which Hollywood and for that matter myself could be tested and found wanting or not. For years Teddy was obsessed with the story of Charlie Chamberlain, one of the postwar Ivy League adventurers of the early CIA, a guy who'd had a good war, parachuting behind enemy lines in France, once getting a whole German platoon single-handedly to surrender by shooting wildly and running around it until they thought they were surrounded;

so good a war that when it was over he didn't want to be a banker and play squash and take the train home to Greenwich, and instead of that death-in-shades-of-gray joined Central Intelligence the year it was formed, and rose in it with more such inspired, slightly hare-brained schemes as he'd come up with in the French village, some of which worked but more of which didn't, so that in the end, when the whole country turned its back after Vietnam, he had a fall from grace and came to see the world for what it was. Teddy himself being from Greenwich, it seemed that he would be telling something of his own life, with dashing, failed covert ops standing in for his own reckless dare as a writer. Not that Teddy had ever got shot at or shot anybody. But still. The upper class bravado that later got bent out of shape. Irony here or satire, something hard and irreducible? Learning the moral lessons of the world, finally not being so sure you were right. Being actually, finally, confused. And doing a kind of late twentieth-century American penance, working with ghetto kids on the streets of New Haven.

Perhaps even more than he loved Chamberlain's story, Teddy felt it must be his ticket out. He would sell it and be gone from this place of weenie cops and overstuffed, tasteless omelets. But a sale proved not so easy. He refined his story, rewrote it, pitched it, changed the title and pitched it again, and meanwhile the years slipped by. One got the feeling about Teddy that he'd come to Los Angeles with Charlie Chamberlain in his luggage and he wasn't going to leave until this great ghost was no longer there.

Although it was true that I sometimes felt, even after thirty years being his friend, that I didn't know enough about Teddy Redmond to make him the spine of my book, I probably would have done it, would have gone that way or tried, if I had not, as

I wrote earlier, found Amos Oz's wonderful book in December of 2004 and come to believe that wherever a writer is, there is the center of his universe.

*

If I had kept Teddy, I could also have kept Eve. Eve Merriman. Or I suppose I am keeping her, since I'm writing about her now, maybe not as much as I otherwise would have, but enough. She was Teddy's girlfriend when he came to Los Angeles. A Bennington girl, she had poise, brains, long brown hair, ambition, and she could run hot or cold. Eve fashioned herself a writer like the rest of us, only she didn't write much, she was better at getting into meetings than writing, and she got into meetings that maybe it would have been better for Teddy to have gotten into. After a while they split apart and then Eve called up everybody she could, including me, looking for work and not getting much. Eventually Zacky made a pass at her. This was after his separation. I never knew exactly what came of it, but it must have been something, because he got her a script to write.

But the chief reason to keep Eve in the story had less to do with Teddy or Zacky as the fact that she fulfilled every vestige of fantasy of an upper-class Protestant Katharine Hepburn–style woman that I still might have had. Eve could sail, ride, and think, she combined a Bennington girl's accommodating views on sex and politics with knowing what Abercrombie's used to be like, and though she couldn't cook worth a damn, she knew where the forks and spoons went. To boot, her family had a summer house on Mount Desert in Maine, like the family of my old crush Sascha Maclaren and her sister, my one-time lover Maisie. In a way, she was a last, slightly watered-down incarnation of these. She wasn't great and complicated like Sascha or big-hearted like Maisie but she had the looks and she knew the jokes and she was tough enough. And so, perhaps inevitably, she became a kind of dark alternative against which I placed my affair with Melissa. Dark because she embodied the world and its demands and weight the way that Melissa could not. Melissa was all about promise, Eve was about what was. And I knew, for a little while anyway, that I could have had her. When she called me up, after she left Teddy, it was in her voice. Talking about Teddy, talking about Maine, talking about some people maybe I should have known, as if there was no need for the conversation to end. Her voice itself a little flat and cattish like Hepburn's but so unaccented that you could not pin one thing on her. And her knowingness. Eve had knowingness. She knew what I was about. The only thing was, I could never save her life. It wasn't the kind of life that someone like me could save. It was as if that part had already been taken care of. Betty and Veronica and I chose Betty, because her heart was always broken? But the argument kept coming back. Wasn't Veronica the one you were supposed to choose? I even fashioned it once as a neoclassical plot. I would be with someone like Melissa and someone like Eve would come along and I would drop the someone like Melissa in favor of the someone like Eve and too late I would find that the someone like Eve either lacked a heart or had a witch's heart or hated me with such heart as she had in a way that left nothing to chance and no escape, except by waking from the nightmare and running all the way back without stopping once to the someone like Melissa, who would be either gone by then or not, but most probably she would be gone.

The chase at the end of the film? But beware, there'll be no film version at all if the someone like Melissa is utterly gone. She mustn't have her dignity, she mustn't have her freedom or her defiance or pride, or even her hurt, tragic confusion; the audience must be served its curdled dessert, its happy ending without end.

*

My father finally got a show on CBS, a half hour, a sitcom. This time he had not only a well-known, highly regarded Broadway playwright to write it, but a well-known, highly regarded Hollywood sitcom director who'd done the pilots for a string of hits to direct it, and the cute premise of a cooking show where they'd give out real recipes between the jokes. He also had a dame of the London stage to play the cooking show's big mama, and I thought, when I heard about it, *maybe*. Maybe, and why not, and it sounds as good as anything else, and the oldest weasel words of all, *nobody knows anything*.

I suppose I should put in here—remind you, really, since it must be very nearly universally known—that most new television shows fail. Although "fail" is in a way a phony word for it, a show gets too few viewers and it goes off the air and the actors and everybody else go on to other jobs if they can, but whether the show had a few decent laughs, or said something or other about something, or nothing about nothing, or was crazy different from anything that had ever gone on before, doesn't usually get recorded in the record books, any more than Jimmy Piersall's stunts in centerfield or Satch Paige pitching on no days' rest ever made it into the encyclopedia of baseball. I don't even know if the phrase "noble failure" has a place in the annals of television.

But maybe that's what *Big Lady* was. I didn't think so at the time. I thought the dame of the West End stage still sounded English when she was supposed to sound like Brooklyn, and the premise wasn't old-fashioned but the characters were. Big mama solves everything. I was embarrassed by it. I told no one at *Northie* that my father even had this show, or if I told anyone, it was only in passing. I knew even less about sitcoms than I knew about the rest, but I wasn't surprised when *Big Lady* failed.

I called my father when the show was canceled. I told him only things he already knew. I told him it's hard to get shows on. I told him it was even harder at his age, and if you left like he did and tried to come back, that had to be harder still. All the things that he could take pride in, and he said thank you.

But then he started to talk about money. "If I'd stayed at Universal, my stock options would have vested," he said. "I made a mistake."

But I didn't want to talk about money then, it made me even sadder than the rest of it, and it frightened me a little.

"You took your shot," I said. "You should feel lucky you got to take it."

"It wasn't a good show," he said.

"It had a few problems," I said.

"Of course the critics were flattering. They loved Dame Alna."

"Well so there's that then."

"She even got Brooklyn right."

"I didn't think so, but neither here nor there."

"You didn't? Really?"

"Neither here nor there."

"The *Times* thought she was marvelous. Even the *Post.* Three stars in the *Daily News.*"

"I was just talking about her accent."

"You know how many times MCA's stock has doubled?"

"Is that a question?"

"It was a lot of money."

"The stock options."

"I made a mistake," he said.

*

But even a show that has too few viewers only has too few compared to some dream of what some other show that would take its place might have, or too few compared to the show that came before it, or to the shows on the other stations. It was still millions. My father failed before millions, or in spite of millions.

And how many will ever read this book?

*

Early on when I knew her, Melissa said something like, "I don't want to get pregnant. I don't want to get fat." I didn't believe her then or it made me sad or I thought it was a joke. She had to be kidding me or herself. But it made me think how much I wanted to make her pregnant. Every time I looked at her I thought I saw every tool that a mother ought to have, and she didn't seem to believe it. Another seduction? Was I just a simple guy who falls for such things? Anyway she changed her mind. After I knew her a couple years, she said, "I want to have a baby. Even if you don't."

The last part I could have lived without, because it was after all I who'd brought it up in the first place. But bringing things up in the first place never scored many points with Melissa. She needed to think she had done things by herself, or thought things by herself. She needed to come to her own conclusions and I suppose she still wasn't sure about me.

Or perhaps it was my dubious potential as a family man. I didn't much believe in nuclear families because my father ran away and because my mother became bitter about men and because of the "group" I was in where families and conditioning were said to be the problem and because of the times we lived in. What point in courting the most predictable of disasters? Live free or die, as they say on the license plates of New Hampshire. I suppose my cock put in a word or two as well. Its wish to roam.

None of which I hid from her, except for my cock's wish to roam, which I'd been reliably told by Zacky Kurtz, old Hollywood hand on the subject, that you never, ever, ever, ever, never, on pain of death-by-sliding-down-a-bannister-of-razor-blades-into-a-vat-of-boiling-sulphuric-acid told the woman you were with, and anyway when I was in Melissa's presence my cock never had that wish. I seldom trusted Zacky's wisdom on anything, but on this one I did. Melissa wanted to get knocked up and so we did that.

And next the question of the health insurance. Now you could say for a guy making millions you shouldn't predicate your whole future domestic life on extending your generous health insurance benefits to the girl you got knocked up and your un-born child, if everything else is saying no, no, no, and wait-just-a-gosh-darn-minute here. But waste not, want not. I'd learned that when I was poor. Melissa had no health insurance.

I was happy, in a way, that I now had a way to make good use of mine.

It was as if I might extend, to the whole nine yards of it, this fantasy of saving her life. Or still, maybe it wasn't fantasy, maybe it was the first real thing I'd ever done or might do.

I've previously written about how Melissa didn't always like me very much, and seemingly the less so, the closer we got. No use picking over those scabs again. No use adding to the list. She had her reasons, her distrust, her defiance. But the day I asked her to marry me, she didn't say no. She was a few months pregnant. The insurance would pay for the ultrasound.

*

What did we sound like together? I realize I've written so little dialogue between us.

We sounded a lot like some old married couple.

*

Melissa was never so much about the words. She could be painfully articulate when desperate or on the phone with one of her girlfriends, but you would never pick her out from her words. Her look that was a little bit ghost-like, her sure hands, the way she bounced back from sadness, something would happen she did not like and she would fret and take a shower and get dressed again and go back out, like a fighter in the late rounds.

*

Now you can say there are a lot of different kinds of old married couples, so which kind did we sound like? It depended, on which day.

*

The whole question, again, of leaving. I asked her to marry me and share my health insurance with me and still she did not leave. Even though I was too smart and got rich too easily, taking money out of the mouths of worthwhile gentiles? Melissa as Robin Hood, righting a kind of imbalance? She who said yes to giving her child a name other than hers and to redistributing the wealth in ways maybe not middle-American and Republican but anyway in ways other than mine.

Maid Melissa of Ocean Park.

*

So we sounded like different kinds of old married couples depending on which day. But on the different days, which different kinds? The carping kind, the careful kind, the silent kind, the ruthless kind, the trying-hard-to-be-loving kind, the after dinner and maybe a glass of wine kind, the sexual kind, the Noel Coward amusing kind, the forgiving kind, the forgetting kind, the buy-things-to-get-past-problems kind, the articulate kind, the too-articulate kind, the little bit sad kind, the kind that wishes for revenge, the lying-around-reading-a-book-or-listening-to-the-heart-of-your-baby kind, the kind that just *is* for a little while. And we weren't even married yet.

*

A conversation we had once.

"Are you just going to smother me because your own parents broke up?" she asked.

But it wasn't really a conversation, because I didn't have an answer.

*

To take possession by a kind of force. A coercion. To use the law and custom and money to get your way about something, to have something. Is even a proposal of marriage an action of unimaginable violence?

*

Melissa had her problems with my father and Irene. Though it's possible her problems with them were really her problems with me, her fears for me, how I might turn out some day. She did not identify with Irene at all. She almost seemed to feel, as if it were a battle over the pieces of who I was, that she must take my mother's part and root out or oppose everything that was not. She liked my mother. They sometimes talked on the phone. And of course she knew what my mother would have called "the whole story."

I would remind her once in a while that passion is an unruly beast; and that she herself had had her affairs with married men. This was not an effective line of argument. And why was I arguing at all? I didn't really disagree with her. Or I did disagree with her but I also agreed.

All I knew was that I wanted to hold no grudges against my father. I wanted to be too big for that, too old for that, even too spiritually evolved for that. The problem was that he would call up and he would patronize Melissa, and Irene would, or that's how Melissa saw it anyway. For sure they thought they were only ingratiating themselves. But they didn't know how to do it, nor was Melissa letting them in on the secret. Nor was I. I didn't know what the secret was. Their politeness, their microscopic concern with whatever she said, their endless praise of her dresses, even their offers to give them to some friend or other who turned out the deeper you got into the conversation to be someone terribly important. All the encounters we had seemed like subsequent impressions off the same block of our first dinner together in Beverly Hills.

Nor did the fact that Irene seemed to be doing badly excite much pity in Melissa. She was too afraid of her to have pity. She may not even have seen that Irene was doing badly. I would say so and it would end up in a fight, as if I were somehow betraying my mother all over again or revealing how I would some day betray Melissa herself. All of it made me wonder whether I had chosen Melissa as revenge against my father and Irene. Or perhaps it was a deep seeking of justice, finding the person who would treat them now as Irene had once treated my mother and me. Offhandedly, without real interest, as an inconvenience. Or as some sort of vague threat, guilt-inducing, our complaints and entreaties like people from the servants quarters popping their heads out when they weren't supposed to. Yet Melissa might have seen that Irene was doing badly, because Melissa had so often done badly herself. Or does similarity make us blind to the other? Irene's depressions, Melissa's depressions, Irene's insecurity, Melissa's insecurity, Irene's fussing with food in restaurants and Melissa's faddish diets, Irene's isolation, Melissa's isolation, none of them necessarily overlapping in time, but they had been there, in these same two people. Melissa was doing better now and Irene was doing worse.

As I say, none of this I wanted, or seemed to anyway. I wanted peace. I wanted the peace of the conqueror, where things weren't all my way but mostly were, and everyone would acknowledge that I had brought something off. And hadn't I? I was on speaking terms with everybody. We were living in a civilized world, more or less. There was money to patch things up. I had brought my mother out to the Emmys. And yet, my father and I drifted apart.

And none of it was his fault. None of it. If by "fault" you meant now, if by "fault" you meant the last conversations and present kindness and even expressions of love. I could not mistake this. The upcoming baby, the upcoming marriage. I was bringing fresh breezes into his life. For god's sake I was making him a grandfather at a time when Irene was only making him unhappy. I said to him once, "Let's do one together."

"A show?"

"Why not? Next season. Whenever. We'll come up with something."

"Marvelous. Really. That would be marvelous. Just let me know. Whenever you'd like to talk. When you have time, of course. I know you've got *Northie*."

But I never seemed to have the time. And he didn't bring it up again, I'm sure because he didn't want to be a pest. I didn't bring it up either.

*

There came a time when I made Teddy Redmond something of a project. Maybe this is in comparison to my father, or maybe it isn't. Friends are different from relatives, aren't they? Anyway, Teddy made the rounds with his story of Charlie Chamberlain, and when he got as far as he could go and it was nowhere, I offered to try to help him. My thinking was that maybe Adam Bloch could be persuaded to take an interest. We had all been classmates, after all, Yale sixty-six. Adam had known Teddy a little bit through Harry Nolan, and then there was the weekend of the crash. As I wrote earlier, I had never forgiven Adam for it, but with me at least it didn't seem to be something he expected. It was part of our past that was simply there, a story that came out the same way every time you looked at it. You could start to root for a different ending, but there never was one. This much we shared, and I suppose Adam's guilt, and my own for being unforgiving. But with Teddy I didn't know. Teddy had been the harshest of us all with Bloch, had blamed him the most, had seen the least excuse. And they hadn't spoken since, except a few words at a dinner I gave once in Los Angeles, but there were a lot of people there.

I didn't think I was trying to rewrite the past, I thought I was trying to help Teddy get his film done. His idea was to go to HBO with it. HBO was his mantra, HBO HBO HBO, HBO would have the taste and subtlety to film the story of Charlie Chamberlain. But Teddy had no track record as a producer, nor as a writer for that matter, and he needed a strong production company behind him to get in the door there. And so that's where I thought to bring Bloch in. Cangaroo wasn't a company that had ever made movies, its whole history was in series television, but could Adam be persuaded to break the mold for once?

Though it wouldn't have to be framed to him as "for once"— the company had from time to time financed the vanity projects of its producers, before Bloch's arrival. All the vanity projects had been disasters.

I invited them out for a drink, the old Yale guys, twenty years out, and look where we all were. In college Bloch had been a weenie but smart, and Teddy had been a preppie but fidgety, and I had been whatever I was, a little bit of neither of those, a little bit writerly maybe, but mostly pure aspiration. Or we had all been pure aspiration, the only difference being that Bloch and I knew it and Teddy then did not. It took years of losing for Teddy to realize that he secretly wanted to win. And then there had been this terrible accident where the one we all loved died, and most of us blamed Bloch, who'd been driving.

The place in Brentwood was dark and wood-paneled the way places in Los Angeles seldom are unless they want to suggest somewhere else. I was the only one who ordered anything but iced tea. Bloch had to go back to work afterward and Teddy was uneasy enough. He had first ignored Bloch in college, then patronized him.

Bloch with his millions, and still an isolate. He had come to California without even leaving a girl behind. No one knew exactly what his private life was like. The common suspicion, voiced by Zacky, was that he had none, that he went home and worked some more. But how could that be? Even mama's boys got to the point where they wanted a family, unless they were queer. Or that's what the sociology of the street said anyway, and Bloch wasn't queer. On this point everyone agreed. Maybe he devoted his private time to charity, a secret Mother Teresa, fulfilling the Talmud's mandate to keep your good deeds quiet. Maybe he just needed a little time to get used to things out here. Maybe he suspected people of being after his money. I had this recurring daydream of Bloch looking in the mirror each night and despising himself. He was compact, his hair was wiry, his nose a little bulbous, his complexion ruddy and rough as if he'd been recently under a sunlamp, and yet he wasn't really an ugly man. He was less ugly than when he was young. He was presentable, really, he dressed neatly in a manner to suggest the department stores and took care to give no offense, spoke softly to underlings, listened more than he spoke. There was a quiet anonymity to him. In an age of accountants, which we might have been in, he would fit. But he never blinked. He had never blinked, not much anyway, for as long as any of us had known him.

Our conversation drifted from Yale to New York to where we were. For awhile it seemed like we all might have been the best of friends. No feints, no exploratory jabs. Members of the same tribe fallen into enemy territory. Or maybe that's what happens. You don't have to have been the best of friends, if you're from the same tribe and in enemy lands, you start thinking you're the best of friends. You share a common perspective that was invisible before. L.A.'s shortcomings, Hollywood's shortcomings, Reagan's shortcomings. When Teddy changed the subject, the incredible thing was how awkward he was about it. Teddy had always been a little jumpy, but his jumps came with wit and they landed him on his feet. He knew how to handle people. He knew where their weaknesses were and he wasn't afraid. He wasn't the kind who'd start something with, "Not to change the subject or anything, but . . ." He wasn't one to get his forehead furrowed or fix some strange stare on you. That was what Bloch used to do, and didn't do so much anymore.

But now he said, "Adam, I don't know how to say this." He did something funny with his nose, scrunched it up. "I'm not sure

I even thought I'd see you in my life again. I wanted this arranged so I could talk to you about a project. It's a good project. I think it could be good. But I can't talk to you without saying this other thing first."

And then it was like he couldn't say what that other thing was. He got as quiet as Bloch. I thought I should jump in and say something, keep the flow, whatever. But there was no flow.

All of us knew what the other thing had to be.

"I'm having a hard time remembering why it was your fault," Teddy said, about the thing that was long enough ago it seemed like a legend.

But then legends are always with us. Bloch put his iced tea down. "Because I was driving," he said, about the crash that killed Sascha Maclaren. We were at a table towards the back, where it was darker even than in the front of the faux-dark bar in Brentwood, and I was on the side of the table with Adam, and in the darkness I could see that he wasn't blinking. I could see the steady gleam of his nearer eye. "You thought I caused it by being a bad driver."

"You were a bad driver," Teddy said.

"I was," Bloch said.

"But even if you were," Teddy said.

"It was an accident," Bloch said. "I believe that. I always have. But she died. And there had to be somebody to blame."

"You were easy to blame," Teddy said.

Through all this I said nothing, as if I were listening in on the gods. Though why do I say that, "gods"? The most ordinary guys in the world, trying to figure something out, get past something that had long been there. And actually I felt a part of it too, by saying nothing, by letting it go.

I was the part of it that wasn't going to mess it up.

Though should there be exposition here? At the end of summer in 1966 we were driving on a road late at night and Bloch was the only sober one and in the fog that came up he thought he saw a deer and he swerved to miss it and went off the road. And there was no deer.

"But if the rest of us hadn't been drunk," Teddy said, "then you wouldn't have had to drive. You were making up for us being fools."

"I said that then," Adam said.

"I remember," I said, and hated the sound of my voice, the way you hate the cold when you jump in the water.

"But I wanted to be the hero," Bloch said, and took his iced tea again, and had a very tiny sip of it. And then, sarcastic in a way he never was, "I learned it was better not to be helpful after that."

"We were cruel," I said.

"It's only because I was trying," Bloch said. "It's what happens when you try. That's when you get in trouble. When you have to try to be helpful."

"I'm sorry," Teddy said.

"So what can I do for you today?" Bloch said.

Bloch trying maybe to be witty, trying to put an end to something. As if he could take it all but Teddy saying he was sorry.

Of course Bloch was wrong to say that then. It wasn't what Teddy meant. Yet it was the most honest thing Adam could say, it came with feeling pushing it out.

Then that was pretty much the end of it. It had been a try. And there we still were, twenty years later, as if meeting in some bar in some foreign country, expats and their stories.

Thank god for the waitress. More iced tea, more whatever I had. We seemed to like being with each other after that. Smaller and smaller talk, until we were down to gossip, who in our class had done this or that, been divorced three times, got a job in the Reagan administration, ran an investment house, farmed oysters in Indonesia, was CIA, was queer, died of AIDS, lived in Moscow, lived in Arizona with Tibetan Buddhists, grew pinot noir in the central coast, became a vet and pioneered an extraordinary technique for artificially inseminating sheep, fucked Sharon Stone or somebody who looked just like her at a resort where everybody was incognito. At the end of it Teddy told Adam about Charlie Chamberlain.

Adam didn't look surprised. But then, he never looked surprised. He didn't look interested or intrigued or eager or skeptical either. He was back to being his leaden self. You couldn't tell.

"Let me think about it," Bloch said, but he didn't blink.

We really didn't know.

The next day I called his office to see what he thought. His assistant said he was on a conference call. Now it happens there must have been a memo some years ago that went out to all the assistants in Los Angeles that the excuse you should make for your boss when an unwelcome call comes in is that he's on a conference call. The "conference" part of it is particularly key, it sounds important and precise, and lets you know that even though it's a lie you hear all over town, it's a lie that somebody took some care with. Hours later the assistant called back to say that Mr. Bloch had to go into a meeting but he wanted me to know that we could go ahead.

I still didn't know what he really thought. About any of it, really.

"What a screwed-up thing forgiveness is," I said to Teddy, thinking I was ironic or profound, then thinking I was anything but.

"Let's go to HBO," Teddy said.

*

I didn't invite my father to the wedding, nor my mother. It got too complicated, the thought of who would sit next to who, and Irene. We made it a small wedding. Melissa didn't invite her parents either. A kind of wedding of our hopes, two people who had made themselves over. We had bought a house in Santa Monica canyon, a log cabin sort of thing, so that our baby wouldn't be born in a welfare hotel. The wedding was at the house. Teddy came, and Bloch and Zacky, and Morty, and Sterner, and a few of Melissa's friends, and a guy I knew from our old group in New York, Philip Deschayne, a *New Yorker* writer who happened to be in Los Angeles on a speaking tour the weekend of the wedding. For some reason we had a rabbi. Melissa's soft spot for rabbis.

The smallness of the occasion was mostly my idea, and Melissa interpreted it as also my fault in a certain way, in that if my parents didn't present such problems, there wouldn't be a problem at all. She was five months pregnant. "Log cabin" might not quite do justice to the house. It was bigger than my father's old house in Bel Air. It didn't have a kidney-shaped pool, but by the eighties kidney-shaped pools were *déclassé*. Anything but a lap pool was *déclassé*, and we were putting in one of those. All these facts I duly noted and wondered why I noted them. Then in the city where, so it's been said, everything is commoditized, we made the best of our little vows. No formal stuff, no made up stuff. The rabbi managed not to put in his cautionary little shtick about "mixed marriages." People felt Melissa's belly. She made her own dress. That night we didn't make love, because she was still mad about not having her parents there.

Whereas I had my parents there that night, in a dream that was once in a lifetime. In the dream I was my mother and I was invited to the wedding after all, and so was *he*. But the wedding is in the Poconos, not California, the "log cabin" is on a lake, and I see *him* first at breakfast, where we chat a bit. I am not frightened to see him. I am not *anything* to see him. He is a little older than I remembered. What's forty years in a dream? And just as my only son is observing this and thinking there couldn't be two people on earth less suited to one another and how did they ever get together in the first place . . . we're having another little conversation on the porch of the "log cabin," which the son can't hear but it's about him and would he be proud of us now, chatting so civilized, so mature, like in the movies, like strangers on a train. Which leads to a dinner in a restaurant in town. Irene is nowhere in sight. He takes me in an old car that is the only car he has now and is not even a convertible and is older than my own. He tells me he saw me at the Emmys—on TV of course, he wasn't *at* the Emmys, he saw me on TV. I register the simplicity of his car, the way the cocksureness of his life has been shed. I do not feel intimidated. And what does he feel? Charitable? Virtuous?

At the restaurant I order fried clams. Why not? It's my favorite. I am aware that it's slightly vulgar, or so he the big food snob might think, but I don't care. It's sustained me, my love of HoJo's fried clams. He talks more about seeing me at the Emmys— on TV, of course, he saw me on TV.

"Why did you do this, why did you come?" one of us asks, I'm not sure which, and the other of us replies, "To not let you have what you want."

Then one of us, I'm not sure which, says, "What do you want? To feel good about yourself, the final triumph of self?"

"Sorry about her death," I say, referencing Irene, realizing she's dead, or otherwise she'd be here.

He nods. "Don't have to say that," he says. "She ruined your life."

"It's true, I don't have to. I take it back," I say.

"I have a new friend," he says.

"I never had a *friend*," I say, at some point later, in indirect response.

"Blame me for that one," he says, referencing my lost trust in men.

"I did but I don't," I say. "What did you ever see in me?" And, when he doesn't answer right away, I become what I feel is very bold and say, "I remember what I saw in you. A way out. A handsome choice. Intense, but kind. Gone to Yale."

He couldn't remember when such kind words had been said to him, when even the word "kind" had been used.

I go on: "I know what you saw in me. Someone available. Someone to touch you."

"No!" he shouts, "No, no, no!"

Then it's the next day and he rows me in a boat. He is the only one who ever rowed me in a boat and his strokes are choppy and slow the way they weren't once long ago and the weeds are slow and the moonlight is as pale as skim milk and while he's rowing he tells me that he's sick, which somehow I already knew, a nurse's instinct or whatever that is. And now everything goes very fast, with the illness that will be fatal and he telling me again how he saw me at the Emmys and how happy he was to see me there, it was the right place for me to be and what a mistake his life has been, including this *friend* of his, he's giving up this *friend* of his. For which I am not prepared to give up in turn one bit of my bitterness and disdain and anger and resentment and hurt for all time, until all time is over and I am. I take pity on him then and will care for him for the rest of his days. Or that's the feeling anyway, the feeling that that's what I am going to do. The feeling, too, that he goes into remission from whatever illness it was, and I die shoveling snow because I always liked shoveling snow, I never liked California, I liked places where you could shovel snow, and he dies of a broken heart. That's his punishment. A broken heart.

*

I neglected to mention: our house in Santa Monica Canyon, our log cabin, had an orange tree.

*

They sent a piece of glass as a wedding present. I'm not sure what it looked like but it had a little tag that came with it and the tag said it was called "The Swan." I don't know. Maybe it looked like a swan. It didn't seem very personal. It came a couple of months after the wedding. It occurred to me they might have been angry that they weren't invited, or reached the arguably logical conclusion that if we didn't think it was an important enough event to invite our relations, then they didn't think it was important enough to think up a gift with personal feeling. It didn't occur to me that in those months Irene may have been too distracted to shop for wedding gifts and that my father didn't know how to shop for gifts. "The Swan" reminded me of the legendary fruitcake of Malibu, an ageless and inedible concoction that for years had been going from house to house, as a house gift at Christmas parties. Receiving the legendary fruitcake of Malibu came to be like a Chinese good omen, promising luck for the whole next year. Melissa wrote a thank-you note. "The Swan" was in the dining room for awhile. It was only weeks later that my father called to say that Irene had shot herself.

*

The reasons for such a thing. There are always reasons and there are never reasons. People make up reasons but they diminish the act. The act has mystery to it. Even in the most pitiful circumstances, it embraces mystery. We step back from it. Perhaps we avert our eyes. There is so little to discuss, yet we discuss. Fred and Irene. Irene and Fred. She had acted as if life was short and so it was. I knew so little about either one of them.

*

I went back to see my father. Melissa was due with the baby in a week. I drove a rental car from Kennedy up to the place in Connecticut on the lake that was still in Irene's family. It wasn't where they had lived, but it was where he would later wish to throw her ashes. She had left no note, expressed no preference, said no goodbyes. Or perhaps she had and I just hadn't heard about them.

Something to my father, something to Thomas? There were things that were none of my business. Of course there were.

I had expected other people to be there. Thomas, at least; but he wasn't, he'd been up the day before. The place itself I barely remembered. Small and clapboard, painted barn red. A dirt path down to the water. It was November and it felt like grief, like the season that takes people away. A few leaves clung to naked branches. Maybe you notice these things more if you live long enough in California. And then my father at the door of the place. It still had the screen door on. He held it open. I came in with my carry-on bag. We embraced, a little awkwardly, because the carry-on was still on my shoulder. I was taller than he was now. All my life, I thought, he had been a little taller than me.

He didn't want to be back in Chappaqua, where she had shot herself and the blood was still on the bathroom wall. He said that to me, more or less. His words weren't exactly those. I don't re-member what they exactly were, they were less articulate, left more for me to fill in, as if the one thing I could do now was give him a hand with words.

But there wasn't really so much for either of us to say. Or of course there might have been a million things, but we didn't say them. It was as if we only wanted to say something that would change something. The main room of the house had many pic-tures of Irene and her brother. On the tables, on the walls. Irene with her horse in the hunt country of Virginia. Irene and her brother with the Duomo in the back of the frame. Irene and her brother and parents and grandparents and vacations and a school graduation, some private girls' school in New York, for the Jew-ish girls who couldn't go to Spence, but the school's gone now because Spence lets the Jewish girls in. Irene as a part of a family that seemed tightly knit and happy and rich, and that I had never known at all. Only a little short of an Old World family, with a patriarch who made things right. But then what had gone so wrong? My eyes wandered over these pictures. Though I felt embarrassed to look too closely, as if why look so closely now when I never had in her life? But then, I'd never quite been invited to in her life. I'd been invited to look from a bit of a distance, and then later I didn't care. A few photos of Thomas as well, and of Fred, their bright Kodacolor, even when beginning to fade, like a garish intrusion on a settled world. While in my feelings I searched for one more image, of Irene in our front yard in Scarsdale shaking and kissing Fred, and me watching with a boy's astonishment.

Wishing it was me. Was that really what I had wished? I guess it was.

None of which I told my father, but maybe I could have then. Or maybe, just as I knew much about him, he knew much about me. We spent our afternoon mostly silent. They sometimes call such silences eloquent, but I don't know. My father in a checked sport shirt, tan pants, and a belt that was a little too long. Always neat, even today. Must have run a shaver over his face and looked in the mirror and seen what? Eyes as if they'd like an excuse not to look back, hooded by lids that were even heavier today. So little light in those eyes. A mottled complexion that had spent too many summers in the California sun. A long nose like an old companion, nothing to write home about but what can you do. That had been his feeling anyway, a feeling that his nose had never really interfered with his life. And now?

An old guy. But neither of us was young anymore. The same build, the same kind of pants more or less, receding hair though his was more gone than mine, and mine had more color and my eyes had more light. Yet it was as if someone in the silence could have said: just wait.

My father was so considerate that day. That was one thing he could still do, he could be polite and considerate and ask about my flight and Melissa and the show and whether it had been easy to get the rental car and find the way to the place in Connecticut and what was I thinking about for dinner, because there was nothing much in the fridge but we could go out to dinner later, there was either a sandwich shop nearby or a little farther away there was a place like an inn. These bits of conversation were like little sprinkles of rain in the desert of our silence.

They say, they're always making these films that say, that the desert has so much life in it. I have no opinion about this. I only report what they tell me. Thomas my half-brother whom I'd seen only rarely since he was a shy child by the kidney-shaped pool in Bel Air where we'd played when he lost his real older brother, was coming back up on Thursday. There would be a cremation, then a scattering of the ashes. Of course he didn't expect I would be there for these, with the baby coming. I did find some room sometime in the day to tell him a couple funny stories about Zacky. Zacky Kurtz as comic relief. A good thing, really. Though my father had a lot of time for Zacky, who had given his kid his job. And too, my father still had a kind of wary respect for people who were big in the business, as if you never knew who you still might want to pull a favor from someday. The 1970s "King of TV." My father liked to hear about the kings of the industry, even if he felt in his heart of hearts that in his day the kings were more royal and longer-lasting.

We went to the inn for dinner after all. My father felt the sandwich shop wouldn't be to my liking. I ordered the lamb chops and he ordered the chicken and he barely touched it. And I felt so ashamed and sorry. All the times when he and Irene enjoyed their food and fussed and "shared" and put things on my plate or his or hers and talked out what they would order and read the menu half out loud and taught me how to send things back if they weren't right because the chef would want to know, and then the desserts, which were always "marvelous" and in the middle with many forks, all of which I had liked at first but came to feel embarrassed about, as if in some magical reversal it turned out it was they who didn't know quite how to behave and not me. And now my father barely touched his roast chicken and I wanted nothing more in the world than for him to have his appetite back and be hearty and love food and start over. I felt ashamed for having turned against him what was good about him, and why shouldn't he have enjoyed life? Why shouldn't he have been extravagant in the ways that he could be? And why shouldn't he have been thankful?

That's what seemed missing now. My father's thankfulness for life. We went back to the house and there was a tape of one of his old shows that he must have left there on a weekend and we put it in the VCR. He apologized for the bad reproduction, but I didn't think it was so bad. An old black-and-white western where you knew who the good guys were. *The Dooley Boys.* His most popular show, went eleven seasons, set in gold-rush country, the forty-niners, the wicked banker, the fallen doves, the sheriff and the new guy who comes into town with a dark stare and rumors around him. A surprise or two, it's not the new guy but the wicked banker who's the bad guy this week, and a flash of a young Clint Eastwood in the back of the bar somewhere, which my father pointed out, stopped the play, went back, froze, pointed out again, more animated than he had been all night. At the end, over the end credits, "Oh My Darling Clementine." I had forgotten over so many years where my love of that song must have come from. Or did I come to my love of it independently, or could it have been another thing passed in our genes or secret minds? Some old-timer like Gabby Hayes sang that song with his banjo, you saw him for a flash just at the end of the credits, and silly tears were in our eyes, in the eyes of my father and me. There was a room with twin beds where my father had slept the night before and another with a bed unmade, and my father began to look for sheets to make up that unmade bed. "The twin beds are fine. I'll sleep in there," I said.

"But I play the radio to get to sleep. It'll keep you up."

"It's okay. Really."

"Are you sure?"

So we slept in the same room. My father had striped pajamas as he had when I was a boy. I remembered these. I was sure of that. And he had brought his pajamas with him. I had not and slept in my underwear. I went to sleep easily enough but he did not. I woke up at four and he was up, lying on his back listening to the WINS weather. I got up and kissed his forehead and got back into bed and went back to sleep.

*

As in a late medieval allegory, Passion and Responsibility in their separate realms. Is *The Faerie Queene* late medieval? I forget. *Piers the Ploughman*? Stuff from college, not so much forgotten as back there somewhere, under other stuff. Waiting to be useful, hoping to be useful, as if you never knew, one day there might be the call and there they'd be, ready to dust themselves off, ready to explain the world. Passion with its one great ally Death. Responsibility with a whole host of them, Reason and Culture and Amity and Society and Life Itself but the lot of them were maybe not as strong as Death, which by the way had a beautiful child called Romance. The Courts of the Two Realms. Two Languages, and not a word of either language translated into the other. Oh sure, each had a word for Love, in fact it was the exact same word, but in each of the languages it meant something totally different.

All Passion and Responsibility could do was fight it out. The old ignorant armies clashing by night, blind to each other, uncomprehending, without words. And did God turn his back, or did he at last send his emissary, called Tragedy, to go and see what was going on and come back with a report?

This is not a bedtime story I ever told Melissa. Nor anyone else, until just now. But in my ongoing effort to understand and forgive, to be a man, and not a bigger man than my father was, but just a man, a little bit taller than he or a little bit shorter . . .

There are even occasionally sentences that begin and do not end.

*

Our baby was born December 6, 1986. We called her Carolyn. Our second child, Stephen, was born four years later. I'm not really jumping ahead in the story, I just wanted you to know, that we stayed together. We tried to make a family.

Which was something, I think, for people like us, for people who came where we came from.

I told Melissa that I wanted to be married only once. I told her this a lot, actually. Or a few times. And she would be suitably impressed and blame it on my fucked-up family and my fear of being left all over again.

But she didn't leave. Still she didn't leave. I don't know much about marriage, I feel I could hardly write about it at all, the daily intricacies, the millions of moments, of angles, of looking at the two hearts. Modern marriage, I guess that's what it's called. Or is it called postmodern marriage by now? All I really know about it, for sure, is that she did not leave. Though to me that was kind of a miracle.

Why wouldn't she leave? Especially after a few years, after you could see what it was all about and there was still only one kid. You took your child and your half-the-money and your looks that were still great and your own ideas about the way things should be and your guts and your wish to go dancing and your aspiration to a better or at least more varied sex life where your soul would be either more exposed or less and you started over, because that's what the law and all the magazines and the TV and your friends who did it before you and the counselors who heard your complaints and the lawyer and good common late twentieth century sense said you could do and even ought to do if a, b, or c went wrong or if you didn't want your spirit to get frumpy and staid or if you didn't want to wait until it was *too late*, by which they meant when your good looks would be gone. Get back in the pool, get back to the gym.

And yet, I still didn't believe in the thing myself. Not in the vows part, the "death-do-us-part" part. I believed in the day-to-day part, today I didn't want anybody to be left. I didn't want the tears, the lies, or the loss. I wanted to build something a brick at a time, even though most of the time the thing fell down and you had to start over. Or even that's not quite so. I thought it was a nice description of what was going on. I didn't mean it to be that way. I hadn't the will. I was too confused. I imagined that if Melissa left, or if I left, I would root around and find someone and there would be love again and it would all be the same again. Not in the details. Of course not the details. And of course it would not seem like "rooting around." It would seem like chance, it would seem like living a life. But the most unlikely thing in the world was that anything would really be better, and the most likely thing in the world was that it would be worse. A conservative view? A cynical view? When I said to Melissa I wanted to marry only one time, I did not mean that I would *stay* married. I just meant that I would not make the same mistake again. Maybe it's just that I was in love with her.

And of course if she didn't leave, like Maryanna, she would not take half. Good point. Can you go off and write your novel when half the money's gone and there are alimony payments to make and child support and second houses?

It was a miracle that she didn't leave. When we met, we were not even young. As if by accident, we undertook this strange project.

I always thought I'd saved her life, but with the birth of Carolyn did she save mine?

"You know what I hated about you most?" Melissa said one night when the baby was in her arms. "That I could never do anything for you, you always had everything, you were always giving me. Your money, your ideas, your advice. Or that's what you thought. How could you think that?"

"I didn't."

"You did."

"Maybe I did."

"You want to hold her?"

I did and she passed her over.

*

My father came out to see the baby in March. It was the first time he stayed in my house. My house, our house. I wasn't sure what to call it then, I'd never had a house at all, nor a bride. My father would lift Carolyn up, put his finger in her fingers, watch from a distance of respect while Melissa gave her a bath. We didn't talk about Irene, even in the evening, when he and I sat together. We talked about Carolyn, and when we exhausted that we talked about the business and the show and Zacky, and when we exhausted that we talked about sports. We talked as if the sun would rise as well as set. And wouldn't it? Why not? What else could we say about the past? I suppose I didn't want to hurt his feelings. I told him that in a matter of years I would take my winnings and quit and go write my books even if I had no idea yet what my books would be. I just thought, somehow, they must be there. When I was twenty I had wanted to write them. I had filled my drawers with drafts. My father didn't say anything, as if he couldn't decide whether to be cautionary or supportive.

The next day Melissa's parents arrived from Seattle. A full house. The possibilities for a comedy of manners. The Republicans from way out there, the old Jew with his letters to the editor and feelings about Reagan and now Bush and when would that part of it ever end. Gave him something to think about, anyway, something other than Irene. Everybody on their best behavior. Melissa's father not knowing quite what to talk about with mine, so he tried fishing. My father said he used to fish. He could remember when he would fish. Then my father asked him about Boeing and airplanes. That one actually worked out well. My father loved planes and Melissa's father knew all about them. And it gave my father a chance to talk about all the planes he'd flown on, and where he'd flown on them to, and to remember what all that had been like, which was the past but it was not a cruel past.

In the afternoon outside we did something for Carolyn that we called a "blessing" but we didn't really know what it was. Melissa's parents weren't going to get a baptism out of us, that's all we really knew for sure. Yet both of us possibly felt that we had brought Carolyn into a world where God was as likely as anything else and if not then we had better step in. Agnostics' roulette, why take a chance. Or as the young mystic who'd almost forgotten that's what he'd been might have put it, why not take a chance. Each of the grandfathers spoke. Melissa's father mentioned Jesus a few times. My father mentioned the United Nations. I must have winced a few times. An actor we knew who had a mail-order minister's license from the Universal Life Church read Blake and spritzed our child with a few drops of water. I may have winced again, but what the hell. When something's the best you can do, you do it. The truth of it is it made me proud. Though could I really say why?

Afterward my father decided to take a dip in the new pool. I loaned him some trunks and he wore his shirt. I don't think he really knew that lap pools were the only kind of pool that in Los Angeles in 1987 wasn't *déclassé*. He asked me why we didn't put in a bigger pool. I told him we didn't want the upkeep, Melissa only wanted to swim laps. He walked to the edge of the pool, to where the steps were. I was a little distance away, clipping my new old roses. I looked his way and was surprised by the skinniness of his legs. They seemed disproportionate to the rest of him, the way you look at certain features of reconstructed dinosaurs and wonder how they ever could have worked, and if the people who put all the bones together could have got it wrong. He walked down the steps into the pool, stood a few minutes with the water to his waist, splashed water on his face. He seemed like pictures you see of bathers in the Ganges. When he climbed back out, his dark wet hair clung to his legs, and they appeared even skinnier than before. I had an urge to feed him up. I had an urge to say, "My father was a bigger man than this." And to add, so that whoever the hearer was wouldn't take it wrong, "He had bigger bones than this." Where had he gone to, or had he always been that way?

FATHERS AND SONS

TIME FOR THE PLOT TO find its final shape. The approach of
a key date. At the point where I was going to put all my story
into one day, so that it would be like a surreal night on *Northie*,
the date I chose was November 9, 1989. I chose it in part because
enough did happen close to me that day, and because there were
some other things that could be made to fit, some of them things
I've already written about. But also because November 9, 1989 was
the day the Berlin Wall opened. There would be the symbol of
this but also how the rumble of the distant storm played or did
not play on my characters. It was like the end of the decade, but
really it was more than that, it was the end of the Cold War that
had thrown its shadows like an enormous hungry bird incessantly
over our whole generation. Or it was close to the end, anyway,
close enough to tell what was coming. But I could never quite fit
my father into that one day scheme. It's most of why it always
seemed false. After the day when I saw his skinny legs by the lap
pool, he went back to New York and I began to think how I had
to do something for him. A gesture anyway. Probably it wouldn't

work, but a gesture. I had no time to start another new show. There was *Northie* and there was the series commitment with Zacky. But I could get him some money, maybe, and I could get him something to do. Or I thought I could, with a little creative budgeting from Bloch. In the eighth season of a big show, there ought to be room somewhere for a show-runner's dad who after all had been one of the industry's early guys. Yet I resisted the idea for weeks. I told myself he didn't really want to come back to California. I told myself he didn't want handouts. I told myself he would be embarrassed. None of these I believed. What I really believed is that I would be embarrassed, that his taste would be old and off, that he would introduce himself into places where he didn't belong, that he would somehow undermine my own authority or weaken people's belief in my own creativity or expose myself to the old joke that all a producer really produces is relatives. I didn't want him close enough to *noodge*. I didn't want to have to deal with him and Melissa all the time. I didn't want, in a sense, the unexpected. Things were going nicely enough. I didn't want to jinx them. After a month of knowing every reason why it was a bad idea, I got Bloch to hire my father on a five-thousand-dollar-an-episode consultancy. His job would be to submit a set of comments on each script. He could do this from either New York or California.

But he chose to come to California. He seemed reborn. He found a place in Santa Monica. He took walks in Palisades Park. He put on five pounds. He called up all his old friends and let them know he was back in the business. And his rich friends from London came and they didn't stay with him but he took them to the set. I didn't see him every day. More like once a week. He'd come over, see Carolyn, or we'd have lunch. His comments would come in on two single-spaced pages and I would read them and sometimes Zacky read them. They were invariably polite and cautious, maybe questioning the exact meaning of a line here, suggesting a snip there. I can't remember when they ever caused us to change even one thing. And he knew this. He didn't mind. He would say things like, "Can't hurt to have an extra pair of eyes on it." And this was true. He was happy for the checks every couple weeks and happy to keep in motion. He had no illusions; none that he himself couldn't see through when he wished to, anyway. And he got along famously with Zacky. One day the television academy came to interview him, they were interviewing all the old-timers left, and he talked for several hours. It was these stories that attracted Zacky. Since he felt himself to be a moment in television history, he was eager to know what had come before him, as if to place himself in the larger scheme. Stories of Wasserman and Schreiber and Desi Arnaz and Astaire and Hitchcock and Aubrey and Stanton and Gleason and Laughton and Reagan and the day Walter Wanger shot Jennings Lang in the balls. Some of the names you know and some of them you don't. It looked different from the inside. Zacky felt my father was a gentleman.

About four months after my father started his consultancy, we got one of those calls from the network that you only get when your show's reached the top of the hill and started on the road down. It had to do with a twenty-five share. We needed to have a twenty-five share. That is, if we didn't have twenty-five percent of the audience watching television during our time period by the end of the year, they'd think about canceling the show. But the company needed one more year of producing the show in order to make its profit. Bloch asked us to try to come up with something that would boost our ratings at the end of the season. This call came toward the end of October. The whole task was complicated by the fact that Zacky and I refused to do cliffhangers. They were stupid, they were beneath the dignity of *Northie*. Or to put it more crassly and in a way we hoped the suits at the network would understand, it would *undermine our brand*. What a phrase. Like calling everything that's done in the world "product." Another product of the eighties, calling everything done in the world "product." Anyway, Zacky and I put our heads together and came up with having our show's irredeemably bad cop, Schlessing, seem to get away with murdering his snitch. The snitch himself was a fairly popular character and we would do this in the last episode and it wouldn't be a cliffhanger because we wouldn't play it like a cliffhanger, it would be in the mix with everything else, only it would give the network suits something lurid to promote. It was my idea but it pleased Zacky especially, because it seemed to be answering the hardass approach of Morty's show tit-for-tat. Or hooter-for-hooter, as Zacky more likely would have said. Anyway, he wasn't going to be out-pigged by Morty, our pig could be piggier than his. In Zacky's mind the network would never have called if it hadn't been for Morty's new hit.

The two of us called up Jaworsky with our idea. Jaworsky said he was excited about it, which in industry-speak meant about the same as saying it didn't put him immediately to sleep, but then he had an *even better* idea. What if Schlessing doesn't quite get away with it—the crime's found out by Lieutenant O'Brien, and O'Brien in turn covers it up, saving Schlessing. "Now *there* would be a real cliffhanger," Jaworsky said.

"We don't do cliffhangers," Zacky and I said, in a discordant sort-of unison that should have been comical but wasn't.

We hung up more depressed than if we had never come up with the idea. We cursed network executives and their "even better" ideas with the usual curses, the fuck did they know, they weren't writers, they just took credit for what writers did. Zacky seemed to be one with me on this. It would tear the heart out of the show. Donald O'Brien stood for the decent man caught in impossible circumstances. Destroy his character and there was no show left. But then, wasn't that Jaworsky's point? It was an old show. Who would care if there was nothing left? Feed the wallboard into the fire and we'd stay warm a few minutes more. Tear out the floorboards and pull off the roof to feed the flames.

*

Have I said enough how much my father liked his job? He would call me if his script was more than a few hours late. He would also call if after he got it he found typographical errors. These calls were not part of his "notes," they were his diligence. He banked his checks with his old broker, he put in calls to his old lawyer. He was fond of thinking, of saying if he could ever fit it in, that he was the only one from *The Dooley Boys* still working, "except for Clint, of course." He may even have had a few dates that I never heard about. Widows and divorcees, why not? He had things to talk about again, and money to go out to dinner. I told him he ought to be saving some, because *Northie* wasn't going to last forever. I didn't have to tell him this.

In the meantime Zacky and I had received the call from Jaworsky that wound up with his "even better idea" and we went to Bloch to complain and strategize. But Adam didn't see our point of view. "I'm not a writer."

"Of course you're not a writer. Adam. Listen. Please. Once O'Brien goes down as a character, there's nothing left to the show."

We were in his office and I was aware of doing all the talking. Maybe Zacky was thinking that I was the one who knew him better and I was the one he'd listen to, since he'd listened to me once before, when he bought the company and sacked Zacky. Or maybe Zacky was just lying low.

"You can't do something the next season?" Bloch asked.

"To excuse covering up a murder? To explain what? To *redeem* him?"

"All I need is one more year," Bloch said.

"Has Jaworsky called you?"

"Called? He calls every day."

"Fuck."

Maybe Zacky said "Fuck" as well. If he did, it was all he said. It was beginning to bother me. In the elevator down I said we should go see Hagle. The guy you'd think would have the most to lose, the former bit player who'd become *Northie*'s star by playing Donald O'Brien with a wry, surprised detachment, as if to ask was it a cosmic mistake that he wound up being a lieutenant of police. Surely Hagle would find some threat to his recently acquired lifestyle in having O'Brien reduced to a criminal. Get Hagle on our side and we'd have enough to say no, even without Bloch, I said to Zacky, or really I asked, because he was senior to me in everything that was political and I wanted him to know that I knew that. Zacky nodded that it was so. "You can't shoot if you don't have your star," he said. *"Nullum astrum, nullum spectaculum."* Well, really. Zacky said he couldn't go see Hagle because he had to get his hair cut. Which might have sounded lame coming from anybody else, but oddly not from Zacky, whose harmonious view of life seemed to depend on regularly getting his hair cut, his boots shined, and his end wet.

I went to see Flip Hagle alone. I found him in his trailer watching a soap, a pink-nosed, pink-cheeked Canadian from the prairies of Manitoba who looked as Irish as anybody. Or enough Irish to play Donald D. O'Brien anyway. I told him what was being planned for his character, expecting him to be shocked and outraged but instead he looked at me with the straight face of a pawn and said we'd come up with something brilliant.

"Are you crazy? Flip! Come on!"

He looked sheepishly back toward his soap opera on his thirteen-inch set. I was hoping it would remind him where he could still wind up, if this thing came to pass. Daytime soaps, Flip, remember those? That could be *you*! I didn't shout that but I could have. Maybe I should have. Instead it dawned on me that what I was telling him was no surprise.

"Somebody already talk to you about this?" I asked.

Flip shrugged. He was not a talented man at hiding his feelings. Neither am I, I suppose, nor probably a lot of people, but for an actor it seemed odd, as if the one thing you might have expected of him was an ability to fool you.

"The network?"

He shrugged again.

"The company?"

"I'm thinking about it," he said.

"Thinking about *what*? It's a disaster."

"I've got that situation."

"What situation?"

"You know. That situation."

Flip had the look of a sixth grader whose teacher just told him to get his hand out of his pocket. More rueful than embarrassed, really. I knew it all then. Six months before, during lunch hour, Flip had been arrested in his car on Ventura Boulevard and charged with soliciting. One of the grips had told him that if you didn't mention money or a specific sex act you could never get in trouble, but the undercover cop in a miniskirt that Flip pulled his Jag over for disagreed with the grip's interpretation of the law. *All I did was point down*, Hagle was heard to say, leaving out that his pants were unzipped at the time. Zacky had to call the chief of police to get the thing disappeared.

"So Zacky told you?"

Not even a shrug from Flip. Staring at the soap again, but the soap had gone to commercial. Flip was studying, with the concentration of a great master of his craft, an ad for Windex.

I waited for Zacky in his office. When he came back, he was proud of his hundred twenty dollar haircut. "Doreen knows hairs," he said. Zacky had a way, when he was feeling good, of kind of gliding along, of following some inner rhythm, like a bird more graceful in flight than at rest. And his haircut somehow seemed to amplify that impression. He had the look, especially after he was shorn, with his thinning blond-white hair like a crest atop his large square head, of some exotic, quite beautiful bird of prey.

"Did you talk to Hagle?" I asked.

"Me? Of course not. You were going to."

"Did you talk to his agent?"

"About what?"

"About this. About where Jaworsky wants to go with his character. And also about his arrest."

"I don't remember. Possibly. He called."

"Today?"

"I don't know. Yesterday. Hey, Mr. D.A., go back to the prosecutor's office. They've got lots of people you can interrogate there."

He was checking his phone messages, not paying me much mind.

"I thought you were against the idea," I said. "I thought you were with me on this."

"If you're saying I'm blackmailing Hagle to get him to accept Jaw's lame idea, when I don't even like Jaw's lame idea, you're quite wrong."

He was prioritizing his phone slips now, deciding who to call back first.

"But not entirely wrong," I said.

"You heard Bloch today. And he's *your* friend. Doing this show isn't a suicide pact."

"Why didn't you tell me you'd folded? You could have saved us a lot of trouble."

"I haven't folded. We'll just see. We'll wait things out."

When I didn't know what else to do or who else to commiserate with, I told my father. This had an unexpected result. He said nothing. Or rather, he seemed to say the equivalent of nothing, he said greeting card things, what a shame, get well soon, the network was too smart, it wouldn't let a good show be destroyed this way. It was the end of the run, I said. He said nothing then. We were walking in Palisades Park. It was a clear day of Santa Ana winds and you could see Catalina. He pointed it out. He said the smog seemed to be less these days.

It appears my father called Zacky himself. If I'd known about this, I would have been furious. He called to make sure that what I was saying was so. Zacky apparently told him that it was not so, that nothing had been decided. But my father understood otherwise. Old enough to hear between the words.

A few days later, he wrote a letter to Bloch and copied the network.

> *Dear Mr. Bloch,*
>
> *I am resigning my consultancy position on* Northie *as of the next episode. I am doing so to protest the ill-advised destruction of the moral center of the show.*
>
> *I have known Lieutenant O'Brien for the several years that my son has worked on* Northie. *It's obvious that that character would never cover up a murder committed by one of his men or by anybody else. What are you going to blame it on, amnesia? It's ridiculous.*
>
> *You're taking a marvelous show and turning it over to all those who glorify the increasing brutality of our country, to those who cynically say it's okay for our police to get away with anything since everybody else does.*
>
> *What you're doing is symptomatic of this era, but it's also worse than that. It's validating it, as only television in our culture can. Anything for money, anything for power. Call me an old fogy, but I want no more part of it.*
>
> *Thank you for your kind support until now. I've been honored.*
>
> *Sincerely yours.*

Bloch called him, Zacky called him, even Jaworsky wrote him a note. "He sent me a very polite note." My father's own last dance with power. My guess was they were afraid that he'd go to the papers with it, that he'd copy the *New York Times*. Though what's the oldest thing they say about publicity, just get the names spelled right? Anyway, they all told him nothing had been decided yet, or, in Jaworsky's words, we were exploring options to keep this historic show viable. Bloch thanked him for his service. Zacky told him he was a great guy, and a brave guy.

We had dinner before he left Los Angeles. "I'm sorry if I caused you any trouble," he said. "It probably wasn't a good idea to start with."

"Hiring you as a consultant?"

"I just caused you trouble."

"It was one of the better ideas I ever had. Better than Schlessing killing his snitch anyway."

"Maybe they still won't do it."

"Maybe your letter will have some effect."

"Do you think so?"

"I don't know."

"It makes me so mad. That people can be so stupid."

"You don't have to resign, you know. You could still take it back."

He pressed his lips together. Then they softened and he sipped his wine. "Nice. A nice Pommard. And very reasonable."

*

The day the Berlin Wall opened. November 9, 1989. If I had told the whole story that day, Zacky would have shat his pants and Melissa would have thrown her pills at her shrink and we would have made love and broken apart and come back together and

Teddy would have despaired of L.A. and Jaworsky would have had his "even better idea" and Morty's new show would have come on and been a smash and Zacky would have blackmailed Hagle and plied Jaw with the pathos of his divorce in order to get from him "bare ass" and some other things would have happened, as well, that really did happen on that day, all of it crunched together the way shows like *Northie* crunched their worlds together. Time as the great organizer, or time as the great trickster. But in this scheme of time my father would have been left out. Left the country by then. Gone to London. It's where he went after Los Angeles.

Teddy Redmond got up that day and went to the Omelet Parlor on Main for breakfast and by then it was already on the news about Berlin. The nine-hour time difference. Teddy heard about it at breakfast and the rest of the morning was a struggle to focus on Charlie Chamberlain. We were having lunch that day, he and I, to plot our plans to take his story to HBO. He kept turning on CNN to see what was happening with the Wall. By noon Pacific Standard Time the gates were thrown open, the Easties in their plastic cars were pouring through the Wall like lemmings, strangers embraced in the street, couples fucked on top of the Wall. Teddy wished he could be joyful, and perhaps he almost was, but he also had darker intimations. He faulted himself for what he took to be a constitutional resistance to the sight of happy people. But then CNN found a right-wing commentator, a Soviet era scholar from Johns Hopkins, who predicted it all: the Cold War was over, communism was finished, even our war in Vietnam was redeemed, it was only a matter of time but *we had won*. Teddy recognized that this was what he had been sensing. Why wasn't he happier? He thought he knew why.

We met at a white box of a place on Ventura Boulevard for lunch. I was inexcusably late, but if I'd written the book all taking place on one day I would have been late because I would have been at the Sav-On for Zacky and the question of whether to buy him the drums and bugles or the cows and cowboy hats would have consumed me and caused me to forget for a little while my lunch with Teddy and been my lame excuse. The clatter of deals being made in every corner of the place was oppressive. It was one of those restaurants designed to let every sound bang around so that people will think it's lively. But it was near the studio, and Teddy didn't work and I did. By the time I arrived, Teddy's patience was plaintive, the way silence can be when it doesn't have the fight left in it to be accusatory. We talked about the Wall. I hadn't been paying it much attention, heard a few bits on the radio driving in to work, but of course the last weeks had been raising hopes. I was facile, reflexively optimistic, failed at first to catch Teddy's mood. He was worried that somehow the opening of the Wall would hurt his chances of selling a script about Charlie Chamberlain.

"Why the fuck couldn't they have waited a month?"

"You know they called me about the scheduling of it. Sorry. I didn't think."

"You should've gotten back to them," he said.

"The Communists don't listen to anybody," I said.

Trying to be sardonic, trying to play it through. Both of us were, but Teddy stumbled over what he really felt. "The world is full of bad luck," he said.

And I could see his point. The Cold War broke Charlie Chamberlain. And now that we'd apparently won, were we really going to be in the mood to hear about the martyrs, the complicated ones? I tried to cheer him up.

"Nothing's won yet," I said, "Nothing's clear cut yet."

But he didn't believe me, he'd been watching the joy at the Wall all morning and listening to the right-wing commentator.

"Well so, good, then," I said "I mean, isn't it a good thing?"

"Of course it's a good thing," Teddy said, but he was still miffed and he said again that the timing was bad.

I put on my producer's hat, as they call it, but really it was to buck him up that I said, "Maybe the timing could be just fine if we tweak the character a bit. Charlie Chamberlain as unabashed hero, wouldn't HBO go for that? Maybe even a network would go for that. He died thinking he was a pawn of history when it turned out he was one of its kings. Or better, what about this? Forget the whole drowning-in-the-Sound stuff, forget the suicide, have him live long enough to see his triumph, have him tell the story looking back from the opening of the Wall, couples fucking on top of the Wall."

But Teddy was still glum. "Charlie wouldn't believe any of that," he said, and then I was glum too.

He returned from our lunch thinking I'd gone over to the other side and maybe I had. Teddy was living in the Ocean Park Apartments by then, he'd gotten my old place when Melissa and I bought the house. Never give up a rent-controlled apartment, it's like an heirloom that you pass on through the generations if you can, just like rent control itself, the succor of hungry souls.

As soon as Teddy entered the lobby, he was accosted by Red, the building's self-appointed historian, who was gathering names for a petition of congratulations to the people of Berlin from the residents of what had formerly been known as the Brandenburg Apartments. Perhaps Teddy wasn't aware of that, that when the building was owned by the Elks it was called the Brandenburg?

Must have been some German Elks or something, Red speculated. Red was a retired member of the Screen Actors Guild, having had bit parts in westerns in the fifties, and I knew him, too, from my days in the building. Before I had work I'd sit around the lobby and listen to Red talk about the old days. The father figure for when all else failed?

Teddy signed Red's petition, unloaded on him the gripes of his day. Mostly about me, actually, me in and for myself and me as stand-in for the world. So quick to adapt, so quick to forget, money rains on the world and people bathe in it. "Now the ya-hoos will do anything they want," Teddy complained. Communism not as a good thing but as a brake on our own worst instincts. And what role for the man in the middle, the ambassadors, the interlocutors, the men of reason? Put out to pasture? Inconvenient, like daffy aunts in the attic, when it comes to compiling new editions of the national myth. Let the plutocrats take it all, fuck 'em, then. Teddy said most of this and implied the rest. Red looked at him with the unfazed expression of a guy who'd heard crazier than this. "But it's a great day for America," he said. "It's a great day for freedom." Teddy told me all this later, in an apologetic mood. But I don't know that he had anything to apologize for. Then he and Red went upstairs and turned on CNN and began to drink.

Many hours later they had finished off Teddy's Bacardi and watched Ted Koppel. Teddy carried Red back to his apartment because it was the only way Red was going to get there. Teddy dumped him just inside Red's door, left, decided he'd been cheap, returned, lifted Red again, and carried him to Red's daybed where he put him down and put the covers over him and patted them smoothly across Red's chest, so that the bed seemed to have been made with Red in it. This last Teddy couldn't quite explain. Red was mumbling in his stupor about a pinko friend of his who'd had it all wrong according to Red and good riddance to him now, may the landlord evict him and may swallows eat him alive. Teddy was gone before he realized that it was probably Teddy himself that Red was mumbling about.

That same night I hardly thought about Teddy at all. I watched a little of the reruns on the news from Berlin. I said to Melissa something about Teddy being a stubborn case. But she didn't seem interested and I let it pass. It must have been midnight when Zacky called.

"Hey. Sorry if I'm interrupting a conjugal visit. Give my regards to your long-suffering bride."

"What's up?"

"I just got off the phone with Jaworsky. He says we're not going to get bare ass on the new show if we don't do this thing with O'Brien."

"I thought we weren't going to get renewed if we didn't do this thing with O'Brien."

"We didn't respond. So he's upped the stakes."

"This is bullshit."

"Guy, it's *their* network. You can't rewrite that one."

"No, but you can go out with dignity. Or I don't know. I'm not saying I know. But there was a time we were together on this."

"That's why I'm calling you now."

"Let's call Bloch."

"I talked to Adam. He understands what's at stake."

"You talked to Adam? . . . You've been a busy guy, Zack."

"I understand what's at stake too."

"*Bare ass?*"

"It's historic."

"Watch the news. That's historic."

"Just write the scene, would you? If it sucks, that's another conversation."

"I thought nothing was decided yet, I thought we were playing for time."

"We were. Time's up."

*

In the middle of the night I woke up to the sort of conclusion that nights are for. Zacky was right about it all. He was the showman, he was the man who knew what the people wanted, he was the man who'd been around television his whole adult life and cared about it and endured the slings and arrows and fought back and connived because he had to or otherwise he'd long be dead, he'd been the king and kings had scars, and if he said "bare ass" was what television needed and he wanted to be the one to bring it off before his rivals did, who was I to say no? I who could not have cared less if you said fuck or piss or shit on TV, who thought it was all a joke, that people could still think it was daring or an advance or "free speech" or anything just to say dirty words to millions. Or to show a tit or two or a cheek of bare ass, when in France you could see guys blowing themselves on television. Now *there* would be something, a contortionist who could blow himself on TV. What a flat world we were living in. Weren't there real things to be daring about? My smart kid's attitude, my sophisticated cosmopolitan intellectual give-a-fuck attitude. Too good for it all, too good for TV, only got into it for the fast bucks so I could go off and be superior. Zacky would be there when I was long gone, still politicking with the network guys, still leaving no fingerprints, still trying to get his way and once again be called the king.

Fifteen years later, for what it's worth, I can say that some version of it came to pass. Zacky wasn't the first to get a bit of "bare ass" on television, Jaworsky bait-and-switched him and that honor went elsewhere, but Zacky did go on to three more sparkling hits—an hilarious comedy set in a morgue, a touching and remarkably candid show about a Methodist minister, and a reality show involving intercultural dating—and his star on various Walks of Fame and so much money that he forgot how much he gave to Maryanna. Maybe he never got shaved pussy on network TV, but he eventually got a few cheeks.

And who's to say that's not an affirmation of free speech? Why not? Zacky must have felt the whole world was kissing his ass. Though I haven't seen him in a while now.

That night I also wondered: superior to who? The answer was obvious enough but I turned it around and around. Because he too had left the business. He too had faulted its vulgarity and lying and cost to the larger culture. He too had wished to be superior. An uphill battle, then? Did Tantalus have a father? Probably, since we all do. Melissa slept beside me, her light pure downy beginnings of a snore, as if just enough to touch the air passing through her. Letting it know, letting the air know, that she was alive? I hoped so. And what about me, who had all these big ideas. It wasn't so much that I had a book to write as that I thought I ought to write one. I ought to quit lying. But Zacky wasn't lying. Or Zacky lied about a few things, but not about his work, in his work he thought he was telling the truth. "Bare ass" he thought was the truth. So why shouldn't he stay right where he was? It was only me for whom it was fatuous and lies and the slow death that comes from wasting all your time. The critics would love "bare ass." It would give them something to write about. And they would love O'Brien covering up murder for the same reasons. We were entering a new America. I didn't know why, but we were. Something about the Wall, something about the day just passed? But it had already been going on, it didn't just start today, as if prophecy and intimation were just as real as facts. One thing I believed, anyway.

The world goes slowly or the world goes fast. America quietly, unconsciously, toughening itself up for the day soon coming when it would not be embarrassed by the word "empire"? Or was that day today? I counted up all my money as I once used to count up all the girls I'd fucked. Then I counted up what I thought I'd need and doubled it in case Melissa one day left. Then I asked myself if it was enough to double it, if Melissa one day left. Then I asked myself if I was crazy. Then I got up and wrote the scene that Zacky and Jaworsky and Bloch wanted me to write. Not that Zacky couldn't have written it himself. He could have and he would have. A simple scene, really. They were just giving me the chance to come along.

I won't trouble you with all the details, what O'Brien said, what Schlessing said. Just the facts, ma'am. Or cut to the chase, or whatever.

```
INT. O'BRIEN'S OFFICE — NIGHT

Schlessing leaves the lieutenant's office, rat-
tling the door, not looking back. O'Brien looks
after him. The squad room is emptying out.

O'Brien flicks the blinds of his office. It's
something he's never done.
```

Will it attract suspicion? Will someone think he's sick?

He opens his top desk drawer and stares into it. A long BEAT, then he reaches into his back pocket and withdraws a handkerchief and with it lifts the piece out of the drawer. He puts the piece into his briefcase.

He reveals nothing. His face is like a dreamer's face.

INT. SQUAD ROOM — NIGHT

O'Brien traversing the squad room with his brief-case, saying his good-nights. Kovel, LaRocca, Williams, McBride, the new desk officer Tommy. As he's exiting, Weiss and Limestead wrestle in a speeded-up guy who goes nuts when he sees where he's headed, breaks free, bites Weiss, smashes the vending machine which topples over in the ensuing melee, and O'Brien doesn't notice. Or he doesn't turn back, anyway. His walk is like a dreamer's walk.

From a corner of the squad room, like Iago, Schlessing watches him go.

EXT. AN AVENUE NEAR THE WATER — NIGHT

O'Brien, on foot, crosses in front of a darkened warehouse.

A COUPLE OF HOMELESS MEN

Asleep in the warehouse doorway under newspa-pers. O'Brien passes them by, rounds a bend so they cannot see.

A sixteen-wheeler clatters along the cobblestone avenue.

EXT. A DESERTED WHARF — NIGHT

O'Brien walks out onto the wharf.

When he's far enough away, so that it seems like he's the only man left on earth, O'Brien goes to

```
the water's edge, opens his briefcase, reaches
into it with the handkerchief in his hand, re-
moves the piece, and throws it into Boston Harbor.

He rubs his hands with the handkerchief as though
to get the dirt out, then drops the handkerchief
into his briefcase.

He walks back up the wharf. We see the tears in
his eyes.
```

Then I also wrote, for Zacky's eyes only:

```
THE HOMELESS GUYS AGAIN

They're stirring. They've got a bottle of Night
Train. They salute O'Brien as he walks past.

O'Brien, to return the greeting, pulls the belt
of his pants, drops his trousers and underwear,
and moons the homeless men.

CLOSE — O'BRIEN'S CHEEKS

As he wiggles them and shakes them.

THE HOMELESS GUYS

Amused, toasting him back.

RESUME

O'Brien pulls his pants back up, cinches his belt,
and continues on.
```

Got to get your cheap laughs somewhere. Show you're a
sport. Show you know how to behave. And why did O'Brien cover
up for Schlessing? A case of amnesia? The good of the force?
Someone told him to and he did what he was told? Somebody
who had something on him, somebody who could squeeze him,
somebody who would have the last word? In the end I decided it

was better not to explain it at all. A mystery, wrapped in an absurdity? Somebody somewhere might buy that. Or a case of amnesia? Tune in next time. Wasn't that the point?

The next day I called Bloch and told him I wouldn't be coming back to *Northie* the next year. That is, if there was a next year. Bloch assured me now there would be.

*

It was the only time I can remember that my father became angry with me. When there's a divorce, when you go away, I suppose that already diminishes your authority. What else can you threaten, what more can you do? I suppose my father had never been angry with me because he didn't think he had the right to be. Or anyway not to show it to my face. But he was angry when I called him in London to tell him I was quitting the show.

"You're only doing this because I did it! Are you crazy? You worked hard for this! You're not going to get another deal, you know. Not as good as this one. You're on top of a top show! You could ride that for another ten years. Think of Melissa! Have you talked to Melissa? What if you have more kids? You never know what's going to happen. And you're giving up the series commitment too? Series commitments are like gold, and you just throw it back in the creek?"

Funny thing for me to say, but I didn't know he could be so angry. Or of course I must have imagined it. But hearing it was different, hearing it was as if I was hearing *him*. The way my mother would put the word *him* into italics, in her voice, in her bitter sarcasm, whenever the subject was *him*.

"I think it's different between you and me," I said. "You were doing it more as a protest. Because the business was your life. I'm doing it more to save my life."

"Don't get melodramatic with me now!"

But his anger was already softening, turning more toward pleading.

"Have you asked yourself, if there are two hundred fifty million people in America, how many of them would be quick to change places with you?"

"And the starving children in China."

"And those too. Right. Those too."

"I'm an ingrate, I guess. I'm leaving food on my plate."

The line went dead then. It's what I'd always hated about phones. The person at the other end of the line, my father at the end of the line, out in California in the sunshine, could just stop talking if he wanted to and I'd never know if he'd ever talk again. And yet my father had never actually done that, until now. I wished I could see his face. I wished I knew what was inside him.

"Dad?" Did I say that, "Dad?" In that pleading way that was like his own.

I thought I heard his voice break. "I caused this. I'm sorry. I caused this."

"I don't think you did," I said.

*

All the chances in the world to change my mind. Or it seemed that way at first. Everybody assumed, that is, Zacky assumed, Bloch assumed, my agent and over at the network they assumed, that I was just playing hard to get. Or that I was planning to test my free agency, that I would shop myself all over town. I told them all it wasn't so. I told them I just wanted to go write my books. Didn't Morty leave to go print beautiful books, or chase French girls, or whatever that was? But Morty came back, everyone pointed out. Bloch even sent Morty to see me. His emissary, the guy I'd listen to if I had a brain left. There's an old axiom in Hollywood that the more you don't want them, the more they want you. But Morty cautioned me this could be taken too far. There would come a point where it was too much trouble, where I was too far out to sea, and they would turn and move on. They, whoever *they* were, were superstitious and insecure but they were not crazy. I told Morty one reason I was leaving was that I felt envy for him, and he was my friend. Morty laughed as if I was the crazy one. "Envy's part of the sport," he said.

"I just want to do this one thing with a friend of mine," I said, and I told him about Charlie Chamberlain and the Cold War and the ending of the Cold War and Teddy's problems.

Morty had no answer for that one. Then Zacky called Melissa, to tell her of the hole in the show that I would leave. Then the company called my agent to say more money could be found. Then Jaworsky called to say that my scene with O'Brien made him cry. Then Bloch called. I don't remember every word, but I remember where we got to. "The best thing you can do if you want to get Teddy's project going is stay on the show another year."

"Because you'll quit backing us if I leave?"

"Because you'll be so busy they'll think they're stealing you," Bloch said.

"I want to write my books," I said.

"Nobody reads books anymore," he said. "Or I don't anyway. I don't have the time."

The things you hear. The things that must be true, if enough people say them.

The power of the created universe in your hands, you shmuck, and you throw it all away.

Bloch stopped calling after that. The company stopped making better offers. Zacky was polite but acted betrayed, almost as if I'd gone over to Morty. "Just do what you have to do." He said that a few times. An act of disloyalty, I guess, to question his world.

And then Sterner the agent heard something funny, he heard Adam was mad at me about something, and it wasn't that I meant to leave.

"What was it then?"

"I don't know. Nobody knows. You've got history with him, don't you?"

Which had to mean what I'd thought likely enough when it happened, that Bloch hated Teddy's apology and hated me for scheming to set it up. As if it had been more than he could look at. Better a billionaire isolate than a billionaire chump.

But Teddy hadn't really tried to make him a chump. He had tried, from the disadvantageous position of a supplicant, to open something in Adam. I suppose I wondered, if Bloch didn't have his billion dollars, would it have been different; if he had no gilded cage to retreat to, could he have been brought back to life? Too grand a way to put it, maybe, but at the time it seemed true enough.

All the emissaries, all the seductions.

But nobody ever came to me and said, "We'll stop this whole business with O'Brien, we'll throw those scenes out, if you'll stay." Not that I would have wanted them to. If they had, it would have only caused me problems. They would be taking away my easy excuse.

*

Not as simple a thing as maybe I've made it seem, by the way. To chuck it all, the attentions, the flatteries, the miracle money, your picture in the paper, NPR or the *Wall Street Journal* or *Playboy* calling up, the tickets to games, the easy awards, the assumption you know something about the culture or are even doing your little bit to make the culture, people knowing who you are. Addictive the way everything's addictive, after awhile it gives you no pleasure but it keeps you from feeling bad. You withdraw the way you withdraw from anything else. As if it were seasickness you're trying to get rid of, you keep your eyes on the horizon.

It didn't hurt that I had already written a lot of the same thing. It may even have been, if I'd kept at it, that one morning soon I'd have awakened with no more urban fairy tales to tell. Another mild observation of mine, or maybe it was Morty's: television would be better off if they didn't hire the same people over and over again to do it. Few guys have that much to say, or if they do it's their compulsion talking, recycling the same things over and over in ways they can't even hear. Though isn't that the point? Product, again. What do producers produce if not product? Twenty-odd hours a year. Thousands of pages of script. I say the people doing it now, the geniuses, the new kings, but only because PR guys get paid to call them that, should do the right thing and politely step aside. Why not? A one series limit, or maybe two, like the two-term limit on the presidency. Bring in the new blood. It's a big country and there's lots of people who'd like the dough. All this is very likely to happen tomorrow.

I went with Teddy to HBO. Teddy told the story of Charlie Chamberlain as he wanted it to be told. They listened and asked a few questions. Two weeks later one of their guys called and said they'd talked it over and Chamberlain was surely a fascinating and dashing figure and they were quite interested in him as a character but his story was sort of a downer for the times. But what if we could change it so he was more of an unalloyed hero, he fought the commies with all his heart and now we've won? Would we be interested in that? I gave Teddy every chance to say yes. He needed the money, he needed the job. Sure we could take it to Showtime or Turner or the movies. But HBO had been his idea of heaven. We went out and got drunk on tequila and wine. We pieced to-gether the way drunk guys do that I was a dancing bear in a gypsy bar. Dance a few clumsy steps with a leash around my neck then stumble off the stage. Or he was, or we both were. We were friends again. We said no.

A few years later Teddy got somebody, an independent pro-ducer in Boston, to put up the money for a script about Charlie Chamberlain along the lines of what Teddy believed. But the script languished. Someone else rewrote it. Teddy got the rights back. As far as I know, he's still trying to set it up today.

I became unemployed and started to write and still Melissa did not leave.

*

Alternative theories of why I quit TV. There aren't any. Leave space blank.

None that I want to put forward, anyway. None that I really believe.

Fun while it lasted.

*

At some point I went over to London to see my father. We'd spoken on the phone, we'd even exchanged letters once or twice, but somehow I had expected to find him not as I found him. I'd imagined he'd be more with his rich friends, taken up by them, maybe going out with one of the widows or divorcees. He was after all in a fairly enviable spot. *Northie* was big in Britain. He could rightly claim to have been a recent consultant, he could be out there voicing his complaints and arguments, he could be writing fresh letters to the editor. And maybe he was. But he would have told me if they'd been printed. I found him in a one-bedroom furnished flat off Baker Street. Hardly the high-rent district. He told me about the tennis court where he played every day. He pointed out to me the stack of pages that was the novel he had begun to write. This I said nothing about, but it seemed so odd to me, he had never been a writer, even as a producer he had only made notes, little suggestions, rearranged or complained, hired and fired, he was from before the time when writers took over TV, and yet here he was . . . imitating me? It was as if life had reversed itself entirely.

I took him to lunch at the Ivy. Got him dressed up, so to speak. He was in his element there, the West End types, whoever else. An old agent came up and shook his hand, didn't know he was living in London now. He ordered the biggest plate of fresh berries I'd ever seen. Bigger than you could get at Michael's in Los Angeles. It made his eyes big and cheerful and a little conspiratorial and he called the waiter for a second plate. "There! There we are!" I felt as if he were talking to a little boy. "Look at *those!*" With the back of his fork he plowed berries onto the smaller plate. But really he wasn't talking to a little boy, it was just his happy fussing, a little like Zacky's *delectatio*. It's not true, as I wrote once, that I didn't like Zacky Kurtz much. In a way, I loved him. He just reminded me too much of my father.

When I had my plate of berries, he asked me, "Do you mind that I'm writing? I'm much worse than you, don't worry. No competition from me. But there's a few little things I thought I wanted to say."

"How's it going?"

"Terrible. I may quit."

"Don't."

"I start . . . but I get so tired."

"Just do a very little bit every day."

"I'm trying that. I'll get back to it."

But I didn't think he would. I thought he would get a certain ways and then I could hear it in his voice, how he would stop.

"Why don't you write about Irene?" Something I shouldn't have said.

He shrugged. "Maybe," he said.

I never saw anything he wrote. But I'm sure he didn't need my stupid suggestion. It must already have been about Irene. Something about Irene, and it got too painful.

Or probably such thoughts comforted me. I didn't really want him to turn out to be a writer. It could be like his last shows all over again, and then what would I say? And what would I feel about my own prospects, if I came from dry seed? Or what if he was really good, what if he out-wrote me, what if that was the point of it all? The spur to my father's writing, if that pipsqueak can do it, then surely I can. I was afraid, somehow, of losing something. One way or the other, losing something. But what? Was there absolutely nothing about me that couldn't be taken away?

Questions that go all the way back and never really have answers. Unless the answer, put forward by the same folks that brought you the late medieval allegory of Passion and Responsibility, is somehow, awkwardly, Love? Did I become my father's voice because he would not be that voice himself? The berries were a little sour, but I added sugar, then they were good.

From the Ivy that afternoon we walked over to the National Gallery. I hadn't been in the place since I was there with my father and Irene, half a lifetime gone by. When I'd been in London with Melissa or on business, the Tate and the galleries were more our speed. Or even the British Museum. I loved the invisible dust of the British Museum. But my father was a National Gallery man. The Titians, the Raphaels, the Rembrandts. The canon of the West. His bible, I guess. I walked from gallery to gallery with him, often a little behind, not moving to the next picture until he was ready, until he had his say. Usually just a few words. "Marvelous."

But in the room with the Rembrandts he said nothing at all. I thought it was maybe because like me he was slightly bored. I almost said it, that I was slightly bored, that I had a hard time looking into the pictures' darkness. But it was in his silence that I saw those Rembrandts. He sat down on one of the benches. His legs may have been tiring, or he simply stopped to look. His face was a Rembrandt face then, shadowed, enduring, aware. Almost all the light gone except what was left, and what was left was more than I had imagined. As if when you take almost everything away is when you can see what everything is.

We went to his tennis court after that. It could have been private or it could have been public but it was not a fancy place. My father played in white shorts because he always played in white, but hardly anybody else did. He had an old guys' doubles game. He hustled around and I heard someone say that his forehand was strong. Don't go by me, I wouldn't know, I've forgotten what tennis I ever knew. But he seemed limber enough, he looked pretty good. When he was done, he introduced me around. The way he did things, "a writer," and then a few minutes into it something about *Northie*, and then everyone with their questions and comments and nice things to say. Though it couldn't really have been a surprise. They all knew about his own connection to the show.

"Why did you move here?" I asked him a little later.

"I have friends here. I always loved London."

"But do you see your old friends?"

"Of course. From time to time," he said. "But you know I don't really have their kind of money. This city is so expensive. Sometimes you can feel like a nuisance."

"Do they think that about you?"

"It's not what *they* think that matters."

"So why did you move here? You must have known all that."

"I was mad at Ronnie. And now Bush. What they're doing to our country."

"I'm glad you still call him 'Ronnie,'" I said.

"Reagan? That's his name. Did I tell you when I played chess with him in the Universal commissary and he didn't know that if you got a pawn to the end of the board you got any piece you wanted back?"

The part of the conversation that made me feel better about it all. "Ronnie." Great. If he'd lost his gift for name-dropping, it would have been as bad as losing his appetite. We both ate well that night, in an Indian place in his neighborhood. In stops and starts he began to tell me an idea he'd had for a screenplay. He was almost embarrassed to tell me, like a boy bringing home a new girl. The story line was this: a Texan television producer like or unlike Zacky Kurtz does a show where the hero is a brutal guy who beats people up or shoots them and then feels occasionally bad about it. One day the producer is flying his new plane, runs out of gas, and crash lands in the desert. Even his clothes get burned up, and most particularly his wallet with all his identification. He makes his way over the desert in his underwear and when he finds a deserted shack he breaks in and goes to sleep. In the morning a sheriff is there and arrests him. The shack was the site of a murder. The sheriff is a bully, almost a copy of the producer's TV character, except that after he beats people up or shoots them he doesn't feel bad about it. He is certain the producer did the crime, disbelieves everything the producer says, and proceeds to torture him to get him to confess. Beatings, shocks, hooks. The producer keeps trying to get on the good side of the sheriff, uses all his self-vaunted charm, tells him about his show and his hero/cop who is in fact a role model to the sheriff. It makes the sheriff even madder to hear all these lies and blasphemies about his role model coming from this "killer." It goes on from there. The producer suffers a lot. He eventually confesses and that only makes matters worse. And is there redemption in the end? Does the producer do penance, does he see any sort of light, does he even survive? To be continued, to be figured out.

"Write *that*," I said. "Don't write about Irene."

"Maybe I will."

"You could probably sell it for a bundle."

"I'm not really a writer, you know," my father said. "Maybe you should do it."

"Maybe," I said.

My father picked up the check.

*

I suppose I always imagined that if I wrote about him, he would forgive me. A producer, after all, is the one who does whatever it takes in order to get whatever it is done. Why else have producers? But would he understand my urgency to write it, the urgency of unsaid things? Dear father, I understood this urgency so late.

How powerfully I missed him in those early years. I laid a sort of trap for him. This book I wrote, dark flower with thorns of rage and betrayal, these books, would be worth less to me if he did not approve. You can say that's wrong, but you can't tell a reflex that it's wrong. Something so far in there that you dig, you excavate, you try to act like some accomplished surgeon of the soul, at your peril, at the peril of it all.

*

Though something else, not unrelated. Somebody said to me once, in a fit of irony, "The Germans have never forgiven the Jews for Auschwitz." Was it possible my father never forgave me for his leaving?

*

I flew back the next day. He died the following summer, playing tennis on a hot afternoon. The preferred way to go, I think, if you're a certain kind of guy. A Japanese eats *fugu* until it gets him or it doesn't and an old Jew who's mad at America plays tennis through a London hot spell. When I got the news I didn't cry, but what does that mean? I told Carolyn, we told Carolyn. I said a kind of silent prayer that also had no words. His ashes went into the lake in Connecticut with Irene's. Thomas took care of that one. Thomas and his new family, his wife and the two kids she came with. And my sister was there, who'd seen him only twice in her adult life, had stayed away from him at every chance. There was a memorial gathering a few months later in Beverly Hills, at the house of old friends. I went with Melissa. We were the youngest there and in a way we were like the stars. Doted on and introduced, Melissa especially. My father must have told them all about Melissa, must have bragged, must have said how much he adored her.

All the old friends reminded me a lot of my father and Irene. A couple of retired directors and a lawyer who wasn't retired yet and their wives and the people involved with the County Museum and a woman who owned a lot of property in Santa Barbara and in a wheelchair with Parkinson's Gene Lang the composer whom I'd named my imaginary city of Langden after and some others I didn't quite figure out. No clergy, no rabbi, no Unitarian minister. It impressed me how many people came. There were few at first, but they kept showing up. In the middle of it, Thomas arrived. Just off the plane. We chatted for a while. He was getting started with a software business and had to go from there up north. I kept thinking, every moment I talked with him, how much he looked like Irene. It was as if I took all the resemblances we shared for granted, the dark eyes that were his and mine and our father's, our lips, our hair, our whatever else, and what was left, looking at me with an expression that might have been critical or might have been tragic, was Irene.

It doesn't seem fair to say what people said about him. You could go to all the memorials there ever were and never hear anything really different. But I would say that people seemed to think my father, whose name was Bill, had a gift for friendship. A few wept. Several mentioned his letters to the editor. Thomas told me in London he had had a lady friend. Someone from the tennis club, a schoolteacher, forty-five years old. It must have gotten going only toward the end. I hadn't heard a word about it. Then they played an episode of *The Dooley Boys*. Gene Lang had brought a cassette. It wasn't the episode I'd seen in Connecticut but it might have been. The wicked banker again. And at the end, the old Gabby Hayes type, over the end credits, singing "Oh My Darling Clementine." Somebody told me that my father had liked that song. I'd never known that.

Then I had this silly producer's thought that the song must be out of copyright, or they couldn't have afforded to play it each week at the end of the show. My father's thought? Or no thought at all. But by the time Melissa and I left, I couldn't get its tune out of my mind. It was like that song at Disneyland, when you take your kid to the Small World ride and then you can't get rid of it for days. The first verse. The chorus. I'd never really known the rest. Something about the miner's daughter drowning because she went too close to the water.

It was driving me a little crazy. It was driving me to tears. It was driving me back to my childhood.

In the car, Melissa said, "Try singing it out loud."

"I can't carry a tune," I said.

"Just do it. It's like hiccups. It'll get rid of it."

So I sang as much as I knew of the song.

"In a canyon, in a cavern, excavating for a mine, dwelt a miner, forty-niner, and his daughter Clementine."

My voice as flat and hoarse, maybe, as that old miner's. I remembered that my father couldn't sing either, or he said he couldn't anyway. I had never heard him sing. Not that I could remember. Not even "The Star Spangled Banner" at a ballgame, nor a song in a children's book.

"Oh my darling, oh my darling, oh my darling Clementine, you are lost and gone forever, dreadful sorry, Clementine."

I sang in our car parked in the street in Beverly Hills in front of my father's friends' house. When I was done Melissa was weeping. I held her in my arms.

ALL SHALL BE WELL;
AND ALL SHALL BE WELL;
AND ALL MANNER OF
THINGS SHALL BE WELL

ALL SHALL BE WELL; AND ALL SHALL BE WELL; AND ALL MANNER OF THINGS SHALL BE WELL

Tod Wodicka

PANTHEON BOOKS

NEW YORK

Copyright © 2007 by Tod Wodicka

All rights reserved. Published in the United States by Pantheon Books, a division of Random House, Inc., New York. Originally published in Great Britain by Jonathan Cape, an imprint of the Random House Group, Ltd., London, in 2007.

Pantheon Books and colophon are registered trademarks of Random House, Inc.

Library of Congress Cataloging-in-Publication Data
Wodicka, Tod, [date]
All shall be well; and all shall be well; and all manner of things shall be well / Tod Wodicka.
p.   cm.
ISBN 978-0-375-42473-1
1. Older men—Germany—Fiction.   2. Self-realization—Fiction.
3. Psychological fiction.   4. Germany—Fiction.   I. Title.
PS3623.O43A45 2007   813'.6—dc22   2007019233

www.pantheonbooks.com

Printed in the United States of America

First United States Edition

2 4 6 8 9 7 5 3 1

This novel is dedicated to my son,
Louis

You are, and have been from the moment of your birth, perilously close to the abyss. You are fourteen years old, a girl. The year is AD 1105.

You are quiet and you are willful. You are prone to seeing things that are not there. Your mother's name is Mechthilde and your father's name is Hildebert, or perhaps it is the other way around. It matters not, for they do not love you. You were not a choice. You are a hole for food and a frame for clothing, another set of eyes to turn towards the everlasting – a thing of mystery and necessity. They call you Hildegard.

Hell is the daily darkening of the sun. Hell is a mouse frozen in a block of ice. Nine siblings, nine other faces and moving limbs and dirty needs to prepare for eternity, and it is decided that you are to be the sacrifice. You, at least, will be saved.

They bury you alive so that you will never have a chance to sin. The ceremony is frightening but you cannot cry because Christ is there. The bishop explains this; the priest, your father, everyone explains to you that He is there as you are enclosed in the stone cell, the anchorage. There is no light, no door. It is little more than a consecrated dungeon attached to the Benedictine monastery at Disibodenberg. You hold your breath.

Funeral rites are administered. You are bathed in holy water,

1

scrubbed – and you will not cry. The village has come to watch the monks bury you. They stare. The stones are arranged. Lighted torches, autumn breeze, woodsmoke, braying beasts, whispers and owls and tumbling bats; and suddenly you feel not abandoned but exalted. There are burial hymns. You are a gift this day, and you pray that you are worthy.

Summers, minutes, winters, years. In this darkness, time is different. One day light trickles in, whistling from a crack in the ceiling. It splashes your palms, forming a puddle in the dirt. You dig a small hole, no bigger than your fist, but enough to collect more, you hope, deep enough to prevent the light from evaporating so quickly at the end of the day. Probably this is not a sin.

Others join you – girls, young women. But you are not permitted to speak with them. They are different places of the dark; rustles, prayers, breathing. Sometimes men and children taunt you, sometimes they laugh, striking the anchorage walls with rocks. You pray for them, you ask their forgiveness. Women come, too, often during the night. The older ones frighten you, demanding miracles.

Because the anchorage is attached to the monastery, you hear the monks perform their eight daily offices. The Opus Dei, the Work of God. The bells that announce its coming. Their chant becomes the sound of your existence, a true and smarting joy. Into the cell, into your slumber and the endless dark, the chanting inflates your dreams. You pray that they will never let you leave.

'Girls.' A voice, my voice.

Your eyes fix on the nylon ceiling, which, for three days, has been your anchorage. The other six shift in their sleeping bags. They still sleep. You light a candle, you pull yourself to your knees. Humming, you lift a glass of wine to your lips and you drink.

2

Part One
AD 1998
The Emigrants

I

Dawn, or its German equivalent, cannot be far off. But here, at the top of the hill, night still clogs the forest. Being sixty-three years old and sleepy, I find it nearly impossible to differentiate now between the stray grapevines, the trees, and the waist-high shrubs that I know surround me. They could all be wild animals.

'Is everyone awake?'

Three days ago I imprisoned six middle-aged women and one pre-pubescent girl in a tent on this hilltop. The time has come to set them free.

'Pray undo the lock,' an anchorite whispers. Then, sensing my hesitation, 'Did thou forget the key?'

There is no key because there is no lock. My hand waits on the zipper. I stand there in my dagged-edged taffeta tunic, my sandaled feet wet from dew. My bald little head. My nose. Somewhere behind me sleeps the great stone Benedictine Abbey St Hildegard, its vineyards cascading down the hill over Eibingen, over Rudesheim, and into the river Rhine.

Zipper down, the tent gives us Tivona Henry. Forty years old and not unlovely, Tivona is skinny in a way that suggests intense concentration; more simian, maybe, than outright undernourished. Her head feeds a nest of gray-streaked frizz.

It's Tivona's medieval chant workshop that I've accompanied on this German vacation. She smiles.

I have only myself to blame. Weeks prior to the journey I'd sowed the idea of re-enacting Hildegard von Bingen's first days in the anchorage, more or less on a lark, knowing full well these women's anchorite longings and their propensity for outlandish re-enactment schemes. I expected nothing to come of it. Then, a day before departure, it was announced that several of the women would be enduring three days in the tent; three entire days and nights atop the hill overlooking the Abbey, reliving Hildegard's girlhood. One meal a day, only wine to drink, no idle chatter, absolutely no grumbling; just chanting and the occasional prayer. I have never had a problem with the concept of medieval re-enactment. In fact, many believe that I actually invented it. The world is riddled with far worse activities and I altogether refuse to even feign embarrassment, especially at my age. Dressing up in period-specific costume? The re-creation of history through practical workshops and group scholarship? For some, in this day and age, there's simply no place left to retreat.

Tivona steps free from the tent. Others follow, one by one. Blinking, grinning heads, then arms, then bodies. Tivona leading her cortège of part-time anchorites back into the twentieth century. Each holds a candle made by the nuns here at the Abbey St Hildegard, most ennobled with now-grotesque melting effigies of their patron saint. White tunics glow in what is left of the moon.

Some stumble, others laugh; they are very obviously inebriated. They sing. Soon I am surrounded, my flame-flickered face a mask of potent infirmities, adhering, so I've been told, to the long tradition of Christian mysticism insisting that those impaired in body are somehow healthier in spirit. Which is another way of saying that because I am ugly I am going to get a reward. Specifically, I have a misshapen nose.

There is a deep silence despite the amateur medieval plain-chant which clouds behind me. It's nearing lauds, first light. Single file, we begin our descent back towards the Abbey and the event of our first public performance.

'Burt?' Tivona asks.

In three days the women will return home to Queens Falls, New York. They do not yet know that I have no intention of accompanying them.

'Are you well, m'lord?' Tivona continues.

'No,' I say. 'I am not.'

Two years ago I joined Tivona Henry's medieval chant work-shop as a way to better manage the anger that New York State's Board of Parole believed they had good reason to be wary of. Following a late-night Confraternity of Times Lost Regained revel, I'd been apprehended while attempting to transport myself home in a borrowed Saab. I didn't have a license to operate such a vehicle, or any vehicle, or the requisite skills; and, worse, I'd consumed much homemade mead. I really don't remember the specifics. It's a matter of public record, however, that I altogether refused to walk in a straight line or touch my nose with my finger. They'd never detained anybody dressed in period-specific, histori-cally accurate costume before, and once installed in the Queens Falls police depot I was treated genially, like a time traveler who couldn't comprehend the vigorous modernity which had enveloped him. Because I was old they supposed I was demented.

For one thing, they refused to immediately imprison me. This I found offensive. I was made to sit on something aluminum, and handed beverages I could not possibly drink. (Coffee, I did my best to explain, was OOP. Out of Period. Such beans did not exist in medieval Europe, so I assiduously avoided them.) My portrait was snapped, the air from my lungs scientifically tested. To the best of my memory, I was wearing a simple woolen tunic, nothing extravagant or untoward.

'Let's do this one more time. Just for the record, what year is this again?'

I liked the police officer charged with interrogating me. In him I noted the same pious dreaminess that often overtakes a medieval re-enactor after a long, involving Confraternity of Times Lost Regained weekend.

'AD 1256,' I answered. I was inebriated enough to imagine that he would see in me what I saw in him, and that he would not only recognize but applaud our similar life choices. Our costumes.

'Your name?'

'Eckbert Attquiet.'

'Right. This your wallet, Eckbert?'

'It is my pouch.'

The police officer removed some cards from my leather pouch. The first was a wallet-sized, laminated reproduction of a painting of my son, Tristan, and me. Domenico Ghirlandaio's *Portrait of an Elderly Man with His Son*.

I raised my voice and rose to my feet. I did something which required another police officer to restrain my hands in metal cuffs.

'Take it easy, old man. Nobody is going to steal your library card.' The officer looked at me carefully. Slowly, he placed my Ghirlandaio back inside the pouch. He held another card. 'Burt Hecker,' he read. 'Well, and here's another, also says Burt Hecker. Confraternity of Times Lost Regained. That your thing, Mr Hecker? Medieval re-enactment?'

History, when you devote your life to it, can be either a weight into a premature old age or a release from the troublesome, promiscuous present: eternal immaturity as an occupational boon. Since I was thirty, most have considered me retired, unemployed, or fundamentally unemployable. I have devoted my adult life to amateur scholarship and the Confraternity of Times Lost Regained, the re-enactment society I founded. I've since been left a considerable fortune.

'Mr Hecker?'

The fluorescence made me sneeze. 'I'm just an old man,' I said. 'Do with me what you will.' Telephones trilled and voices barked from small boxes full of static. Flags, bowls of peanuts, guns, computer screens imitating aquariums – lunacy, plain and simple. Me in my tunic and homemade sandals.

'You do not have a New York State driver's license.'

'Correct.'

The CTLR revel had not yet ended when I had absconded, stealing the automobile. It was the first time in my life that I had ever been behind the wheel of such a vehicle. I had had much mead. The last image I recall was of dozens of men, women, and children dressed in all manner of medieval garb – princesses, squires, knights, blacksmiths, peasants, and monks – my twentieth-century secessionists arm in arm around a bonfire, dancing, leaping, singing, with all that desperate blackness surrounding them, pulling at them, devouring the edges of their perfect, historically accurate illusion. Way too much night, I thought. They don't stand a chance. In any event, the idea with the Saab had not been to transport myself to any physical realm.

'Who is Lonna Katsav?'

'What?' Lonna Katsav was my best friend and my lawyer. 'She has nothing to do with this,' I added, finally shocked back into AD 1996. It was Lonna's Saab that I had stolen. On the wall was a framed photograph of the Governor of New York State, and one of the President of the United States. Since when, I wondered, did those wielding great authority begin smiling like nineteenth-century barkers? How could anyone take these men seriously? If everyone loses their mind at the same time does anyone really notice? I looked around me at the game being played, the idea of order and duty and society and justice being re-enacted, that stern idiotic bustle, and I knew, suddenly, that it was all over. I had crashed my best friend's car into a point of no return.

'Well, Lonna Katsav is coming to pick you up.' The police officer offered me a stick of chewing gum. 'She's not going to press charges, you'll be happy to know. Though she thought about it.'

I held up my shackles. I sighed. 'Make sure that she sees me in these at least, would you?'

It should be said that throughout the whole ordeal my officer did an admirable job of not once gawping at my nose. The first fellow I encountered at the station had demanded that I actually remove it, thinking it was part of my medieval garb.

The punishment for drunk driving without a license in a

stolen car consisted of a fine and the recommendation that I serve my parole in thrice-weekly Anger Management & Self-Betterment Workshops. However, because my late wife knew some people who knew some people who knew the judge, I was allowed a unique alternative. Thus, I became the first male member of Tivona's medieval music therapy workshop. Truth is, nobody was particularly worried that I'd anger. I rarely did. They simply knew that I would, on principle, risk six months in the threatened cage rather than submit myself to the group hugs with mountain people I was certain such Self-Bettermenting entailed. Better, finally, to chant. Better eighteen months of intuitive healing with Tivona Henry.

Because no previous musical skills were needed to join Tivona's chant workshop, none had any. Only Tivona Henry and, to everyone's surprise, my best friend, Lonna, who only joined, she'd said, in order to protect me from the dawning of the Age of Aquarius. But more on Lonna Katsav later.

Tivona mostly taught us the music of Hildegard von Bingen (1098–1179), that medieval anchoress, theologian, visionary, naturalist, and composer so adored by today's more esoterically disposed females. And though Hildegard affirmed the lowliness of womankind and the subjugation of female sexuality, Tivona and the girls saw her as a proto-feminist New Age icon, not the Catholic scold she undoubtedly was. No matter. History is ever ours for the reliving. They were Hildegard's devotional songs we crooned, her visions we dissected and manipulated over tea. To the girls, the medieval woman was a person capable of great self-assertion, so they studied what they believed to be instances of this, ferreting out kernels of sassiness from the most minor

11

of references, building a fairy-tale history and peopling it with sisters-in-arms. The medieval woman was them, only more real. Them, with a less cluttered connection to the eternal. Tivona utilized a tedious if ultimately effective call-and-response technique in teaching us to chant; no attempt was ever made to expose us to musical notation or Latin. She sang something, we sang it right back. And I would be lying if I said that the results were anything less than extraordinary.

Chanting was performed in a circle, at night, facing inwards. The circle's center held a pumpkin-sized ball of twined electrical Christmas lights. Bed sheets hung from the ceiling like clouds and I always closed my eyes. It was quite enough hearing the startling music, I didn't wish upon myself the mind-wracking task of reconciling what I heard and felt to be true with what I would see: a dumpy circle of primarily middle-aged women in the costume of modern practicality and routine. That pampered circle of burghers' wives, den mothers, Confraternity of Times Lost Regained romantics, spinster insurance representatives, and doughy, dreamy elementary school teachers. Nor could I help thinking that all of these women, most in the process of passing their prime, were now starting to resemble men in drag. I saw the petty gnawed fingers that did bills, worried pennies, and thrust sandwiches into paper bags. I would sniff a sudden flush of chemical or animal odor. Deodorants, perfumes, perspiration, hand creams. Tivona insisted we remove our shoes. Shoes hamper chant. If I opened my eyes everything collapsed and there I was, out of period, wearing uncomfortable twentieth-century slacks, wearing socks, standing in a circle in a small room above Tivona's Second Hand, Third

Eye shop, the sound of trucks passing on the slushy street below.

I recognized many of the women from the CTLR – though, in keeping with policy, I refused to acknowledge their mundane, modern selves. I insisted on introductions. They humored me. From the very beginning I was welcomed with a bright muddle of pity, curiosity, and genuine warmth. The events of my recent past had aged me, and my age had neutered me; I was in mourning, I was in need of maternal condescension, I lived alone in a big house and only wore medieval garb and rarely answered the telephone. But mostly I was an opportunity to put into practice all that healing stuff they seemed so convinced was an integral part of performing medieval plainchant. My presence thoroughly invigorated them: I was a project that became something of a friend, something of a mascot. But, besides my endearing personal tragedies, I do think that I had a lot to offer those seeking a more than cursory knowledge of medieval times. That I took my lawyer with me was, for them, perhaps my only snag – Lonna Katsav had something of a reputation. But things, for the most part, went smoothly. Early on, Lonna and I made a pact to not begin drinking until after the chant workshops had ended, an agreement we only broke when absolutely necessary.

So it was that two weeks ago we arrived in Germany to celebrate Hildegard von Bingen's nine-hundredth birthday. Early Music performers, nuns, medievalists, and all manner of mystical individuals from all over the world made this pilgrimage to Germany and the Abbey St Hildegard. The Hildegard 900 Symposium was to be something of a spiritual culmination for the girls and, for many of them, myself

13

included, their first taste of Europe. It was also part of my plan to elude the United States of America and, more importantly, my own history. Specifically my middle ages. I'd arranged everything, even helped finance it. None suspected that my ticket was one-way, not even Lonna, who'd recently helped organize the sale of the Mansion Inn. The Mansion Inn was my late wife's Victorian bed and breakfast. It is where I had lived for the last thirty years, where my children were born and raised. Let me be as clear as possible. I had sold the only home that I'd ever known, flown to Germany, and I didn't even pretend to know what I was doing. I pretended that this was somehow a virtue.

There is a story by Sercambi about an aged furrier from Lucca. One day this clever and respected man visits a Tuscan bathhouse. There he becomes convinced, suddenly, that simply by undressing and entering the public bath he will forfeit his identity. One more step, he fears, and all that he is, and has worked for his entire life, will cease to exist. He will be lost or, even worse, he will be just like everyone else. To prevent this, the furrier attaches a straw cross to his shoulder. In this manner he at least will know who he is: for won't his be the only naked body with a cross stuck to its shoulder? Some minutes after entering the bath the cross slips from his shoulder and floats away. The furrier tries to retrieve it but is too late. 'See here!' crows another bather, snatching the cross up from the water and sticking it onto his own shoulder. 'Now I am you! Begone, you are dead!'

Similarly, I worried that the authorities at the Frankfurt

International Airport's Passport Control would somehow be able to prove that I was not the man my documentation purported I was. But questions asked, answers given, my identity was approved and, moreover, stamped. How easy it was to undress, I thought. How simple to emigrate. The tenuousness of it all both troubled and delighted me: what would it be like when I tossed my straw cross away? Would I drown in a panic like Sercambi's old furrier, or could I not be reborn? Couldn't I step out of this pool and into someone else's clothing?

From our departing, Rudesheim-bound bus, the Frankfurt skyline looked like New York City with eighty percent of its teeth punched out. The girls talked away, excited, as I rested my head against the window. The country was sterile, prim, suburban, green, and industrial. The factories we passed seemed rubbed raw, as if their sole purpose was keeping themselves clean. They were precocious teenagers compared to the chain-smoking, no-nonsense factories of the New World.

Finally, after what seemed like hours, the machine stopped, the doors opened, and our landing party stormed the suburban Rudesheim asphalt, cameras at the ready, as if something medieval might suddenly leap from behind a semi-detached house once the bus was safely out of sight. Before her ascent to the heavenly bridegroom, Hildegard von Bingen had lived her Middle Ages here. But where?

Very peculiar, those first few moments in Rhineland. For instance, where exactly was the Rhine? Where was the Abbey, the nuns, the cobbled roads, toothy cemeteries, moss-eaten towers – the history? Even the hills of perfectly cross-hatched vineyards we'd seen but minutes before from the win-

15

dows of the bus: gone. By God, I thought, where is the wine?

The Germans – who had something of the sad, silent delicacy of gorillas – planted their homes inside manias of flowers. I'd no idea that Europe would be like this. This stillness. Beneath a leaden sky, we marched past desperate, immaculate homes, looking for Hildegard's abbey. Somehow it was all so much more modern than America, more sterile, stunned, like they'd long since washed themselves of history and were hiding, hoping nobody would notice. There were no people anywhere. Where were they, what were they up to? Did they take the summer off, I wondered; did they get to stop being Germans for a few months, time off for good behavior? If so, who pruned the shrubs? The yards we passed were inhabited solely by a worrying array of gnomes, elves, penguins, water falls, wind mills, and plastic pools on which the occasional beach ball floated like a doomed aria. Intermittently, you could hear a television or the disruptive hint of a far-off train. The girls had never seen such meticulous and extraordinarily abundant gardens. Many of the homes had metal porches aflame with flowers, frozen explosions of them, vines pouring up and down the walls like vegetable smoke. There were birds but they didn't sing.

The homes gave way to the rising vineyards, which shaved the road of its suburban barnacles and drew it nakedly onwards and upwards towards the lofty, stone Benedictine Abbey. There it was. Even Lonna, still quite drunk on Lufthansa's complimentary vodka, mumbled an approval.

The remainder of our pilgrimage was soon banked on either side by stone walls, behind which the sea of ancient

16

vineyards spread grasping to meet the horizon. Single file, we tramped up the hill. Beneath us, the suburban encampment from which we had recently escaped was now but a huddle of gray and brown roofs on which birds, great companies of them, settled like debris. Further below, the thuggish, thick-waisted Rhine.

It was difficult to imagine that a full day hadn't yet passed since we boarded the airliner in New York. I paused. Medieval man believed that one was placed beyond the touch of time, and therefore aging, while attending Mass. What, I wondered, would he have made of those hours we left up in the sky? I would not change my watch until I gave the matter more thought.

The gray sky began to soften, sun spilling out here and then there, splashing the hills on the other side of the Rhine like, I imagined, the light from the cracks in the ceiling of little Hildegard's anchorage. I thought again of the journey. The juxtaposition of the slow tilt of the earth – so sad, so unaccountably patient – with the complimentary movie silently playing, the smiles of our stewardesses, the plastic walls. I'd never been in an airplane before and I'd not be setting foot in one again.

'Burt, c'mon!' They had ascended the hill, reached the Abbey.

'Shush, leave him. He's in the Zone.'

'Adorable.'

'Wait, quick, who's got the cancer?' someone blurted.

'*Camera*,' another corrected.

I didn't even flinch. Sometimes I thought that my wife's illness and death didn't cling to me so much as it had actually replaced me.

'Hey, Burt, turn around! Say cheese!'

I watched then as a cloud of debris rose from a roof, swarmed, arched insanely in the still air and settled on another roof, or the same roof. It was becoming impossible to tell.

II

Two weeks later, on the night before I was to release my anchorites, Lonna Katsav was sober. The two of us sat in the Pension's room hoping the other would soon venture forth to procure more wine. We watched TV. Historically, pilgrimages had been occasions for all manner of depravity, not unlike the North American tradition of 'spring break'; public wantonness, rampant promiscuity, and gluttony had been the scene around even the most hallowed of Christendom's medieval shrines. Lonna, noting the precedent, had once again started to smoke.

Cigarette dispensers could be found on even the quietest residential street; mailbox-like rectangles on stilts, lurking behind low-hanging branches. 'Nelson would love it here,' Lonna said. She dangled then dropped a burning butt into an empty bottle of noble rot. It frizzled.

'Have you called him yet?' Ten-year-old Nelson lived with Lonna's ex-husband, safe from his mother's idiosyncrasies. I said, 'You ought to give Nelson a call.'

Instead, she gave me a withering look and violently ripped through television channels. 'Oh, way to go. Look who's talking.'

'The least you could do is pretend.'

'Father of the Year here.'

Profundity uttered, she leaned back and blew smoke, her new form of punctuation, a way of stepping back and observing her greatness impartially. Briefly, however, in the recoil of her eyes, I saw that I'd hurt her. She loved her boy even more than she hated herself.

I had known Lonna Katsav ever since my late wife had hired her to clean up some legal difficulties we had concerning a former Mansion Inn guest who had shattered her left wrist in a tumble from the top of our showpiece Victorian staircase. Basically, it had been Lonna's job to prove that the woman was, in fact, right handed, and that two and a half million dollars was slightly excessive compensation for a retired New Jersey homemaker, even if the fall – executed in a bright yellow evening gown – was embarrassing and quite obviously the fault of our historic house not being equipped with an elevator. Lonna was young then, as were we all. (Though, at twenty years my junior, I suppose that she is still rather young.) Anyway, Lonna won the case, we paid her, had a party, and she was soon an unexpected and intractable member of our family.

We both tended not to mix well, or at all, and both for different reasons. My excuse should be apparent by now. Lonna's was equally complex. I believe that many of her problems stemmed from the fact that she was fiercely, cripplingly intelligent, and she was trapped. Just out of Yale, she had relocated to our small upstate New York town with her then-husband, a moneyed urban-expatriate, who had decided to realize his dreams of becoming a gentleman farmer. Lonna had loved her husband. She believed agriculture was only a phase, and a cute one at that. They'd be back in their

20

Manhattan nook before the end of their first upstate winter, and oh the stories they would tell. But she was wrong. Her husband quickly began to live for his Colonial re-enactment – grubby jeans, feeding animals, reading books about soil, about seeds, sweating without antiperspirant, waking up before light, he even refused to go to the cinema or dine in restaurants ('not,' Lonna qualified, 'that Queens Falls had any restaurants worth dining in'). His stated goal became to only consume what he could grow or kill himself, which was difficult at first because he really had no idea what he was doing. Lonna fought back as best she could. She bought expensive, enticing groceries. She ordered minimalist furniture. She clothed her impossibly tall, sometimes elegant, sometimes skinny frame in designer clothing: Ms Katsav would not wear anything that could possibly enable her to walk out onto her husband's fields or visit the old barn he'd repaired and stuffed full of animals she could see perfectly well from the bay window, thank you very much. They divorced soon after Nelson's birth and Lonna's realization that they would never get out of Queens Falls alive.

  Both of us were fond of alcohol. We would spend hours sitting on the Mansion Inn's renowned porch, me drinking my homemade mead, Lonna her cocktails, talking and laughing into the night. To outsiders we made an unusual pair. On the few occasions that we stepped out together in public, people who didn't know of me and my medieval garb tended to think that Lonna was taking her hospitalized grandfather out for a walk. 'They're looking at your nose,' she would whisper to me. 'They think your tunic is a hospital gown. Burt, start barking or something.' She had no interest in the CTLR or medieval history as I had none in her legal profession or her sexual conquests, but sometimes it felt as if we were siblings, and at other times it felt odder than that: like two survivors living amongst the ruins. Perhaps it was only our ability to find these ruins so funny, so perfectly absurd, that connected us. Neither of us belonged, neither of us wanted to. She was great friends with my wife, too, I should add. They often escaped down to New York City for lost weekends of what Lonna called 'a breath of fresh air'.

Lonna and I shared a double room at Pension Konigsbergstr, a vigorously unremarkable home in a suburban neighborhood at the top of the hill near the Abbey St Hildegard. Some of the other chant workshop women also lodged there, also two to a room. The rest, primarily Tivona and her anchorite faction, were able to stay with the nuns in the Abbey St Hildegard itself.

Lonna stood. 'I'll go see if Hansel and Gretel have any more of that Riesling. Want anything?'

I silenced the television. 'No.'

The dining room of Pension Konigsbergstr, where a terrifyingly premeditated breakfast was deposited for us each morning and where one could buy bottle after bottle of their superb Riesling, opened directly onto a living room. There, two Pension keepers kept watch. The woman had red ears, and the man, heavy and pink, we generally observed topless. Occasionally, they would enter into our daily breakfast service in search of a fork or a chipped saucer, which they would snap up, examine, and remove to the living room from where one could sometimes hear them contradicting the television. Never, not once, did we witness one speak to the other. It was Lonna's belief that they had not yet been properly introduced.

Germany was all kind of like that: full of perfectly arranged, uncommunicative objects. I'd spent the past fortnight eschewing the chant workshop girls' surgical ambushes on historical Rhineland, even avoiding Hildegard-related sites, preferring to do nothing but wander the rolling vineyards. There, I'd found a sort of contentment. Because there were no fences, and sometimes only the slightest of stone walls, the vineyards really did seem to lap at the edges of every-thing, like green waves, their spray of leaves hanging over every road. One could just walk right in, and, once in, keep walking. Lonna, meanwhile, had been on the other side of this line of production, swallowing magnificent quantities of Rhenish vintages. Once or twice I spotted her figure in the distance, tall and alone, a shark fin piercing through grape-vines, pocket book swinging, following trails specifically marked through the countryside, wine cellar to wine cellar. Lonna, to nobody's surprise, procured as many bottles as she did European admirers, who never ceased calling Frau Katsav on our room's telephone. She was that most delightful of anomalies: a sarcastic, ironic, fading flapper of a middle-aged American woman who knew when to drink (all the time) and when to smile (never, unless something horrible was occurring).

There were more reconstructed castles between Rudesheim and Koblenz than in any other region of the world. Long ago, they'd all been ruins. Haunted by robber barons, the unwell and the perverse, by all those seeking shelter from the gregariousness of the late-medieval hearth, the castles had been entangled in budding flowers, and they'd been pulled apart by grapes. Now private homes, hotels, museums, and theme restaurants. Not even allowed a night's repose, there the castles stood, one after another, searching in vain for their reflection in the Rhine, permanently lit by spotlights, ceaselessly interrogated by our shallow modernity. Their dungeons and towers glutted with armies of nut crackers, T-shirts, and anthropomorphic miniatures. To tell you the truth, hand-sewing my own tunic for a CTLR revel has contained more true history than I felt standing beneath the wall of such a defiled corpse. To the surprise of everyone – myself especially – I hadn't yet entered a single one.

Lonna returned with two bottles of Riesling.

'There,' she said. Then: 'Burt, can we talk?'

'OK.'

'I just want you to know that it's still completely in your power to back out. Look at me, hey. I want you to tell me right now that you honestly haven't been having second thoughts.'

'Back out of what?'

Lonna exhaled. Lonna knew.

'The one-way ticket,' I said.

'Burt, what the hell are you thinking?'

Six months ago I paid a surprise visit to Lonna Katsav's Albany, New York, law practise. It was the first time that I'd ever been to Albany. For this I'd had to hire a taxicab all the way from Queens Falls, a sixty-mile journey that had cost me roughly the same as a plane ticket to someplace like Baltimore, or so my chauffeur maintained.

I entered the old brownstone as if in a dream. I passed through the mock-Roman chill of a marble hallway. I sunk into the leather of the waiting-room sofa, opened and closed a *National Geographic* magazine, then another, then something called *Entertainment Weekly*, my mead-sticky fingers all the while troubling a medieval pouch of fresh Rosemary (which is good against brain weakness, moths, nightmares, and gout, as well as helping to stimulate the memory). My good shoes were pinching my toes. I really should have worn my CTLR sandals.

Would I like a coffee? The question had made no sense. Coffee while I waited? I don't know how long I gawped at the receptionist, an expressionless girl who trilled several other offers. Would I maybe – a glass of water, sir? Mineral water? Perhaps I would prefer tea? Herbal? Black? Sugar? Milk?

Finally, somehow in motion again, I had been guided down another hallway and into the warm oak of Lonna Katsav's office, where I had managed to request – to demand – that my friend take immediate control of my not inconsiderable assets and liquidize them. Even if I didn't know for sure if that was the correct terminology. But I liked the smooth sleepy finality of the word – 'liquidize' – and, anyway, she had understood. Too well Lonna understood. I was wearing my only twentieth-century formal attire, the suit I had no doubt donned to the funeral that people assure me I attended. I meant business.

I would sell the motorcars I could not legally operate, along with the antique furniture, the appliances, the heirlooms in the attic, the real-estate holdings I knew precious little about, and, finally, the Mansion Inn itself, the famed Victorian bed and breakfast that I'd owned, lived in, and watched my wife and children manage ever since I retired at the age of thirty from teaching High School history to those doomed to repeat it. Even my beloved library. Even that. Put a price on the past and sell. The resulting capital I had decided to spend on escaping the empirical borders of New York State. Then America itself. You emigrate from, you immigrate to. Germany seemed as good a kingdom as any. Did Lonna know all along that the ticket was one-way? I had told her only that I needed to move – desired a change, a respite from memories and the past, a smaller place made of logs, maybe a condominium. I couldn't bear the emptiness of the Mansion Inn, the echo. I told her life had become a kind of nightmarish, solitary re-enactment of something I was never totally certain of in the first place. Waking up now, alone, and preparing breakfast for myself felt like a bloodless, terrifying reliving of a time when I used to wake up and prepare breakfast for a family who would tell me that my primary-source medieval food was nauseating, or that they didn't care if oranges were OOP, they were going to have orange juice with their eggs and oat gruel. Lonna understood and supported my decision – the sale part of it, anyway. I even told her I would buy a cat. Isn't that what the hopeless did? Buy pets? But first – a holiday. Wisely, if weakly, I made it look like a chant work-shop field trip which I had proposed and organized and partly sponsored – I would take the girls with me to the Hildegard 900 Symposium for cover and support, and then, while there, I would slice the strings and watch them fly away from me forever. I would stay and . . . begin again? Modern Europe interested me as much as modern anywhere, it should be said. I had vague ideas and I had substantial capital. But what was I doing? What was I thinking?

'Lonna,' I said. 'I don't understand you. I can back out of what exactly? You already sold the Mansion.'
    'Here, shall we – some wine?'

I nodded.

'I haven't invested your entire estate yet, no? Where's your –?'

I handed Lonna my glass. She poured. 'Our man out there was wearing a shirt. God knows why.'

'What?'

'Fucking wine isn't chilled.' Lonna Katsav occasionally spoke like a peasant, I think, because she was extraordinarily intelligent and no longer wished to be.

I said, 'But you have sold some of it?'

'Some. The BMW,' and a civilized sip of warm wine.

'The BMWs.'

'No, just the one. The whitish one. Burt, look at me. You didn't really want me to go through with it anyway. I know you. Don't I know you? You think this has been easy on me?'

'What are you talking about?'

'They're waiting,' Lonna said. 'Our buyers.'

'I am not a child.'

Lonna eyed my taffeta tunic and sandals. 'Believe it or not you've got a lot of people worried about you.'

'Sell it,' I said. 'I want it all sold.'

She paused, lips frozen to the rim of her wine glass. 'Fine.' She put the glass down. She started to chew, though I knew very well that she had nothing in her mouth.

'Good,' I said.

Still nothing.

'I can take care of myself, you know.'

'You can take care of yourself.'

I looked at the carpet.

'It's been two years – Burt, look at me – it's been two years and I just don't see how this is going to solve anything. Can you blame me for waiting? Jesus, look at you. Here we are a couple of weeks in Hildegard-land and you haven't shown even a bit of interest in anything except walking around vine-yards? Have you even discussed this with Tristan? With June? This silly – this post-midlife Middle Ages crisis or whatever the fuck you think it is you're doing.'

Tristan my son, June my daughter. 'This has nothing to do with them,' I lied. I placed my glass of wine carefully down upon the bedside table. I picked it up again.

'Bastard.' Lonna stood. She walked across the room and entered the bathroom.

I was left with the room's mirror, which hung there like a scream. I looked into it. Positioned neatly on the bed, a compact, childlike man gazed nervously back. When would he grow up? I tried a smile, he smiled back wearily. The face of a what? The face of a widower – not so much missing as half-removed. But how small he looked, and how terribly odd; wrinkles cut with a fine knife, drawn onto his other-wise smooth skin with undeserved diligence and care. His head was petite, a boiled peanut. Its top bald, its sides and back unweeded with curly, overgrown gray. In preparation for releasing the anchorites from their tent, he wore his taffeta tunic. Ridiculous, utterly and truly. His equally ridiculous signature black suit sat shed and deflated on the bed next to him. It looked like him, only melted. Two tiny silver eyes opened wider, as they always did when confronted with a reflective surface. Their owner despised how pebble-like they appeared and strove to compensate, lending his mirror-face a choked, terrified expression. The eyes, of course, were small because the nose was not. *Portrait of an Elderly Man without His Son.* I could almost superimpose the Ghirlandaio

28

masterpiece over the mirror. The nose, like a beetle-ruined fruit about to drop. The time-honored medieval cloth. The gathering dark. Everything but my son, Tristan. If I looked down there would be nothing now holding my eyes. I looked down.

Two years ago, at the age of twenty-two, Tristan dropped out of Julliard, where he had been finishing a degree in Early Music and Eastern European Folk Instruments. Overnight, and without alerting me, my son departed for Poland to live with his maternal grandmother and study the traditional Carpathian Mountain folk instruments of her Lemko people; how to play them, and how to chop down the trees and cure the wood from which to build them with his own two hands. The cymbaly, the trembita, the sopilka. I have not laid eyes on Tristan since, receiving only the tersest replies to the letters I've written him. The serious, silent boy had been my best friend.

Lonna kissed the top of my head. 'I don't know,' she said. Lifting my suit and wiping invisible diseases from the bed, she sat next to me. She aimed the remote control. There followed a luxurious stretch of television. Lawyer and client adjusting their attentions into the spasmodic flashings, the oversped newspeak, as if it all constituted a third party who had suddenly been sprung upon us, demanding to say his piece. It soon became clear, however, that this third party wished to bring ailing British cows into it. Their pretty eyes filled the screen.

'I've told the others,' Lonna said. She muted the machine.
'What?'
'They're pissed. You should know that they're waiting for you to tell them. They mistake your weakness for drama.'

'What did you tell them?'

'What do you think I told them, Burt? I was at the end of my rope, believe it or not. Should've told them sooner,' she held a cigarette but did not light it. 'Maybe Tivona could talk some sense into you, I thought. But she just, you know, *sagely nodded*. Fucking Tivona. Like she suspected all along.'

'How long have they –?'

'Before the medieval campout thing. I don't know. Three days ago, I guess. They adore you, Burt. It was all I could do to stop some of them from contacting the US Embassy to try and work out some kind of intervention. I seriously had to talk them out of declaring you legally insane and God knows what else. Told them that you just needed a little extended vacation, that you would find your way home eventually.'

I sighed.

'The least of your worries. Here,' Lonna took out a piece of paper. 'You'll be wanting this. Tristan's address. New address. Phone number too. And a map.'

I stared at Lonna in incomprehension. 'How?'

'Your daughter.'

June lived in California with her husband, Jack, and their son, Sammy. Our relationship, my daughter's and mine, had not been the most exemplary, it must be said. By all accounts, June had had an unhappy childhood.

'Does she know?'

'No.'

'Have you talked to Tristan? Lonna? Have you?'

'Yes.'

I looked down at his address. 'He's not in Poland.' I turned the paper over, as if the other, more expected, more Polish address would be found there.

'Hasn't been in Poland for – well, for a while, I think.'

Prague, Czech Republic. Bohemia. I stifled a laugh, I grinned; and hope sprung in my chest, further distorting my face. Hope felt like a heart attack. Tristan was close. Tristan was not in Poland with his maternal grandmother.

'Thought you'd like that,' Lonna said. 'But be – I don't know, just be careful. Be cool. Two years, it still might not be enough. He seemed cold, Burt, frankly.'

I had never touched Lonna in an affectionate way, but I feared that circumstances might now warrant such a breach. Yawning hugely, I dropped my arm around her high shoulders, drawing my friend close. She was warmer than I expected. I shifted my weight. I did not know if I was required to leave my arm there for a specified period of time or whether it was best to hastily remove it, benediction having been placed. So there we sat, shyly, watching ourselves in the mirror. It helped abstract things. *Portrait of an Elderly Man with His Very Tall Lawyer*. Lonna smiled lightly, registering my discomfort.

'The anchorites,' I said. 'They're waiting. I have to bring them dinner.' I made to stand but Lonna held me.

'Please come home.'

'Home?' I shook my head.

'Don't give me that. Burt, you are not an Irish Sailing Monk.'

'I never claimed to be an Irish Sailing Monk.'

Though, I suppose, I had been talking about them a lot recently. Medieval Irish monks who, boarding a coracle, gave themselves to the ocean without the slightest of provisions, trusting God's will. One man, the cold crashing sea. I'd become enamored with photographs of the stark, weather-cragged

31

monasteries still standing on remote Irish islands, seeing in them testaments to His occasional mercy. History's weird soulful details.

Lonna said, 'This is a mistake. I'm just – look at me. You know me.'

'There's nothing to worry about.'

'I'm exaggerating?'

'I didn't say that.'

'Burt, really. Who do you think's going to take care of you now?'

'Are you well, m'lord?'

'No,' I say. 'I am not.'

Released from the tent, our part-time anchorites float behind us, candles in hand, intoxicated and of uncertain feet, all of them chanting softly. Tunics whisper over the long grass and wild-flowers. The vineyards wake, rolling the distance out before us. Birds spray upwards. An anchorite scuttles off into the shrubs, and it's difficult to ignore the angry rush of her urination.

I swat an insect that turns out to be Tivona's hair.

'Thou art running at the brain,' she says.

'T'would seem so.'

'I like it not, Eckbert.'

I am holding a staff. The anchorites follow me, one by one, like the rootless poor of the thirteenth century. The few Germans we pass pretend not to see us, but they immediately stop tending their insane gardens and return from whence they came. Our performance will begin at 6:30 a.m. The hulking stone Abbey St Hildegard and its two towers wait below.

I adjust my tunic. I imagine that the grapes are using the cover of morning mist to push the sleeping village of Rudesheim down the hill and into the Rhine. Slowly, imperceptibly. Someday they'll reclaim this land entirely. I hear what sounds like a drunken, plainchant version of *O Tannenbaum*. I trace the progress of three gleaming, dewy automobiles as they wind through the vineyards towards the Abbey.

Hildegard von Bingen herself wrote that the wind holds the firmament together just as the soul stops the body from disintegrating. But there is no wind this morning. One of the anchorites, our youngest, a seven-year-old named Heather, tunic held up over her knees, breaks from our procession and scampers past us down the hill, laughing, carving a trail through a spread of waist-high weeds and wild, untended vines. Her mother calls after her in a fruity, Hollywood Old English. Heather has been a part of my Confraternity of Times Lost Regained and Tivona's chant workshop pretty much since birth and already has a reputation as a fearsome pedant. ('This,' – I've seen her pinch and hold a Burger King crown before her, like a mouse pulled from a swimming pool's filter – 'this isn't a crown. This is a ducal coronet.') She's tolerated, I think, because her mother is even worse, and religious to boot, and so many of the women take it upon themselves to give the little girl as normal an upbringing as possible. Where keeping her in a tent for three days comes into this, I do not know. But free from the nylon anchorage, the little girl twirls, chasing birds from their breakfast, no longer chanting or laughing, but shouting. 'Good morning, Germany! Hallo! Hallo!'

Lonna Katsav and the remaining non-anchorite members of the chant workshop penguin the stone steps of the Abbey St Hildegard, their suitcase-fresh blouses and skirts and shower-pink faces in bold contrast to the plain anchorite tunics of our inebriated procession. Tivona beams beneath her heavy head of curls. Planted about the enclosed stone garden are two dozen nuns. If we were an army of lepers, castanets rattling and scabbed mouths open for alms, I don't think we could have made a more scandalous impression.

For two weeks I've wandered among the nuns of St Hildegard, the slow hive of their Abbey crafts shop and restoration workshop, their prayer mongering and daily singing of the offices; their moon faces, round and bespectacled, many with buck teeth, rising like bubbles from an unfathomable interior. Silently, I've watched them, enjoying their assurance. Once in a while, one has even shown me a smile as I kneeled and pretended to contemplate salvation.

Bells clong. Pink clouds pull across the sky and the rising sun burns off the mist, antagonizing the shy steeples and roofs of Rudesheim. It's nearly time for our performance to begin. During the last war this abbey's bells had become casing for Nazi bombs. The nuns themselves scattered down the hillside, many never returning, their abbey requisitioned by the injured and dying. Did those expelled women think of bells, I wonder, as the bombs began to explode around them? In the sound of one was all trace of the other lost? The eternal malleability of every intention, of everything, both good and bad, sends a pleasant, oddly hopeful, shiver down my spine: because maybe I wasn't making a mistake.

The nuns are joined this morning by a good number of

the Hildegard 900 guests; visiting sisters from across Christendom, fidgeting monks with sunglasses, oblates, tourists, a hirsute huddle of sympathetic New Agers, and, finally, a clutch of professional Early Music performers with voices like ice-water. They have, all of them, arrived early. They've come to mock us, to silently bare witness to their own cultural superiority. Their firm backs, their meek leather bags; their dead, officious talk of antiphons, responsories, psalm verses, doxologies, introits, neumatic styles, melismatic melodies, graduals, kyries, and the like. Bunk. They have come for our tunics and candles. Our vulgar, unself-conscious land of American make-believe. Later, as before, they'll ask questions of my girls, subtle jabs of knowledge and irony that many of the women won't begin to fathom. The girls' excited, good-natured squawking has done much to sully their symposium: you don't need to be a dentist to see the fangs in their smiles. Lonna is chain-smoking for their benefit. She's smarter than they are and this gives her some kind of leverage.

Our little pedant, Heather, not to be outdone, begins praying before a metallic statue of Hildegard von Bingen. Kneeling, she prays loudly, with the sloppy, staccato exuberance of a cheerleader. Twice she punches in the sign of the cross as if emergency-dialing a telephone. The nuns don't know what to make of it. Some turn away, others do not. I really couldn't tell you what obscure sect of Christianity Heather and her mother subscribe to. (During the flight, the little girl had been inconsolable, convinced that the turbulence was caused by the aircraft 'running over angels'.) But I will not be embarrassed. Nine hundred years ago only the wealthiest of the mentally ill were allowed the luxury of an asylum. The rest could be found therapeutically harnessed to the rood screens of churches. Or they were left alone, naked and howling in the forest as the good Lord intended, maybe a cross shaved into their head for good luck. Sometimes they were burned alive. So where's the harm here? They invariably numbered among the armies of pilgrims at shrines such as these – though today the pilgrims are not the paralytics, the flagellants, the wretches, the outlaws, the scrofulous, or the crippled. Today they are us.

I join my girls on the steps. I wave good morning to the nun I've decided is my favorite. Someone asks me for the time.

'Lord Eckbert? Oh, he's on his own time,' Lonna smiles.

Eckbert Attquiet is, of course, my Confraternity of Times Lost Regained persona. I remove my pocket-watch from the leather purse I've attached to my belt. 'Eleven,' I say. 'Eleven p.m.'

'Burt, sweetie, it's six in the morning.'

'I don't believe one can lose or gain hours,' I say, finding solace as the Eccentric Old Man. 'I'm an island of time.'

The sun warms and I feel happy, at peace with these women. They laugh, groaning at my obtuseness, and I realize how much I've come to depend on them over the last two years. They will not mention the one-way ticket, but they don't need to: standing among them, I feel as if it were stuck to my nose. We speak about how nervous we are and how special this morning is. And maybe I'd always expected them to stop me, to not let this go so far. But something has happened, and I know now that they are not going to stop me. They are not even going to try.

Tivona gathers us in a semi-circle around her. There is about her a thoughtful, tactile slowness, an air of ritual. Lonna and I have a joke where we imagine Tivona Henry brushing her teeth, guiding some kind of homemade wooden toothbrush in imperceptible circles, very slowly and for many hours, gently easing her plaque into its afterlife, smiling.

Our performance today will be a medley, an unorthodox cut-and-paste of some of Hildegard von Bingen's more moving passages. 'Our Jubilee Year remix,' Tivona calls it.

It is here, finally, that I am introduced to Max Werfel, the Brazilian dermatologist. The spherical, shiny middle-aged man is upon us, and I avert my head as from an explosion. Even his eyes prance. For the last two weeks he has been the women's constant companion; they'd met at some Hildegard 900 workshop that I'd refused to attend, and since then he has apparently accompanied them on all of their Rhineland excursions, no doubt sprinkling that high giggle all over situations better left unadorned. He is adorable. Hands lost to a bundle of flowers, he bounds first to Tivona, kissing her forehead and sticking a single purple bloom in her hair; and then to each girl in turn, planting one behind their ears, between their breasts, or on their shirts and tunics, and, in the case of an inexplicably charmed Lonna Katsav, into the bottle of Evian she carries as proof of her European sympathies. I instantly dislike him.

Tivona presents Werfel to me and I study my sandaled feet, wiggling my toes. He does not speak English. This, evidently, only adds to the allure. His hair is very black, like a helmet attached to his perfectly round head. White socks nearly obscure his knees. He speaks what the women, incredibly, refer to as 'Brazilian', but which is only Portuguese or a sunny, rainforest German. He speaks and Tivona translates. My hand is held, squeezed, shook – and with Lonna looking on I get the feeling that this is not the last I will see of the dermatologist. I mumble hello. I turn, leading the women into the church.

'Someone's jealous,' Lonna whispers.

I rebuke her with silence.

'You and Max are going to be such buddies. You'll see.'

Jesus commands from high up in the church's apse, His numb blind stare giving one the tantalizing impression that someone has just stabbed Him in the back. He is shocked, frozen, mere seconds from toppling forward out of the mock-Byzantine painting and onto His father's altar.

Behind me, Heather asks her mother what's wrong with Jesus, and her mother makes the little girl repeat the question so everyone can hear her before concluding that there is nothing wrong with Jesus.

The nuns and their affiliates enter and assemble on the wooden pews. The professional Early Music people like nineteenth-century students at a public autopsy, their clean hands floating on their clean laps. I bristle. Nine hundred years ago there would be no benches, no pews, and this floor would be covered with straw. Peasants, stinking and often inebriated, would've come to hear a Mass in a language that none of them understood. God was never meant to be understood.

We stand before our audience. Those with tunics stand in front of those without tunics. I hold the center; my tunic and bald head a likely focal point, my nose a perfect handle for the Europeans' budding mirth and disbelief.

One of our anchorites walks down the aisle lighting candles. She is not wearing shoes. Two others begin a vocal warm-up exercise of indecorous moans, and I'm reminded of the Feast of the Fools, the medieval New Year's tradition when priests led their congregations through a series of wanton songs, all the while devouring sausages before the altar. We watch as an anchorite runs from the church, hand over mouth.

'Christ,' Lonna says in what she knows isn't a whisper. 'What are we doing? Historically valid or not, did they have to drink so much?'

Tivona stands before us. She exhales. Collectively, we do the same. Two people out there begin to cough in the manner of people who do not want to laugh; others actually go right ahead and giggle.

Tivona lifts her chin, then her right hand. For a minute her voice holds the room. It occurs to me that I will never hear this music again, not like this. Lonna, then, from nowhere, is above us all, even Tivona. She booms, answering Tivona's plaintive calm. The other girls, taking this cue, explode. Wavering and wobbly, they're ecstatically off-key. Technically speaking, they've never sounded worse. But despite all this, something possibly true and very nearly timeless suddenly fills the Abbey St Hildegard. Some of the nuns smile, impressed. The Early Music professionals bare their teeth in horror. Tivona's hands rise theatrically and our volume increases, we increase, and I imagine actual clouds being pushed above us, the vineyards around us flattened, the castles re-ruined, the past reinstated, and the terrible future put on hold. I close my eyes and I hum.

Besides Hildegard von Bingen's tongue and heart, Eibingen's parish church keeps a trophy case full of bones. Skulls swaddled in silk, golden crosses set with teeth, a coronet knobbled with human knuckles; there are all manner of leg and arm bones, also wrapped in silk and hung in crosses, tied with gold trim like the Christmas offerings of Victorian pirates. The names of the men and women who once made use of these bones are written in calligraphy across the silk. Standing alone, gazing into this case, I see my own face reflected in the glass, superimposed over a gift-wrapped skull.

'Now I am you! Begone, you are dead!'

When Saint Elizabeth of Hungary lay dying, a crowd of souvenir-seeking worshippers came and pre-emptively sliced off her nipples, hair, and toenails to add to medieval Christendom's stock of relics. Charlemagne's ears. Drops of the Virgin's milk. Christ's baby teeth. A relic from the Lord's circumcision. Enough splinters of the True Cross to build an ark. Two arks, three. The Crusaders even brought back two of John the Baptist's heads from Jerusalem, leading Guibert of Nogent to ask, 'Was this saint then bicephalous?'

I step away from the bones, inexplicably happy. There's nobody but me here and the silence of the parish roars. An orange bird shoots in through the opened doors and begins to sweep frantic circles in the air, stirring the dust, splattering peeps and sunny trills over the walls.

Tonight we'll have one final Rhineland feast, my much ballyhooed Farewell Revel in a wine cellar on Rudesheim's famed Drosselgasse or Happy Alley, 'The Happiest Street in the World'. Tomorrow morning Lonna will be taking a vacation from this vacation, flying directly to Paris, where she'll spend a few days recovering from the Middle Ages before returning home. The rest of the girls are heading back to New York.

I walk down the stone steps into the parking lot that laps

at this modern parish from all sides. It's like someone momentarily parked the unsightly building here while running across the street to purchase eggs and milk.

'Now I am you!' Two bicycles thrum by. 'Begone, you are dead!'

I walk along the edge of a vineyard. Motorcars pass like spirits. Children, prim and joyless, occasionally wander across the landscape and I can't stop smiling. I have a map of Bohemia. In my pocket I have a Bohemian address and a Bohemian phone number written on a folded sheet of legal paper. My son is not in Poland.

III

I still remember how the United States of America smeared on the other side of our BMW's windows, and how that solidified us. The time that I'm thinking about, my family and I had been driving to Florida. If only I could've always kept them like that, time rushing past as painlessly as Georgia or Virginia or Maryland or wherever it was we were. Tristan was probably about five. I was old enough to know better. Florida meant chlorine and Florida meant space travel.

My wife and my daughter, June, were entangled in a game involving license plates. She was lengthy, my wife, a woman of large appetites leaning over a little steering wheel, pushing us onwards, prematurely-white hair snapping in the highway's bluster. June was hidden behind the front seat's headrest. Occasionally they'd turn back towards us, the folksy keepers of the map and the exact toll-booth coinage – my wife over her right shoulder, my daughter over her left. Their heads would inevitably bump and they would comically exclaim, 'Ouch!' in unison. It had been their idea to go again to Cape Canaveral. ('Dad, if you were living in your Middle Ages, wouldn't you want to go visit Copernicus? NASA is like our –' 'Copernicus was a Polish troublemaker.') The only thing my daughter liked more than space travel was collecting rocks. My wife liked disappearing.

'Being small,' she called it, craving that momentary loss when she surrendered her expansiveness to Florida's ocean, wading out as far as she could. My wife liked collecting seashells at dawn, alone, sipping mimosas, her footprints the only ones on the beach. But sometimes my son would follow her, making a game of hopping from one of her footprints to the next, doing his best to leave no trace of himself behind. 'I'm your ghost,' he'd say. 'Don't look. You can't see me.'

But Tristan was much more than that. He was our sad little immigrant. So deliberate, mannered; his high forehead, magnifying-glass spectacles, long Renaissance hair, and, of course, that quiet, oddly accented voice rising and falling, chopped up by unnecessary commas. When you could actually hear him, strangers sometimes assumed that English was Tristan's second language. In those early years, I acted as the little man's buffer from and conduit to the world. 'My two little antiques,' my wife would say. And for many years I couldn't imagine my hands without Tristan attached to one of them.

'I know what, Dad,' he whispered. 'Let's get Mom to turn left.'

'Left?'

'Just please.'

'What? You need us to stop at a rest station?'

'Shhhh,' and the five-year-old pointed to the sun. He shook his head. His hair settled over his glasses. 'Just shhhh.'

'The sun?'

'It's following us.'

The girls, meanwhile, had become excited. One of them had spotted the highway's equivalent to the Loch Ness Monster.

Even Tristan and I marked the Hawaiian vehicle with

wonder. It was pink. The driver was brown, shirtless. Squealing, my daughter flung off her seatbelt and began rustling through the plastic bags at her feet. 'My camera,' she moaned. 'Jesus, Mom, where's my –?'

The pink automobile sailed by Tristan's window. June, camera suddenly in hand, hooted. She began snapping photographs. My wife, a forty-year veteran of the License Plate Game, actually clobbered the steering wheel with glee.

'But why would Hawaii drive to Florida? Is that even possible?' my teenage daughter turned back to me. Because she had a big nose – not deformed like mine, but a larger than average nose she couldn't help see future traces of mine in – June abused cosmetics. 'Burt, any grand theories?' She took my photograph – snap – and righted herself to better admire her itinerant Hawaiian.

'Copernicus,' I said. 'Evidently.'

'Evidently,' my daughter mimicked. She tossed a Frito back at me.

'Anyway, 100 points,' my wife said. 'I win.'

'Not if I can spot an Alaska you won't. Or ten North Dakotas. Fifteen – what? Fifteen Montanas. Burt, Tristy, you guys keep your eyes peeled, OK?'

Tristan continued to gaze skyward. The sun was rolling, shadowing our every turn.

June began lazily defenestrating Fritos. My wife slapped her hand. 'Bio-degradable,' June said, popping one in her mouth and opening her geological map of wherever we were. She had such a map for every region of every state in the Union.

My wife and June generally distributed the cloven fruit, sausage pies, bashed neeps, and carrot juice my son and I depended on. The two of us were wearing our Confraternity of Times Lost Regained medieval garb: matching brown tunics and sandals. Our passive resistance to the twentieth century. Stealing a sip of my homemade mead, my wife passed the earthen jug back to me. 'This the rhodomel? The rose petal one?' she asked.

I drank.

'Partly,' I said, honey alcohol warming my throat. 'Though I mixed it with a touch of . . . of cyser. Which is like melomel but made with –'

'Apples, mmm,' she said. 'That's it. That's what I'm tasting.'

I touched my son's head. The sun was really bothering him. He would stare at it, and then quickly turn away. Then he'd peek from between his fingers. I think that I had always known I would eventually lose them, my family. 'Tristan,' I began – but, really, what did I know about the solar system?

I coddle the memory. Nineteen years later and to my immediate right, Tristan's sun pummels through houses, factories, trees, hills, and churches. The sun, at least, seems to have some idea as to where I'm now going. This German countryside is a utilitarian fugue, and Max Werfel is an exceptionally poor driver. It's almost exciting.

For safety reasons, and because I hated him, I'd begun our journey strapped into the backseat, behind the dermatologist. Then, operating under the illusion that I could better prevent an automotive misfortune by having a less-obstructed view of the autobahn, I capitulated and joined Werfel up front. This afforded the man many opportunities to touch me, particularly my shoulder. Brazilians are friendly, demonstrative people. Religious, too. Which is good, because, really, you have to have a tremendous amount of faith to drive like Max Werfel. The only thing, I think, that has saved us is that the Germans are preternaturally skilled drivers, easily parting and re-forming around whatever spectacular automotive feat he decides to pull. Sometimes I think that he's actually testing them.

My ears clog with the true tonal opposite of chant. Werfel likes all of the windows opened all of the time. Sun-drunk, he yawns, stretching an arm outside, palm upward as if awaiting a tossed apple or a long-in-coming blessing. His round head rolls in my direction.

'The road,' I say. 'Please, attend to the road.'

The man has too many teeth. 'Burt,' he says. He laughs and slaps my shoulder.

But he is intelligent. Self-contained at one moment – lost looking, grinning sadly – the next moment he's trying to speak English, or making noises for my benefit. Like in war or at sea, the constant nearness of annihilation accelerates something, and I eventually stop hating him altogether.

The solitary medieval traveler was a man wholly lacking in any sense of self-preservation. He was most certainly mad, heretical, a Satanic emissary, and it was generally considered the Christian duty to relieve him of his possessions or, if the wanderer was lacking in those, his life. For these reasons, journeys in the Middle Ages were undertaken by what my chant workshop girls would call a car-pool. No fewer than two should undertake a journey together, and even two could be too little in times of particular strife and lawlessness, which, of course, was most of the time. Nothing less would have been advisable.

Such was Lonna's logic, anyway, when she made it quite clear that I was to travel with Max Werfel or I wasn't to travel at all.

This was her final request upon me, the end of my parole. Tivona and the girls, of course, happily made this their sticking point too. I would journey and lodge with Max Werfel until reaching Prague; and if, for some 'reason' (which, to my further distress and curiosity, Lonna found likely), my stay in Prague was to be shortened, I was to continue with the Brazilian to Vienna, and finally Budapest. The mischievous smirks that'd been so freely tossed between Lonna and the others were as difficult to miss as they were to gauge properly. I had been given no instruction past Budapest.

My facts relating to this South American are scant. Obviously of German descent and having no more than forty-five years behind him, Max Werfel comes from the city of Porto Alegre, Brazil (or 'Port Algae', as one girl boasted), and had been invited to attend the Hildegard 900 Symposium with regards to a recently-published work on the history of dermatology. Werfel's book cites our St Hildegard von Bingen as a foremother of the science, and devotes – so Tivona told me – an entire chapter to Hildegard's musing on scabies, lice, insect bites, rhinophyma, rubbing baths, and poisonous shrubbery. It was widely agreed that his well-attended presentation on the saint's *The Subtleties of the Diverse Nature of Created Things* was as rousing a success as one might hope to pull from the jaws of Historical Dermatology. Werfel is heading to Prague to meet with his half-sister, whom he only very recently learned existed. Apparently, it is something of a surprise visit. In that respect, we are both very much in the same boat.

I plunge my thoughts back into the roadside tumult of greens and browns. How to reconcile these lands, this scroll of Bundesrepublik Deutschland with my Middle Ages? It happened here once. But where? Despite the castles and churches, and all those townships still adhering to thousand-year-old plans, modern Germany seems a most non-historical kingdom. Safe, well-ordered, tame, all mystery long since burned away in the conflagrations of this last century.

Still, it's not difficult to peel back the facade and poke around into what once was. I imagine the puddle-pocked auto-bahn which once carried fourteenth-century peddlers, merchants and their pack trains, tax collectors, knights, monks, pilgrims, wandering scholars, jongleurs, prostitutes, madmen, bishops and pardoners and murderers and horses. I imagine horses running alongside our vehicle, past candlelit windows, ponds, spires, past the citadels, inns, and wattle-and-daub villages with names no one now living has ever spoken.

Night falls and I look for stars. But there are precious few with all the headlights and streetlights and the dull, watery glow of civilization. Those I see I urge to refill the flat, empty European sky, to turn up their volume. It's been a long day.

Soon a star appears, and appears to draw nearer. I watch, and because of my trance nearly a full minute elapses before I realize that the blinking, gliding star is a commercial airliner. Another cluster of seconds passes before I'm able to place the flying machine in the context of my recent past, because I'm certain that there, by what odd angle of their journey I know not, hang my friends, thousands of feet above me, going home.

They are talking too loud. I can very nearly hear them. Talking too loud to strangers who wish not to be talked to. They are showing one another photographs and postcards, fussing over the anthropomorphic miniatures and trinkets and Christmas ornaments which they bought, and all those things which they should've bought but, for some reason or another, didn't. Little Heather is counting stars or angels, cities, maybe even cars – perhaps she's already added us to her survey, spotted us among the glowing ants, beatified us or mistaken us for a slow, blazing seraph. Some of the girls are reading magazines. Others are dreamily lost to medieval romances. They are turning their watches back in anticipation, winding themselves in time, in unison, towards home. Still others are writing Rhineland postcards they see no quandary in sending their families and friends when they finally get home, dispatched with the blessings of stamps and postal regulations they better comprehend. They are missing their children and husbands, their pets and their sisters and their colleagues, the clean known scent of their own bedsheets and the water pressure of their own showers. They are dreading what their homes will look like after two weeks of their absence. They even begin chanting quietly, some of them, using the drone of the engine as their substitute hum. Their substitute me. I have been left behind. And in the dark of the highway ahead of us I watch my future open like a hole.

Max Werfel stretches and hops in place, applying emulsions, re-Velcroing his footwear, and drawing his white socks up over his legs. His knees are his face doubled and shrunken and scoured of features. He glows in the buzzing, fluorescent night-time parking lot.

'Warp speed,' he says, shyly, getting into the car. I smile back. Unable to accept that I wanted nothing to eat, he has brought me some French fries.

'Thank you, Max.' Though hungry, I would really rather have my head smitten off with an axe. Potatoes, like tomatoes, tobacco, coffee, corn, bananas, chocolate, and sugar cane are totally OOP. Out of Period. These foods did not exist in medieval Europe.

Werfel pulls three tiny metallic pillows of ketchup out of his pocket. He drops them on my lap. Like Eskimos with their thousand words for snow, Werfel seems to have a smile for a thousand occasions. This one manages to be hopeful, affectionate, confused, proud, and snappy all at once. I haven't eaten potato in at least two decades. I put a French fry in my mouth and chew.

The car starts. 'Burt? *Star Trek*, ja?'

I shudder. Ja, more than that, I actually cough, recalling my daughter June's contrary childhood obsession with that utopian space-opera. 'June Gwendolyn Hecker,' the sign on her bedroom door read, 'Star Fleet Academy.'

To this day, I'm certain that June became a 'Trekkie' solely as an affront to her father, his Middle Ages, and, in particular, the slightly larger than average nose she thought he had bequeathed her. If I would brew medieval mead and dodder about the Mansion Inn's grounds in full CTLR garb, then she would wear Vulcan ears, she would learn to speak Klingon. 'Why shouldn't I? Look at me, Burt. I already am a Klingon!'

Where her mother was tall, sultry, and big-boned, June was small, and always slightly frazzled. June walked like a man, balled fists attached to swinging, stubby arms; knees apart, brows down. Like mine, her hair was lanky and dull at best. Usually a mess. Her eyes were my wife's however, and tremendous. Just beautiful.

She constantly watched herself in mirrors, in windows, in the reflective surfaces of televisions; not in a vain manner but with painful, private faces. Especially when she thought she was not being observed. But even accompanied, she could hardly pass a mirror without raising her eyebrows, or tightening them, or inflating her cheeks. There was a constant, worrying dialog going on between June and the image of June. She would pull faces full of torture and snarls, as well as those terrible dead looks that could occupy her for minutes on end. She would suddenly stop eating during dinner, catching her face reflected in the kitchen window, or curved in a spoon. What held her so, I wondered. What was she trying to squeeze from that image? Every word you spoke, every sound and stimuli played itself over June's face. She would flinch, twitch. My daughter watched TV under great heaps of blankets, even in the summer. And I will always remember her like that, all swaddled, wrapped up like a suburban leper, only those two eyes peering out, motionless, storming with reflected light.

To everyone's chagrin, one year I allowed June to join the Confraternity of Times Lost Regained. It was cute, at first – or at least I thought so. Shy June of Star Fleet Academy, landing at our CTLR revel with her silver suit, Vulcan ears, and ray gun. In those early years, the CTLR had been home to the odd hobbit or wizard, so why not an extra-terrestrial visitor? Wasn't it possible, she'd argued, that the thirteenth century had had its share of alien visitations too? June's alien campaign was probably done only to upset me, expecting me to say no. But I couldn't deny her anything, and had hoped that maybe it would bring us closer together.

But I've never found a path through June's sarcasm and

bile, a way past the warden of her mouth. Though I've often seen my daughter there, in those eyes, waiting, pleading almost, for me to hurry up and figure her out. She spent her first and only CTLR event either zapping people with her ray gun, telling knights and ladies that they'd been 'abducted', or making snide and disagreeable comments. ('Look, medieval Americans, up there, a commercial aircraft! The nerve. Don't they know we're trying to have a re-enactment down here?') She wasn't allowed back. This too she blamed on me, even though I'd been the only one to stand up for her, to plead with the others to please, please give my little girl another chance.

June sought, above all, a legitimate validation of the state she saw herself born into: she would suffer alone and she would suffer at all costs. She felt like an outsider and so that is what she would be, an outsider, joining various clubs and orders just to be kicked out, craving banishment. June collected stamps of disapproval. She failed history on purpose, proudly, and only to rile her father.

In one of her dreamy moods, I clearly recall a summer afternoon she shared with me, lining a family of stones across the kitchen table. She did this maternally, intently, and to her own logic. To occupy space and time with my daughter I had to ignore her. If I showed any interest she'd attack. She would laugh at me. If she knew that I knew she was there then that was it, she'd up and leave. I was a nuisance and an embarrassment. Maybe in my face she saw what she hated so much in her own, I don't know. I had hoped that her childhood was only a phase.

But lost to her rocks, June, on that particular occasion, had said, suddenly, 'It's history too. To hold them. To hold in your hand something from the beginning of everything. They're like bones, like skeletons.'

I looked at her rocks. I found a particularly interesting one, I thought. I pointed and, delicately, as delicately as possible, I said, 'That one's pretty.'

My daughter cringed. 'Pretty?' She blinked, mumbled. She said, 'Yeah.' She began to collect her rocks and put them back into their box. Carefully, one by one.

'No, wait, I'm sorry,' I said. 'Finish what you were saying. I'm interested in what you were saying. One of these is a bone?'

'Right, that's what I said.' Her eyes never met mine when we spoke. They hovered, flitting somewhere across my chest. 'It's OK,' she said. 'You don't have to pretend.'

June lived for her rocks and her science fiction, growing more quiet and underweight as her teenage ordeal progressed, biding her time, hunkering down before she could at last fall under the plastic surgeon's promised blade, as if that would cut loose the real life waiting for her on the other side of her father's nose. By that point, of course, it was too late. With her medieval mind for lists, collecting, and divining enchantment in the natural world, June moved to California, eventually accepting a position as a geologist's assistant. She was far too romantic to be a true geologist, just as her father before her had been far too romantic to become a true historian. I haven't seen her in two years.

Werfel blinks his high-beams into the road before us. 'Czech,' he intones. 'The final frontier.'

Germany, at last, appears to be retreating. Bohemia looms and I find myself giddy at the promise of poverty and uncleanness. There are less lights here, slower automobiles. There are stars.

I remove my *Portrait of an Elderly Man with His Son* from my wallet. Under the cold blush of the ceiling light, I allow Werfel to inspect it. Why not? He carefully appraises the Ghirlandaio, holding it in his right hand as his left aims us into the void. The dermatologist's eyes flick from nose to nose until they slot back into the rushing autobahn, more in order to process the oddness of that shared, century-crossing proboscis, I think, than out of any responsible consideration for the road ahead. He wags his head, hushing the radio's aural halitosis.

'But not the nose, here, see – my son,' I say, indicating the boy. 'Tristan.'

My companion furrows his brow.

'I am going to rescue my son, Tristan. He's in Bohemia,' I explain. He doesn't understand a word I am saying, so I add, 'I love him very much. I am going to find him and bring him home.' Then I tell him something about why Tristan emigrated, and what I did to cause it. And why that will never happen again.

Werfel slips the laminated card into the pocket of his Hawaiian shirt. '*Vielen Dank,*' he says.

Then, before I can protest, I'm instructed to remove four black-and-white photographs from his wallet. The first is a skinny blonde boy, crisp in a military uniform. *Baden-Baden, AD 1937*. The second is a woman. She commands a field of yellow flowers, a spill of black hair, and wind; the mountains behind her have the faded look of a water stain. The third photograph is of a small girl: a sad, papery thing in a large jacket, posing before Prague Castle, two elderly wraiths clasping each of her hands. This must be Werfel's half-sister, the woman he is now traveling to Prague to find. Like me, he has only an address and a phone number, both written on the back of the photograph by God only knows who. The last photograph pulls itself back, withdrawing behind a screen of fingerprints and decay, long-unfolded folds squaring it like rotting window panes. I hold it to the ceiling light. It is, I believe, the woman and the Nazi, now much older, though perhaps no more than fifteen winters have passed since AD 1937. Now bearded and balding, his eyes are buttons, his face boiled. They are both clad as pre-war holiday makers who, having had their luggage lost and their money stolen, have been too long stranded without a change of clothing. The woman holds the man's arm, and too tightly it would seem. Her black hair is short now, possibly graying. Her cheeks are sallow and her eyes hidden in pose, erased by the patient subjection to the act of being photographed. Werfel's parents. They are on a beach. Behind them, a jungle.

'*Mutter*,' Max Werfel says. Then, more hesitantly, and probably still musing on *Star Trek*, '. . . Captain?'

'Father,' I presume. 'Dad.'

He nods sadly. '*Ja*, Captain dead.'

I inquire about the child, and who the child's mother might be, and how he learned of her existence. He momentarily smiles and says, proudly, '*Schwester*.' Then he begins telling me all about it, I think. Perhaps not. In any event, he occasionally becomes upset, and once comes close to tears. He ends the story with a triumphant noise, a few more Germanic snorts, and a giggling coda. I feel as if we have shared something intimate, the more so for not understanding a single word said. Still, I consider holding his photographs hostage. There's no way I can allow the silly man to filch my Ghirlandaio.

St Thomas Aquinas maintained that acrobats, jongleurs, minstrels, actors, and players of every sort were wholly reprehensible, allies of the Devil, and wanton spreaders of evil. They were, in his august eyes, even worse than cripples, vagabonds, and beggars. John of Salisbury, meanwhile, held that musicians, like prostitutes, were monsters with human bodies. He advocated their extermination.

My son, Tristan, is a musician. Two years ago, following the death of his mother, Tristan bought a one-way plane ticket to post-communist Poland, where his maternal grandmother and my arch enemy, Anna Bibko, had been living since AD 1991, trying to help her Lemko people regain their Carpathian Mountain homeland. (More on both her and them later.) I only discovered my son's defection when my daughter, June, before the sentencing at my operating-a-vehicle-without-a-license/DWI trial, decided to speak with me again. She was in California. I think she was hoping that I would have already been installed in a penitentiary or, at the very least, a mental institution. She expressed much surprise that I hadn't been.

She said it served me right. By this, I think, she meant Tristan's abandonment. She said, 'What did you expect, Burt? I think Europe's going to do him some good. And no way, before you ask, I will not give you his phone number. I'm under instructions. You messed him up enough, don't you think? Tristy will contact you if and when he's ready.'

'How can you do this?'

'You've got to be kidding me. You fuck, Burt. Just fuck you.'

Eventually, Tristan did write me a letter. But this was worse than silence, and contained no return address. I've no way of knowing if the letters I addressed to him via his grand-mother's Hospodar Rusyn Democratic Circle of Lemkos office in Warsaw ever met his eyes. I do doubt it. But placing a phone call to that Warsaw office one year ago, I was finally able to connect myself to my mother-in-law. For this, I pretended to be Vaclav Havel, President of the Czech Republic. The receptionist put me through.

'How can I help?' is how Anna Bibko addressed the President of the Czech Republic. Her English heavily accented. Her manner metallic, as usual, and already odious to me.

'Anna,' I said. 'It's me.'

'You.'

'Please, can we talk? For only a moment, I –'

'Woah. I thought you did not talk into such things as tele-phones. Is very OOP, no?'

'I'm only –'

'Only nothing. Mister, the time for talking is end.'

'Tristan,' I said, because suddenly that was all. 'Please, I just want to – wait, please, Anna.'

'Nothing.'

'Stop. This is –'

'Nothing!'

'Important! Listen to me! I know that what happened –'

'Burt Hecker, I am sorry, but you know nothing.'

In the letter, Tristan wrote that he was now playing Lemko folk music exclusively. He was no longer studying Early Music. His grandmother had won. The cymbaly, the trembita, the sopilka, and the flojara had replaced his medieval shawms and crumhorns, his organistrum and hurdy-gurdy, his heavenly vielle, his rebecs, lutes, psalteries, and tabors. But now Bohemia – why, what could've happened? Prague? I can't imagine it. My son traveling Europe, spreading evil with a costumed Lemko folk ensemble.

With slow jerks, our motorcar is finally drawn towards the glowing edge of Germany. I uncork a bottle of Abtei St Hildegard Riesling. The traffic congeals and we toast to new lands.

The border itself resembles nothing so much as an uppity complex of toll booths. Or a gas station putting on airs. It's bright, but seems abandoned. The two of us ready our passports. Two or three mustached attendants mill woefully about, leaning into cars, tapping firearms, half-heartedly sniffing through trunks, trading passports, poking and prodding the soft underbellies of vans and buses and trucks, conspiring, joking, taking documents and handing documents back, no doubt fantasizing about the powers enjoyed by their occupational forefathers, all of them half-unreal in this fluorescent fog. They wave us through.

In no time the women materialize, gilding those first hesitant miles of Bohemia farmland, field, and forest. Every half minute one emerges from the darkness, garish and numb in the sweep of our headlights. Then gone, swallowed by the night we pull in our wake. Perhaps there exists a precedent somewhere in this land's folklore where at the setting of the sun the cows become whores.

'*Schlampen*,' Werfel calls these woodland sex workers, whistling. 'Diseasing peoples, *ja?*'

I repeat this. '*Schlampen*.'

Or, perhaps these are the ghosts of the highway dead, warning us back. Seek not, ye travelers, lest you find.

The dermatologist is a serious, thoughtful drinker. He seems to like the Riesling. He shows me the pink skin on his hands, his neck, and, once, his belly, all the while expounding upon God knows what. He has a purposeful, gentle, yet always enthusiastic manner which is only ridiculous when one remembers that he is more than likely expounding upon obscure skin conditions and ways to properly treat them. But it is impossible not to respect one who genuinely loves what he does.

The window wipers smear stars of exploded insect into gray frowns. I yawn, hoping Werfel soon locates an inn, if indeed that is his current intention. Judging by the number of prostitutes in this kingdom's employ, I don't think it'll be very difficult procuring accommodation at any hour.

The wine has either improved Werfel's driving or significantly deadened my sense of self-preservation. I have another draught. It is good. Indeed, it is excellent being under the control of one whose intentions are unknowable.

'Window wiper,' I say, continuing a game I had started in which I teach the Brazilian practical English. I have begun to slur my words.

'Widower,' Werfel says and is satisfied. Misreading my silence, he repeats it, '*Widower,*' and pats my shoulder.

IV

I awake to a scattering of thumps and the car skidding to a stop. Then the door opens. Max Werfel throws himself from the door.

I hadn't even known that I'd been asleep and there, suddenly, I'm awake. Werfel is hunched over, sort of lurching around the car, erupting in odd exclamations. My first thought is that he's sustained a head injury, but he seems fine. I undo my seatbelt.

Furry, volcanic hills surround us. There is no light but moonlight, which muddies the stars. Bats ricochet overhead. It looks like the road has been equipped with fishing holes, and in the distance a flat spill of clouds seep towards us: all these things I note in an instant. Werfel had finally veered from the road and run down at least half a dozen chickens. The feathers make it look worse than it probably is.

I help clear the poultry from the road, putting the carcasses in a neat, respectful row. I place my hand on Werfel's shoulder. You can hear the wind ruffling up the blackness before it finds us, finally, bringing with it the promise of rain. Nearby, the bark of a dog.

'*Entschuldigung,*' Werfel says. 'Sorry.'

'People shouldn't leave chickens in the road,' I say. 'Or near the road. It's not your fault.'

Minutes later, we drive into a medieval village. I can hardly contain myself. Stones in varying states of crumble and the shadows of roofs cowering around the stiff warning of a spire; everything haphazardly set out, as if grown. Trees molest each other across dirt roads and many of the fences are sunk lower than the weeds that they once protected from God only knows what. Even the moon, caught in the mangled branches of an old apple tree, is cracked.

I tell Werfel to stop the car. He understands, and does so. The windows open. Cows, hay, a certain green, mossy wetness, even a hint of coal: the air is perfect. In the dark, the dwellings appear to be wattle and daub. Noting the unabashed penury, my spirits rise. With a draft of Riesling, I tell Werfel how medieval malefactors were known to actually dig through the walls of wattle-and-daub homes in order to procure items which did not belong to them. He nods politely, seeing in this an opportunity to start the car and get moving. I imagine the automobile-shaped quiet we leave behind, and wish I could luxuriate there indefinitely.

'Sabina's Nite Klub,' says a sign. And another: 'Sexy Motel!' The sudden grin that rattles Werfel's concentration makes it quite clear that we now have a destination, and I close my eyes, remembering the village to our back and the roughshod peasants still slumbering in their straw beds. I know that in the morning they'll be gone. In the morning they will drink instant coffee like everyone else.

The man behind the counter mumbles what can only be a warning or a curse, emitting a low garlic apocalypse from beneath his mustache as he hands us our key. 'Thank you,' I say. The man shakes his head. But I cannot stop smiling, and I slap Werfel's back in a chummy manner as we go in search of our room. Bohemia, it would seem, is an entire kingdom of unwitting medieval re-enactors.

In keeping with this, our room is far from sumptuous. Because Werfel failed to explain to our hosteller that we aren't involved in a sexual liaison, we'd been provided with a single queen-sized bed. Which, on closer inspection, appears to be two twin beds pushed together. On even closer inspection they aren't the same height or length and don't have a mattress, only a thin layer of foam. There are no sheets. There is, however, a blanket, or a very old towel, folded at the bottom of the bed. There are three different carpets – all shades of green – doing their best to cover a patchwork of linoleum, also green. On the wall, a framed poster of a Corvette. I have little desire to examine the bathroom. Werfel sits on the bed, tries and fails to bounce, removes his shoes, looks about him, then at me. He uncorks another bottle of wine, our second. From the curtainless window we can see the rain-smeared neon signs of the disco some several yards away. The thump of the music makes the globules of water vibrate anxiously on our window. It sounds like something trying to escape. I remove my shoes. Then I think better of it.

The women dance around exposed plumbing. They hastily denude, encouraged by slot machines, neon, Germans, plastic flora, and mirrors which reflect and compound a manifold pestilence of vices. I have never seen anything like it. Their breasts have the shape and firmness of baby skulls.

'Burt, what is that noise?' Lonna asks.

'Max is asleep.'

'What?' Then: 'You're alone?'

Three women approach my wallside telephone booth. In

my left hand I clutch a bottle of Abtei St Hildegard Riesling. 'Excuse me, Lonna.'

The one with imitation eyebrows touches my elbow. 'Please, no, I'm sorry,' I whisper kindly, trying to make her understand. 'Long distance? Paris?' Under no circumstances do I wish to purchase this woman, or her associates. But she is persuasive. '*American*,' I explain, finally. But the wretch continues to woo me in German. Then in gutter Bohemian.

Lonna says, 'It's three in the morning, old man. So glad you called and I'm all kinds of shocked right now and certainly enjoying being privy to your nocturnal adventures but –'

The whores depart. 'Here, listen,' I hold the telephone in the direction of the disco dancing.

'What is going on?'

'Bohemians have a stench,' I continue. I laugh. 'It's macabre. The women terrify me.'

And of course, one cannot now help but recall the victims of the Rhineland's own 'dancing mania', or 'St Vitus' Dance', the medieval craze of flagellant dancers who, believing they were possessed, spent entire days leaping and flailing, foaming at the mouth, copulating, howling, and thumping one another in an attempt to loosen Satan's grasp. Sabina's Nite Klub is kind of like that.

'Speak up. How long you been in Prague, anyway? Tivona, she says she's been there, likely in a past life or something, and she thinks you'll just love it. The architecture and the poverty. The food, apparently, is all sorts of awful.'

'I'm nowhere near Prague.'

'Darling, I'm tired. You're where?'

'Got lost,' I say. 'Actually, we've been drinking. The Brazilian, particularly. I left him at the Sexy Motel.'

63

'Burt, you're drunk as a skunk.'

Frantically, then, with my bottle of Riesling, I shoo away a skeletal woman, obviously a victim of scrofula, who approaches me with a beer, obviously poisoned. Two mustached peasants drinking in the corner have marked this interaction with distaste. I describe the scene for Lonna.

In no time, the skeletal woman returns with a bottle of Bohemian vinegar. '1,000 Czech crowns,' she demands, grabbing at my bottle and thrusting hers into my hands. There we struggle for a moment until, between clenched teeth, I say, 'I am speaking to Paris. Please, gratify your flesh elsewhere,' and free my Abtei St Hildegard Riesling from her claws. Benedictine nuns picked the grapes that made that wine, and so, for good measure, I slap the woman soundly on the arm. I drop the phone. The hussy squeals.

I can hear a tiny, sizzling Lonna shouting from the floor. I pick her up.

'Are you all right?' she asks.

'I think so. Hold on a moment.'

The bartender, who'd been watching the proceedings, nods to a cluster of youths. They stand, cigarettes igniting like a line a street lights at dusk. They saunter in my direction. 'OK, I get it, no trouble,' I tell my tormentor, pulling out my medieval money pouch. 'Here. You win. 1,000 crowns.' I present her with the silly notes, and tuck both my superior German wine as well as this recently purchased bottle of Bohemian rot behind me. The youths, monitoring the transaction, settle back down into a low-hanging stratocumulus.

'I'm in a bawdy house,' I say. 'A house of ill repute. It's really remarkably medieval.'

'Seriously, Burt. Isn't Max supposed to be taking care of you?'

'Lonna,' I say. 'The reason I'm calling –'

So she tells me that she spent the previous day 'putting the fun in finagle', her voice and my money beaming off of satellites in outer space. It has been done. The liquidation of my past. Lonna outlines this, the specifics, as I watch the denizens of Sabina's Nite Club re-enact some of Hieronymus Bosch's more fiendish visions of justice. But that is not all. 'Oh, yeah,' she says. 'June called.'

Approximately fifteen years my daughter's senior, Lonna had been June's favorite ever since the brash, handsome attorney had entered our life. Teenage June used to follow her dream big-sister around, aping her expressions and even her habits: the profanity, the Lucky Strikes, plucked eyebrows and cocktails. Lonna did spend a good amount of time at the Mansion Inn, courting her moneyed clients in the 'Timeless Victorian Splendor' of the sitting room, even renting our facilities for conferences and high-stakes arbitrations. Or, more often, just relaxing, throwing down highballs on the porch with me, or bonding with my wife over what it was like to financially support an impractical spouse. To June, Lonna was everything that she wanted to be: fiercely independent, naturally sarcastic, and not without a certain hard-won glamour. Though I don't know for certain, it is my belief that Lonna and my daughter have kept in fairly regular contact ever since California's faults swallowed June all those years ago.

'June called you in Paris?'

'The Mansion Inn really is gone, Burt. This you should know.'

'I don't understand. Lonna, speak up. Did you tell my daughter?'

Lonna taps a pen against the receiver, a legal affectation. It sounds like gunshots. 'Let me just say this. Today, tomorrow, soon – you better call her, Burt. And Burt? You be nice.'

Using the Calling Card that Lonna took such great pains to instruct me in the proper usage of, I punch in June's Long Beach, California, telephone number. It is roughly 9:00 p.m. US Eastern Standard Time. I have no idea what time it is here, at Sabina's Nite Club, and even less of an idea of how time operates in California. It is a disagreeable business.

My grandson answers the telephone. He hangs up almost instantly. I look up at the roving red and blue lights, then at the telephone in my hand. Once again, I dial. I've not laid eyes on June or her son, Sammy, since AD 1996, at the funeral that people assure me I attended. Sammy should be seven now, though it's been made clear that that's none of my business. 'Hello?' he says.

'It's Grampa Burt. Please, don't hang up. It's your grandfather.'

'From jail?'

'From Europe,' I say. 'I never went to jail. Could I talk with your mother, please?'

Sammy thinks about this. 'She's locked in the bathroom,' he says. And I believe him.

The last time we spoke, Sammy had been forced to converse with me because his mother had refused to. 'Or no dessert,' I'd even heard June stipulate as she passed the phone over. I sensed then from the tight silence mounting behind Sammy's voice how his every word was being monitored – how they watched him, encouraged him, and, more than that, humorously identified with the boy's plight. They'd made me into a vegetable, something to be endured. Speaking with Grampa Burt required compensation.

'Please,' I say. 'Try and get her. It's long distance.'

Sammy drops the phone. Eventually, after some yelling, he picks it up again. 'She says tomorrow. Because she's on errands.'

'In the bathroom?'

Sammy, who apparently shares his mother's enthusiasm for subterfuge, whispers, 'Mom's always crying.'

'I know she is, Sammy.'

'She won't come out of the bathroom.'

There is the click of another telephone being picked up. The bathroom phone, I assume, remembering that in California nothing is sacred. My daughter says, 'Please, Sammy. Enough. Put the phone down, would you?'

'It's Grampa Burt. I told him like you said. Like you're shopping.'

'Well, I'm back.'

'She's back,' Sammy corroborates.

I watch three Germans order beer. Before the bartender serves these beverages he pretends to do something else just long enough so that the Germans believe he's forgotten them and just short enough so that he can become irate at their pushiness when they remind him. I hear my grandson hang up.

'June,' I say. 'I'm at a strip club.'

'*Dad* –' and she laughs.

I can't recall the last time I made my little girl smile even. Moreover, since childhood, she's rarely called me anything but 'Burt'. 'Well, and how are you?' I ask.

'I was just – only a few hours ago I was on with Lon in

Paris. I guess that's why you've called,' June pauses. 'Did she tell you? Wow, really, what is that noise?'

'Sammy's out of school?'

'It's like five p.m. It's the summer. Honestly, where are you?'

'June, I have no idea where I am.'

She's separated from her husband, Jack, she tells me, and soon to be divorced. She begins to talk quickly, then angrily, and then she weeps. I cling to the phone. There's another woman involved, a Mexican woman. June is exacting. She outlines the events thoroughly at first, as if I was a friend or geological colleague, as if each marital hiccup were a rock to be labeled, categorized, and placed inside a box, but soon her tone changes and I feel as if I was a judge, or someone who doesn't believe her, let alone love her. Injuries are listed and injustices related – possibly savored. June's perennial garb of woe. Everything is bad, everything has always been bad, and it's still somehow my fault. Chastisements, maledictions, sobs: I helplessly listen, trying to get a foothold somewhere in my daughter's emotional vortex. I want to help her. Here is my chance to help her, I think. She says, 'Dad, we're coming back home.'

'What?'

She falters. 'Dad? Is – so is that cool with you?'

'*What?*'

I listen to California. I can almost hear the highway lapping at June's ranch or condo or wherever it is she's never once invited me to visit. Home?

'Are you there?' she says. Then growing angry: 'Burt!'

'Lonna told you where I am, right?'

'Listen, I knew you'd freak but don't, OK, you don't have

68

to do a thing. I've already arranged everything for the move and Sammy starting school and so on in September. I've got it under control. We're going to – I mean, we'd like to help you run the Mansion. Like Mom wanted. You know, re-open it. Like how it was before,' June says. 'Dad? Burt –?'

The construction of our home, the Mansion Inn, was completed in AD 1866 for George West, inventor of the Flat-Bottomed, Folding Paper Bag. It had been his summer residence. His permanent seat, which must have been palatial indeed, was fifteen miles away and by all accounts far too grand to survive the coming century of convenience the industrialist's paper bags helped birth. Fittingly, a gas station and mini-market now serve as this other mansion's headstone. The big joke being that it's not uncommon to find paper bags decomposing among the mini-market debris, left there in lieu of flowers. 'Oddly respectful for litter,' as my wife once said.

She had been born there in AD 1930. It was hers, everything as far as you could see or cared to walk, inherited several days after her father changed his will to exclude his wife, Anna Bibko, and subsequently committed suicide. My wife had been the nominal manager and owner of the bed and breakfast since she was eight years old.

The Mansion sat across from the ruins of George 'The Paper Bag King' West's old Excelsior Mill and the part of the Kayaderosseras Creek known as Queens Falls itself. If one stood near the top of the waterfall, by the half-sunken tracks and trestles of the old Kayaderosseras Railroad, the Mansion Inn, our home and livelihood, would look right back at you with all the soul of a stuffed, glass-eyed badger. In truth, it was a grand piece of architecture, and one of the most historically significant estates in Saratoga County. An enormous square thing, it owed as much to the classic Venetian Villa as it did to the Georgian school of stockiness. An ornate Victorian cupola crowned its top, rising from the center of the building, giving the whole structure the look of an upside-down dreidel. But to me, it'd always appeared the most petrified of houses, like a comatose Victorian matron overly decked-out for the big Hospital Christmas Party. Or, later, when things had gotten bad: like the tip of an iceberg.

The cupola was June's place. She'd give her summers to its heights, sleeping up there in a sleeping bag, taking her meals there, perhaps dreaming she was imprisoned in a tower or watching the green sea of treetops for the ship that might any day come to carry her off, away from her miserable childhood. Even as a teenager she would laze her quiet moments in the cupola, taking a break from the hospitality industry she'd been born into, smoking marijuana cigarettes and pouring over her geological surveys and books, perhaps imagining the molten beginnings of Queens Falls, a time long before her hated nose had been called into being. Her long, knotty hair set loose after a morning of cooking, socializing with guests, and cleaning with her mother, grandmother, and, sometimes, her brother. The cupola was June's private peace, and I can't remember ever spending more than a collective hour up there in my entire life. We all knew better. Only Tristan was ever allowed up there with her, but only before he could speak. Local children, Tristan once told me, spooked themselves with talk of the Dead Girl of the Cupola.

The interior of the Mansion Inn had been preserved in a more or less pristine condition since the days of George West.

70

Marble fireplaces, chandeliers, wood floors, and brass fixtures: all original. The garish antique furniture, however, was a hodgepodge collected from countless auctions and estate sales. There were nine guest rooms in all. Each had its own name – The Excelsior, The Empire, The George West, The Sophia, The Queens Falls, The Saratoga, The Lemkovyna, The Kayaderosseras, The Ballston Spa – as well as its own particular decorative motif I am hardly the man to comment on. One had a whirlpool tub. Disconsolate old oil paintings crowded the walls, Victorian style, our most famous being a glowering portrait of Ralph Waldo Emerson done by a contemporary of his. He had a spot all to himself on the wall above the landing of the grand staircase, and June used to tell guests that he was George West, inventor of the Flat-Bottomed, Folding Paper Bag. There was a dining room, three parlors, and a library which contained a grand piano once owned by Mimi Eisenhower.

Like how it was before.

Our best business was done during August when the nearby Saratoga Racing Season attracted high-end gamblers, low-class snobs, and equestrians from all over the country. This was also the time that we held many weekend Confraternity of Times Lost Regained tourneys and festivals, to the bafflement of our non-regular guests. It was something of a local curiosity, my annual CTLR gatherings; and about two dozen 'Human Interest' newspaper articles with titles like 'History Clashes as the Middle Ages Meets the Victorian at Historic Inn' had been written about us over the last few decades, some from as far away as Miami, Florida.

My family lived behind the Mansion Inn in a simple two story Colonial-style house built when Anna Bibko, my wife's mother, decided to convert their living quarters in the Mansion into more guest rooms. Sometime in the 1930s, I think. Our front windows were portraits of the inn, its gardens, lawns, and our suitably aristocratic Tiger Tail Pines, which gave our second floor some degree of verdant, dusky privacy. These trees prickled the sky around the Mansion Inn, bursting up on all sides like explosions, a great deal taller than any of the surrounding flora. My beloved Ensemble Guillaume de Machaut de Paris on the phonograph, I will always remember lying in bed together with a ten-month-old Tristan, watching those trees shake birds out into the upstate New York sky. How the breeze brought the scent of manure from the nearby farms, as well as flowers, mowed lawn, burning leaves and forest, and breakfast. My wife, daughter, and mother-in-law already there, always there, working, serving our guests their celebrated Grand Marnier French Toast breakfasts, setting the cutlery just so, washing sheets and dishes and towels, vacuuming carpets, squeezing oranges, and answering questions about the estate's well-publicized ghosts. Tristan would grab at the birds, or their shadows, and I would do the same. He was my responsibility. The Mansion Inn was my wife's.

From our back windows waited a forest of normal, plebian trees. There was one stream, two ponds, and, if you walked for a good day or two, Vermont. This was a great place for CTLR melees, or CTLR stag-hunts – a really nice environment for the Middle Ages in general. Deer, fox, wild turkey, and the occasional bear were seasonally spotted, though never captured or killed. From the kitchen window, through the foliage, you could just about see the old barn that Tristan and I had reconstructed into our library and music workshop. The barn predated the Mansion Inn by about twenty years, implying that at one time there were no trees, no forest back there at all. It had all been fields. The ruins of stone walls tumbled through that relatively new forest of ours, obscurely demarking land that, at one time, had had access to the sun. June loved that forest, loved digging for rocks there, or just hiding out, climbing trees. She always maintained that George 'The Paper Bag King' West himself, in both penance and gratitude, planted each and every one of those trees. 'And if he didn't,' she said, 'he damn well should've.'

'I'm not coming home,' I say. 'End of discussion.'

June's dead mother hangs in the air, filling the silence. They've identical silences, June and her dead mother. 'Of course you are,' June says.

I cannot possibly tell her, not yet. But now that the trammels of her marriage have broken, maybe I can speak to my daughter as one failure to another. Or is there no way to revivify a relationship that was trying at best. Every stark altercation of her fortune, hasn't it been set into spin by her father? The old, inexhaustible lament. And here I have ruined her life again, a lifelong passion for ruins thrown back in my face. Even after her eighteenth birthday cosmetic surgery and the vengeful social life that ensued, it was my fault. (It's my belief that she wasn't fully prepared for life without the nose, and many of her post-operation failures and disappointments wouldn't have occurred if the nose had been left unmolested.) Goddamn her. How is it, I want to ask, that she can always find the splinter in her father's eye, and never notice the plank in her own?

'I assure you I'm serious.'

73

'You're unbelievable. This,' she says, 'is unbelievable. Are you – you're drinking, Burt. Jesus fucking Christ. Of course you're drinking. Look, I don't know what you're talking about. I'm sorry, but we both know that you can't take care of yourself. Well, you can't. You cannot take care of yourself.'

'I am not drinking,' I say.

I can hardly believe a place like California exists. June is pleading with me from outer space. I look at my bottle of Bohemian wine, now serving as a spa for insects. Endowed with reason, I prefer folly. Shall I tell her that my follies are all I have left? I am going to be ill.

'Dad, please. For once in your life,' my daughter says, sobbing. 'I need help, Dad. I need help. I hate it here. I want to come home.'

For once in my life?

I back away. I stand there, colored lights swooping down and picking at me like seagulls. I've hung up the telephone – I stare at it. Is it ringing? Something is ringing. Why is everybody dancing, I wonder as I stumble towards what is presumably an exit. Why is everyone dancing to that terrible ringing?

Emptying my stomach in the parking lot, I try and stop crying. Dozens of worms have emerged from the wet earth, forming a desperate calligraphy on the pavement. Help us. 'Too late,' I mumble. It is too late.

I find Max Werfel lying across both mattresses. His Hawaiian shirt is restless, feeding off his body like fire.

I remove one of the wallet-thin pillows from the bed. The floor, I place it on the floor. I follow it. On to the floor. The carpet is a swamp that somebody has attempted to temper with chemical citrus, and I stretch my body out.

Hanging above me is Max Werfel's smile. It opens, laughs; and, despite everything, I laugh also. His round head, his hair. He says something German that seems to rhyme, I think, as a dog's bark might seem to rhyme with another dog's bark. Beyond him, the ceiling ripples like a milky lake someone keeps dropping stones into. Then he too is gone. The room lightens. I can't close my eyes for fear of tumbling into space. I imagine the safety of winter, and I populate the ceiling above me with Christmas, with children, woodsmoke, carols, and decorated trees. Werfel, it turns out, has a velveteen snore.

V

Reaching Prague by highway you've first got to pass through a graveyard of concrete housing projects, huddling tombstone cities erected by Czechoslovakian communists as if to finally, irrevocably mark the burial of some ancient Bohemian disorder. The old city is besieged. Max Werfel studies his map. This is not what he expected.

The speed at which we pierce through these atrocities makes me feel like something of a liberator, and the empty blue sky gives the abruptness with which the old city finally presents itself the piercing quality of a nightmare. The road has brought us to a high point adjacent to the castle, above the city. There are the forest of spires, towers, and orange-red roofed buildings. Werfel tosses the map into the backseat, vindicated. He applauds the metropolis as if its appearance was a conjuror's trick, and down past the castle we wind.

The city is overrun, being eaten from the inside out. Contemporary man scratching together, swarming cheek by jowl, squatters in this historical shell. Overfed red trams burrow through streets full of small, smelly automobiles, pornographic advertisements, clanging heat, confusion, smog, and hysterical clusters of tourists. The Brazilian drives ecstatically on, but I feel as though I am watching an invasion that hasn't had the common decency to raze what it's already destroyed.

Like this entire country, our hotel appears to crave nothing more than a release into easy superficiality. Its facade is heart-breakingly Renaissance, but the inside has long since been hollowed out and refitted in a parody of the comfort one might find on the side of any New World highway. Plastic ferns, brochures, and screaming, dwarfish Italian holiday-makers predominate in the lobby.

I've learned to defer to Werfel in all things. I trust him implicitly. Though the hosteller can speak English, I have my friend handle everything in German, a language more suit-able to demands and distance. The dermatologist and I will once again be sharing a room.

Before setting out on our first Prague expedition, Werfel fills a bath. I wait while he steeps himself. The window of our room affords a view greatly at odds with my desultory musings: the walls of Prague Castle rising up above us, and the gardens and paths clinging to it. Such a soothing reminder of the limitless-ness of human anxiety and will, and I suddenly yearn for the music of Hildegard or Machaut, or even Dowland. There is a kind of voluptuousness in sorrow, and I think of the Speculatores, those Monkish scouts whose sole occupation was to watch for, categorize, and interpret the signs which were to herald the ever-imminent Day of Reckoning. From the sound of splashing, it's evident that the Brazilian is a rapturous, energetic bather. I smile. When, I wonder, has the world not been about to end?

I call Lonna and hang up before she answers. Prevaricating, I decide that it would not be in my best interest to call June again today. Though I'm not at all certain, I believe that today, in California, is still more or less yesterday.

Werfel emerges from the bathroom. He boasts a new Hawaiian shirt and the aromatic glow of an oiled piglet. 'Tristan,' he says, reading my mind, and pulling me towards the crashing promiscuity of the century waiting outside.

Tristan has not once, to my knowledge, ever shaved his face. Far taller than medieval me, my son had brown hair which he kept in a long ponytail, and thick spectacles which kept his blue eyes in a state of suspended surprise. By his twentieth year, a reddish beard obscured his neck.

When he wasn't wearing medieval garb with me or one of those accursed Lemko folk outfits with his grandmother, Tristan dressed in denim trousers, white cotton button-down shirts, and homemade CTLR sandals. Strolling through the Mansion Inn's grounds, he looked like a twentieth-century Robinson Crusoe, stranded and starving in our desert culture. He was a monk among strip-malls, dodging footballs, stepping over sunbathers; reality wading through a population with its eyes glued so rapturously to the false. He has never changed and I don't believe that he ever will.

The boy spoke little. His words, when they came and when you could hear them, came in halting, painfully thought-out wisps. He was movement, for the most part, and, of course, he was music.

So while my wife, her mother, and June handled the Mansion Inn, Tristan concerned himself with his instruments. Together we had converted the nineteenth-century barn which hung on the edge of our vast property into a mead brewing center, library, and medieval music workshop. It was a quiet, deliciously ruined place. In the summer the wood still smelled of hay, and large flies charged endlessly into the brown windows which looked out onto that forest which, two hundred years ago, was a field. Foxes lived under the floorboards. Tristan and I loved taking our lunches together, more often than not in silence, sitting on one of the forest's old stone walls, which now demarcated little more than random squares of trees. The barn roof we repaired together when Tristan was six. He'd insisted on painting stars on the ceiling afterwards, and he had begged that this be done to a very high degree of astronomical accuracy: it wasn't, of course, because we had too much fun creating our own constellations. The Crabby Uncle. The Spitting Lamb. The Big Battle Axe. The Little Battle Axe. The Pizza. We were always getting stung by bees and it even became a contest one year, if I remember correctly, seeing who the bees hated least. (Not using them to produce an intoxicant, Tristan won.) And so I would brew my mead or drink my mead, reading from my medieval collection while Tristan, growing older, would play his music and smoke marijuana cigarettes, a vice I couldn't exactly approve of – being OOP – but one which had no noticeably negative side effects. If my family wished to ingest a home-grown plant, then my family would ingest a home-grown plant. I would dress in period-specific, historically accurate clothing and all would be well. There, in that barn, we shared time like two very old men, brothers perhaps, who'd long ago discarded conversation as too limited a mode of communication.

'You think he's so special, and sure he is. But also he's just a kid. Please just promise me you'll remember, Burt. You and my mother, I swear, neither of you do him any favors.

Trust me, he's not as together as you think he is. I think it's important that you let him be confused and stupid now and then, you know?' my wife once told me. 'Otherwise, how's he ever gonna appreciate getting old?'

My wife and I agreed, more or less, that music was one of the safest avenues left for creating a decent human in this day and age. But the boy needed little encouragement. The muddle-minded perversities of the modern church, political punditry, television, or organized sports were never for Tristan. With pride I can say that he was something of a prodigy, and I can even more proudly say that, as a prodigy, and against the wishes of every baffled and jealous instructor that ever thought it their duty to mold him, Tristan refused to delve into any sort of 'classical' music that postdated the sixteenth century, not to mention most of whatever it is his generation regarded as music. Folk music he liked, however, and he learned to play an astounding repertoire of old English and Scottish ballads, carols, hymns, and rounds. From the age of five, my son was a star feature of the Confraternity of Times Lost Regained's Bardic Circle evenings. His singing voice was everything his speaking voice was not. For one, you could actually hear it. But when not singing, plain-chanting, or leading the CTLR madrigal group, he played every medieval instrument one could purchase for him or, later, that he could make for himself in our barn: shawms, crumhorns, the thunderous medieval organ, bagpipes, tabor pipes, hurdy-gurdies, organistrums, vielles.

'Dad,' I remember Tristan looking up from some instrument he'd been sanding. 'What's wrong with me?'

He was about thirteen, I think.

'Nothing's wrong with you,' I said.

He nodded, and went back to work.

Ten minutes later he looked up again. 'Are you sure?'

'Do not mingle with the throngs in the public houses, for the number of parasites is infinite. Actors, jesters, smooth-skinned lads, Moors, flatterers, pretty boys, effeminates, pederasts, singing and dancing girls, quacks, belly dancers, users, perfumers, alchemists, statuaries, foreigners, swindlers, gluttons, jesters, sorceresses, extortionists, night-wanderers, lepers, magicians, mimes, Jews, beggars, buffoons: all this tribe fill all the houses. Therefore, if you do not wish to dwell with evildoers, dearest son, do not live in Prague.'

Such was the advice – cribbed from Richard of Devizes and the irascible Petrarch – that I planned on reciting for Tristan, as a joke, in my Eckbert Attquiet CTLR voice, when we were finally reunited.

But really, the best I can say of Prague's remaining medieval streets is the historically accurate predominance of dogs and their excrement. No, perhaps it's not as bad as that. There is much to be said of streets still following their ancient paths, unstraightened at least, if now prey to automobiles and those seeking recreation. The frequent churches and cathedrals can hardly fail to inspire, even if they are now as mute as they are deaf to this age, boldly weathering the shifting humors of novelty. Stepping past the old stone buildings, gates, and passageways, I occasionally find myself holding my breath, as if at any moment the dam will break and the past will come back like a flood, destroying all that's transient here.

Feral geese, dogs, rats, cats, trampling horse hooves, the garbage and dung, the fishmongers, linen makers, lice-pickers, tooth-pulling barbers, and the pungent urine-stink of the tanners; the chickens, ducks, rabbits, and hares, their legs trussed, floundering on the ground in wide-eyed terror: all long since gone.

But so are the corpses. The gibbeting, burning, and quartering has ceased; and no fly-haloed heads are impaled on the stakes of this city's wall. That, at least, is progress.

But still, I feel as if I'm a time traveler here, as if my Confraternity of Times Lost Regained medieval sensibilities are being trampled on by these modern, more or less blameless people.

The day is humid. The sky is a thick, lonely bronze. We cross the Charles Bridge in a maniacal parade, the Brazilian occasionally holding my arm, adding significantly to my sense of the surreal. Enclosed in a tangible web of expectation and then disappointment, we admire the Astronomical Clock and the bombastic, mostly post-medieval architecture of Old Town Square: all that sickly sweet Austro-Hungarian kitsch. We become thoroughly lost in mazes of streets, impasses, and courtyards which might be spectacular under harsher, less hospitable conditions. Surely the best time to visit Prague is during a blizzard. Werfel desires to ride a tram, so we do so. And he is delighted. It is safer, I learn, to gravitate towards the tourists on such a tram, for their scent and disposition, though less medieval, is more palatable than that of the natives. The natives, you learn, are the unhappy ones who do not speak in public or, it would seem, bathe at home. The elderly are positively venomous. (Two assaulted Werfel in two unrelated incidents, both because he failed to relinquish his tram seat to them quickly enough. One whacked his leg with an aluminum cane, the other told the entire tram how monstrous foreigners were, especially German foreigners – or so this tirade was translated to us by a kind little Bohemian with glasses.) Wenceslas Square is foul. Prague's Old Jewish Synagogue tries too hard to be poignant. In all these sights I achieve solace only in bringing forth trees, picturing them blooming like smoke from the roofs of gutted buildings, dreaming of what a fine and picturesque pile of rubble this city will someday make.

In a public house, we dispose of a noteworthy feast of roast duck, soggy purple cabbage, beer, and dumplings. I enjoy both the meal and the scullion thieves who attend us; their dead eyes and princely impertinence. I add these CTLR-esque Bohemian waiters and a majority of their meals to the canine excrement as some of the truly medieval things alive and well in modern-day Prague. How can I begrudge the young men the 200 Czech crowns they brazenly add to our check? 'Good show,' I say, as Eckbert Attquiet. 'We did enjoy the repast right heartily!'

Tomorrow night my son and his Lemko folk ensemble will be performing at Jazz Club Z. If I can trust Lonna's handwriting, they are called 'The Sound Defenestration Collective'. I will not telephone him. Nor will I seek out his apartment. Tomorrow I will simply buy a ticket and find myself a seat.

The club, an unlikely place for Lemko folk music as any I can conceive, is located in a cellar near Old Town Square. Lemko folk music should be performed in the hills to an audience of goats and clouds. Trust me, the stuff is unpalatable to human ears. But two years have led me here, to tomorrow, and I will not stumble. I will cheer, and I will applaud, and I cannot wait to see my son and hear his music. This mess will be cleaned.

The sign outside the club says,

THE SOUND DEFENESTRATION COLLECTIVE
(US/CZ)
with special guests
20:00

For a moment I grant myself the luxury of thinking that I'm included among those special guests. But that idea passes quickly enough.

My son's birth was the beginning of another pregnancy, one which was to develop imperceptibly alongside the boy for twenty-two years. I've often thought of the cancer as such: like another child in my wife's womb, as if the tumors consisted of nothing but residual traits, those defects my son had managed to shake off before being born. Envy, wrath, gluttony, lechery, avarice and cupidity, pride, sloth: a festering pocket of vices unwittingly left behind, an evil twin who was one day fated to clamor for the attention he felt himself due. My wife had been forty-four when Tristan was born. He was a surprise, and one which her health never fully recovered from. It is my belief that Tristan never forgave himself for being born. But because there is nobody who blames him for his mother's death, there is also nobody to absolve him. Why else would he have left me? What else could he be looking for with his equally guilt-racked grandmother and her Lemko culture?

Anna Bibko lived for her grandson, and Tristan, I must admit, dearly loved the cantankerous emigrant. There was a time when they had been difficult to separate, as if she were his true mother. This all began when Anna Bibko, shortly before Tristan's birth, announced to us that the child would be the reincarnation of her Lemko grandfather. She had had a dream. Then, when he was four or five months old, Tristan began making sounds. Anna Bibko, of course, claimed that these curious gurgles and cries were very nearly words, even muddied phrases, in her own native Lemko language, an East Slavic tongue not dissimilar to Polish or Ukrainian. There was nothing you could say to dissuade her from this line of thinking, even when she could not entirely translate what the infant was saying. It became a joke. June, to my delight, began maintaining that the sounds were very obviously Klingon in origin. Klingov, she started calling Tristan in order to rile her grandmother: Klingov the Eastern European from Outer Space. My wife would smile and say it was like seeing the Virgin Mary in a water stain, or faces in the whorls of wood. 'It's just weird crying is what it is. It's gurgling. Let Mom have her reincarnated grandfather if it makes her happy. God knows it's good that something makes her happy. It's harmless. Don't let it spook you.' But Anna Bibko didn't spook me. She enraged me. The whole thing was absurd, and time has proven, I think, that it was not harmless at all. Because, to this day, my mother-in-law remains convinced that Tristan is her grandfather. That my son is his own great-great-grandfather reborn.

Situated in the Carpathian Mountains, Lemkovyna, the Lemko homeland, was unfortuitously smeared over the borders of Poland, Slovakia, and the Ukraine. There, sometime around the turn of the century, she was born. Anna Bibko, my mother-in-law and nemesis.

Basically a kind of Eastern European hillbilly, the Lemkos

were known – when they were known at all – as everything from Rusyn, Rusnak, Carpatho-Ruthenian, Ukrainian, and, even, in certain circles, as a 'Lost Tribe of the Poles' (only the Poles, it is implied, could lose an entire tribe of their own people and do so in Poland). If there was a central European land still clinging as doggedly to a way of life linked to that of the medieval peasant then I have not heard of it. They were stateless, seemingly forgotten up in those mountains; and for hundreds of years they'd been ignored. While the lowland nations around them industrialized and set one another ablaze, the Lemkos made pottery. They tanned leather, collected mushrooms, and carved wood. They made and sold brooms, juniper bush baskets, wagon whips, millstones, chests, church furnishings, icons, and a pathological variety of twig-based curiosities. Dairy farming was important, as was bee-keeping, ox-grazing, shepherding, and weaving. Until the Second World War and its denouement, most of the Lemkos still used wooden wagons, wooden plows, and wooden harrows to farm their poor, hilly soil. They cut straw and hay with homemade knives a less-discerning student of history might expect to find in the Bronze Age wing of a natural history museum. Their women were known to sing incessantly. And until I met my wife, I hadn't known that such a place even existed. Of course, by that time – AD 1965 – it no longer did.

I don't know why the Bibkos emigrated from Lemkovyna to the United States in AD 1912, how they afforded such a journey, or what promises they made to themselves in order to see it to its conclusion. The economics, the politics; the ugly specifics. Their hopes could only be normal hopes.

My wife always imagined a sloshing, summer afternoon in

Romania. She had a funny way of telling the story, of making her own family history a fairy tale: the Bibkos respectfully removing their hats and shoes as they finally passed into the ship, the hull of which was larger than any man-made structure that they had ever entered. Little Tristan would listen rapt to the story. Not only her grandparents first time off of dry land, my wife would say, but their first time at sea level. The journey through the Black Sea, the Mediterranean Sea, and across the Atlantic Ocean. The stenches, petty disputes, and deprivation. The buzzing they mistook for a million flies when they stepped off of the ship and into New York City. And the way those three months of traveling seemed like three hundred years; Lemko time travelers, their clothing suddenly folk costumes, their ears overwhelmed by the hysteria of a growing country. So from New York City they fled north, ever upwards, perhaps reverse tracing the same journey they had made from Lemkovyna to the Black Sea port, working under the belief that if they followed this logic they might encounter a land not dissimilar to the land they left so many thousands of miles and years behind. The red and gold autumn leaves, the sun, everything would have been recognizable but ever so slightly different. My wife had them partake in fantastic adventures. The country was a dreamland; and perhaps it even reminded my wife's grandfather of the night he woke up drunk in his friend's house, beside his friend's wife, everything similar but new, different, better. The United States of America was like an eternity of those first disorientating seconds of not knowing and not wanting to.

They settled in Queens Falls, New York. That, at least, was a verifiable fact. The three of them: my wife's mother, Anna Bibko, age eight, and her parents. Anna's father found employment in a paper mill situated along Kayaderosseras Creek. He was never to return to Lemkovyna, though nearly every year he shipped Anna and her mother back as a kind of boastful tribute, bearing US currency and excuses.

Lowlanders. That is what they were called after a year in America, the worst insult one Lemko could throw at another. Only Anna's grandfather – who, if one wishes to believe her now, has been reborn as my son – recognized Anna and her mother as family. He was a shepherd and a musician. He would sing to them, play his cymbaly or trembita or sopilka; he would paint them pysankas, Lemko Easter eggs. In those days, apart from her grandfather, Anna loathed Lemkovyna. The sweat, the homemade cheese, the singing women watching the river wash their clothes; the language itself seemed stupid, backwards, ever on the verge of devolving into barnyard babble. It must have terrified the little girl, time traveling on an annual basis.

Then, on returning from one such Lemkovyna sojourn, Anna and her mother found their five empty cupboards open and their shard of a bathroom mirror covered with oily black cloth. Four days earlier, Anna's father had taken his own life after a disabling accident at the paper mill. Anna's mother, who never learned to speak English – never tried – soon moved her and Anna into the attic of an old farmhouse on the outside of Queens Falls. There the Lemko woman began to regress into the near-imbecilic state of joy which was to occupy the remainder of her life. There her daughter, listening to the boisterous family stomp beneath them, decided to become an American at all costs.

This she did. One week before her twentieth birthday, in AD 1924, Anna Bibko became Anna Steed, and moved into the George West Mansion (not yet the Mansion Inn bed and breakfast). I still have a photograph somewhere. Like my daughter, she was a small woman with prominent fists: in the photograph, these fists, both of them, choke a bridal bouquet as if it were a deserving neck, black-and-white flowers forced up in an explosion which manages to take out half of her groom's face. He could be anyone. She could almost be said to smile.

She'd been courting Henry R. Steed, scion of Queens Falls' richest family, for nearly as long as she'd been speaking English. They had been classmates. Though economic differences, not to mention the bulwarks of religion and culture, should have kept them apart, Anna was beautiful. What's more, she was intelligent. My wife disagreed with me, but it's my opinion that Anna connived to keep her spoken English just porous enough to be endearing, feminine, and adorably foreign. Haunted by her limited mother on one side, and the limitless country on the other, Anna Bibko must have burned especially bright.

It's of some interest to point out that Anna's mother had been employed at the George West Mansion as a maid. I imagine her haunting the Steed's historic home, drifting from room to room, singing quietly in a language her daughter refused to acknowledge. Did mother serve daughter? I can only assume so. The Lemko ghost probably as proud as her daughter was mortified, watching from the side as the New World and its ways erased her from her daughter's life. In any event, they were celebrated, Henry and Anna, as far as a town the size of Queens Falls can celebrate two people of little or no practical worth.

Thirteen years later, seven years after the birth of my wife,

Henry R. Steed, like the father of his wife, took his own life. The George West Mansion, which under Henry R.'s spectral watch had become the renowned Mansion Inn, was inherited by my wife and not his because he had changed the will to specify that Anna got nothing. Even Anna's guardianship of my eight-year-old wife's claim to the Mansion Inn was challenged – unsuccessfully – via a protracted legal battle between the young widow and old Mrs Steed, Henry's mother, who had never liked the 'frigid little Slav' that had stolen her only son's heart and then, it is assumed, broken it in two. To my knowledge, Anna Bibko never spoke of Henry Steed as anything other than a means to an end. My wife, however, insisted that there had once been love between her parents. She remembered her father as two hands and a book. His face was the book, always some great leather-bound tome; when you spoke with him, she said, when you crawled into his study to find him in his chair, you looked up at the rings on his fingers as if they were eyes. He would only lower the book and speak directly to you if he was angry.

My wife visited Lemkovyna but once, in AD 1934, when she was four years old. It was called Poland then, but would be called worse in the years only then beginning to gather at its border. But that summer was a fairy tale. It was one of the happiest times of my wife's life, and one she never tired of talking about. The chickens, the straw roofs, the magical forests, costumes and singing. They had arrived just in time to witness the death of Anna's beloved grandfather, and Anna had left vowing to never return.

Following the end of World War II and the signing of the Yalta Treaty, the Lemkos, occupying a borderland apparently crawling with Ukrainian anti-communist insurgents, had been asked by the Red Poles to immediately vacate their mountains, culture, and history. They were officially invited to the 'Happiest Country in the World', which at that time was Siberia, lowland Poland, the Ukraine, East Germany, or Russia, depending on where the train happened to be coming from. So, between AD 1944 and AD 1946 over 200,000 Lemkos were made a great deal 'happier'. Then, in AD 1947, the hundreds of thousands who refused to leave were either forcefully repatriated or massacred by the Wojsko Polskie – a Soviet-commanded army of Poles – in what was noted as 'an atmosphere of mutual accord and agreement'.

The Poles went house to house, slaughtering men, women, and children. Then onto the next village, then the next. They were not as efficient as the Germans – and this fact is supported in the manner in which they massacred, and the fact that many Lemkos were able to hide and escape; while many, too, were sloppily left as witnesses. Guns, it seems, were primarily used to scare the Lemkos enough so that the Poles might be able to cut off their breasts or ears, or shove bayonets into their eyes. Men, women, children. Entire families burned alive. Sometimes they would return to a village, raze every building, and tell the survivors that they had one day to leave. For what had they to stay for now? Then, when the Lemkos did not leave – because, really, what on earth had they to go to now? – the Poles set about killing them. Eventually, numbed by the flames blooming one after another over their dark, otherwise silent hills, most Lemkos allowed themselves to be herded down to the trains. My wife believed that at that point they would have allowed themselves to be herded off the edge of the world. It simply couldn't matter to most of them anymore. Within the span of six or seven months, Lemkovyna, for all purposes, no longer existed. The mountains were emptied. New weeds were already sprouting where families had lived for countless generations, smoke was already indistinguishable from cloud.

The Anna that I've always known is the one forged in the fires of those Carpathian Mountains. My wife says that the change was overnight. She thought it was a joke, at first, coming downstairs and finding her mother dressed in a Lemko folk costume. But, no. Anna hated jokes. Where once she was disgusted with her fellow immigrants and their nationalistic fantasies, after receiving numerous reports of the massacre, lists of the dead, and, worse, the atrocious way in which they had been dispatched, Anna began reaching backwards with the same tenacity that she'd once reached forwards. She legally reverted from Steed to Bibko. She joined and soon took over every Lemko organization she could find, and when she couldn't find one to suit a particular cause, she started one. In Yonkers, New York, she debated whether a Lemko was best affiliated with the Byzantine Catholic Church or the Orthodox Church. In Toronto, Canada, she discussed how to better integrate the Lemko language with the Ukrainian language. Everywhere in the free West Anna's Lemkos seriously talked about returning to their homeland behind the Iron Curtain and living just like they used to live, or just like their great-grandparents used to live. They donned folk costumes on the weekend. They cooked food, danced dances. They painted their Easter eggs out of season. They created a Lemko flag. These organizations were not at all unlike a more deluded Confraternity of Times Lost Regained, as my wife would so often point out. They were re-enactors, practicing customs most of them couldn't even remember from childhood, customs their grand-parents probably would have found old-fashioned or comi-cally inaccurate.

She still ran the Mansion Inn like a good American, but now she ruled over a staff consisting entirely of Eastern and Central European refugees – Jews mostly, it turned out, but even Poles, even Russians. To her all were victims, and there was nobody who wasn't welcome under Anna's wing. Yalta was an enemy; Communism, Capitalism, Fascism, and Nazism: enemies all. Because a person, even a communist person, even a signer of the treacherous treaty of Yalta, could never be Communism or the Yalta Treaty. Anna Bibko would never recover from wishing devastation upon Lemkovyna, from all her American hatreds.

In fact, Anna's policy towards Jews got the Mansion Inn featured in *The New Yorker*, then the *New York Times*, *Time* magazine, and, finally, *Life* magazine, which photographed Anna and my wife, both dressed in full Lemko garb, standing outside the Victorian mansion with their staff of post-war misfits, under the heading 'New World Unity, Old World Hospitality'. None of this was premeditated. Not once did Anna use the media's attention to draw attention to the plight of the Lemko people; a plight, it must be said, that she spent all of her non–Mansion Inn hours trying to draw people's attention to. This is only slightly baffling and only to those who do not know her. To Anna, *The New Yorker* was friv-olous, non-existent. *The New Yorker* was not President Dwight David Eisenhower. *Life* magazine was not the US Senate. The *New York Times* was not former Secretary of State Dean Gooderham Acheson. She had put *Life* magazine on the antique rose wood coffee table of the Mansion Inn for twenty years and she rarely saw anybody reading it, and those she saw reading it didn't look particularly important. They did not look like Vice President Richard Millhouse Nixon. Those that had time to look at pictures and read magazines looked like her late husband or, worse, like me. These were not people able to help anyone. We could not even help ourselves. Perhaps in this she was wise. People who read *The New Yorker*, she once told my daughter, like only stories. 'Pah! And what is that? Stories are no good at nothing.' The Lemkos didn't have a fully codified language. If one wanted something done one went to another Lemko who might or might not help get that thing done. One spoke. Life and thought were not abstract, or separate.

Obviously, Anna Bibko never approved of me and fully expected that, like all the fathers she'd ever known, in time I would kill myself.

'It's sad,' she would tell my wife, or son, or daughter. If asked to elaborate she would shrug.

I pretended to be other people. I sewed my own period-specific clothing. To compound these failings, I also, like a father, retreated to my study in order to peruse books, while my wife, mother-in-law, and my daughter worked to earn a living. I spent evenings drinking home-brewed mead, listening to recordings of Early Music. In Anna's experience, art led either to suicide or homosexuality. 'Nobody kills self or goes gay in Lemkovyna because in Lemkovyna nobody got books. Laugh, make funny. But in Lemkovyna only pysanka Easter eggs get painted – and get painted only gorgeously, color-fully, with many colors, because when someone tries to express himself with masterpiece Easter egg then village destroy egg and say, who is going to want that?'

June, until Tristan's birth, most acutely suffered her grand-mother's Lemkomania. June was forced to paint pysankas. June was taught to shout '*Chrystos voskres!*' ('Christ is risen!') as a greeting. To June went the task of remembering the Lemko dead; Anna, against our wishes, would tell the girl stories of her brief girlhood tenure in Lemkovyna, stories which never failed to end in mass-murder. But Lemkovyna was a fairy-tale world for my daughter, luckily, and the mass-murdering only real in the way that the wolf bloodlessly devouring Little Red Riding Hood's grandmother was real. It was June who took her the least seriously. June just thought she was nuts. She cared not a bit for Anna's past as she cared not a bit for my Middle Ages. June navigated between us, asserting her unformed, detached individuality. In this, of course, she was only following in her grandmother's American footsteps. Anna noted this, and pushed harder. 'I was as you, you know. I wanted to be American, to be something new and not like everything around me, everything that come before. Stupid parents, stupid Lemko village, stupid language. I tell you this. But this is wrong. OK, Little Miss USA with your super smiles. But someday maybe your friends and family are mass-murdered and you remember these things you find so full of funny and they will be very important to you. I hope not but –' and she would shrug.

In my more self-defeating moods, I see Anna as the only thing that ever really united my daughter and me – in the same way that it can be said that she was the only thing that eventually divided me from my son. Because from the moment of Tristan's birth, Anna relinquished June. June was not a Lemko. Tristan was a vindication, an answered prayer, redemption for the mass-murder it is not hard to imagine

Anna somehow blaming herself for. Even June acknowledged, in her particular way, that there was something odd between the old woman and my son. Never sharing a relationship that could even be considered cordial, Anna and I went into open warfare sometime after the boy's birth. Tristan was our battle-ground.

VI

Kids strut and bob past, propelled by their own laughter. They smoke cigarettes in a vaguely affluent, naughty manner. They enter Jazz Club Z. I've been in Prague long enough to know that the fact that these young people are smiling and talking aloud in public marks them as foreigners – and, anyway, they are every last one of them speaking English. My nose is conspicuously not noticed, and I must say that these days I really do prefer the honesty of an open stare. If I have learned anything in my sixty-three years, it is that one should strive to meet ugliness head-on.

I wait. Brazilian foibles being what they are, Max Werfel could be anywhere, involved in nearly anything. He is late, in any event. I nip into an earthen flask of mead.

Finally opening Jazz Club Z's seventeenth-century wooden door is like tearing off a bandage which has long been covering a particularly sensitive part of the body. In my case, something left to fester for two years. The door shuts behind me. I think: I have now entered the wound. I descend. Then I wince, thinking: you preposterous old man! Idiot! You haven't learned a goddamn thing!

I'm apprehended on an under-lit landing half way down the stairs. There, a girl behind a wooden table demands currency for the privilege of seeing my son.

'I'm a special guest,' I try. 'I'm Tristan's father.'

The girl exhales. 'Here is no Tristan.'

'My son,' I continue. 'He's performing tonight. Tristan Hecker. My name is Burt Hecker?'

This guardian of the underworld lowers her head to examine a piece of paper. 'Burt Hecker,' I say again.

Finally, she holds the piece of paper before my face. She says, 'You are not special.'

I rattle an international conspiracy of currency upon the table. German, American, Czech. The girl shakes her head, takes what is required, gives herself a tip, and stamps my hand with a purple smiley face. 'Please,' she concludes.

'Thank you.'

I had thought the cacophony I'd been hearing to be furious workers in another part of the building or, more likely, cataclysms from the cobbled street above. But the sounds are originating from the bowels of Jazz Club Z itself. I ingest a pinch of Betony (which, besides being a panacea for all ailments, is rumored to be particularly good against witches). I purchase two beers. It is a prank. It is Lonna's big joke. My son isn't in this Bohemia at all, he's still with his grandmother in Poland and this hellish miasma, this music, is Lonna's idea of a practical joke. But, no; how could even she possibly plan this? A worse idea occurs. It could be Tristan's joke on all of us.

Negotiating another stone passageway, I follow the noise to the arched, candlelit medieval wine cellar. Or dungeon. I note the heads of the young adults gathered here – mostly shaved – and the obscure shapes of the creatures producing the tumult. There are four of them, hunched over their instruments. The clamor is the accumulated woe of centuries of torment, deprivation, madness, death; the horror of the medieval world externalized in sound. I wait for my eyes to adjust to the candlelight. They do not. How old I feel. How quickly these young ones move, even sitting down; all around me, breathing smoke, chattering, nodding to the noise: a quickness in their very skin. I search the faces. Young, unformed, ecstatically stupid. They've just been released from wherever it was they began, and they're tumbling. I become lost in watching them laugh, finally free, grabbing at anything they can to mark their tumble, to soften its inevitable landing. It is imperative that I sit down. Tristan is nowhere to be seen. But I will wait. I drink my beer, then its lukewarm sequel.

Saint Bonaventure taught contemplation of atrocious death as a means of attaining spiritual purity. My guess is that the four men of the Sound Defenestration Collective, loitering more than standing, appear to have taken a lesson like this to heart. They are illuminated by candles and electronics. They casually, sometimes viciously, lash out at objects that at one time or another may have been instruments. Even the drummer, who, on closer inspection, turns out to be a female, doesn't play the drums in the normally prescribed manner – that is, for rhythm. Instead, she mostly just splashes a collection of cymbals and bells randomly, sometimes pounding out a tribal beat. There are microphones on these drums, I think, and their wires lead to a very tall fellow who stands behind an array of scientific experiments: this man is recording the drums and playing them back altered in tone and speed. They echo and explode. This is not the traditional folk music of the Lemko people.

The other two members, actually positioned behind the drums, are more difficult to see.

Undernourished and bald, the saxophonist keeps his back to the audience and the rest of his collective. I am no expert, but the sounds he makes are probably the focal point of whatever might be considered the Sound Defenestration Collective's song. He screams into the instrument – which, it soon transpires, is also connected to the voodoo of the tall gentleman's electronics, causing the screams to multiply like a host of angry ducks. When not screeching, this fellow induces his brass cornucopia to burp, sputter, skonk, and bray. Sometimes it is hard to tell whether the saxophone is making the noise or if it is not the man's mouth: there is growling, moaning, and what appears to be some kind of chanting. Occasionally, a genuine melody appears to escape from the instrument, but it's so quickly subsumed by the chaos around it to seem accidental, like the soul of the instrument attempting an escape from the torments of the song.

Lastly, there's a pianist. He's hirsute, and for this I like him best. Indeed, when I first registered his beard and hair I thought that he might be my Tristan. Not my son, thank God, the pianist plays forgetful, noncommittal chords. His demeanor and playing both rather like Bohemia's own King Charles IV, who was known to concentrate more on the whittling of sticks than on the myriad of supplicants presented before him. The pianist, I decide, has absolutely no idea where he is.

'Excuse me?'

It is a girl, a mistake. I ignore her, pretending not to hear. The girl says something else then that I couldn't hear even if I wasn't pretending to not hear her: a few sentences ending in a smile. Short yellow hair, pudgy face. Her nose mutilated in the tribal fashion. 'Mmm,' I reply. I turn away.

She touches my shoulder. 'Sorry,' she says. 'Hallo?'

'No thank you.' That she does not look like a whore is no way indicative of whether or not she actually is a whore. 'I don't have any money,' I say.

Brazenly, then, she launches her mouth towards the side of my skull. I clutch at my purse. She holds my head and says into my ear, *'You are Tim's dad, yes?'*

I look about. I nod yes, then no, then I say, quite loudly, 'What?'

'Tim's father.'

'No, no, sorry. What? I'm Tristan's father.'

'Tristan. Yes, this also.'

'Burt,' I shout. 'My name is Burt Hecker. I'm Tristan's father.'

'Lenka Vackova. I'm Tristan's friend.'

I look past her. 'But where is – you know Tristan? You know my son?'

'Moment.' She bends down to my ear again. 'I'm sorry. Is very loud. He was so nervous about tonight already, I never see him so nervous.'

Even in the fug of smoke and spilled beer, she smells of musk, cloves, nutmeg, cardamom. I cannot speak. She says, 'Is perfect to meet you finally. Welcome to Czech Republic.'

The pianist begins assaulting the small electronic keyboard, pecking it. But suddenly there is something else. I stand up.

Hildegard von Bingen's 'Columba aspexit – Sequentia de Sancto Maximino': the first piece on Gothic Voices' AD 1983 recording, *A Feather on the Breath of God*, a Hecker family favorite. Hildegard's voice. Tivona's voice. Lonna's. My girls from the chant workshop, all of them gently, almost perfectly transcribed into the terrible brass instrument. The saxophone. The sound sighs in slow, eternal exultation. The sound of the moon moving through the night sky. The rest of the Sound Defenestration Collective have ceased their agitation, rumble, and clang. The saxophone plays,

calor solis exarsit

et in tenebras resplenduit

unde gemma surrexit

in edificatione templi

purissimi cordis benivoli.[1]

Then in my ear, Lenka's voice. 'This is for you. All week he is nervous practicing this for you.'

His eyes dart, drowning in the sudden spiritual calm of his own music. His eyes so suddenly small. I sit again, I stand again, but he cannot see me. He has lost his glasses. He cannot possibly see without his glasses. His elbows and skinny arms, long legs, standing with that ridiculous instrument sticking out of a mouth and a familiar face that I've never ever seen before: glistening, pale, covered in sweat. Is this what his beard was busy creating all those years? That is my son's face? *The heat of the sun burned dazzling into the*

---

[1] *The heat of the sun burned dazzling into the gloom: whence a jewel sprang forth in the building of the temple of the purest loving heart.*

gloom. Frantically, I stare. Because his hair is gone, he has no hair, my son has no hair on his face or on his head, and chemotherapy is all I can think. Tristan is punishing himself. He is – that person up there with the saxophone is my son and my son has given himself cancer.

Tristan and his Sound Defenestration Collective entertain us for another hour. I collect myself. I proceed through a selection of fine Bohemian beers with Lenka, who keeps pace quietly by my side. Between the songs I do not applaud, as those around me are doing quite enough of that. It's not so wise an occupation, I think, to encourage the aural recreation of a fatal illness.

Shorn of his tresses, his beard, and his magnifying-glass spectacles, I'm seeing my son for the first time. This nakedness is as hard to endure as his saxophone's bright, violent bleating. His tabor, psaltery, clavichord, chordophones, lute – smashed to bits. My itinerant musician, my jongleur, spreading evil on a saxophone. How sick he looks without his beard, how young. How like his mother in those last days. It's like seeing them both again, but not seeing them. What have they become?

The band, relinquishing their instruments and leaving their amplifiers to replicate the sounds of an angry hive, weaves through the audience. Overhead, light bulbs ignite. My son draws near.

Lenka runs towards him. He pauses, several yards from his father, staring past Lenka while she speaks to him, while she points towards me. Tristan nods. Lenka leaves him and returns to my side.

The Sound Defenestration Collective are upon me. The

percussionist is Margot, from the USA. The hirsute pianist is Martin, from Prague. The tall gentleman is Honza, also from Prague.

Honza shakes my hand, soliciting my opinion on the night's entertainment. 'You've got to be kidding,' I say. I can hardly think. I watch Tristan talking to people across the room – talking to people, Tristan, my quiet boy, talking to so many people. I cannot account for it.

'Our performance?' Honza repeats.

Martin rolls his eyes, grooming his beard. I explain to Honza that it was ghastly. He is delighted.

'Improvisational music is for some complicated, not satisfactory. For your people it is rather too intellectual, I think. And so,' he opens his hands sadly.

'My people?'

'Americans,' he offers, as if the very word pains him. 'Your son is the only exceptional one, I conclude.'

Tristan, crowded by people, laughs affectedly. Hand movements equally exaggerated.

'Only exceptional what?' Margot pinches Honza's arm.

He laughs. 'Do not mind her, Mr Hecker, she is from California.'

'In California, people are orange,' Martin adds.

These are Tristan's friends?

Lenka touches my shoulder. 'I have to be home. But we're going to see you soon, yes?'

'What is going on?'

'You know, he's just coming, I think –' But she is embarrassed. Tristan is not coming.

Then he is there, standing above me. He extends his hand. And I shake it, my son's hand. But before I can stand, or cry, or laugh, or even begin to formulate a way of asking his forgiveness, Lenka says something about getting home, and, after also shaking my hand, she departs. Tristan hesitates only a moment before following her from the room.

You could feel him listening. That is something else about my son. Tristan often said that listening was a very difficult thing for him, and, judging by his demonstrative concentration, I believe that this was the truth. He never seemed aware that most people don't actually listen to one another, or only superficially at best. Or maybe he was only too aware. To my son, the spoken word was a crack in the mask, a rope from one drowning, confused organism to another; and he could discern meaning in the most banal of statements – in advertisements and political speeches, for example – and usually not the meaning the speaker intended. He almost always knew when you were lying. Some – Lonna Katsav, say – found this 'creepy'. But why and how to listen is perhaps the biggest lesson he has taught me and the one I'm most fundamentally unequipped to benefit from. It took Hildegard von Bingen and Tivona's chant workshop to bring me closer to Tristan's natural state of true listening, and even now I don't think that I'll ever be able to totally forget myself in another's presence.

What else? Tristan gathered flowers for the marble mantelpieces in Mansion Inn's guest rooms. That was his job. Tristan helped his grandmother with her potatoes. Tristan spent summers with his grandmother in Poland, after she moved back, dressing like a Lemko, perfecting his command of the Lemko tongue. Tristan read all of the science-fiction books his big sister recommended, and watched all of June's movies and television serials with her, under her nest of blankets, their heads poking out like two Easter eggs. He alone escaped June's troubled claws. Likewise, he didn't suffer much schoolroom bullying outside the typical ostracizing granted to any individual existing naturally on the periphery of the accepted modes of New World behavior. He simply didn't have many friends, preferring solitude or, failing that, the company of us, his family.

But loving Tristan often felt like loving something once removed. He could be cold and indifferent to others' suffering, especially if he was causing it. Even when he was small, there was the sense that he could leave at any time. That maybe part of him had already emigrated and was only waiting for the rest of him to catch up. Sandy, the pretty daughter of the Mansion Inn's electrician, and the only girlfriend my son ever had, once carried out a minor tantrum in our backyard, screaming, 'I can't take this anymore! Where are you? Hello?' seizing Tristan's hands and placing them on her breasts. I had watched from a window.

Tristan, then sixteen, had kept his hands where she had placed them. He was silent.

But 'Oh, you freaking shut up!' she screamed. 'Shut up! Shut up! Shut up! Shut up!' and she fled.

Eventually he did develop a sense of humor. This was shortly before his mother's death. Suddenly childlike, playful, he might break into song or do light-hearted impressions of people. He had the rare ability of amusing and even honoring the person he aped. His heart grew lighter as he aged. His grandmother would say that this was to be expected; the same had happened to her Lemko grandfather.

Once, I sought Tristan out across the Mansion Inn grounds. This was before Anna Bibko had moved back to Poland, so Tristan must have been about fifteen, maybe sixteen. I had decided that I needed his help preparing for a CTLR revel which was to take place that evening. I was in full medieval garb, though not yet my Eckbert Attquiet persona.

I found him, finally, across the street from the Mansion Inn, sitting with his grandmother on the edge of the Kayaderosseras Creek. He was carving something from wood. She was speaking Lemko. I paused, watching them. Both were smiling, oblivious to the occasional automobile that passed them by. Tristan looked so gentle, almost besotted with his old grandmother; and in a flash I saw Anna Bibko when she was still a little girl, before she had decided to be an American, long before her people and their homeland had been destroyed. She was telling my son stories in a most animated fashion, and she really resembled a teenager wearing an old woman costume, one that she could easily just slouch off whensoever she wished. Tristan would occasionally scoop some of his wood shavings from the ground and sprinkle them into the creek, and they would watch them float off before disappearing down the Queens Falls. Instead of letting well enough alone, I thumped across the road. I shouted: 'Tristan! Hey! You promised to help with the new batch of mead! The melomel!'

Grandmother and grandson flinched, Anna's face visibly graying, aging, her smile crackling back into her signature frown. Tristan stood up, ridiculous in his colorful Lemko folk costume. He did not say anything, looking between myself, Anna, and the curly snails of wood at his feet.

'Well, what are you standing there for,' I shouted. 'I need your help!'

'I love you too, Dad,' Tristan only said. And he sat back down with his grandmother, who could not for the life of her tell whether this round had been a victory or a defeat.

'Mr Hecker,' Margot says. 'Is he yours?'

I follow her finger to the outer-dark at the edge of the room. Instantly, I try and stand. Because there is Max Werfel, his round head beaming back at me like a spotlight. Standing, I collapse, catching something of mine on something else, possibly a chair, possibly Honza. Martin rises and prevents me from toppling. 'OK, it's OK, OK,' I hear my laugh. 'OK, it's OK. Drunk. Only drunk. Everything OK.' In the commotion, a woman appears. She is the same height as Max Werfel, hair short and black, skin glowing in a similarly infantile manner: she looks like a neglected, ill-intentioned wax museum version of Werfel. Sitting back down, I vaguely wonder why everyone is staring at me and not these two oddities. Werfel, it would seem, has successfully located his half-sister and, for whatever reason, decided to take the poor woman to meet me here in the dungeons of Jazz Club Z. I laugh, perhaps a touch manically, but I am genuinely happy for him. For them both.

The woman scans the room in understandable distaste. Werfel simply shines. Looking only at me, he begins explaining something important in German, while the woman translates this information into Bohemian. I nod dumbly. Honza or Martin translate the best they can into English. The gist of this conversation being computers, incredibly, and how Werfel used one to identify and locate his half-sister after discovering a photograph and a name in some of his father's old

Nazi memorabilia. I try to appear interested. Finally, citing the smoke, Werfel and his sister depart as quickly as they appeared, but not before instructing me to check out of the hotel tomorrow morning. It seems that I'll be lodging with Werfel at his half-sister's apartment. So be it.

The ghost of my wife watches all of this from the far end of the room. Bald again, and alone, she holds a cigarette to her thin lips and disappears for a moment behind its smoke. 'Kitty,' I say. I stand. But when she reappears she is holding a saxophone, and a boyish look of disgust.

My son sits across the table from me, drinking mineral water. Jazz Club Z has hollowed, and the few patrons it has managed to retain no longer look entirely capable of going anywhere else. That witch's familiar of an instrument rests curled in Tristan's lap.

'What is this, Burt?'

Tristan has never called me anything but Dad.

'I don't know,' I say.

'There's a surprise.'

This is not Domenico Ghirlandaio's Elderly Man's son. Sarcasm? 'What has happened to you?' I ask. He won't even look at me. Envy, wrath, gluttony, lechery, avarice and cupidity, pride, sloth . . . sipping his mineral water, holding a saxophone, refusing to look at his father. This is Tristan's evil twin.

'Lenka's mother is Lemko,' he offers. 'We'd been writing letters – to each other, Lenka and me. Pen pals. For over a – a long time, you know? Since we were little kids.'

'She seems very nice.'

'I never lived in Poland.'

The silence between us is the evil twin of our former silences. It sounds exactly the same but it is not the same.

I say, 'You look good, Tristan. Different.'

'Tim. People call me Tim now.'

The air is ripped from my chest. 'People.'

'What did you think of my music?'

'I don't know. Lemko folk music certainly has changed.'

'Did you like it?'

'Did you want me to like it?'

'I did,' he says, 'until I saw you.'

'Tristan –'

'Tim.'

I bring an empty glass of beer to my face. This is not happening. I become angry, greedy for that other thing, that lost thing that should be happening. 'And Anna,' I spit, 'your grandmother?'

'I see her.'

'Often?'

Tristan shakes his head. It is disgusting, my jealousy.

'How often do you see her?'

'Stop,' he whispers.

'Just a question.'

'After what you did. Why are you even here, Burt?'

'Why are *you* here?'

'Stop. OK. This is useless.'

I slam the glass on the table. 'This is not! Not useless! This is not useless! Look at me.'

'I can't do this.'

'Do what?' I say. 'I don't even know what this is.'

'Just leave.'

'What? Leave you here? You were – you used to be – look at you up there tonight, so lost up there, walking around trying to impress these base idiots, these morons, these low goddamn –'

'Then I'll go.'

'Don't. I'm sorry. There's so much to say. No, wait –'

He says something that I cannot hear.

'What?'

'June was right,' then even louder, 'I said, that June was always right.'

'I never claimed to walk without blemish.'

'Oh, grow up.'

'I love you.'

He pushes his chair back. He doesn't move. 'I spoke with – to Lonna. You're not better. Lonna said you were better. This knight-errantry, what is this, what do you expect? I'm not who you think. I'm not going to take care of you.'

'I thought I could help.'

'Please.'

'I sold it. The Mansion Inn.'

His eyes meet mine for the first time in two years.

'Everything, Tristan. I sold everything.'

'My name is Tim.'

'I have no place left to go,' I say. 'I thought that we might start again, you and me. Like before. Look at me, wait. It's important you know that it's not your fault. Your mother. That I don't blame you. Nobody ever blamed you.'

'You don't what?'

I indicate his shaved head.

He repeats, 'You don't *what*?'

'The cancer,' I whisper.

Tristan's saxophone hits the ground. It is not himself that he has blamed. He shouts something, my quiet boy. He grabs my arm from across the table and shouts something unspeakable.

Part Two
AD 1934–1996
Kitty

VII

I met Kitty in March, the month, according to Chaucer, in which the world began, when God first made man. I remember the melting of that month. AD 1965, apparently in a popularity contest with the loquacious AD 1964, had proclaimed spring a few weeks early. Creeks and rivers, greedy with runoff, turned brown and impatient, lifting the lips of their banks back to expose rocky grins. I remember watching from the window of my Queens Falls High School classroom. Even the trees seemed to be sweating the season off, or mourning its early passing, weeping, and for days the only things that didn't drip were the puddles themselves. They became ambitious. One or two looked like they'd actually manage to prolong their life as ponds.

I was a bad teacher. I was thirty years old. I had relocated to Queens Falls three years earlier in order to accept a position as a high school European history teacher, having been asked to resign from my short-lived reign at the Saint Mary's Catholic High School in Syracuse, New York. History doesn't mix well with mythology, being the lesson there. In Queens Falls, on the other hand, I barely taught at all. I had a New York State Teacher's Book, and this prevented me from doing much of anything except preparing the children for New York

State exams. History as dates, facts, and a scientific, easy-to-digest compendium of causes and effects. The effect, the light at the end of the tunnel in almost every case, the New York State Teacher's Book made quite clear, was Democracy. Something loosely lauded as the American Way of Life.

'Will this be in the examination, Mr Hecker?' was the limit of my students' interest in any given subject. If it was going to be in the test they took notes, if it was not going to be in the test they did not take notes. Their silent, depthless stares were unnerving. I told myself that they were not stupid – for how could the final attainment of thousands of years of human progress be stupid?

In the end, I simply got into the habit of writing the New York State Tests directly onto the blackboard, both the questions and the answers, and giving these peculiarly well-behaved, often good-natured teenagers a chance to write them down as well. This they did, assiduously. Still, on the day of the test, it was guaranteed that nearly one-third of the class came close to failing. These optimistic, truly gifted New Worlders were raised to look forward, not backwards. They would not repeat history. Hadn't they transcended it?

Some weeks after recognizing the extent of my folly in accepting the QFHS European history teaching position, I endeavored to remedy things by organizing the Living History Club, which I opened to all interested boys and girls. I made posters. I spent late nights and solitary weekends planning (though, to be honest, all my nights were late and all my weekends were solitary); and I barely kept my head above the flood of primary-sources from which I collected enough material to quench what I was certain was a whole young village of untapped interest and vague historical cravings –

cravings that the New York State School Board knew next to nothing about. Well, wouldn't I show them? I'd fill those gullets, I'd bring them history. It felt like a calling. Every Friday we would meet; then, when things took off, we would meet every day, each afternoon. Children of all ages from all different school districts would flock to my Middle Ages, and eventually the Living History Club would extend into a sort of national extra-curricular society, like the Boy Scouts or Little League. It was an idea whose time had come. I promised, in those posters, a type of weekly, proto-re-enactment event: medieval food tasting and feasting etiquette, clothing and armor workshops, even mock medieval trials and battles based closely on sources. Chaucer would be read aloud, twelfth-century art discussed, Early Music phonographic records listened to, and the world of heraldic arts explained. Someday, I hoped, we would hunt stags with authentic weapons. I even planned mock pilgrimages and, to titillate the youngsters, a mock heretic burning or two. 'Re-create history!' trumpeted the posters in my best Gothic lettering. 'Reclaim lost times! Journey through the Living Past!'

Not a single student joined. One little thing, cow-eyed and, I thought, almost desperately lonely, showed up that first Friday, alone, after school, an entire medieval feast set before her. I in my tunic brooding glumly behind a desk stacked with hand-copied piles of the Magna Carta, staring at the empty classroom I had done my best to decorate as if it were a thirteenth-century revel. Had I not made enough posters? I had certainly made enough food. Was my painstakingly accurate uncial lettering even legible? (It was not, someone later told me.) Sitting alone at her desk at the very back of the room and as far from me as possible, the girl had been too alarmed to even glance at the many foodstuffs I'd spent the better part of two weeks preparing. For my part, I could hardly bear to look at her, such was my shame. Those hectoring mazers filled with mustard, venison, plums, pomegranates, blankmanger, and eel. I think we both stared out the window. I do not know what she hoped for. Perhaps only an opportunity to meet new people, to make friends. Perhaps she really wished to learn about the Middle Ages and my own wretchedness chased her away. I still don't know why I couldn't reach out to that girl. I didn't have any friends either. The Living History Club could have worked with two. That wasn't such a bad start. I was a bad teacher. Of course, the girl asked if the Living History Club would be in the test. 'No,' I sighed. 'Oh,' she said, 'oh.' She ate not a thing and never returned. 'Thank you for attending. Fare thee well.' 'Bye, Sir.' Years later, Kitty chided me, saying that I had given up too soon, that I was boar-headed, obtuse, wildly unrealistic, and probably had no right teaching anyone anything. Kitty insisted that they were probably frightened of me, those boys and girls, wary of my nose and my longish hair (which had not yet fallen out), and, especially, my eyes when Ye Olde Obsessions were in ascendance.

In those days I lived in a book-stuffed rented room in the attic of an old farmhouse. I had no real friends, nor family, and Queens Falls had been the furthest I had ever traveled from my hometown of Syracuse, New York. Owing to a nature that had not yet found full expression in re-enactment and, therefore, had not yet found any means of expression at all, I left behind me a trail of perplexed semi-friends and semi-girlfriends, mostly fellow outsiders who had at one time or another reached out to me, only for me to push myself away as soon as something like intimacy began to develop. Nothing felt right. I liked people, and people often liked me, but not for the long, tedious stretches of time necessary for bonding or mating. I spent most of my time safely reading, abusing alcohol, and dreaming myself into some kind of life that would fit. Back in teacher's college I had had a friend for a few months, a slow, careful girl by the name of Susie, and Susie had confessed to me that she had always felt fundamentally wrong inside herself. She had always known, she said, since she could remember knowing anything, that she was actually a boy. She said that it was quite simple and obvious, this feeling. The same as knowing you have blue eyes, or that your hair is brown, she had said. She was not crazy. But she was so deeply unhappy, so unfulfilled, and I could not be around her for very long without becoming slightly panicked myself. By the age of thirty I had more or less resigned myself to not being what I was, whatever that might have been. Unlike Susie, my displacement was historical. I simply felt as if I were a remnant from something long since passed, and only ever half there in a modern world that I did my very best to ignore. The more I concentrated on reality, the less real it became. Back then it even made me angry. But that soon passed.

Even without the nose, I looked odd. In the conservative kingdom of upstate New York – where AD 1965 was still very much AD 1955, make no mistake – I was really quite radically made out. I was a compact, tightly wound man; and my hair, among those dated Korean conflict styles, was very much of its time. I resembled, people always told me, the percussionist from the Beatles, albeit with a larger nose. Of course, I had no interest in the Beatles or the social changes being instigated by the hair salons of our nation's urban centers. I wore my hair longish because of the Middle Ages; my garb, also, on the weekends, was as close to tunic-like as I thought I could get away with without being committed to an institution. I had nothing to do with the so-called counter culture apparently sweeping the nation, and thought neither positively nor negatively about it. Let it sweep. But people took me for a free-thinker, a hippie, so called, and it was useless pointing out that many of our nation's Founding Fathers had had far longer hair and more flamboyant manners of dress than I.

In any event, I gave up on my Living History Club and, weeks later, in last-ditch desperation, I formed the Queens Falls Historical Society. There were already several historical clubs and societies in nearby Saratoga Springs, but these mainly concerned Saratoga itself, horse racing, the Revolutionary War, and the amassment and appraisal of Victorian hoo-dads. I was interested in something a little more outlandish.

Towards the end of February, a woman named Anna Bibko contacted me. 'Dear President of the Queens Falls Historical Society,' her letter opened. 'I would like to teach you about atrocities.'

Included in the fifteen-page epistle was information pertaining to the Yalta Treaty, the Vistula Operation, the Molotov-Ribbentrop Line, the Lemko people, and a forty-page list.

MAKSYM, ANASTASIA – 14, breasts cut off, rifle shot to the neck
MAKSYM, MARIA – 18, stabbed with bayonet in eyes, gashed stomach
MAKSYM, YAROSLAV – 50, head split open

120

NECHYSTY, MYKOLA – 27, shot through the stomach,
burned alive
NECHYSTY, CATHRINE – 10 months old, burned alive

How could I say no?

The day of Anna Bibko's presentation, only five of us had
showed. My female companion, Marla, myself, and our three
Great War veterans. It was disgraceful. It was the first time
I had scheduled a guest speaker and I had gone to some effort,
as usual, preparing a variety of primary-source refreshments,
including a very tricky mazer of honey carrots, as well as a
selection of cloven fruit.

There were normally about twelve of us in the Queens
Falls Historical Society. We were a dysfunctional and unhappy
bunch. Each week we gathered in order to argue about what
we would argue about the following week, and I was not a
very persuasive leader: it was a pitiable failure. In fact, I was
not a leader at all, though I was the nominal President and,
as such, I was left each week with the task of cleaning up
both the physical and emotional vestiges of our increasingly
contentious meetings. Every one of us knew precisely what
the Queens Falls Historical Society was not. My medieval
faction wanted the Society to be something of a workshop
on the Middle Ages; but we were, as you might guess, the
most socially ill-equipped to state our case, so usually we
did not. We grumbled meekly and occasionally made painful,
fruity Old English speeches about this or that glory of the
medieval world. Shyly, however, and importantly, we'd started
meeting in private, even dressing in homemade medieval
garb. What would have been easy to do with children – as
had been my plan for the Living History Club – caused us

adults certain pangs of embarrassment, the like of which I imagine transvestites or others partaking in socially transgressive behavior might feel. Our three haunted Great War veterans wanted to talk of the Great War and those they saw killed and those who survived the Great War only to be killed later by things like boundless despair. I liked and thought I understood these elderly gentlemen, even the browbeating Lieutenant Michniewicz. They came because they had nowhere else to go. All that history but no place to put it.

The veterans had arranged themselves in the corner of my Queens Falls High School classroom, obsessing over a faded map of France. Marla fidgeted at my side, actively uncomfortable and overdressed. I was curious to see how she reacted to atrocities.

'Well,' she sighed. It was a question.

Marla taught folkloric US History to elementary school children. She obsessed about the order of the US Presidents, occasionally quizzing me in bed, imagining fantasy orders, rankings from best to worst. She knew which First Ladies were bitches and which shrews, and all of the Founding Fathers' dates of birth by heart, as well as the basic gist of all of the fourth-grade New York State textbook principles on our beloved Union. These she interpreted, when pushed, as eternal. Johnny Appleseed, George Washington and the Cherry Tree, Plymouth Rock, the Pony Express, Thanksgiving, Betsy Ross, and hiding under desks in order to survive Atomic Warfare. Marla was recently divorced from Queens Falls High's very own Coach Buck. Several years my senior, she had a ten-year-old boy I would never meet, also named Buck. Marla and I had been involved for four or five months, and

I do not now wish to be so unkind. She had a forgetful, watercolored way about her eyes.

I'd met Marla at a PTA meeting. I didn't want to be there and neither did she. 'We're both drunk,' she had said, drawing close to me, brushing a breast against my arm. 'Drunk teachers.' Also, at that time, I was a virgin.

'You are so special, Burt. I mean it.' Later on, weeks later, she kneaded my thigh and we discussed what I was. 'So smart. So different from the other guys, you know? Intuitive.' Meaning, I thought, that Marla was willing to overlook my nose and inexperience if I was willing to be discreet about us in front of 'other guys'. Specifically, her ex-husband, Coach Buck.

She had a deal.

Because I had never really touched a naked female before and, more importantly, did not immediately force her mouth onto my penis, Marla also decided that I was sensitive. I was not and have never been a particularly sensitive or empathetic individual. I simply didn't yet know that I was supposed to force Marla's mouth onto my penis. It took weeks before I figured this out. Coach Buck, she said, used to bump her around. *Wife-beating, in the Middle Ages, was a husband's sacred right, but if he availed himself of it while under the influence of drink or in a bad humor, the consequences for the couple could be serious.* This, or something like this, I told Marla in an attempt to give her past troubles a little historical context one dark and stormy night. I had thought that we were both creatures of history. I explained that in the Middle Ages an adequate diet was usually offered as protection against this evil. But Marla had told me in no uncertain terms that she was through dieting, and if I didn't like her body then I knew where I could stick it.

123

I found that she entered into such relations with the gusto of a third-century Christian martyr. Eyes clamped, she'd wantonly thrash and shriek as if I were ravishing her, and not vice versa. In the beginning, I often wondered if I were causing pain and halted the stabbings, asking if she were OK, which only made her thrash all the more until I got the hint. She was generally OK. I wasn't too inexperienced to know that by being taken by Burt Hecker, the shut-in with the facial disfigurement, she was punishing Coach Buck. Nor did I care much. (Hildegard von Bingen believed that semen was a type of blood which sexual desire and the moon whipped into foam.) I grew to greatly enjoy and even somewhat crave the solaces of Marla's lower part, and I have little desire to relate here the many unconsummated romantic failures I had accumulated over the preceding decade. Needless to say, I had no right to be choosy.

'What is it?' Marla asked.

The schoolroom clock was worn raw by stares; and you couldn't look up at the big Puritanical face of it and not feel the countless years of young eyes reflected in it, urging it onwards. It was a dark, old spirit that didn't so much mark time as bequeath it.

'Clocks,' I said.

Marla rolled her eyes.

I can still picture Anna Bibko as she was, entering that room. Exactly on time, right on the click. The way she was impervious to nearly everything around her, including the remains of the Queens Falls Historical Society.

She was elderly in the way of fourteenth-century donjons and large, celebrated trees. She moved in yanks: pausing, yanking herself forward, pausing, looking, and yanking herself forward again until she had found the best vantage point by which to assert her history. Her hair was gray, thick, curly. The wrinkles on her skin rippled outwards from her large blue eyes, as if they'd been dropped down into her face from a great height. Most strikingly, she was dressed in the bright, complex, and wildly festive manner of a Lemko peasant, pre–Vistula Operation. She donned a decorative blouse spattered with intricate embroidery, cherry-colored velvet, red needle work, brass buttons, and a short yellow sheepskin wool-lined jacket.

Our Great War veterans stared, sitting at their children's school desks, the fluorescence imbuing their uniforms with ghostly, nightmarish menace. They were monstrously sad. I did not invent historical re-enactment, as some today claim. Reality is re-enactment.

'Goodnight,' Anna read from her prepared presentation. 'My name is Anna Bibko and I am Lemko.'

'Oh, my,' Marla whispered.

I stood, proffering my hand. I had prepared a few words of my own but, as I was to soon learn, there was no time for formalities in the face of atrocities. The veterans began applauding. She had actually gotten their attention, I thought. Goodness God. Perhaps they had seen her kind during the Great War, or, more likely, perhaps they thought this was all some kind of USO Entertainment.

She began, with no further ado, to recount the history of the Lemko people. She surged, sucking the whistle from a veteran's lungs. Everyone hushed. Even the clock, I thought, tempered its occasional click. Anna Bibko did her people no disservice. She gave life to their dead, weight and shape to times lost. She spoke with a spare, odd grace and authority. In fact, so much did her story involve us, and so immediate and surprising was that involvement, that her ridiculous costume slowly, perceptively, over the long telling, became necessary. Even noble. By the end of her presentation, with hundreds of her people murdered, and untold thousands evicted from their mountains, their culture, and their past – shipped off to the Happiest Countries in the World and their mines and factories – Anna Bibko and her past were a good deal more real than our surly, florescent present. Time was regained, momentarily, if not redeemed.

Thus was born my medieval re-enactment society, then and there, with Anna Bibko as its midwife. If she only knew. It wasn't an idea, necessarily, it was something that had always been there, in me, something that I finally chose to acknowledge. I suddenly knew what I had been looking for, and what I would do. It could be done.

'Questions?' the Lemko asked.

I had a million.

Marla, genuinely moved, squeezed my hand. The veterans even seemed fully engaged with the subject at hand. The one with the watery eyes had made angry huffs, and slapped the desk in front of him many times during Anna's history, ready to lead an army back into the past to safeguard the Lemko people from those Polish bayonets.

'Thank you very much. It was a very interesting presentation, Mrs Bibko,' I said. Nobody had any questions. I tapped Marla's leg. She asked if there was anything we could do to help the Lemko people, and I nodded eagerly. So Anna Bibko told us, quite seriously, what we could do if we were or knew anyone who was the President of the United States of America, or maybe a Senator, or Vice President. Marla, bless her, took notes.

Lieutenant Michniewicz stood up. He announced his name, rank, and company. Sheepishly, his comrades looked elsewhere.

'This is Polish second name, yes?'

'American, ma'am,' the Lieutenant said. I noted the pugnacious silver flask on the desk before him. 'Michniewicz is an American name.'

'Your question, American?'

'Ma'am, my question? How dare you come in here and try,' his voice like soggy thunder, 'try and spread goddamn communistical propaganda? I should know, see. Polish people never did nothing like you said!'

'How you know?'

'How do I know?' Lieutenant Michniewicz laughed. 'You're a goddamn communist, ma'am. There's how I know!'

I stood up to intervene but the Lemko stopped me. Her sudden smile chilled like a mouthful of snow.

My head rested upon a desk on which had been carved, 'All shall be well; and all shall be well; and . . .' by me, in desperation, in defiance, with the kitchen knife I should have used to cut the medieval food I had prepared but nobody had so much as glanced at. Marla had gone to the Teachers' Room kitchen to put the stuff away, and good riddance to them both. Down empty halls her high heels echoed, backfiring like dainty mufflers. I hated the school at night. I hated the school during the day. I had no friends. My occupation was, as they say, unfulfilling and undignified; and my not infrequent attempts at fostering a community here in Queens Falls were even worse, often culminating in violence. I was having an affair with a woman who thought what my small, book-stuffed rented room needed was a plant. Ten minutes ago, I'd had to prevent a crippled World War I veteran from attacking – and thus humiliating himself by getting brained by – an elderly Lemko woman in full folk costume. The clock gave us 8:23 p.m. Take it back, I thought. 8:23 p.m. was utterly superfluous.

'Excuse me,' said a voice. 'Need some help there?'

I looked up, knife in hand. I saw a tall woman.

'What?' I said. Gigantic, actually.

'Help vandalizing New York State School property. I won't tell. Got some paint back in my car, actually.' She was not joking. Her face opened into the most vulgar smile that I had ever seen, and it was clear that if I'd asked her to collaborate with me in defacing more Queens Falls High School desks with medieval clichés, well, I believe that she would've been enthusiastic, as well as capable. Premature white streaks shot through her dark hair like jet-plumes. She wore a billowing, loose dress of paisley.

I said, 'I'm quitting, anyway.'

She glanced back at my classroom door, and read, 'Mr Hecker, Historian.' She added, 'Quitter.'

'Teaching, I mean.' There it was: and I don't now think that I really knew I was quitting teaching until I had said it, until I had notified that stranger. 'I guess I just decided to quit.'

'Just now?'

'Just now.'

I must have seemed a little out of sorts, more than a touch befuddled, because the woman laughed. It was tremendous, eruptive, but not at all sarcastic or unkind. There's never been another human being with such a laugh, as there has never been another human being to find such boundless joy in the simple, wondrous absurdity of everything and everyone.

'I'm sorry. But you just look so perfect there, so naughty and sad with your little knife. Just came to, you know. To thank you. It's good that you let her speak. I only hope she behaved herself. She had that look coming out to the car and I just wanted to poke my head in and make sure there weren't any black eyes in here. Guess not if you do these things armed,' she winked. I put away the knife. 'You can't know how important these sort of evenings are to my mother. To me, too, I guess. It gets her out of the house. I was there, once, when I was a little girl, just in case you're wondering if it really exists – or existed. It did. Lemkovyna. Mom's crazy, but not like that.'

I had no idea where to go with what I had been given. 'It was a very nice presentation,' I managed.

'Nice?'

'Well,' I shrugged. I grinned. And Anna Bibko's daughter erupted again. It was sink or swim, so I jumped in and laughed. My high titter complimented her deep, gusty mirth. Then, when our duet seemed to be dying down, I cleared my throat manfully. 'I'm just sorry we had such poor attendance.'

Behind her, written on the blackboard in Anna Bibko's strident hand was, 'LEMKOVYNA: LAND OF EARTH'S FIRST EASTER EGG, LAND OF COMMUNIST ATROCITIES'. This was probably what had set poor Lieutenant Michniewicz off. Hard of hearing, or just a bad listener, he'd no doubt thought that Lemkovyna had invented both the Easter egg and communist atrocities.

'I told her,' she sighed. 'But she's convinced about those eggs. She's really got it in her head that if more Americans knew about all the pretty Lemko Easter eggs they'd go liberate Lemkovyna. God knows, maybe she's right.'

I made a joke then, and not a bad one. Something to the effect of that it might be better to let the military think that they were going to liberate the Easter Bunny. Then, following that, another less successful joke about sending the US Marines on an Easter egg hunt: and Anna Bibko's daughter touched my shoulder as she laughed, more at me than with me, I think, but not in an entirely negative way. I was funny, her touch said, even if my jokes were not.

'1946,' the blackboard also said, 'BIESZCADY COUNTY. 34,026 LEMKO PEOPLE DEPORTED.' There followed a grisly and detailed list of the dead.

For a moment, we tested a silence. The nothing was comfortable. More than that, it wasn't lonely in the least. I felt perfectly engaged and encapsulated by that minute of March 6, AD 1965, more so than any minute I could ever remember. 8:37 p.m. And I wondered if we could make it to 8:38 together, and what that might be like. The future.

She said. 'Nice to meet you. Finally.'

I'd forgotten to ask her name.

'Nice to meet you too,' I said, still sitting at a school desk for children. I was, I suddenly feared, far too short to stand. 'Thank you,' I continued. 'For meeting with me.' I felt like hitting my head against the desk.

But she laughed, almost crossing her eyes. 'You're welcome, Historian. By the way, if Mom comes back and starts up about running for the United States Congress, you, Mr Hecker,' she said, pulling out a pen from her purse, 'are to call me. Immediately.' This was, I believe, long before it was common for people to write things on other people's arms.

'I could write it on the desk too,' she laughed, putting her pen away. 'It's just that she really doesn't have the stomach for it,' and she turned. She began walking towards the door, then out the door.

'Stomach for what?' I called, hoping to hold her, thinking: I have another arm, write something on my other arm!

'For a congressional election,' she said, winking and closing the door. Then, through the door's window, just over the 'Mr Hecker, Historian' sign, she reappeared, making her hand into a phone. Call me, she mimed.

Marla returned.

'What on earth?' she said.

I was staring at my arm. 'Nothing.'

'You cut yourself?'

'It's –' I said. 'I'm fine.'

'I told you about the knife.'

'It's nothing.'

Marla picked up my arm. She snorted. 'Kitty Steed,' she read. '793-8354.' Obviously, either Marla didn't think that Kitty posed any threat whatsoever or, what was more likely, Marla simply didn't care. 'The stories I could tell you, boy. Kitty Steed. Never married, which isn't to say that she never tried. I thought that's who I saw skipping down the hall. I mean, that dress at her age? Talk about homemade.'

131

VIII

I splashed through the roadside puddles, potholes, and ponds, dousing Marla's legs with my sloppy joy. I had no stomach for the sexual act that evening. The air was too clean. To our right, the Kayaderosseras Creek gurgled and poured invisibly. It sounded like its neck had been cut. There was no moon. Nothing but the two of us, walking one after the other, alone, down the black bank of Route 29 under an excessive spill of stars.

A car passed, wetting us. Marla yelled, 'Inconsiderate! Inconsiderate!'

It was a twenty-minute walk from Queens Falls High School to my rented room. Marla's own house was closer. Stomping a puddle, I accidentally splashed her again.

'What are you, deficient? Hold up, would you?' she said. 'I'm drowning back here!'

'Then take your heels off,' I said. 'It's a wonderful night. You want to break your ankles?'

'Some gentleman. What is with you all of a sudden?'

I splashed her again.

'Burt! I swear to God.'

Then again.

Then one of Marla's high-heel shoes collided with the back

of my head. I scrambled, running away. The other shoe hit me in the shoulder before tumbling into the Kayaderosseras.

'I'm sorry,' she said. She'd started to cry. 'That was rude.'

I brought a broken heel to her.

'Good to know I haven't lost my aim,' she half-laughed. She took the shoe, sobbed, and tossed it at a mountain. 'Coach Buck. The things I used to throw at him. You're lucky, Burt. Once, I got him right over the eye with a television.' Marla was really laughing now. 'He was asleep.'

I don't think that I'd ever liked her more.

'Your feet,' I said, after another minute of walking. Her bare feet punched puddles. 'They must be cold.'

'I should have gotten a ride with Mr Shepard.'

'Who?'

'The veteran. The one with the eyes.'

In the darkness, I listened to Marla struggle behind me. 'I'm sorry,' I said.

She didn't deserve mud, and I didn't deserve her. She was lost. Wasn't she following me? Who in their right mind would follow me? It wasn't revenge Marla wanted with Burt Hecker; not for revenge did she claw, scream, and pull me down each night, holding me tighter the more I drifted away. She had chosen me because, for whatever reason, she had actually wanted me. Marla liked me. Until then, until I heard the gastric slop and suck of her bare feet in the mud, I had never even considered that a possibility. She had actually convinced herself that I was what she was looking for. She was not stupid, just over simplified. Damn me for letting it go so far. She had tried to understand me. She, at least, knew she was sinking; she knew when to grab, just not who. Her heels, dress, the hysterical reds and blues of her make-up, perfume, jewelry: a thirty-seven-year-old divorcée's attempt at not being alone, of trying to get something, someone, to stick. It was all for me. I was supposed to help her, and her me. That costume wasn't ridiculous, it was hopeful, and she'd taken her heels off and thrown them at my head in order to wake me up, the heels she had chosen hours before, standing alone at her mirror preparing herself for someone who didn't think she had a brain in her head.

'It wasn't a good evening, was it?' I asked.

'I don't know. Wasn't what I expected, I guess.'

I knew, or thought I knew, what she expected. The two of us trudged onwards. 'I'd carry you,' I began.

'But I'm too fat.'

I turned back, stopped. 'But I'm too weak,' I snapped. She was not too fat. 'I'm quitting,' I said. 'Look, I wanted to tell you before I told anybody else.'

'What do you mean "quitting"?'

I told her. I had enough money saved up for a year of nothing, I knew. But I was not going to do nothing. I was going to re-enact the Middle Ages. I was going to call Kitty 793-8354. 'It was all a mistake,' I said. I thought of Anna Bibko in costume, and how the truly foolish and absurd are the ones who don't do exactly what they want and how they feel. I wasn't happy but I would be soon.

'You're right. It's not really working,' Marla said, or asked. 'Me and you.'

'I don't know.'

'Is it working between us?' There was hope in Marla's voice.

I shook my head no.

She became quiet. Then, 'That's what I thought,' she

said. Surprising me again, from behind, she rubbed my hair affectionately. 'Probably need someone more your age, huh?'

'Maybe,' I said, and I felt the blood drain from my face.

But she only laughed. 'There's what I'll miss about you. That right there. You're just too fucking weird, you know that?'

'I still want to see you,' I said. Marla, I realized, possibly too late, was my friend.

She said, 'You don't know what you want, Burt.'

The car glided to a sloshing stop some feet ahead of us, its red taillights turning the water to wine. Kitty Steed called to us from the window.

She said, 'Marla, your shoes?'

'I had to throw them at Burt.'

Kitty drove a Corvette. I squeezed into the backseat, while Marla took the front. They were around the same age, old schoolmates I gathered. Marla was a fountain of pleasantries, a modern mess of neutral inauthenticity. But I could no longer blame her. She was in pain, and she was trying her best with what she had, which tonight was little more than a lot of mud between her toes. It was obvious that Marla found Kitty odd, and that Kitty found Marla dull. They were both only partly correct. But still, I wasn't paying attention when we pulled into Marla's driveway, and she got out. She slammed once and then opening the door with a comic flourish, she slammed it again in order to get my attention. This was deemed pretty droll. 'The Historian's never been in a horse-less carriage before,' said Marla. 'He's in shock.' Marla's house looked like a jack-o'-lantern. She came to my side of the car, touched the window and mouthed either, 'Good luck' or 'You fuck'. Then she sang, 'Thanks, Kitty. Tell your Mom I hope she gets her homeland back!'

I got out of the car, bade Marla farewell, and ducked into the front seat of Kitty's Corvette. I sat as high in the seat as possible.

'Marla,' Kitty said, and we were off. 'Boy, I could tell you stories. But isn't she married to that lumberjack?'

I felt sucked into the oncoming rush of road, the life of it; the sweep of the lights freezing the countryside, startling it in the act, making slow flashes of the puddles and potholes. This was not the way to my farmhouse apartment. 'Divorced,' I said. 'Coach Buck.'

Kitty laughed. 'That makes you?'

Confused.

'None of my business,' Kitty said. 'Sorry.'

'It's only –'

Kitty lit a cigarette. 'Only my big mouth.'

I told Kitty that, until four months ago, I had been inexperienced in the ways of love. Kitty's laughter almost shook us off the road. Her cigarette jumped from her mouth, and its wicked little red eye made for her sandaled feet. She stamped at it, bumping the automobile nearer to oblivion. 'The ways of love,' she repeated. Things eventually stabilized and I felt very strange indeed. I felt as if I could tell this person anything, almost as if I were supposed to.

Turning down another dark, rolling country road, Kitty said, 'So, let's get this out of the way.' She looked me full in the face.

'My nose,' I said.

'Is it fatal?'

I laughed. 'Is it contagious, you mean.'

Kitty didn't deny it. She reached over, touched it. Marla had always gone out of her way to avoid my nose touching her skin or anything that might come in contact with her skin. Every time I returned to her house there were new pillowcases, new sheets, and new towels to be sullied by my admittedly diseased-looking proboscis.

'Feels more rubbery than rubber,' Kitty mused. 'It's nice. Better question, then. Permanent or temporary?'

'Permanent.'

'Good. You don't drive?'

'Not really.'

'Meaning?'

I told her, more or less, what that meant. I made it all sound somewhat amusing, charming even; and I wondered why I had never thought to try and make my eccentricities sound funny before.

'I've seen you around, you know,' Kitty said. 'Well, who hasn't? Nobody knows what to think of you. Walking up and down the highway every day, hauling those books. That nose, your shaggy hair. Personally, I've always thought how sweet you looked. But a lot of people around here aren't used to such a hairstyle and think you're a vagabond, or a Beatle. They take the British Invasion very seriously,' Kitty was enjoying herself. 'They're simple people and it scares them.'

Then, at the exact same time, in almost the exact same manner, we stopped, looked at each other, and said, 'Ringo Starr'.

9:23 p.m.

The road rolled. Signs gave us numbers and jumping deer,

but they never, not once, told us to stop. Ringo Starr had been more intimate than sex.

Kitty turned the headlights off. But it was more like she had flicked the stars on, and for one meditative moment, as the car buckled up invisibly over some hill, it seemed as if the stars were our only destination. Kitty, again, guffawed. She honked the horn. 'Scared?' she asked.

'No.'

But maybe she was, because in a few minutes the head-lights turned Queens Falls back on. You couldn't have both Queens Falls and the stars, in Kitty's automobile it was either one or the other. There was no turning back.

'I grew up at an orphanage, I was raised by nuns,' I told her.

'You're kidding me.'

I was not.

I told Kitty about the Latin. The fake Gothic arches and the fake Gothic morals, the genuine stone hallways, hollow and cool, and the genuine feeling, even though I was in Syracuse, New York, that the past breathed through this architecture and ritual. The feeling that time moved differ-ently inside different modes of thought, of life, inside different buildings. I was, I told Kitty, from someplace else entirely. Rain falling on stone, all those gloomy statues with their staring secrets. The high Gothic walls with their windows, and the candle constellations we put up there every Christmas, the muffling snow, all that sourceless winter light – no, I told Kitty, actually it wasn't fake at all. The mysterious history books and the nuns, many of them intelligent as well as kind, who had abandoned me to reprints of medieval illuminated manuscripts; and their music, their chant, sitting alone in that New York Gothic, listening to their parched and puckered and unworldly souls pour out in Latin which was anything but dead. I told Kitty of the other children who beat me, pitied me, tried to get me to play like them; the other boys, always bigger than me, even when they were smaller, outside with cigarettes and cursing, their footballs and swaggering Major League dreams of automobiles, motion pictures, jazz and war and ice cream; scuffing the dirt with their charity-shop sneakers, dreaming of buying things with money, all that money they'd someday gain control of once they got the hell out and joined the century the orphanage did its best to deny, and for good reason.

I told Kitty much more. Things which I once thought defined me, but really only helped form me, which is an important distinction. My mother, a devout Catholic, had died shortly after my birth, or during my birth. Nobody would tell me anything about my father, who had likely raped her, and was quite possibly her father, or grandfather, or so I used to imagine in my own well-stoked Gothic manner back when those things seemed so awfully important. Decades ago. How long ago that was now. My mother's name, I told it to Kitty. It left my lips for the first time in my life and I felt nothing. I could, I knew, trace her family if I wished. But it wasn't my history anymore. No, it was never mine to begin with.

I liked Kitty's listening. It was aware, without hamming up the sympathy or her presence in the proceedings. She listened like our son someday would, like a fine musician. I would have stopped the story at the first coo, the first audible or physical signifier of sympathy. Instead, she listened, and so did I. It was like hearing my story for the first time. Re-enacting memories and feelings I'd had but hadn't bothered with in many years. It was almost boring.

'Then you became a teacher,' Kitty said. We were in New Hampshire now for all I knew. The road just kept coming.

'It was either that or become a priest.'

'But this was out of the question?'

'I never had the faith. Even when I thought I did, I didn't. Not really. I memorized the saints, you see, hagiography being my first love.' I told Kitty of those saints. How the medieval people believed that Saint Cyriac had a pet devil he kept on a chain, Saint Denis and his removable head, how Saint Maur gave you gout, Saint Pius made you lame, Saint Vitus made you dance, Saint Fiacrius was lord of the ulcer, and how poor Saint Erasmus was perpetually disemboweled. I had loved their stories and, to the great chagrin of my nuns, the history of their corporal remains. The saint pieces. How saint hearts, bones, hair, lungs, fingers and breasts and toetails and tongues spread all over Europe, being squabbled over and founding trade routes, towns, churches, causing wars even. Massacres on occasion. I told Kitty how the saints were the comic-book superheroes of medieval Christendom, the first comic-book heroes. Some kids had Superman, I had had Saint Anthony, the Fire Demon.

Kitty looked at me funny.

'Faith was never for me,' I concluded. I laughed.

'Good for you.' It was obvious that she had a rational dislike for religion. This made me slightly sad, as if someone you loved disliked a parent you yourself knew to be rather terrible and insane, but loved anyway.

'I don't know,' I said, in defense of my stubbornly anachronistic nuns, and their quiet, perfect convictions. Their nobility and patience of purpose. 'I've been away from The Abbey for well on ten years now and it still seems like I'm on vacation, that I'll be called back. That I'll have to go back eventually. I don't think I've ever properly adjusted to the outside world. I don't think I've ever felt that it was particularly necessary.'

'The twentieth century.'

'As if any day now I'll have to return. Sometimes I dream about it. Returning. Often, actually. I guess, growing up, you could say that I had some peculiar role models.'

Kitty gave me a cigarette. 'Burt, are you going to ask me where I'm taking you?'

'No.'

The two of us drank whisky into the early hours of the morning until I tried marijuana and fell promptly asleep. When I awoke, Kitty lay curled next to me on her sofa. She had removed her clothing.

That first evening. Kitty, once in her own environment, which was surprisingly conservative given her mode of behavior and manner of talking, opened up. 'My turn, Historian,' she said. I shared normal tobacco cigarettes with her, one after another, if only to touch her fingers, which lingered on mine with each pass. Kitty told me about the Mansion Inn and her mother; about visiting Lemkovyna when she was four, the nineteenth-century American novelists and poets she loved, the first man she almost married, the second man she almost married, and her father who wouldn't have approved of either. Slowly, I saw the reality she'd made for herself out in the middle of this teeming nowhere, running a bed and breakfast inn on the outside, and cultivating a solidarity on the inside. 'I've always felt I was preparing for something,' she told me. 'The older I get, the more terrifying that is.' Kitty was joyous in everything, even loneliness. Even futility. Kitty laughed at my stories and observations, which came freely in her company; and when she had asked me why I hadn't become a real historian, or an archaeologist, I even told her the truth. I wasn't smart enough. 'You're too dreamy, Burt,' she said, then laughed so hard she frightened me, adding, finally, as an annex to her madness: 'I'm sorry. Funny thing is I meant it. I really think that's the best way to describe you. But it's one of those words you're not allowed to say. Dreamy.'

She played me phonograph records, shyly excited that I'd never heard a single one. Bob Dylan mostly. But she also had a small box of very old records which had belonged to her father, Henry Steed. She'd heard her father's voice so rarely as a child, seen him so rarely before he took his own life, that nowadays, when she thought of him, of his face, she saw instead the wild wigged Europeans gracing the cover of these records.

'Which one do you want to hear?'

I flipped through them. Henry Steed had nothing predating Bach.

'I guess this Bach will have to do,' I said.

'Don't look so glum.' She held Bach in her hands, thinking. 'Nope. Actually, no. Not yet, sorry. I don't think you're ready to hear my father yet.' I would not be allowed to listen to those records for many years.

Breakfast we ate at noon across from the Mansion Inn, at the Mill Pond, beside the almost medieval ruin of the Excelsior Mill, there in all that sun and dripping, breathing in March's best imitation of June. Queens Falls itself beneath our dangling, bare feet. I should've been teaching at that very moment, so we made that our joke and I stood before her and the Mansion Inn and lectured about European History, primarily, if I remember correctly, the Papal Schism of the fourteenth century. Frequently, Kitty would raise her hands and ask questions in a silly voice. I told her about how I dressed up in medieval clothing sometimes, secretly, in the woods, with other members of the Society. Kitty laughed, saying that that didn't surprise her. Her mother had been re-enacting history for over fifteen years. I told her about the idea of starting a medieval re-enacting community and we spent some time deciding on an appropriate name. She proposed The Weirdos.

'Will you join?' I asked her, having decided on the Confraternity of Times Lost Regained as a fine enough moniker.

'No way, are you kidding? Not me,' she said. 'But I'll help you cook. Those regurgitated carrots I saw Marla carrying down the hall last night looked pretty sorry.'

'They were historically accurate.'

'So are lice.'

'That's not the point,' I said.

'Right. The point is you didn't even try and kiss me,' Kitty said. 'Not once all evening.' To kick the point home, a breeze swept through her long, white-streaked hair.

I chewed my toast. The bloated creek at the bottom of the waterfall exposed the roots of trees. They twisted like boa constrictors. 'This is good toast,' I said. I smiled.

Kitty laughed. 'You've seen me naked but you haven't kissed me,' she continued.

'Toast,' I said.

'Kiss,' Kitty insisted. 'You can't chew that toast forever. Wow, Burt. You're so square you're hip, you know that?' She made a diagram. On one side was hip, on the other side was most decidedly not hip. I was on the most decidedly not hip side but so far over that I had circled back over to the hip side. 'Truth is, when I first saw you walking Route 29, before someone told me you were the new history teacher, I thought you were a painter. How romantic, right?'

I kissed her. I kissed her poorly. Gently, Kitty pulled herself back.

'I'm sorry, I –' burned with shame.

Kitty stood up and did a funny little dance. 'Wow,' she said.

Six months later we eloped in Syracuse, New York, deep within the steady, bracing Gothic dusk of the orphanage everyone called The Abbey. The only guests were those medieval re-enacting nuns I'd come to think of as ancestors, role models existing concurrently in the past and the present, and three dozen little boys who couldn't sit still. They lived in the future. Of course, everything was smaller than I remembered, more mean. Mean little prayers, scattered and mumbled and fudged, and all those little boys running around. Kitty and I had brought them fourteen gallons of ice cream for the wedding reception, and we didn't stick around to see even half of it consumed.

To my initial shock and disappointment, Anna Bibko despised me. The old Lemko had pulled herself out of poverty, and her daughter seemed to want to pull herself, and everything, gleefully back down into it; at least Anna's useless, romantic husband had had the good sense to be wealthy and suicidal. Me? I was unfathomable. I had disparaged her only child. The Confraternity of Times Lost Regained, whose meetings and workshops we held on the Mansion Inn's grounds, quickly became something of a phenomenon. 'Who knew there were so many historically displaced people in upstate New York,' Kitty joked. But she was right. Meanwhile, Anna Bibko became silent as the knife that slices your neck. Our histories clashed. My medieval garb and ways belittled Anna's own re-enactment, both in exposing the lunacy of it as well as highlighting and spitting on its supposed purer purpose. In those days I was as eager to seek her council as she was to snarl. Kitty, for her part, and as usual, was untouched. Her mother was her mother and it wasn't worth worrying about or trying to change. 'Just don't kill yourself,' Kitty told me. 'I'll never hear the end of it if you kill yourself.'

In bed, one morning, the next winter, we held each other's hand. The windows were frosted, the trees white as the rivers that ran through Kitty's dark hair. The giant Mansion Inn, outside our window and decorated for Christmas and the coming AD 1966, was buried in snow. I'd brought Kitty a mug of coffee and an ashtray. I drank warm milk with honey. Machaut on the phonograph.

'Delicious,' I said.

'I love you.'

Kitty had opened the window a crack; a clean, icy wash of winter sent us under the softness of our covers. She knew how I loved the smell of woodsmoke from the Mansion Inn's old fireplaces.

I kissed her.

145

'Maybe we can go back here someday, maybe we're already back here now,' my wife mused.

'What?'

'This is the sort of morning you remember, that becomes a memory. Those simple memories that you never think are going to be memories at the time they're happening. I'll smell woodsmoke someday and I'll be right back here.'

'Ten years from now.'

'Thirty years from now. We'll come back here when we're old. I believe that. I'm serious. I believe we're already here, our old selves. I can feel myself almost. Old Kitty laying next to me. She's happy too.'

'Good.'

'Old Burt is just like young Burt, I think. Good ol' Burt. Only younger.'

I ducked my head under the blankets and kissed Kitty between her breasts. She dragged on her joint. I poked my head out. 'Can you talk to them?'

'Nope. Well, sort of. But I don't have to. I am them and they're me. Right now anyway.'

'You're stoned,' I said. The winter light glazed Kitty's skin. Her hair was like a wild wigged European composer, like Beethoven, like the father she had no real photographs of. 'You're nuts.'

'They've come here as a refuge. To refuel. Life isn't always going to be easy for us. You know that, right?'

'It will,' I said.

'It won't. Only today will be like today.' Kitty propped herself up in bed, into a sitting position. Better to keep the coffee under her nose. She liked the smell of it more than the taste. My mouth moved down to her lap and she ran her free hand through my hair. She looked out the window at the Mansion Inn.

'We'll have children. Two, I think. Girl and a boy. Children are never what you think they'll be.'

'Well, the boy will be Tristan,' I said. 'And we'll call the girl Gwendolyn.'

'The girl will not be Gwendolyn!' Kitty laughed. She slapped my head.

'Genevieve?'

'Old Kitty is telling me that old Burt is bonkers. That you'll get even worse. That life is going to be hard for me and the kids with someone like you doddering about dressed up as a fourteenth-century monk. That right now, in bed – that it won't get better than right now in this bed. Smell that air.'

'I don't believe that.'

'Well,' Kitty thought. 'We'll grow apart. But we'll find each other anew every once in a while; we'll come back here. We'll always have here. You'll lose your hair. I'll lose whatever's left of my figure. I'll have the Mansion, and you your Middle Ages.' Kitty laughed, but quietly, as if we really did have guests from the future in bed with us. Whispering, 'Old Kitty tells me that many days and weeks we'll only pass each other. Servants to different obsessions. But I'll never get annoyed at your ways and you'll always love me. I might take lovers, but discreetly. It's my nature. You might take me for granted. That's yours. But in the evening, sometimes, no matter what, we'll lie together and we'll talk about boring things and feel safe. The future has fewer and fewer places where we can feel safe.'

'Kitty.'

147

'I'm older than you. I'll be the first to go. Old Kitty tells me that someday you'll be alone.'

'Can't you tell old Kitty to reconsider?'

Young Burt and young Kitty held each other then; his hand, my hand, combing through her pubic hair. And young Kitty moaned as old Kitty watched.

IX

There was my wife, my Kitty, and there was my wife's body. Between them, now, there was something else, a third thing. Curing the disease, I knew, would've been like curing a thunderstorm.

The old woman pointed to the wall. 'Holes,' she moaned. 'There are holes in the wall.'

I held her hand, standing over the bed. There were no holes in the wall. 'Shhh,' I said. It would all be over soon. She was not here to see this, to be this, thank God. She was in Lemkovyna again; no longer in her sixties, no longer my dying wife, Kitty was four years old again and she was safe.

The holes were the size of human eyes. They had been drilled into the walls of the house some weeks ago, when it had been decided that the old man would die. The old man, a musician, had been ill for many months.

Kitty and her mother approached the house. They passed two cows, a dog, and some chickens. The larger creatures stopped chewing.

'Such a stupid,' Kitty's mother, Anna, pointed. 'Look at the stupid. Holes. And for what?'

For breathing was for what. Kitty knew, even if her mother didn't. Her great-grandfather was very sick.

'Be normal,' Anna said. 'Ach, Kitty, please. Not today.'

Kitty was holding her breath. Today was Sunday back home in Queens Falls, but here? 'I am normal,' Kitty deflated her cheeks. 'See? Normal.' Here it couldn't possibly be Sunday.

'And don't with fingers in your mouth.'

Kitty removed her fingers from her mouth. 'I'm not.'

Anna smiled at her four-year-old daughter, her perfect thing. She didn't know what she would find within that house, or what was expected of her now. How could she have possibly come from such a place? Why on earth had she come back?

It was the summer of AD 1934 and Henry, Kitty's father, had decided to close the Mansion Inn for renovations. They were installing toilets and bathing units in every guest room of the old Victorian mansion, no small project. Anna, for reasons she didn't yet understand, had chosen to forgo a summer of babysitting plumbers and her increasingly polite husband to visit the village where she had been born and, more specifically, the grandfather she loved. Kitty accompanied her mother across the sea as a trophy and a shield, proof of what Anna could do. Anna had made an American. What had those she'd left behind made? Butter? Hay? Kitty and the English language were a deflection, a border, because the young mother was terrified.

Cheers erupted around them and Anna jumped. In the sky, a booming. Chickens scattered. Dogs barked. And the entire village watched the beautiful German airplanes pass overhead.

The old woman giggled. She clapped, whistled. The airplanes were on the ceiling, and she watched them move from one corner to the other. Then back again. Until – there! – they appeared to hang motionless, three silver warplanes, dipping their wings, as if bowing to a standing ovation.

'Kitty, please.'

She shouted, she pointed. 'Hurrah!'

It is a concerted, humiliating effort. The way they leap, shout, applaud, and wave into the sky. This happens twice a week now, sometimes more. The Lemkos believe that as long as they show the airplanes that they are friendly, then the airplanes will be their friends.

Kitty, ignoring her mother, joins in on the fun. It is a great thing, waving at Germans in the sky. How the little girl loves Lemkovyna!

But when the heavens empty, the men and women of the village begin to mutter. They go indoors to think, while the children, unafraid, throw sticks at trees. And Kitty stands before the fairy-tale house with the holes, holding her mother's hand, and she watches the clouds that the three silver warplanes have disappeared into.

'Goodbye,' she said. 'Bye-bye!'

I lifted an earthen jug of mead to my lips. I rubbed my eyes. I will not now describe my wife's body, or the cancer. To begin with I'll describe the rocking chair upon which I sat, month after month, waiting, hoping Kitty's body died before she did. It was oak, brown; orange in the sunlight. Of an old New England design, the chair was grandmotherly, brittle, and sanctimonious. You've seen this type before. It chirped, commenting on one's every shift, puritanically condemning one for succumbing to the need to rock. The armrest had swirls, fingerprints, hurricanes, infernos: it had faces in there, of that I'm quite certain. Faces I grew to know better than my own during those months of watching my wife, my giant girl, disappear. Sometimes they were tormented, screaming for help, petitioning for an axe to break them from their frozen Presbyterian misery, and sometimes those same faces were laughing. Sometimes they were Kitty. This chair, of course, hadn't rocked since I shoveled some of June's childhood science-fiction paperbacks beneath its runners, books whose covers I subsequently found myself obsessing upon. Other, better worlds; gear and sprocket cities overrun with creatures startling even for one accustomed to medieval demonology and Hieronymus Bosch; spaceships that resembled microscopic diseases scraping smoke trails over planets like something from one of Hildegard von Bingen's visions. Stars, black holes, infinity. Sometimes, despite myself, I could even see the attraction of it all. To such an extent has religion failed us, I thought. And I missed my daughter. I conducted conversations in my head with June, which often began asking her about the books and ended begging for her forgiveness. The chirping of the chair had terrified my wife.

I held her hand. 'Promise me,' she said.

'Promise what?'

I will not describe her body. I will not describe the air that still left her lips. Nor will I describe what remained of Kitty's hair, or what had happened to her teeth, her neck, her fingers. Nor the flesh around her eyes. Her veins, her breasts? Her pain? You've got to be kidding.

'Only promise,' she said.

Because she wanted a Lemko funeral now. She'd been talking about it all morning, or afternoon, or whenever it was. But maybe talking is a very loose way to describe what

152

she had been doing. She was dreaming out loud, leaking. The room had no clock and this day had no sun and, of course, I'd been drinking homemade mead for the better part of a month or two, on and off, between sleeping and sitting in the non-rocking chair and not helping my son do whatever he was doing at the Mansion Inn to keep us all solvent. I wasn't, as they say, holding together. It was AD 1996. But not for Kitty. Because Kitty wanted a Lemko funeral now. This was because she was temporarily insane. Or because of the medication, or the dreams which had leisurely, over the course of the illness, supplanted reality, as the illness had supplanted Kitty herself. In all honesty, it felt sometimes as if I was guarding the disease, that chipper assassin, spending time with the cancer, getting to know my enemy, sleeping with it, keeping it close and healthy and obscenely innocent. Come here, I'd tell it. Get out of there, friend. Come here. The cancer and I had got on pretty good terms while my wife had been in Lemkovyna.

'I promise,' I said.

This was not the first lie I'd told her, nor was it the worst. The reason that Kitty's mother was not with us was because I hadn't yet telephoned her. Anna Bibko was in Poland, in Warsaw, no doubt still trying to reconcile herself with history. She had no idea that her daughter would soon be gone because I knew that once she arrived, my wife would disappear from me, from all of us; that Anna would take control of whatever Kitty had left of her life. For once, I thought, I would take care of my family. I would protect them.

'For breathing is for what,' Kitty said, suddenly, looking now to the side of her bedroom, very seriously. She grabbed my arm, pulling me down to her face. '*Holes for breathing.*'

'Shhhh.'

'Pillow,' Kitty whispered. 'What happened to my pillow?'

'Shhhh.' I kissed her forehead.

'My pillow,' and she squeezed my arm. 'Oh, my God. Where's it gone?'

The pillow was under her head.

The holes have been bored into the walls because the old man's death has been protracted, his passage to the next world constipated, to say the least. Unclean spirits have been blamed. More specifically, unclean spirits somehow related to the ludicrous Americans' arrival in the village. Indeed, it is only now, a week into their visit, that Anna is permitted to attend her dying grandfather. It was initially thought that her presence might keep him unnaturally alive. Now it is decided that her presence, gross and inappropriate and disruptive as it has proved to be, might anger the old man into finally letting go. It is traditionally thought that holes drilled into the walls of a dying person's home will entice that individual to fly through them.

Kitty is a novelty, a New Worlder from across the ocean, and, in the general opinion of the village, almost certainly something of an idiot. She cannot speak Lemko, and that is enough for most. There must be something wrong with her. Also, with her large, Protestant face, her long, dark hair, and her bone-doll skin, the little girl looks nothing like a Lemko, who tend to be squat, fair-haired, and of a dark, weathered complexion. Thus, for many, Kitty looks nothing at all like a normal human being.

The Lemko language, which Kitty recognizes from her grandmother, sounds different here. It sounds like singing here. Everyone is always belting songs at one another from doorframes and from across yards, across expanses of green, greeting one another from great distances, like birds. During the day, with the men gone working, the village seems to consist of nothing but busy women, their children, and the aimless elderly. These old Lemkos do not have many teeth. No toothbrushes, no teeth; and Kitty gets into trouble on her first day for giving an old lady her toothbrush to try out. Females in Lemkovyna – Kitty and Anna included – dress in colorful, complex, and many-faceted dresses. Girls and unmarried women wear their hair with bright ribbons, whereas married women and the elderly cover their heads at all times. Kitty has never felt so pretty.

There are far more chickens than people in Lemkovyna. Kitty has the most fun with these, feeding them from her hand and pursuing them around the dusty village center, under the shadow of the wooden church. This is the stuff of storybooks, and every day Kitty expects to see knights, talking bears, castles. Her mother even catches her kissing a toad, and has to explain that there are no longer such things as princes. But Kitty knows a lie when she hears one.

The Lemko dwellings are eked out from the meaty surrounding green. Wood, grass, vegetables, leaves, twigs, great fur coats of moss. Listless smoke from cooking fires attends thatched roofs. There are –

'Flowers everywhere. No pavement, nobody jumps rope, nobody uses rope for jumping, and nobody has a car and nobody has a mansion either. Older girls have these really bright dresses, so pretty. I want one, I tell Mom. I want one just like, as pretty as that, when I am a big girl. And they have baskets too, and inside the baskets are mushrooms. And

155

we go down to the river, at the river, and there are even babies hanging from trees. Apple trees. Babies all snuggled in cloth. And the women don't wash the clothes, the river does. They just watch. We watch too. And, and –'

There are wolves. Bumblebees create a constant hum in the air, often just out of sight. Packs of dusty children wander in costume, following Anna and Kitty wherever they go, crunching carrots and beets. Many of these girls and boys loiter outside the house that the Americans are staying in, the house of their Bibko relatives. Each morning there are always one or two of the curious urchins about, standing together, waiting, though sometimes there are as many as seven, side by side, staring. Crawling with germs. It seems to Anna as if they have been there all night, watching, waiting. The children rarely laugh and their eyes are too big for their heads. It is impossible that Anna had once been one of those. She is different, always has been.

They will stay until the old musician dies or one month elapses, whichever comes first. Thirty days is all Anna can be expected to stomach of this.

The house is low and long, rectangular, not unlike an upstate New York log cabin bleached white. The logs are split, half-round fir, and the stuff between them is dried moss. Traditionally, half of the building is for people and half for livestock, though over time the partition separating the human side of Anna's grandfather's house from the animal side has ceased to exist. It is unclear – and a rather contentious point among certain villagers – as to whether this transgression was instigated by the two cows or by the old man. The thatched roof is balding, clumps of the straw laying among the cow excrement that surrounds the house like bulbous stalagmites.

'Kitty. Look at Mommy.'

'What happens when it rains?'

'What? Kitty, please, listen now. Because Mommy has to go inside great-grandfather's house. To say hello.'

'With the holes when it rains?'

'It doesn't rain. Are you listen? You must be brave girl now and wait right here. Don't move until Mommy come back. Can you be brave little girl?'

Kitty could. 'Can I look in holes?'

'No.'

Anna enters the house, and Kitty stands perfectly still, waiting. Then she runs up to the house. She finds a hole and fits an eye into it.

She's never seen so many candles, not anywhere, not even at Christmas or in the sky at night. The bed is in the center of the room. Kitty's great-grandfather is in the bed. He is bones and skin, he is gray and green and brown; weedy with hair in odd places – his ears, for instance – and he is breathing as if he's been out running for a long time. For a hundred years it looks like. Maybe, Kitty thinks, the house needs more holes. Magic plants are on fire, making strange-smelling fog. Hay and cow excrement still cover the floor. Kitty watches her mother. Anna has entered from a side room.

It is like watching a tree move, the old man's head turning to meet Anna. He attempts to raise himself but cannot. He makes a noise that is a laugh, but not a happy one.

His hand touches Anna's as a gentle look settles his face. He starts softly to sing, occasionally stopping to clatter something in Lemko. Eyes like an overcast sky. 'Where have you been, my child? My Anna, ah,' he says. 'You're surprised? Come closer. You think yourself so changed that your grandfather cannot recognize you? Silly one, little traveler, come.'

Anna bends to wipe his forehead. 'Nobody else recognizes me.'

'You will always be what you are. Come, don't cry. Especially for yourself. I'm the one dying, see.' The old man contorts his face.

Anna smiles. The old man chortles and coughs. 'That is the girl I remember. If only dying were so easy. Tell me, how are my cows?'

This, then, was the old man that Anna remembered. His cows indeed! The old man has lived with the two animals for many years. He doesn't talk to them, or name them; he isn't crazy. Still, it is widely thought that he enjoys their company more than the company of the villagers.

'They're outside, Grandfather.'

'Have you met the priest? Now there's a charming one. You see him, you tell that Lady Legs to come back and visit. Tell him with haste. But more plum brandy and less Bible this time, yes? It's been many days and I've had many sinful dreams I'd like explained.' And he laughs.

Anna touches her grandfather's cheek. 'I remember your music,' she says.

The old man's voice opens up and a weak melody escapes, hounded out by the cough that follows so hot on its heels. 'I hear it all the time now. It doesn't let me alone.'

'What about your instruments?'

'Even worse. Good for nothing, see,' the old man's fingers are mangled, purple. He holds them before Anna as if to toss

*the ghastly wastes of time out of one of the holes in his wall.
'I knew you would come. Did you know? I've been waiting.
Do you remember when we used to dance? In the hills? How
I wish I could die in those hills now, my little Anna. Die like
a raindrop.'*

Anna frowns. *'I'm far away, Grandfather,'* she begins.
*'People here, people from when I was little, they forget. Ivan
won't even look at me. They pretend to forget. But I forget
more, I forget worse. It is too difficult. Grandfather? I come
back to you and I'm even further away.'*

'You're not. You're right here.'

'I have a daughter.'

'I know.'

'She is American.'

'I know, my lamb,' the old man coughs. *'It is better this
way.'* Another cough. *Blood bubbles from between his lips,
pops, and splatters onto his chin.* *'Anyway, what can you
do? I will confess having an American great-granddaughter
when I next see the priest. Can he absolve me, do you think?'*

But Anna is serious. *'How can you live like this, with these
people?'*

'Ach, the people across the ocean, they are so different?'

Anna begins to reply but is cut off by another cough. *'They
are no different,'* the old man says, *with a gust of annoy-
ance. Then he grimaces.* *'Come now. Who knows, maybe I
will visit this United States of America. See where they buried
my son. The land is fine there, is it not? I am told that everything is free in this America. Maybe I can be reborn as an
American? Or an American cow at the very least.'* *More
laughter.*

'American cows aren't allowed inside houses, Grandfather.'

'Are they not? Well, there is something. Not even when they're ill? In the winter? I don't believe it.'

'I missed you.' Anna kisses her grandfather's forehead.

'Do the Americans know how to play the sopilka?'

'No.'

'The flojara then? Does your daughter? I can teach her. I will teach her. Where is she? Do you have snow in America? Does your daughter know about snow? Tell me her name.'

'It is not a Lemko name.'

'So much like your father. Trying so hard. Too strong for your own good. Boulderheads, the pair of you. To make yourself forget your people, your home. It is a sin. And for what? Why?' The old man shuts his eyes. His son, Anna's father, refused to return to the land that he had left and the impractical father he would not take care of. 'But don't think that I can't see how sad it makes you. It is not easy not being what you are.'

'Her name is Kitty.'

'Kitty.'

'It is pretty sounding in English.'

Two flies land on the old man's nose. 'Your husband, why has he not come?'

Anna shoos the two flies. 'He is scared of crossing the road. He knows only books.'

'Ah.'

'He is very rich,' Anna says, her face instantly blazing. She looks away. Why say such a thing? Of course her husband is rich.

The old man says, 'Well, this is also important.'

For several minutes neither speak. Lightly, with her finger, Anna traces the veins on her grandfather's head. 'I'm sorry,' she says.

The old man's breath is shallow. 'Child,' he says, 'I know.'

But Anna wonders what he knows, what he really knows. Crazy peasant. Anna sighs, pulling herself back, feeling like a fool. Old men, especially Lemko old men, they lived for this. And Anna thought: didn't they get to an age and suddenly start speaking like this, like him, all dying and wise and benevolent because what else was there to be but bitter and angry, or drunk, or insane? There is nothing to be sorry for. She is emotional, that is all: and all emotion is always sorry, or should be, or that was Anna's experience anyway. Who is this thing before her, what have they in common but the past? And what is that, where is that now? The medieval room sways, skips and crackles with candles. It is a ghost of itself already. A fading space. It is a dead thing. She is the survivor, and she isn't even here now, not really; she knows this without understanding it. That this isn't real. This is a fairy tale, a ghost story, all of Lemkovyna, an apparition living in the hills, going over the same routines, traditions, customs, the same unchanging stupidity, stuck forever, not even aware that it is dead, dead, dead. Lemko icons are set upon the table. Dumb things. Dumb wood. They could be two days or two hundred years old. The old man's magnificent homemade musical instruments and tools removed, and Anna wonders why the villagers don't just bury him alive and get it over with. Alive or dead, the ghosts will live on. Nothing will change. That is the comfort of these ridiculous hill people. That death doesn't mean anything; that is has lost its howl because life is going to go on as it has always gone on, forever and ever and ever, Amen. Dying isn't so bad, because you aren't going to miss a damn thing, or you know exactly what you're going to miss and adjust your outlook accordingly.

161

Ghosts stay the same, only their houses change. But what happens, Anna wonders, if the house stays the same too? You won't be forgotten because you aren't an individual anyway. You're a story, a village, a forest far away from the real world of progress and comfort. You are what your culture amounts to, and you'll live on, as it will. Or won't. Just another frozen winter morning, another spring, another ridiculous song. The same song.

I'm haunted, Anna realizes then, with clarity unusual for one so focused on the material. She is haunted by these people and she loathes them for it. Because a ghost can't exist without its haunted house. But no. She is strong. She'll shut all her doors, all her windows. She'll renovate. She'll burn herself down if she has to, anything to get them to leave her alone.

'Have you not seen the machines in the sky?' the old man asks, suddenly.

Anna nods.

Closing his eyes, his hand drops from his granddaughter's. 'But you have not gone so far,' he says. 'You can never go far.'

Too normal, a hysterical normality. Kitty, my sixty-six-year-old wife, speaking more or less coherently, as if it were three years ago, three months ago, like she wasn't being swept messily off the earth, stuck to a bed stained with things which I will not describe. Speaking as if I wasn't drunk, garbed in a soiled tunic, a historically accurate beard clinging to a face sticky with homemade honey alcohol. For the most part, she knew who she was talking to and what she was talking about, but I am sure that she probably had no idea where she was or what was happening, really, truly happening, to her body. Talking on autopilot, retracing conversations long since faded. This was worse than when she was four, this momentary, monstrous respite. It was a taunt. I had nothing to say to Kitty anymore. I could not think of a single goddamn thing to say. Bring back the cancer, I thought. I would have a word with the disease.

'What time is it?' she asked.

I didn't know. I shook my head, trying to smile.

She was out of breath. She looked dizzy. 'Tristy?'

'Helping with guests.'

'He's good. Is he alone? Should I get – should I go over and help him?'

She could hardly lift her hand to mine. 'Tristan thinks you should stay in bed a little longer. Until you feel better.'

'Tristy's good. He's right. Don't feel so hot right now. Is tomorrow Wednesday?'

I had no idea what day tomorrow was. 'Amy's there with him. Amy's been over a lot, helping us,' I said, hoping it was true. 'Whenever she can.'

'That's good. She's a little trouper. Amy's so good.'

Amy Sturk was a CTLR member and neighbor. She'd spent her childhood summers working at the Mansion Inn, and it was hard, though not unpleasant, to imagine the place without her. She was married now, with two children, girls who shared their mother's plumpness, freckles, and bossy red hair.

'You look tired,' I said. 'Maybe you should get some sleep.'

'But I remember my grandfather's funeral. How we played games all night, games with his body. These things, how odd. Lemko kids like elves, like fairies, everything a fairy tale. Four years old and I'm drinking plum brandy moonshine stuff, you know. It was so good, sipping it with the big kids, and the cows in the room. I can't believe it was even me sometimes, that I was there before everything. Those games. I remember the names still. The Pear. The Goose. God and the Devil. The Wooden Spades.'

'I love you, Kitty.'

'The Rooster. The Magpie. Are you listening? Where are you? Listen.'

It was like interacting with a phonograph record. She was there and she wasn't there. 'I love you,' I said.

'My mother told me that you were her punishment. Did you know that? Her *punishmentation*,' Kitty smiled, imitating Anna. 'That you were Henry all over again, that . . . Hold my hand.'

'I am holding your hand.'

'Hold it harder.'

'I love you.'

'But.' Kitty was silent for a minute, almost audibly collecting her thoughts. 'I mean that Henry had finally got his daughter away from her. Hank's revenge. She doesn't hate you. Who could hate you? Wait. What was I –?'

'Your grandfather.'

'His funeral, my father's funeral though. Henry's. Don't even – I can't even remember it. I don't think Mom let me go.'

Outside, somebody engaged a lawnmower. There was a world outside this room where people still mowed lawns.

'You have to unbraid my hair. I remember now. Little girls have to unbraid their hair for funerals.'

Kitty no longer had any hair.

'Burt?'

She had her books in a pile next to her bed. Her wild young things, her Young Turks. Hawthorne, Melville, Whitman. I picked one up to hide my face behind, tears running down my cheeks. 'Shall I read to you?'

'Need to talk to Mom now, Burt. Don't feel so hot. Honestly, I really honestly don't. I need my mom.'

'She's on her way,' I lowered the book. The fever had returned. 'I'm here.'

'I want my mommy.'

'Shhhhhhhhh.'

Then, 'They stuck knives in the eyes of children, the children I played with. Later on, after I left, after the war. Most of the village was massacred,' my wife whispered, stricken, as if she had actually seen it and was seeing it again, up there on our ceiling. 'They stuck knives in their eyes. They stuck knives in their eyes and they set them on fire.'

The girls of the village unbraid their hair as a sign of mourning. The women wear black. The men become drunk and the church bell rings three times.

The coffin is built in the old man's house, next to the bed on which he rests, uncovered, dressed in his finest clothing – which is not fine at all, even by Lemko standards. His eyes are covered with US pennies placed there, with some trepidation, by Kitty herself. This had been something of an honor and something of a test.

He is dead but he is still there; and he will be there, still, in the dead body or just outside it, until the top of the coffin is shut for good in three days' time. He holds a candle which bleeds wax onto his fingers. He can see and hear everything, though it's unclear to Kitty how. Probably doesn't much mind the banging of the carpenter, solid and polyrhythmic, almost appropriately musical, though he might mind that the wood being used to build his final resting place has been taken from the walls of his own house. His coffin will have breathing holes too. But, then again, he is smiling. The cows have been allowed back inside.

For Kitty it is a dream. Soon it is normal for her, the body. The bats that live in the ceiling. The candles, the stench. And soon Kitty is talking to the body, introducing herself. Kitty even makes friends with the other Lemko boys and girls. She gives them all pennies, which they also place on their eyes, laughing and moaning like the awakened dead.

They spend all day with him. Kitty and a revolving cast of black-clad Lemkos who come and drink bottles of plum brandy over the body of the old man, who's allowed a dribble of the stuff when the priest isn't looking. It's his party, after all. One nameless, bearded young man plays music over the body. He must be from another village, it is joked, the village where everyone is tall. But he disappears before anyone can find out who he really is, where he's from, and how he knew the old musician. The old man had never had any students, it was thought. 'Perhaps he came for the plum brandy,' someone proposes. People only shake their heads.

Anna is in and out of the house, trying to prepare a feast that is low on germs. To do this she makes sure that nobody touches her or the food. She makes spaghetti. She had actually thought to bring some from America. It was to be her final triumph, she'd decided, introducing the progressive wonders of spaghetti to the peasants. But it doesn't quite turn out like that. How fitting, one woman says, that the Americans should serve worms at a funeral. Worms with squashed tomatoes. Mother Mary, what devilment. They pretend to eat their bowls and slyly, one after another, dump them outside in the dust, joking that they hope the birds won't mind having their breakfast pre-prepared.

The coffin is finished by dusk and the old man lowered into it; and Kitty notices that he's finally stopped smiling. He looks shocked, afraid. The opened coffin is placed on the bed. Kitty tells her great-grandfather not to worry.

The priest returns with the moon and reads from the psalter. Between the psalms, people tell stories about the old man, most of them apparently rather hilarious, many of them untrue. Some of them, Anna thinks, even nasty. Legends and fairy tales are recited for the candlelit children who sit around the coffin, rapt with enjoyment, right up close, like the stories are coming from the dead man, like he's a CBS radio show. Their faces flicker, eyes jumping with wonder. The adults become more jocular with every glass of plum brandy, young men squeezing young women who loudly, and in very uncertain terms, object: and Anna Bibko is forgotten. She's a barnacle in the dark at the back of the room, amidst cows, devouring fistfuls of spaghetti and cursing a culture that could turn a funeral vigil into this uncouth backwoods revelry. But how free she feels, thinking: it is over. Nothing holds her here now. How she loves the air suddenly, the fields of flowers, the apple blossoms, the icy mountain water, the shaggy dance of the trees, the whatever those pretty birds are up in that sky that stretches perfectly away from here, all the way back home to Queens Falls, New York, where even the clouds are a good deal cleaner. How Anna loves her daughter, her little Kitty. To die like a raindrop; let all of Lemkovyna die like a raindrop, Anna thinks, happily. She has Kitty. They will

escape. Anna will bury all of Lemkovyna with her grand-
father, and she won't ever look back again.

But Kitty is happy, ignoring the glower of her mother. It
would be very late, she knows, if the Lemkos had invented
clocks. She never wants to go home again.

The rising sun made tangerines of Tristan's glasses. My son, sitting on the porch, smoking a marijuana cigarette, looking out over the recently mowed lawn, the violent crispness of it. The dew twinkled and the murderous little birds hopped.

No. Sleeping. Tristan had slept there all night, waiting alone for who knows what on the Mansion Inn's antique porch, unlit cigarette in his hand. I would get up and take a bath today. Today I prove them wrong by bringing my son a mug of steaming hot coffee. Today was an important day.

I held up the earthen jug of homemade mead that I'd been drinking since I woke this morning on the floor beside my wife's bed. Rhodomel. *'The rose petal one?'* Similar jugs created a sticky Arabesque city on the hardwood floor. Bees everywhere. Flies. Carpenter ants scurried and stopped, scurried, stopped. *'Partly. Though I mixed it with a touch of – of cyser. Which is like melomel but made with –'* 'Apples, mmm. That's it. That's what I'm tasting.'

Last night I had spoken to the cancer at length about the Children's Crusade, AD 1212. They'd come from France and Hildegard von Bingen's Rhine Valley. Two armies numbering in the thousands, the illiterate sons and daughters of farmers, serfs, and simple tradesmen on a mission to reconquer the Holy Land for Christ. Two boys urging them onwards, ranting, professing divine providence. Precocious brats.

Whelps. Doomed puppies. How I envied their faith in the miraculous. Before they were all starved to death or raped, murdered or shunted onto ships and sold into North African slavery, the children had believed that the Mediterranean Sea would part before their march as, long ago, the Red Sea had for Moses and the Israelites. I can see the mobs of them moving across Europe like locusts, towards Jerusalem by way of the Italian coast, passing and amassing beneath the walls of cities, picking up new recruits with their rusting farm tools, psalms, pointy sticks, and David and Goliath slingshots. Reality is re-enactment. The cancer, of course, hadn't had much to say about the Children's Crusade. Cancer would never have children. That sort of thing didn't interest the cancer at all.

I brought the jug to my lips and heard her voice again. *'Apples, mmm.'* Kitty, I love you. *'Apples, mmm. That's it. That's what I'm tasting.'* Don't go. Please. Don't. *'This the rhodomel? The rose petal one?'* This, I thought, is what happens when someone larger than life stops living.

The next time I looked out the window my son was gone. I would talk to him today. Today we would set things right. I lowered myself back down onto the floor to wait.

Kitty called my name, perhaps she even woke up.

'Good morning,' I whispered.

'Where are you?'

'It's OK. I'm here. I'm on the floor,' I said. 'Praying.'

Kitty laughed weakly. 'You gorilla.' Then, just like old times, 'What am I going to do with you, Burt Hecker?' She thought I was joking.

X

I stepped out of our house, away from Kitty and into the late, late morning. It was another affront, the way the world continued to manufacture such beautiful days. With a swallow of mead, I doused the urge to look back up at the empty glare of her window. Then another swallow for good luck.

I was garbed in a musty brown tunic. My joints ached, popped, and I hadn't washed in some time. Nor had I eaten. In my hand, a jug. Today I would find my son. I would brew my son coffee.

From the Mansion Inn's porch, a middle-aged woman peered down at me as from the deck of a luxury-liner docked at some impoverished, politically unstable Caribbean island. She was, I saw immediately, the type of woman unused to walking on grass. It was August, then. Track Season.

'Do you work here?' she called.

'Work?'

I walked towards her. Tunic, nose, earthenware jug of mead; in quick succession she'd seen all she needed. Fearing infection, she stepped back. My nose has this primordial, subconscious effect: in order to limit their exposure to contagions some dunk their hands in their pockets, whereas others discreetly adjust their intake of oxygen. 'Good morning,' she mustered.

I gave her that.

Judging by her clothing, she appeared to be re-enacting British Rule on the Subcontinent. She told me she was at the end of her rope and wished to speak with the manager. Earlier in the morning she had spoken with the bearded gentleman but she didn't think that he was listening, or capable of listening, if I knew what she meant. I did not know and told her so. The poor woman probably hadn't been listened to in over twenty years, and simply wasn't used to it. 'That was my son,' I said. 'He's a musician. I'm the husband of the owner.'

'There are flies,' she said. 'In my room.'

There was probably a name for the type of hat the woman wore. I realized that I was swaying and stopped myself, sipping some mead, thinking: coffee. I would have to figure out how to work a coffee machine if I was to bring my son that steaming mug of coffee.

'What were we thinking?' she said. 'To think we just came from a four-star resort in Lake Placid. This is so unacceptable.'

'Sorry?'

'Excuse me.'

'Flies,' I tried again.

'I think that maybe I should speak with someone else.'

'No, please,' I would pull myself together. 'Please, speak with me.'

'This is absurd. You obviously –' looking me over.

'I just got out of bed.'

That was another thing: the beds were too soft. Plus, it took her ten minutes to get the conditioner out of her hair, what with the Victorian water pressure. The bathroom itself, she said, felt like a cave. Then she tried to steer the conversation back to insects. She said, 'My husband is allergic to bees.'

Tristan came loping across the lawn, Robinson Crusoe of upstate New York, stranded here at the Mansion Inn, shipwrecked from his final year in Julliard by the storm of his mother's illness. He emerged from the forest, probably from our barn. He was not wearing shoes.

The woman called to my son, who stopped. Seeing me standing out of the house and on the porch momentarily threw him. His forehead furrowed. 'The flies,' he said, almost inaudibly.

I relished the impression he surely made upon the woman, and wanted nothing more than to run down onto the lawn and stand beside him. I felt that she would not be able to pursue us across grass. Tristan repeated, 'Flies in your room.'

'Possibly bees,' she said.

'Well, I was just out back in the forest setting traps,' Tristan drawled, quietly. He would not meet my eyes. 'Flytraps. But one bit me, see,' and my son, grinning, showed us his middle finger.

The woman gasped as Tristan turned, his glasses flashing with menace. He strolled back into the woods. Stunned, I laughed, and laughed heartily, until it occurred to me that, in all likelihood, the intended recipient of the middle finger had not been our guest at all.

They sat at the far end of the Mansion Inn's porch, and probably had been there during the entire altercation. Both hid behind newspapers, giggling. The tip of a shaved head rose over the top of one newspaper like an orange sunrise, and then, just as quickly, set. It was something to watch, the way the Sunday *New York Times* Sports section's horizon fluctuated between dawn and dusk. Sunday then. These two I knew.

Every summer Marie and her husband, Don, spent a fortnight with us. My wife, unbeknownst to them, still charged them the off-season rates of AD 1972, the year of their first visit. It had been their honeymoon. It had also been their first time outside of the greater Long Island/NYC area, something they never ceased reminiscing about. Years later, between the giggles which Marie often substituted for normal breathing, she even recounted that Don had taken a loaded gun and a switchblade knife with him on their first upstate New York nature hike. 'Swiss Army Knife, Marie, c'mon,' Don had corrected.

'OK, but tell them about the socks.'

'I wore five pairs of socks.'

'Because of the cobras!'

'Rattlesnakes, Marie.' Massive and hammy, Don was still very much in love with his doting, mousey Marie.

'But he used to call them cobras, didn't you? King Cobras.'

I hugged them both.

'Still protesting against the twentieth century I see,' Don said, looking my tunic up and down, laughing. 'That bitch you had it out with took the entire pot of decaf to her room this morning. Tell you what –' Don was always telling you what.

'Manners, Donald.'

'People like her, manners don't apply. Am I right, Burt?'

Summer drifted through the Tiger Tail pines above us. I had never seen Don not wearing an athletic uniform of some sort; elementary school teacher, volunteer fireman, and soulful fool, the man had thick, lovely eyelashes.

173

I sat down. 'Welcome back,' I said. 'Some rhodomel?'

'Lay it on me.'

The Mansion Inn's covered porch ran along the entire eastern side of the house. Hundred-year-old vines twisted up the wooden latticework around us, and a very young chipmunk ran past while another rattled through the storm drains above us, sounding bigger and more dangerous than he was. Marie flinched. Don began his annual exposition on fresh air and the extent at which you forgot it existed while living on Long Island. Marie inquired about rabies. Plants embedded with purple and orange flowers hung down from hooks in the ceiling.

'How is she, Burt?' Marie finally asked. 'How are you?'

'She's getting better,' I said. 'I'm fine.'

They put their mugs to their mouths and swallowed. I didn't look so fine. Kitty wasn't getting better. 'If there's anything we can do,' and Marie sniffled. 'I'm so sorry.'

'We're family, Burt,' Don squeezed my upper arm. 'Wasn't I just saying? How many years we been coming, I was just asking Marie, how many years now?'

'Twenty-four years.'

'Summer wouldn't be the summer without Kitty's Mansion.' Long-time guests tended to call it that, Kitty's Mansion.

'It's good to see you both,' I said.

'Damn right.'

I refilled Don's mug.

'Show him, Marie,' Don said. The zippers of his jogging uniform grinned tightly in the sun.

'Oh, but not now.' Marie blew her nose. 'Let's let him breathe. Burt needs to breathe.'

'Show him.'

Marie must have been forty-five, fifty now; still a tumble-down tomboy unself-consciously dressing like a princess. She had a way about her, a tough twinkle. 'It's for Kitty,' she said. She handed me a watercolor painting of the Mansion Inn executed on white construction paper.

Don kneaded my shoulder athletically. 'Little lady's something else, huh?'

'It's beautiful,' I said. 'Thank you.'

Marie began crying. 'I didn't know what else to do.'

'See in the corner,' Don said, patting his wife's leg. 'Up in the window there?' It looked like a pineapple had been painted in the window. 'Marie had me up there posing for hours.'

'Half-hour, Donald.'

'Like that guy who chopped up his face,' Don said. 'His ear. What's-his-name. Remember, Linda at PTA was going off on him. Said we shouldn't have his poster in the cafeteria. Good artist, bad influence on the children.'

There was a zoo of beasts cavorting around Marie's Mansion Inn watercolor. Two deer, cats, and something that might have been a horse or a griffin. Swarms of birds blackened the sky.

'It's really special,' I said. 'I'll show Kitty tonight.'

'Only if you think its good enough.' Marie blew her nose.

'It's good enough,' her husband insisted. 'Burt just said so.'

'Kitty will love it. Thank you.'

'Takes these night classes now and everyone's just going nuts about her drawings, aren't they? Even had some of it shown, where was it, honey?'

'St Edwards Retirement Home.'

'Over in Great Neck. You want to see some real art, Burt? Great Neck, Long Island.'

The three of us drank to that, and Tristan emerged from the parking lot on the other side of the Mansion, more or less from the opposite side of the world I last saw him depart into, as if he'd circled the globe. He carried three large, flat-bottomed, folding paper bags full of groceries. Amy Sturk followed. She carried a pie the size of a bicycle wheel.

My son ignored me.

'Burt,' Amy called from the lawn. She ran a handful of freckles through her red hair. 'I need to see you for a minute.'

I needed to eat, to lie down, to get up and stop drinking and make Tristan some coffee, I needed to call my daughter, June – and now I had to speak with Amy Sturk? 'Ten minutes,' I said. Tomorrow, it occurred to me, must be the Mansion Inn's fabled CTLR End of Summer Feast and Tourney.

'I'm serious,' Amy said, walking away. 'Seriously, Burt. We need to talk. I'll be back at your house.'

Amy Sturk could nurture the skin off your very bones. To be sure, she spent a lot of time at our estate. Even when there was no work to be done and long after we had stopped officially employing her. She was a little older than my daughter, June, though they had never been particular friends growing up. (She's like a mosquito, my daughter once complained to Kitty, a mosquito who *hugs*.) Amy had always gravitated more towards Kitty anyway, on one hand ideal-izing my wife and on the other mothering her when Kitty drank too much, or smoked too much marijuana, or slouched when she walked, behaving as if they were contemporaries or equals. I'd once even come across them exchanging moth-erhood tips, and this long before Amy had even fully exited puberty. Kitty humored the serious, caring, and – Lonna thought – possibly deranged girl. Amy's mother had been killed in an automotive accident a few years after Amy was born, and Amy's father never got over playing high school dances with his rock and blues combo. Amy was her own mother, her father's mother, and, to a certain extent, ours. Really, none of us could much stand the industrious red-head, though we loved her dearly. She was, of course, also a member of Confraternity of Times Lost Regained. There was really no escaping her: she even followed one through time.

Black nubs began popping out of the lawn, sending sneers of water up into the air. Amy and her medieval pie, stranded on the grass, began to run. Don laughed ('Would you look at that,' he said, as if it were the first chubby girl carrying a pie he had ever seen sprinting across a lawn) and Marie told him to cut it out; and I felt myself perched on the edge of a vast sleep. I watched water evaporate in the air. Don calmed, and Marie reached over and rested her hand on my arm. This, then, was the winding down. Nothing could ever be like this again. Don spoke about his high school students, *Braveheart*, and his cousin with the divorces. He asked about Lonna and the CTLR, wondering when he would get to see them both. (It had been weeks since Lonna and I had spoken. The last time she stopped by I refused to emerge from Kitty's room and she had, I believe, legally threatened me with a mental institution.) The three of us lifted our mugs and drank, and I wondered why Don and Marie had never had any children.

The woman with the hat returned without her hat. I could hardly focus my eyes. She speculated aloud as to just what kind of establishment I thought I was trying to run. She meant that we were all inebriated. Don had removed his shirt.

'I am not trying to run anything,' I told her. But I should have been trying and I suddenly despaired over my dirty tunic. My historically accurate stench. She was right. I should have been making Tristan coffee.

'Well, obviously, and just who is? Your son?'

'My wife.'

'Right. Well, we've decided to leave early. Maybe I could have a word with this wife of yours before we check out?'

'Certainly.' I pointed to our house, slurring. 'Be my guest. Want me to go wake her up for you?'

Marie squeezed my hand.

'I think you better go,' Don told her. 'Right now.'

She agreed, further stipulating that I should grant her a full refund if I knew what was good for me; at which point things began to get a little messy. Don called the woman a thief in respect to the entire pot of decaffeinated coffee she may or may not have lifted from the communal breakfast room that morning in order to consume in the privacy of her own bedroom. The woman said that she and her husband had hoped for a little more 'class' from an establishment such as the Mansion Inn. Don, laughing, defending the honor of Kitty's Mansion, called her 'Dumbo' and offered to take her to fucking school if what she wanted was class: at which point I closed my eyes. 'Shut up shut up shut up,' Marie pleaded. I heard her fists collide with Don's arms, or chest. I heard my name. Perhaps I was needed, so I opened my eyes, turning the whole ludicrous world back on, and the woman with it. For some reason she was still right there, standing before me, slightly blurred and threatening the Mansion Inn with some kind of boycott. Her husband, she said, knew people within the Saratoga Racing Community.

'Yeah, well, Burt here has got friends in the Medieval Re-enacting Community,' Don laughed. 'Friends with swords.'

The woman disappeared, and Marie began to cry. She was so sorry, she said, so sorry that her husband had never grown up. Nobody ever really does, I thought to say. But I couldn't. I could not concentrate, even when a grown-up gentleman in a green shirt appeared before us, demanding to know just who had threatened his wife and who was the owner or acting manager.

Don, shirtless, an empty mug of mead in his hand, rose to his feet. 'How can I help?' he said.

Consciousness consolidated in throbs, each more agonizing than the last. The living-room sofa. The ceiling. Someone had wrapped me in a quilt Kitty had knitted to approximate the more thrilling parts of 'The Battle of Poitiers' from *Froissart's Chronicles*. Two horses expired on my belly. Perforated with dozens of arrows some five hundred and thirty-six years ago, their crazy-eyed fury found echo in my head, AD 1996, there, then. I groaned. Turning my head, I saw the Mansion Inn gloat from the large bay window. Perhaps it was the angle, but it seemed that our little house had drawn nearer to the white Victorian heap, that somehow less lawn separated us now than had done that morning. I had always known that my family would someday collide with that iceberg.

Kitty and the cancer were up there, above me. I stared at nothing and tried not to imagine them. But the ceiling seemed to hang lower, if possible, buckling under the weight that had already snapped me in two.

179

A medieval band of clunking Confraternity of Times Lost Regained bellatores marched by the window. Three knights, one Don, and some entrepreneurial serving wenches with their pots and OOP Tupperware containers of 'primary-source' medieval dishes. Stone soup, probably. Waybread, keftedes, sausage hedgehogs, meat and poultry pasties. They were setting up for tomorrow's big End of Summer Feast and Tourney. The horses on my unfed stomach rumbled. There, finally, was my other world, the one I could slip into in order to destroy what I hadn't already destroyed of this one.

Beside the sofa, our coffee table had been laid with a bloody rag, bloody paper towels, Band-Aid wrappers, a pot of herbal tea, a bottle of Saratoga All Natural Spring Water, two empty glasses, and some Children's Chewable Tylenol. I instinctively felt my forehead. It was held together by several Band-Aids. Recognizing that I had cracked my skull open somehow made the pain more eloquent. I laughed. I sorrowed long and marvelously. Perhaps I would die.

Where was my mead?

Confiscated.

What was that noise?

Kitty.

It felt so habitually normal, so comfortable, that I didn't think twice. Kitty in the kitchen. Kitty had pulled herself out of bed and taken the cancer to the kitchen. I could hear her music playing from the small Compact Disc player that lived on the kitchen counter. Kitty's beloved *John Wesley Harding*; and I listened to Bob Dylan pitying the poor immigrant. Dishes were being washed. They were scrubbed, dunked, clattered.

Burt Hecker should have washed the dishes, of course; a

180

long time ago I should have scrubbed, dunked, and clattered them. I had been prepared to wash them that very day, in fact, or so I told myself. The cancer was now taking better care of my family than I was. They began to chop vegetables.

'Kitty,' I called.

The medieval doctor held that recovery depended on a number of variables, including the milk of pulverized almonds, Holy Whims, the phases of the moon, and the position of certain heavenly constellations. Fevers could be tertian, quartan, daily, or pestilential, and the properly trained specialist could learn much by tasting the patient's urine for sugar. If you died, it was because you were supposed to. But if you suddenly got out of bed to wash dishes and chop carrots?

Slowly, carefully, I made my way upstairs to Kitty's room. Besides being wrapped in the Battle of Poitiers, I was unclothed. I didn't have any of my medieval garb there – I kept items of that nature in my library, in the forest – but I did have some mundane clothing. I would dress myself before seeing Kitty.

The door to Kitty's room, our old room, was closed. I turned the doorknob. Locked. That was not possible. I tried again: still very much locked. Next to the door, in the hallway, two large garbage bags were lumpy with empty mead jugs. Someone had cleaned the floor. Despair crashed over me. Then a queer relief. From inside, I heard my son's voice. 'Hello?' it asked.

'Tristan,' I said. 'The door is locked.'

He didn't answer.

'Tristan,' I raised my voice a little. 'What is going on?'

'Shhh,' he said. 'Go away. Mom's sleeping.'

Before I could protest, I heard my name evoked from the kitchen, then the living room. Then again from the bottom of the stairs, then once from each step, my name climbing the stairs towards me: it had been Amy Sturk in the kitchen. 'Burt, Burt, Burt?' I stood there, nearly naked, waiting for the worst, hounded down by myself, an endless bloody Burting. Blood had begun to trickle down from the wound in my forehead. Think, I thought. But I could not. The endless thoughtful days were coming to an end.

'The doctor came by when you were unconscious,' Amy Sturk sighed. 'You've been giving her too much medication, Burt. I'm not blaming you. It's just the truth. She could have died. You could have put her into a coma.'

Amy sat on the sofa, legs crossed, the Battle of Poitiers raging beneath her posterior. She wore a large, factory-made summer dress with floral patterns. I was in Kitty's pink bathrobe. I had wrapped toilet paper around my head to stop the wound, and blood burned a Japanese sun into the center of my forehead; like a kamikaze pilot, I thought. The question now being: on whom would I explode?

'You're lucky I removed all those jugs before the doctor came or she'd be right back in the hospital. Is that what you want for Kitty? I could not believe it. That room. Like some medieval frat party or something. I'm going to be staying here until Anna and June arrive.'

I looked at the ground.

'I love you, Burt. Look at me, please. I love you. You're like a father to me, but what's been happening these last few months – if I had known.'

'I'm trying.'

'Some of the CTLR gals are helping Tristy over at the Mansion right now. Helping for free. He's falling apart, Burt. Your son's been carrying everything on his shoulders. Then today. Finally decide to poke your head outside and you start threatening guests with swords?'

'I don't remember,' seemed to be the most appropriate answer.

'Because you were drunk. You need a bath. You need to stop drinking. You need to shave and you need to start wearing, like, normal clothes and speaking in a normal way and you've got to help Tristan and be there, really be there for Kitty. You could have turned her into a vegetable, Burt. I'm not saying this to upset you.'

'I know you're not.'

'Then please do something. Help us. Stop feeling sorry for yourself and get off your butt, OK? I know this is destroying you, but please, please realize that you're not the only one going through this. Like I said, I'm going to stay here until June and Anna arrive. I'm going to take care of both of you. You and Tristy. But I need some help. No more mead, got it? Lonna seriously wanted to commit you last time she was here, you know that, right? To a mental hospital. Seriously. She wanted to take you to a hospital, Burt. Guess who fought her, told her she was overreacting? But maybe you need help, ever think of that? The drinking. The everything. But first, and for Tristy's sake, I need you to help out at the Mansion for once in your life. I mean vacuuming, among other things. I had no idea that he'd been running the place by himself for, what, four months? Five months? But he doesn't complain, not a peep from our Tristan. I come by and he tells me everything's cool, that he's cool. Like always, keeps everything bottled up inside him. I don't know. Look at me. Is it true that you won't let him see his mother? That he has to ask, Burt? I mean, I came today to start setting up for tomorrow's big tourney and he collapsed in my arms. Tristan, who is uncomfortable shaking hands, collapsed in my arms.'

'Stop,' I said.

'He's not going back to school, by the way. Officially. In case you didn't know. He's dropped out of Julliard.'

I crumpled.

'Here's a list I made you,' Amy said.

The title of Amy's list was, 'MANSION INN TO DO TASKS'. I found that amusing.

Her green eyes pinned me back. 'You think this is a joke?'

Luckily, my bloody toilet-paper headband decided to slip down and rest on my nose. I was bleeding again.

'Jesus, God,' Amy said, standing over me. She arranged Band-Aids.

I said, 'I need to see Kitty.'

'She's asleep.' Breasts brushed my nose. They smelt of freckles. 'Hold still. Kitty's fine.'

'Really brained myself, huh?' I said. 'How bad?'

'Just a –' dab, dab, dab, dab went Amy's fingers. 'Well, a pretty nasty scratch if you want to know. You fell off the porch. There. Better?'

'Thank you.'

Amy bent down and kissed my nose. 'OK.'

'The door,' I tried. 'You locked Kitty in.'

'No. I locked you out. You'll see Kitty when you're ready.'

'When I'm what?'

'She could have died, Burt.'

184

'I'm ready now.'

Amy stared. 'When is Anna coming, by the way? Tristan's confused. Can you tell me that at least?'

'Boats,' I shrugged. 'Soon, I imagine. I don't know. She's afraid of flying.'

To prevent Tristan from calling his grandmother, I'd led him to believe that Anna had already departed from Poland, that she was taking a bus, then a train, then an ocean-liner, then another bus or train or something back home to Queens Falls, New York. She'd been arriving any day now for about a month.

I would call Anna tonight. I would telephone Poland. My head cleared slightly, and some pressure dissipated: there it was, a simple thing. It was not too late to change the course of my family, to divert this catastrophe. I would telephone Anna, I would speak to Tristan, I would atone, and I would prepare June's old bedroom with fresh sheets and, yes, even a small complimentary Mansion Inn chocolate on her pillow. That would make her smile. June would be here any day now. I would bathe. I would place my enemy on the next flight from Warsaw, first class. Consequences be damned.

Things felt better already. I would call my daughter's car phone, I would tell her to hurry. June, I was certain, would convince her little brother to go back to school. June was driving across the country from Long Beach, California, because she had Midwestern in-laws that occasionally required acknowledgement, she'd said. Sammy, my grandson, was with her, and no doubt collecting tribute from distended aunts and uncles he'd never seen or known existed. My sci-fi daughter had had a telephone installed in her automobile, just to be safe. She'd said that if her mother's condition suddenly worsened then to call her immediately, ASAP, and she'd ditch the stupid car wherever and she and Sammy would be on the next plane. June's husband, said June, needed to hold down the fort in California. Meaning, he'd only fly out for the funeral.

I savored the dull, bloated orange of the sinking sun. I was prepared for the future. I had carefully explained to my warden that I needed to go back to the barn for a few moments in order to collect my clothing and thoughts; and Amy sighed consent. She could not argue with general decency, and I had already taken a bath as she requested. Just a sip of mead, actually, was what I craved, if only to stave my throbbing brain and sharpen my emotions; and a new tunic, of course. Mead, tunic, and then I would begin. In my hand were To Do Tasks. In my heart jangled the Yuletide notion that everything would improve, that friendly strangers, bursting into song, would stream out from the forest. Perhaps the crack on my head did me good. But which task to do first? That was the exciting part.

My CTLR brothers and sisters had arranged their things for tomorrow and departed for one last, sordid night in the twentieth century. The Mansion Inn's lawn was strewn gloriously with the Middle Ages. Historically accurate banners snapped in a timeless wind. Tents stood, half-completed. Piles of swords, shields, lances, crossbows, armor, and . . . good Lord, what?

It was three stories high: a Siege Tower. Incredible, beautiful. Never in CTLR history had I seen its like.

Don appeared at my side, wondering if I didn't need to go back inside. I ignored him. He apologized for before, and I started walking towards the forest, towards the barn. But the big man persisted, flapping his eyelashes, following me, and asking me where I was going and what I was doing and if my head didn't maybe need stitches after all. I didn't look so hot, said he.

'I have to get some clothes,' I said, finally. I was still wearing my wife's pink bathrobe.

'Well, yeah.'

We entered the forest. Tree branches brushed the sun like clouds.

'I'm fine,' I said.

'I don't know, Burt, buddy. You keep your clothes in the woods?'

From the outside, it looked like any other abandoned nineteenth-century barn; like it could collapse at any moment, its wood gray and weathered, covered with vines, moss, mushrooms. Saplings and ferns grew from its roof, which sagged. Inside, of course, it was another story. Tristan and I had gone to great effort to stabilize the structure so that the outside could retain its ruin without falling on our heads and killing us: what we had done was not unlike building a house within a house. We had insulated the walls, built a new roof and ceiling under the original collapsing roof and ceiling, and even added a stone fireplace for winter use. The walls we hid behind a scaffolding of bookshelves. The floor space was given to Tristan's music and furniture workshop and my mead brewing, as well as other CTLR projects, including some iron-work, candle making, and sewing. Standing in the shadow of the barn, I instantly felt more at ease. It had been some weeks since I'd been inside our sanctuary, and even then it had only been to retrieve jugs of mead. Probably, it had been months since I had last stopped here to enjoy its historic quiet. Even longer since I shared that quiet with my son. I opened the door.

My son's shawms, crumhorns, lutes. I stepped back, nearly knocking Don over. I covered my mouth. His hurdy-gurdy and his heavenly vielle. It looked like a shipwreck. There was shatter, blood, everything in tiny terrible pieces – all of Tristan's handmade medieval instruments had been destroyed.

Nothing can prepare you for stepping on your son's childhood, for seeing its scattered bones. How memories sound. The crunch of them under foot. I made my way inside. I moved, stumbled: I tripped and fell down and picked myself up again, moaning, almost enjoying the pain. Tristan's Lemko instruments were untouched, loitering, gawking at the scene of the massacre like the surly peasants they were. I kicked one. And for a moment I actually believed that the Lemko instruments had somehow perpetrated this violence. The cymbaly. The trembita. That jealous, bastard sopilka.

The blood was mead. Every one of my jugs had been smashed. Bees and flies steamed up around the dark sticky spill; ants trickled down from the walls and up from the barn's wooden floorboards, and God knows but the end of life as I knew it smelled magnificent.

'Burt!' Don shouted. 'Wait, where you going?'

I was running away. The final time-destroying blast from the archangelical trumpet had blown and I had no idea where I was going. Then I did.

Not good, mostly bad, but ultimately rewarding. So this, I thought, is what it's like to engage with reality. My joints protested, my past rattled against my skull; my purple knees felt as if they were blackening, softening. I was old, hollow, yet still – even after the barn – I felt hopeful. I was more hopeful, actually, than before I had stumbled upon Tristan's butchery. The destruction was cleansing. Because maybe now, after everything, we might finally start to rebuild, to renovate at the very least. Things could not get any worse, anyway, which was a chilling sort of relief. The roar and vibration of the vacuum cleaner felt good. It burned out my insides, my mistakes, and inflated my sense of purpose. It sucked up the bad things, leaving a trail of purity behind it. Just like new. It was simple. Life, it taught, could be just as simple: if you keep running over it, back and forth, back and forth. I pushed the machine from room to room. Occasionally, a guest would appear, stare, and depart, no doubt flabbergasted to see an old man with a deformed nose in a pink bathrobe vacuuming. Well there it is, I thought. A concerned Marie tried to give me something that smelled of Don to wear. But I would do my penance, I would play the fool.

In my fantasy Tristan was crying. 'You've got to help me, Dad. Please.' In that hardly-there voice, standing over the corpses of his instruments; and in my fantasy I was helping him. I was being strong, vacuuming. He had collapsed in Amy's arms. Next time, so help me, he would collapse in mine.

The vacuum cleaner stopped. I turned around. The plug had been snapped from the wall.

The real Tristan stood before me. The real Tristan was also crying, his shoulders heaving. No, I thought, no. I had been locked out. They had locked me out. I hadn't said goodbye.

And I suppose that I raised my voice, perhaps I even screamed. In any event, Tristan hurled an empty jug of mead at my chest. It hit me and I went down. Falling atop the vacuum cleaner, I lost Kitty's pink bathrobe and I lost my breath. The vacuum cleaner was warm.

'Tristan,' I gasped.

My son kicked me. I rolled over. I felt no pain.

'I just called Warsaw,' he said, standing above me. '*You* –'

XI

I should have known that only the dead can be truly born again. I was not yet dead: my son had only kicked in my ribs, and the throbbing of my head was probably caused by a combination of mead-withdrawal and falling off the Mansion Inn's porch. Tristan, for whatever reason, had not bothered to kick my head.

It was the day after the worst of days. I looked around me, awake. The medieval prints on the wall, books everywhere, the Battle of Poitiers gruesome in a heap on the floor, a teapot, bloody toilet paper, Band-Aids, a slice of cheese, and a ribbon of carpenter ants – two Hildegard von Bingen compact discs staring up from the carpet with fanatical serenity. Morning light, pain, the inhuman clamor of birds.

Someone was pounding on the door. Shaking the sleep away, I stood.

Hopefully, I thought, it was Tristan come to finish the job. And how polite of him to first knock. My legs quavered. But I was resolved. I was suicidal. I opened the door.

The mid-morning sun slapped me before the 'Hoobah!' burst in my face. Throughout the Mansion Inn's ground spread my Middle Ages, hundreds of arms raised in salute, fists and weapons, voices booming a hearty, emotionally medieval good morning. The Confraternity of Times Lost Regained. They've come to rescue me, to take me back where I belong. The rebellion against the twentieth century had begun.

Lady Isabella Estrildes, Shimshon Moshe, Hringhere Wytheberd, Edric Coffyn, Willemu Wythe Hameres, Randulfus Ryppringham, Lord Benedictu Conoc, Petronilla Whowood, Gunnora le Bone, Maria Ryppringham, Lucia Warbulton, Avelina Olyngworthe. They arrived in droves. They wore long-sleeved tunics fastened at the neck with brooches; circlets, dagged edged and scalloped fabrics, tabards, pendant belts, sideless surcotes, coronets, elaborate hairpieces; embroidered sleeves, pearled wimples, and ceremonial cloaks. Bright blues, yellows, crimsons, purples, greens, wool, samite, tin foil, taffeta, iron, OOP eye glasses, silver spray-painted plastic and cardboard, goatees, beards, damask. Two steps out into that crowd and, I knew, my problems would cease along with the present century. My problems wouldn't even be born yet: anything was still possible out there in the past.

I gave myself to the re-enaction. I wandered the Middle Ages like one condemned, the past few days became future days and therefore something I could still thwart: I brooded on Tristan's attack, my wife's illness, and my own inability to grow up as one might brood on an upcoming trial, or a difficult task one has to complete. It ceased to be history.

Swords clanged, shields crashed. Shouts of 'Hold!' and 'Clear!' and 'Good morrow!' and 'Aye!' I watched ladies admire one another's handiwork, tittering, trilling, flouncing and strutting before knights, squires, and princes who minced around in their pointed poulaines, the absurd French-style footwear that seemed to be all the rage at the CTLR that year. There were fools juggling and troubadours weaving hackneyed clichés around melodies too ancient to care. I ambled past pavilions, under banners. I greeted one and all, and was greeted warmly by one and all: Eckbert Attquiet, scholar and master mead-maker was home. Groups of children ran through the crowds. I smiled, almost giddy. There was already maypole dancing, and the games pavilion had begun setting up for the outdoor chess and big Jeu de Boules (a thirteenth-century forerunner to lawn bowling) tournament. Some had already begun to play Hoodman's Blind, Last Couple in Hell, and Hot Cockles. The air tasted of smelting iron, burning wood, roasting pig, mowed lawn, wool, and perspiration. I had escaped. My knees stopped hurting, as did my ribs. That was all still in the future, hundreds of years from now in a land not yet discovered, far across the ocean. I felt the wound in my head close up like a zipper. It could all still be prevented.

The CTLR incorporated elements of feudalism, Marxist and feminist revisionism, historical Dungeons & Dragons whimsy, and a not-unhealthy dose of can-do North American spirit. To some it was a costume party, a primary-source bacchanal, or an alternative sports and games center, but to most my Confraternity was still a serious historical workshop. It was a place of learning and discovery through re-enactment. It had long been out of my hands but I still took pride in it and the people who devoted their lives to making it what it was. Since the creation of the CTLR many such societies had sprung up across North America and the world. Some of these were large, unwieldy, bureaucratic, and no doubt prosperous corporations now, consisting of hundreds of thousands of members. They published books of rules and regulations, magazines, and newsletters, and operated rather like franchises ('Burger King Societies', we CTLR stalwarts tended to call them). I had always taken pains to keep our organization relatively small, hands on, and non-hierarchical in a very unmedieval manner. No larger than necessary, our own history and organization structure – when such a structure was deemed necessary – was to be exchanged orally or by illuminated manuscript in a pre-Gutenberg, pre-Xerox, pre-electric manner, or not at all. Among other re-enactment communities, the Confraternity of Times Lost Regained had a reputation as rather libertarian and anarchic, but with a strong focus on authenticity. Unlike other organizations, we had no official royalty.

Many saw us as a rather pedantic bunch. For example, in the medieval world, mead, wine, and beer were the staple beverages, water being unsanitary and dangerous. Thus, the CTLR, alone among other re-enactment organizations, kept a very strict policy concerning alcohol, which was: you had better have a good reason not to drink it. Driving home, back to the twentieth century in an automobile (a 'time machine' in CTLR-speak), was a good reason. Almost anything else was not. If that made us pedants, so be it. For the most part, I tended to think that I hadn't thought big enough. Why only a society? Why only weekends?

'Eckbert, you sack of pepper! How dost thou?'

Even within groups of eccentrics there are eccentrics. Sir Bob of Ghent (aka 'The Bobonic Plague') was just such a man. Pudgy and ever ablink, Bob of Ghent was obsessed with the Black Death. That in itself was normal, or not to be particularly noticed; it was the gregarious good cheer he invested in his obsession that made people slightly wary every time he slipped a Black Death fact or figure into even the most innocuous of exchanges. Once he came to a meeting stuck with rubber buboes, screaming and flailing in a historically accurate manner that nobody could do anything to stop, not even our two chirurgeons, until two hours into the meeting he finally decided to die. He was kindly asked not to do that again. He could die, we had decided, as long as he didn't scream beforehand. Normally, by the end of every revel, tourney, or meeting, Bob of Ghent found a corner to quietly die in, a smile invariably smeared across his face. God only knew what the man did during his weekdays.

That day he was master of the buttery, the beverage pavilion. This was sometimes my role. Jugs and bottles of mead, wine, and beer were arrayed on a large table, which hid, I knew, OOP water-coolers.

'God ye good den. Thou art healthy this day?' I asked. 'Got that Plague under control, Sir Bob?' I scanned the table for some jug small enough to keep under my tunic.

He laughed. ''Tis this Lemon-Nutmeg Mead recipe of thine. It'd get anything under control, I dare say. Prithee, Eckbert, take a draft with me?' then he coughed, and flinched, blinking, as if tugged up by the ear. He looked to his left. 'Or water, I mean to say. Got some water here,' he added in what I assumed was his twentieth-century voice. 'Juice?'

Juice? 'Perchance I shall return anon,' I said. Was Amy Sturk watching? My God, had Bob of Ghent actually been warned about me?

'I'm sorry, Burt,' he said, again out of persona. 'Seriously, you all right? You don't look so – you want to sit down?'

I departed with a bow and the traditional mead master's farewell of 'May your bottles never burst.'

'Buboes,' he corrected, with a sad grin.

'Aye, those too.' Goddamn Amy. Goddamn them all.

If Tristan contacted Anna, then she would be here today. Tomorrow at the latest. Six hundred years from now.

The day rejoiced with the practice of heraldry, archery, lace making and needlecraft, metalwork, manuscript illumination, and brewing. I took a detour to the edge of the gathering, checking on my medieval garden. As historically accurate as the upstate New York soil would permit, I'd planted flowers indiscriminately with the lettuce, sorrel, shallots, beets, scallions, and herbs. The flowers' blossoms could be used in cooking. Lavender, marigolds, and peonies were perfect for decoration, while violets could be minced up with lettuce, carrots, and onions. I said their names, as one says a spell to slow time. Basil. Mint. Agrimony. Hyssop. Dittany. Sage. Fennel. Parsley. Savory. Coriander. Marjoram. Rue. Mallow. Nightshade. Borage. I'd taken this garden over after Anna returned to Poland. She had grown only potatoes. The Mansion Inn always had hundreds more potatoes than it needed, potatoes rotting, going green, black, soft, sprouting roots in big boxes in the basement. 'Laugh now,' she'd say. 'But when World War comes what you going to eat? Books?'

I left the garden, reminding myself that Anna had yet to be born. That none of that had yet happened. My wife wasn't dying. In this world my son didn't hate me.

I passed the ruins of the medieval mew that I built for Tristan when he started elementary school. The boy had loved

196

feathers, so I had thought that he might love birds too. For months the two of us had studied primary-source books on medieval falconry.

'Nails,' I said to myself.

Standing right there, Tristan had once passed me nails. I had hammered nails. Long ago I built a mew and my son sat exactly there in a little aluminum chair, asking questions, watching, reading his books about feathers. 'What color you want to paint it?' I had asked him. And for some reason this question, after much deliberation, had brought the boy to tears. He just didn't know.

'You want what?' I can still hear the pride in Kitty's incredulity. 'Burt did you tell him he could have falcons? Do they even make them anymore?'

Tristan said, 'I want falcons.'

'I told him maybe.'

'Burt,' Kitty sighed.

'Dad and I built a mew. For falcons.'

'Burt, tell him he cannot have falcons. Falcons are dangerous. The mall doesn't even have falcons.'

'Your mom's right. Canaries are better,' I told Tristan. 'Parakeets.'

'They have them in the Middle Ages too, Dad?'

'They can talk.'

Kitty smiled, 'Burt, I don't think canaries can talk.'

'Daddy?' Tristan was so excited. 'They can talk?'

Now there is nothing left but a soggy pile of wood, moss, and garbage bags full of last year's leaves. In the end we had painted the mew gold. Later, some of the canaries had pecked at the paint and were poisoned to death. The others simply disappeared; and we all pretended to not suspect Tristan of setting them free, or killing them for their feathers.

'Burt, really, they can't talk. Tell him.'

'Ours will talk,' I told Tristan. 'Don't worry. We will teach ours to talk.'

I made it a point of not acknowledging any CTLR re-enactor on the street when I saw them in twentieth-century Queens Falls, unless that man or woman, donning his or her CTLR persona, addressed my persona, Eckbert Attquiet. We were others during the weekdays, and it was embarrassing to be caught out of character in mundane garb. Like being caught cheating on a spouse, or unclothed in public.

Our mundane lives, as we called them, were taboo during these weekend re-enactments. Names, jobs, economic woes, dying wives: everything left in the time machines that brought each CTLR member to my Middle Ages. The illusion had to transcend illusion, and it generally did. Though some of us took this more seriously than others. We were known as Authenticity Mavens. For us, the CTLR had become more real than real life, and we lived weekend to weekend, only feeling truly alive when in our so-called persona, at a re-enactment or involved in the uncountable hours of research we devoted to our passion, making sure everything was as authentic as possible. I could always recognize a fellow Authenticity Maven. Simply put, they were the ones that weren't acting; their eyes clear, solid, both far away and very close indeed. They were more comfortable, happy, and, most importantly, relieved: as if they'd just taken off their shoes after walking endless miles. (Also, Authenticity Mavens tended towards facial hair and alcoholism, whereas the less committed tended towards less body fat, ponytails, and inaccurate Celtic tattoos.) I believe that some of us were ourselves only during the act of re-enacting. That is, the truest expression of what we felt ourselves to be. I don't think that the CTLR subsumed personalities, as such; I really think that it set some of us free. The argument being, wasn't our daily life also just a persona? Masks, costumes, roles. Building up one's historical CTLR persona, finding a name, applicable skill, social caste, country of origin, and job, and then researching a historical time-frame within the Middle Ages, the joy of learning all you could about that was time-consuming to say the least, and, for some, even life consuming. For some, their personas repaired aspects of their normal lives that they were uneasy about. The cliché of the accountant becoming a marauding knight every weekend, for instance. It was, said one ex-CTLR member who happened to be a psychologist in his mundane life, rather therapeutic 'if not taken too far'. But we took it too far. Far wasn't far enough for some of us.

In a way, we were all historians in the Confraternity of Times Lost Regained. That is what people from the outside always failed to understand. History books can never lower themselves down from the third person, that false godlike overview, but reality is never lived that way. History did not happen that way. That we looked idiotic is relative. Shouldn't all explorers be brave?

Every moment I expected to be attacked from behind, to be sliced down where I stood, throttled and thrown to the ground by my son.

I lurked on the edges of workshops, wandering, speaking

with peasants and princes, nibbling cloven fruit and meat pies. I clung to my persona, to Eckbert Attquiet, as someone drowning clings to the shoulders of another, no matter that the other is also drowning. So we both began to go down, Eckbert and Burt, into a sucking muddle of the past and the future. Half of the people I spoke with actually broke from their personas and wanted to know how Burt was. 'Burt?' I said. 'Mayhap you're confusing me for another.' God damn them. I needed the truly, purely delusional or I would crumble.

The Mansion Inn, all the while, fumed there sourly. Lording it up, pretending to ignore us. It wouldn't lower itself to our level. I wondered if Tristan was in there, up in that house. Don and Marie and some of our other guests had come to the porch to watch, as if we were a circus. They even interacted good-naturedly with some less authentic CTLR members, having their questions answered, their jokes appreciated, and their glasses and mugs refilled with historically accurate alcohol. It took me some moments to see Lonna Katsav sitting beside Don. He'd contacted her, I guess, and I felt less alone suddenly, less out of control. I hadn't seen Lonna since she told me, some time before, that I ought to be committed to a mental institution. It was good to know that she was still watching over me. I had missed her terribly. Of course, Lonna didn't even try to get my attention. She knew better than to call out across the centuries.

The afternoon waned. The scents of the coming feast wafted over the grounds. Dogs barked, dozens of them, forming investigative packs. Tomorrow, six hundred years from now, this world would be over and then where would I be?

Someone tapped my shoulder. Slowly, expecting a punch in the face, I turned. 'Lady Isabella Estrildes,' I said.

200

'Amy,' corrected Amy Sturk. She held her wimple in her hands.

I took a deep breath.

'How is Kitty?' Burt Hecker managed to ask. Kitty, Burt Hecker's wife, was dying. His son, Tristan, had attacked him. His ribs began to ache at once.

'Tristan's with her. She wanted me to open the windows, which is just great. I was a bit worried but the noise is doing her good. It's made her so happy. She misses you, Burt.'

'Does she know?'

'She knows her mother'll be here soon. That's all she knows.'

'You probably think that I –'

'It doesn't matter what I think,' Amy said. 'Lonna's here, you know.'

'Can I explain?'

'No.'

That was good. Because I had no idea how I would explain any of my actions. Better to simply accept my punishment and let others explain my actions to me, like the child I so obviously was.

'Just try, OK. Just don't be such an idiot,' she whispered into my ear. She hugged me. 'But I'm proud of you today, you goat.' And she laughed, warning me, 'So far.' I hadn't yet imbibed any historically accurate beverages.

'Tristan,' I said.

'Don't worry, he'll cool down.' But she didn't sound convinced. 'Look, I'll come get you after Tristan's left. You can see Kitty then.'

'I can see Kitty whenever I want.'

'No, Burt. I'm sorry. You can't.'

So the two of us stood there, an island of twentieth-century despair, while the randy, gaudy tumult of the medieval world continued about us, lapping at our sides. I was as scared to stay in the center of that emotional vortex as I was to let go, to fall back into the past. The past was as empty of Kitty as the future.

'Sons of iniquity! Miscreants! Hordes of the Anti-Christ!' The crowd we were in parted and from the forest came our knights.

I held on to Amy's hand. But Lady Isabella Estrildes said, 'Stay close, Eckbert. These knights. 'Tis trouble, I do fear.'

'Trouble, aye,' I said. 'Trouble.'

Dirty, vicious, proud, their standards and banners snarling; crossbows, picks, faussars, planchons, axes, guisarmes, shields, bucklers, breastplates, and swords both great and small: two dozen strong, they came bearing the farming tools of a most perfidious harvest. 'This kingdom shall tremble before us!' shouted one. The most anticipated segment of our CTLR event was about to begin. Sneering in the sun with their mail of iron and lead and, yes, plastic and tin-foil. Many had covered their heads with reinforced fencing masks or the traditional CTRL Barrel Helm: an ordinary steel bucket.

In medieval times, contrary to popular belief, most knights were bandits, mercenaries, lawless brigands, skinners, high-waymen, and thieves. The supposed chivalry of Charlemagne and Roland had as much to do with the majority of medieval knights as the historical Jesus with the temporal riches and hypocrisy of the Catholic Church, or any church for that matter. Generally accompanied by their immoral entourage of servants, priests, and whores, they went from tourney to tourney like a touring rock and roll band, sports team, or gang of South Sea pirates. Court to court, skirmish to skirmish, rape to rape. Fighting as the noble's substitution for work. In the Middle Ages, knights tended to form itinerant households. Our CTLR knights had studied their primary sources well.

'War!' roared Domnall mac Luloig. 'How sweet a thing is war!' Sir Domnall, fey and of sallow chest, fancied himself something of a rapist and pillager, his shield snidely quoting St Jerome: 'I PRAISE MARRIAGE AND LAUD MATRIMONY BECAUSE IT PROVIDES ME WITH VIRGINS!' Domnall claimed to be a Cathar, that is, a member of a medieval sect that denied the Redemption and the Incarnation and claimed that God has brought his only begotten son into the world via Mary's ear. Cathars despised the Old Testament and believed that there was no Hell or Purgatory. Our World, they insisted, was Hell enough.

Domnall mac Luloig scanned our faces. He swung his two-handed steel longsword in huge arcs, his body moving in a circle with each swing. The sword gave the illusion of moving slowly through the air, like a landing jumbo jet.

The knights beat their weapons against their shields, growling, stamping their feet, sending all of us back further, enlarging the circle around them. The bloodshed was about to commence.

'You shall pullulate like worms,' announced one, shoving his longsword into the earth. 'Today you shall all pullulate like the worms thou art!'

Quite a few children hid terrified behind their parents, while others stood in open-faced awe. I did not let go of

Lady Isabella's hand. Everyone reacted to the knights as their persona demanded: some cheered, while others swooned, hid, hectored, or cursed. Eckbert Attquiet, as was his wont, thought only of running out onto the field and throwing himself upon a longsword.

The mêlée began. The knights fought not with their historically accurate and highly coveted 'live steel' – which they put to the side, being only for display purposes (there was a bit of Car Show about some of these knights in the way they constantly washed and polished their steel swords) – but a variety of sword made from ethylfoam and rattan. They called these 'boffers'.

'They do die nimbly, do they not?' a goldsmith behind me commented.

They were all – even the most spindly – well trained fighters. They swung, clashed, charged, and circled with ferocious, surprising agility. They did, indeed, die nimbly: falling and twirling and screaming as if their necks were hot fountains of blood. 'Thy sword shall slice naught but air this day!' someone shouted. 'I'm killed! I'm killed!' cried another. I looked up at our house, at that giant dying ear of a window. People screamed and moaned in agony, and Kitty listened. 'Die!' someone cried. 'You dog, die!'

It ended and the deceased, dying, and crippled knights roused themselves with calls for wine and wenches.

I'd fought only once, when Tristan, then just a boy, had urged me to. I had been killed almost immediately. The Cathar, Domnall mac Luloig, had hit me in the head with a foam mace. Failing to revive me, my son had run back out onto the battlefield, weaving between bemused combatants, to avenge my murder. Domnall mac Luloig, offering no quarter, did his best to kill Tristan. But, to everyone's amusement, the boy would not die. He beat his fists on Domnall's legs, he was hit over and over again with that mace, then a short sword, then a longsword, but Tristan would not be killed. One year later, his mother received a concerned telephone call from a Queens Falls elementary school teacher. For the essay topic 'The Saddest Day of My Life', Tristan had written about the day he had been unable to prevent or properly avenge the murder of his father.

The finale of the knights' presentation was the formal unveiling of the huge Mobile Assault Tower. They pulled it from the forest and set it up near my house, as if the rescue of my wife from cancer, that vile kidnapper, was in fact this incredible Siege Tower's purpose. Nobody had ever tried to build something so large or intricate before. Domnall mac Luloig and a small retinue of his more skilled knights must have spent a year on its construction alone. Knowing Domnall, no modern tools would have been used, no wood bought from lumber yards. Not only would he copy a primary-source design but he would also, to the best of his ability, construct the thing in the exact manner of a thirteenth-century carpenter: from the cutting down of the trees to use of medieval systems of measurement. It was a masterpiece. The only tragedy was that we had no castle to lay siege to. No wall to put asunder.

'The Victorians!' someone from Domnall mac Luloig's brigand bellowed, pointing at the Mansion Inn. Don, drinking wine on the porch, got a kick out of that. 'Bring it on!' he shouted. Lonna, catching my eye for the first time, smiled and rested her hand on Don's shoulder. Marie scowled.

'Nay, nay!' another yelled. 'I do think 'tis those Civil War re-enactors we should drown in blood this day!'

'Aye!'

There followed much mirth. 'Onwards, noble knights! To Gettysburg!'

But before they could lay siege to anything, the crowd parted once again. Scattered, actually. Because an automobile, hoarsely honking, drove straight onto the field, snapping fallen weapons and bursting jugs of wine, beer, and water. Peasants shrieked. This was quite an affront on many different levels, and for some in the CTLR it was hard to even process; a few stood staring, stags in the headlights. From the car window there came a torrent of twentieth-century vulgarities, curses, and promises to contact the New York State police if we didn't have the good sense to disappear. People picked up what they could and fled. June seemed to leap from the automobile, slamming the door then slamming her fists on the car's hood while calling on me to present myself forthwith. I had always found that the surgical reduction of my daughter's nose had made her eyes seem vaguely inappropriate, like outsized upgrades. Like she had inflated them, and then had them polished. Needless to say, this effect increased significantly when she was murderous.

The CTLR backed further away, or pretended to make themselves busy, ignoring our twentieth-century interloper altogether. I had never seen June so full of wrath. 'Disrespect! Disrespect!' she shouted. 'You crazy, disrespectful fucks!'

Two goodly knights stood before me, granting me sanctuary behind their capes. 'Think nothing of it, Sir Eckbert,' one whispered.

Lady Isabella emerged from the crowd. 'June, it's OK,' she said. 'Not you too.'

Amy removed her wimple. 'It's a wimple,' she said. 'It's me, it's Amy.'

'You stay away from me, Amy, I'm warning you. Where's my mother? Burt, you unbelievable asshole! Where are you? Where is my mother?'

Lonna sauntered onto the field. She had never seemed so tall, so coldly in control. Even the cocktail in her hand she brandished like a Scepter of Reason.

'Kiddo, shhh,' she said. 'It's OK.'

June fell into the lawyer's arms. 'Oh, my God. Where is he? What is going on?'

'Listen to me,' Lonna said, holding June close. 'It was your mother's idea. She's fine. She's upstairs with your brother. June, your mother wanted them to have this. It was her idea, OK? She wanted to hear the tourney, just like normal, do you understand me? June? More than anything, June, she wants things to go on as normal.'

'I came as soon as I could,' June sobbed. 'I'm sorry. I came as soon as I could.'

'I know,' Lonna said. 'Your mother knows.'

'These people. Oh, God. Where is he, Lonna? I hate these people so much. Where is Burt?'

'Shhh.'

The front door of the house opened. Tristan seemed hung there, dangled. He looked at his sister and burst into tears.

June let go of Lonna and ran to my son. She embraced him, the door closed, and like that my children were gone. I stepped away from the knights. My family now twenty yards and six hundred years away.

Lonna's hand found my shoulder. 'Stay, Burt,' she said. 'Not yet. Look.'

Because in the backseat of June's car, staring out the window at the gathered warriors and damsels, princes and magicians, was Sammy, my grandson, wearing the largest smile that I had ever seen. His mother had crashed their car into a fairy tale.

XII

'She's coming in tomorrow morning. Anna will be here tomorrow,' Amy said. 'I'd keep away for a few days though, Burt. To be honest. From Tristan and from June.'

'So be it.' I downed a mug of mead.

'Just the one,' my friend stipulated. The candlelight, the sound of medieval masticating, belching, shouting, roaring. The players, flatterers, fawners, talebearers, minstrels, and the jongleurs spinning fourteenth-century political satires. The laments and the Dawn Songs. It was a magnificent feast.

'Sir Sammy, you having fun?'

Sammy was having the time of his life. He bounced on my lap, occasionally reaching up to molest a nose he couldn't believe was real. Obviously, he had never seen a pre-operative photograph of his mother.

Nearly three hundred medieval re-enactors eating outside by the light of candles, the moon, the stars; and I tried to see everything through the boy's eyes. This magic world that I helped create. People visited us, paying tribute. Domnall mac Luloig presented the boy with a knight's helmet and a little ethylfoam short sword, and Bob of Ghent even brought Sammy a little goblet of mead before expiring in the corner, his head thumping down on a green wooden picnic table. I had not seen Sammy since he was born. My grandson could talk; he clapped wildly at the jesters, singing along with the jongleurs. He called me Grampa.

The CTLR's donkey boys – the historically accurate appellation for medieval firewood carriers – had outdone themselves this year. The bonfire licked the stars. The Mansion Inn, even, with its electricity switched off, was now only lit by candles. From the dark, and with a little squinting, it could have been a castle, and I imagined the ghost of George West, confused, watching us from the upper windows. The Paper Bag King dethroned. That nothing lasts forever – that was also a hopeful thing.

The feast had started after the typically drawn-out and rather dull CTLR investiture and dubbing ceremonies. Then came the spitmasters and soupmasters and serving wenches with the food. Bashed neeps, sausage pies, cream herb soup in loaves of bread, Cornish game hens, spirited fruit (raisins and dried fruit drowned in apricot brandy), turbot in sauce, vension, suckling pig, and the seven OOP turkeys some of us were willing to pretend were swans. Sammy loved that we ate most of these dishes with our fingers and wiped our hands on our clothing or the tablecloth that served as the communal napkin. He also loved that it was considered bad manners to eat everything on your plate. Some food had to be tossed onto the floor, or, in this case, the Mansion Inn's lawn. I told him how in the Middle Ages it was believed that cinnamon was collected from the nests of giant birds in Arabia, how the Egyptians were thought to harvest spices by stretching a net across the Nile river, and how cassia trees were believed to grow in ponds guarded by winged fiends.

There was even a Mundane Table for our friends from the

future: Lonna, Don, and Marie. Don, loudly inebriated, enlightened all on many different subjects.

'In their past lives most people here were medieval servants, desperately poor, despairing, trod upon,' a woman I had not yet met said. 'It's healthy, what you've created here. It's doing a lot of good. It's a reincarnation workshop whether you know it or not, and I am very impressed. Reclaiming the past in a positive manner. My name is Tivona Henry.'

'Eckbert Attquiet,' I said.

Tivona wore a simple peasant's tunic, like mine. Her massive head of dark curls made her look like a more stable, content version of my daughter or mother-in-law. 'I know,' she smiled. 'Lady Isabella Estrildes invited me tonight. I run a Hildegard von Bingen chant workshop.'

'I brew mead.'

'Your grandson is beautiful,' Tivona said. 'Anyway, nice to meet you, finally. I'd like to speak with you later, if I could. Back in the twentieth century. Until then,' and the peculiar woman hugged me.

'Mommy!' Sammy said, jumping from my lap, into my daughter's. June had appeared at my side, sitting where Amy had been not two minutes before.

'Hey, little guy. You having a good time?' she asked her son, her voice flat, distant. Her eyes were red.

Her son was having a very good time. Sammy hugged June's neck, and June stared over the table, into the Middle Ages. She would not look at me, and I could barely think. I said, 'I'm so happy you are here.'

June began to cry. 'Oh, Daddy,' she said. 'What have you done?'

It was obvious that she had just been to see her mother,

211

but whether Kitty had seen June is another question. I placed my arm on June's shoulder. Shocked, angered, she twisted and flung it off. She said, 'Do not. Don't. I swear to God, Burt.'

'She wanted us to have this,' I said.

June put Sammy on the ground and the boy, surely used to his mother's moods, hit the ground running. 'You know,' she said, laughing strangely, 'I'm glad Grandma isn't here. To be perfectly honest, that woman is way crazier than you are. And harder to deal with. But what you did. My God. Not tell her, lying to Tristan. *Lying to Mom*. This drinking and locking yourself up there with Mom and,' June tried to collect herself, 'and Mom and the pills and Tristan running the place by himself. Tristan all alone here. He's just a little boy, you know? Inside he's just this weird little kid.'

'I'm sorry.'

June nodded. 'I know you are. Sitting there in your fucking tunic with your fucking mead. That's the funny thing. I really know you are sorry.'

I wanted to tell June how beautiful her son was. I said, 'Sammy.'

'Yeah. He likes you.'

'Do you think so?'

June reached for my jug of mead. She put it to her mouth and drank, she drank for a long time. 'Used to steal this stuff, you know. Back in high school.'

'I thought you hated my mead.'

'Oh, I did. I do. I mean, OK, actually, I really liked it. Used to bring it to parties, used to be the only reason I was invited to some parties.' June made a face. 'It was so easy to steal, Tristan would help me. I told myself I was stealing

212

it to piss you off, but you know, this is pretty great stuff.'

'It is pretty good, isn't it?'

June laughed. 'This is fucked up, Burt. You do know that?'

We both looked around at the living history, the CTLR raging on all sides, the medieval clothing, the fire, the uproar. 'We're alike in some ways,' I said, remembering June alone all day with her rocks, and her giant books about lava and the early history of the earth.

June just shook her head. 'Don't.'

'How was your trip here? The Midwest. How is Jake?'

'Wow.'

'Jack,' I corrected.

'Whatever, Burt. Look,' and her face softened. She turned around and up towards her mother's window. 'Never mind,' she concluded. I tried not to think of her nose as missing.

'I'm so happy you are back,' I repeated, desperately.

'You know what?' June said, softly, looking up into the night sky. 'I really despise it over there.'

'What?'

'California. Everything. I don't know. And now I can't believe I'm home again. It's been so long. But all this. And Mom.' Her breathing changed. She wiped her eyes.

'June.'

She looked around her again, and at me. 'Most of all I hate how normal this all is. How good this stupid shit makes me feel. These ridiculous people. How normal it feels.'

'Would you like some more mead?'

'This is not normal,' and June stood, suddenly nervous. 'No,' she said. 'No. I've got to get out of here. I've got to see Mom.'

'I'll come with you.'

'Tristan will kill you,' June said. 'He will kill you, Burt. You've broken his heart, you know that. You've betrayed him and I've never seen him so confused and full of hate. And he's right.'

'I promise things will get better. Anna will be here tomorrow, correct?'

'That's just what we need. A bloodthirsty Lemko. Nice one, Burt. Things won't get better. Just don't do anything stupid. Mom needs you so much.'

'Let me come with you.'

But June turned and left. Sammy, no doubt lurking on the sides and watching us, bounded back, climbing onto my lap. He held in his hand a painted egg.

'Oyez!' a herald boomed. 'The populace is invited to draw nigh and be seated!'

Then Tivona Henry, Amy Sturk, and some other women – both CTLR and twentieth-century – stood and began to chant. Their amateur plainchant was technically awful, but true, in the way that laughter and crying and breathing are true. I held my breath. They chanted a variation of a Hildegard von Bingen piece that I couldn't quite place, their Latin mealy and slurred. The music was timeless though, beneath the heavens, beneath light which had just started its journey towards us when Hildegard had left her anchorage and begun composing music, or so I wished to believe – because, really, what did I know about the solar system? What did I know about anything? The bonfire crackled and sang along. My grandson half asleep in my arms. I looked up at my wife's window. Kitty was awake, listening; and, more than that, I knew she was happy. There was a candle in her window. I knew at that moment that we were together, and that we always would be together. Tivona's singers transcended any idea of history.

Today I can still remember that feeling, and how I wish now that I'd stopped there, capped that evening right there with that final, glorious knowing. But one thing led to another and, God help me, I got an idea.

The last time I had seen Anna Bibko was eight months after Polish Communism had collapsed. She was leaving, she'd announced. Back to Poland for good – and for the good of the ethnic Lemkos all over Eastern Europe and the world. Being the most prominent American Lemko, a legend in the movement, she'd been asked by some newly-founded Lemko Rights organization in Warsaw to take a leading roll in the struggle. 'Born in Lemkovyna, I will die in Lemkovyna. In the mountains of my ancestors, like dropping rain.' I wasn't accompanying my mother-in-law to the Albany airport.

'Say goodbye, at least,' Kitty told me. 'Be the Big Man.'

For over twenty-five years, Anna had been my bane, and I hers. Twenty-five years of Cold War and we'd never gotten used to each other, or learned of a way to cohabitate peacefully, besides the wholesale denial of one another's existence. For Anna, everything was a problem; her words were either lectures or epistles from the darker edges of despondency. There was no compassion, or humor, or joy, only a furrowed seriousness of intent: for what was life but the avoidance and the remembrance of mass-murder? You could trust only work, death, and the unremitting awfulness of everything. What were laughter and happiness but a shallow luxury, an obscenity to the memory of those who could no longer laugh or be happy? She hadn't run the Mansion Inn in thirty years, but still worked there – in much the same capacity as her mother did all those years ago, doing the laundry and washing the dishes – still done up in her Lemko folk costumes and reading her list of the Lemko dead to anyone fool enough to listen. Guests sometimes mistook her for a ghost. She'd become more belligerent, extreme, and the old woman's grip on reality outside her own shrinking world had diminished considerably, but she was not crazy. She was unhappy. Not so much lost as missing, gone. And each year more so. Every year that had taken her further from her fabled Lemkovyna, every new innovation or political cycle that went forward and spared not a glance at the history she had devoted her life to protecting, reliving, and someday returning to. It was my opinion that returning to Poland after over sixty years would kill her spirit and hasten her bodily demise. Her memories would not find fertile soil there, they'd be confronted with a change worse and more ugly than she could possibly imagine. I believed that she had no real idea of what she was going to find in post-communist Warsaw. But maybe she knew this also. It is quite possible that failure was the entire point: her final act of self-castigation for not dying with her people, for all her varied American sins. If the United States wouldn't kill her then Poland would, just like it killed hundreds of her people all those years ago.

'I've come to wish you well, Anna,' I said, and meant it.

She sat alone in the George West Room, propped up in her bright, grotesquely festive Lemko folk costume. She looked stuffed. Like a mummy of colorful ribbons and complex bows. I could almost imagine her as the little Lemko girl she had once been, before her emigration to America eighty years ago, waiting to board the ship that would take her hundreds of years into the future. She looked like someone preparing to hold her breath. It suddenly occurred to me that Anna would never see her family again; my mother-in-law had gone too far this time, and she knew it. She did not want to leave.

'Thank you,' she said. Crisp as a smack across the face.

Though she was almost in her nineties, she could easily pass for, say, seventy, or even younger when indignation fully animated her. Or she could have been one hundred. In fact, she was just as timeless as when I'd first seen her; an oak of a woman, a living, folkloric legend.

'Perhaps you and I have a lot in common after all,' I hazarded, overcome with something like regret. 'I think I understand what you're doing,' I said.

'I remember first meeting you,' she said. 'I remember your nose.'

'You were very persuasive,' I smiled. '"Land of Earth's First Easter Egg", "Land of Communist Atrocities".'

'But you were not the President of the United States of America.'

'No,' I laughed. Her memory was perfect. But one did not laugh around Anna Bibko; to laugh was to deny the atrocities. She was not joking then and she was not joking now: I wasn't the President of the United States of America. Was that really a disappointment of hers? Likely, yes. Yes, it really truly was.

'I have hated you,' she said.

She still had the power to knock the wind out of me. 'I once tried to know you,' I said. 'I never wanted things to be like this. How stupid. I've always respected you, though. Never more so than today.'

217

'You respect nothing.'

'OK,' I conceded. 'Fine. But you, Anna, tell me, will you not now, after all these years, respect your daughter at least? Respect the life we've made together? Kitty and I?'

'Listen to this. Such bullshit. You can never know me or understand or have in common anything with me. How you even dare? I watch you. You I keep close eye on, waiting when you going to suicide. You curse my daughter. You have put the curse on my family.'

For Kitty I would stay calm. 'She loves me, Anna,' I said. 'Kitty loves me.'

'Kitty no love you.'

'Have a nice trip,' I said, walking out. 'Bye. Hope you find your home. Wherever or whatever that might be. You know what, I'm only glad it's no longer here.'

'Kitty pity you!'

'Jesus Christ.' That did it. 'I came here to say goodbye, to wish you well!'

'So noble so suddenly? You and me, why suddenly such stupid fucking bullshit?' And she laughed. She actually laughed! 'Why this wishing well make-believing American bullshit?'

I exhaled, tried to grin, and said, 'Right. You're right. What do you want from me? What could I have done to make you happy, tell me? All these years. Tell me that at least.'

'You? Nothing.'

'There it is.'

'There. Yes. My daughter is worth hundreds of you.'

'I agree.'

'Tristan –' Anna began.

'Let's leave my son out of this, why don't we?'

'*Your* son?'

'You don't even really see Tristan.'

'Yes, and what you see?'

It occurred to me that perhaps we saw the same person, and maybe we were both wrong. I said, 'Goodbye.'

'Tristan isn't from here. Here confused Tristan and you think you know why? I know why. He don't belong here is why. You think you don't belong but you do. Look at you. What could be more America than Burt Hecker?'

'And you?'

'I am Lemko,' she said. 'My history follows behind me and pushes forward of me. You are nothing. Pah. No roots, nothing. I have *place*.'

'You,' I said, 'are as American as apple pie.'

I have never, in all my years of knowing Anna Bibko, seen her angrier than she was just then. 'Kitty never love you!' she squealed.

'Shut your face.'

'You – you only make her into whore!'

'Shut your goddamn face.'

'No! God damn you, listen! Kitty have men friends, I tell you now true! Is true! Truth!'

'I'm warning you. Don't, Anna.'

'I am the mother, I see a thing or two. I see everything. Don't what? Truth? Open you eyes. My daughter is made into whore because of you. Tristan, look and see Tristan, he is not even yours. This I know! This – this is fact. Fact that Kitty, she have other loves, other men. Tristan is mine, he is Lemko, he is of Kitty, but no yours. Never yours. You remember that – you only think about that, Burt Hecker!'

She stared wildly into my face. But I would show her

nothing. For this moment I'd been prepared. For eighteen years prepared, and I would give her nothing to take with her across the ocean but her own smallness, and the knowledge that she'd betrayed both her daughter and her beloved grandson. Let the bitch rot in her own poison. She might know facts, but she would never understand the truth.

'You won't find what you're looking for,' I said. 'For that I'm almost sorry. You inspired me once, Anna, you know that?'

'Find? But idiot, I no even look, why even look?' Anna said. 'Nothing ever end.'

I stared at her, amazed. 'Precisely,' I said. And I laughed then, one last time, at that brave and wise and tormented woman.

It took me nearly three hours to move the Siege Tower to Kitty's window. The process is really not worth relating; suffice to say, it was not easy. Clocks around Queens Falls had probably found 3 a.m. by the time I'd gotten the thing in place and, with something like a prayer, began climbing its wooden ladder. I cannot now remember what I was thinking at that point, beyond the obvious. Do not fall, do not make a noise. Everything was immediate, blessedly unreflective. The bald, chicken-bodied old man with the nose and medieval tunic, limbs shuddering with each pull up that medieval Mobile Assault Tower. My entire body ached, but my heart – my heart was delirious.

Far as I could tell, everyone was asleep. The bonfire only smoldered. Tristan, June, and Sammy were in the Mansion. Luckily, their rooms faced the other side, the parking lot side, so even if I did make a noise, or scream out as I fell to my death, they were unlikely to investigate. Reaching the level of the Siege Tower adjacent to Kitty's window, I took out a small hammer – one of June's old 'rock hound' tools – and a Leonard Nimoy 'Live Long and Prosper' beach towel to muffle the noise and minimize the danger of cutting my hands. And I broke the window. It was an uncontrollable sound, all teeth and stars. It flared and died, this sound, leaving crickets, owls, and the far off rush of the Kayaderosseras. My blood throbbed. Thief! Rapist!

Trees swayed with the night. Kitty, or something, moaned. I stared at the Mansion Inn, daring it to move, to twitch, to turn on a light or open a window, to come and get me if it could. But the Mansion Inn slept. I swept away the shards of glass. They tinkled and clinked like a broken Christmas carol. The window, of course, had been unlocked in the first place. I could have simply opened it. But no matter, I thought. I'm old, the house is old, old people break old things, and what's done is most certainly done. Besides, I enjoyed smashing the window in, giving my transgression some outward, measurable shape. I was serious. I would break this world for Kitty. Carefully, I put half of my body into the dark nothing of the room, the front half, leaving my legs and posterior sticking out of the window like one of those people-trumpets that Hieronymus Bosch's demons tend to blow. Using all the force I could muster, I kicked the Siege Tower over. Now none could follow me. It fell slowly, like the swing of Domnall mac Luloig's longsword, like a jumbo jet, and it landed with a creaking wet crunch upon the huge pile of garbage bags I'd placed there specifically to minimize any noise. The garbage bags were what was left over from our CTLR revel. The question then being:

if a historically accurate medieval Siege Tower is kicked over on upwards to a dozen full plastic garbage bags and everybody is sleeping in a Victorian mansion, does it make a sound loud enough to wake everybody up? I watched, waited. For one last night, Kitty was mine.

She was still breathing. I could see nothing but depthless gray and the purple fuzz which her breath seemed to inflate, giving it dangerous shape. The room was a ghost of itself. Shapes, crags, blurred warnings. It was something half there, it and everything in it, me included, all being erased as I stood there trying to get my own breathing down to a walking pace. I had too much air, she had not enough. There was the memory of a bed. There, the memory of the rocking chair. Kitty I couldn't see at all, she wasn't even a memory. I shuffled towards the rocking chair, took it, and brought it towards the door. It was so light in my blistered hands after moving that medieval Siege Tower. I giggled. I felt unreal. I locked the door. Damn them all, but I was giddy. Then, to be safe, I put the rocking chair under the door handle in a way I hoped would further prevent anyone from coming in and getting me. Getting us. Soon, I thought, Anna will be here soon. Soon this will all be over.

I took off my tunic and stood naked. I felt strong, young. I was young. I was strong. My heart beat wonderfully. I got into bed with my wife.

She shifted. Her body was cool, wet. Her body was so reduced now that I couldn't believe it was her at first. Who was this little girl in the darkness? Who was this old, old woman? She groaned.

I caressed her breasts, and her stomach. Her inner thighs. I lifted her nightgown up to her neck and I ran a finger down her cheek, thinking of our children. Our pink little babies; and those years of pulling away, each from each other, all from me, but I would pull them back, and I would pull Kitty back too. I kissed her lips. They gasped, closed, and then they lifted to mine with surprising, almost rapturous greed. I kissed her lips passionately.

It was the first time we'd lain together, in bed, in over a year. It didn't matter that soon they would come, our family, pounding on that door. Let them come. But even if I'd known what was to happen, the horror just hours away, the urine-soaked mattress, the blood and hysteria, the confusion beginning to gather and rise with the innocent summer sun – even if I had known, I wouldn't have stopped.

I held Kitty more tightly. Her breath caught and she tried to get away, to escape, frantic suddenly. But then she sighed, moaned. I kissed her ears, the cool bald curve of her head. Here was all the home I would ever know. Together we'd wait for the end, the pounding, the pleading and screaming to begin from behind the door. I wouldn't let them in. This was not for them. Let them break the goddamn door down.

There was no cancer. I saw it all so clearly. There was only Kitty, my wife. There had never been any cancer, not really. In the dark she was what she'd always been and always would be. Together we were something else.

'Finally,' she whispered.

Part Three
AD 1998
The Castle

XIII

The sun tells the best joke of a day full of them, setting so spectacularly that you can almost smell the tropical paradise lazing somewhere over this rim of endless, gray socialist towers. Miles of square windows explode orange, red, and purple, like a million TV sets broadcasting the apocalypse. Clouds unspool. The sky drains of birds.

I've been here, manning the outer defenses of Prague, for about two weeks now. I'm on a balcony. Incredible view up here. This city of *paneláky* – the cement, pre-fabricated buildings that surround the historic Bohemian capital, protecting it from the poor. Like being atop a rampart of a walled city, at once part of and yet high above the rabble; and I listen to the clangorous dialogue of the summer evening. I sip my beer. Being on the extreme edge of Prague you can see where these *paneláky* end and the fields, forests, and the curve of the earth begin.

In one hour my lawyer will arrive. Lonna telephoned this morning, finally. She's been in Prague; for one week she's been here in this city searching for me. June is here as well. Everyone, I'm told, is more than a little upset.

I stand up. Below me, children smoke cigarettes and kick balls among concrete statues of comrades with hammers, gas masks, and drills. These peeling, innocent, graffiti-poor *paneláky* and their promise of affordable living for everyone, it is a history still projecting itself into some other, better future. Behind me, inside the apartment, I hear Max Werfel playing with baby Tonda, his great-nephew. Max's half-sister is cooking. Her name is Jana. The television wafts unpleasantly from the apartment, joining together with thousands of others, recreating the same dubbed German helicopter drama many feet above the ground. In the Bohemian home, a television is required to be on at all times. In the late evening there is a weathergirl who removes her clothing as she prophesies meteorological futures. The US–Korean War comedy *M*A*S*H* is very popular, as are ice hockey and zany Czech variety shows. Werfel, Jana, and I sit every night in front of this TV, more accompanying it than watching it, as we drink Kozel Pivo (Male Goat Beer), shots of Becherovka (a medicinal herb liquor), and tiny ornate glasses of acidic Bohemian cooking wine. We eat peanuts that taste of chlorine and greasy fried bread covered in garlic. I thrive on the disconnection of not ever knowing what is being said. I believe that I could live here forever.

I go for walks, but only in these *paneláky* areas. Though it looks like what I imagine the very worst New York City ghetto to look like, the hundreds of thousands of people living here – who I'd first come to think of as historically displaced, banished from the beauty of their own city – are, for the most part, of the lower middle class. Retirees, Gypsies, and young families predominate. The young women dress like prostitutes but usually aren't prostitutes, and many of the young men cop their clothing and attitudes from the colored Americans they see dancing on their televisions. And while it's not at all a friendly place – on the whole, Bohemians are comically unfriendly – it's not a dangerous place either. In any event, I've no desire to be confronted with anything cobbled, medieval, or overtly non–twentieth century, so I acquaint myself with all of the smoky, slot-machine pubs, the innumerable shops where people buy and sell stolen electronic goods, and the small, mean supermarkets that stink of cat food. But I'm not alone in my wanderings. There's a fraternity of us, especially in *paneláky* land. People comfortably beyond real desperation, out taking their miseries for a stroll. Together we navigate between these concrete slabs, never really getting as lost as we should.

Understandably, Werfel spends much time with his half-sister now, touring historic Prague and the other castles and UNESCO theme villages of the Czech Republic. I've been very enthusiastically invited on nearly all of these excursions but, to my own disappointment, I have always declined. I often wonder on the mystery of their relation, the hot and cold wars – not to mention the ocean – that separated them for so long. Max will be leaving in a week. The dermatologist is going home to Brazil, by way of Budapest. I've thought of renting my very own *paneláky* apartment here in the Černý Most (Black Bridge) area of Prague, if only to give myself a chance to plot my next step, whether it's from a twelfth-floor balcony ledge or someplace less exotic. I imagine for myself some Tokyo of the soul: an endless, modern interior of windows, all closed. I've got nearly inexhaustible funds and little else. But nothing belongs to us as fully as time. Wasn't it Seneca who said that everything else is extraneous, that only time is truly ours? But what of failure, I wonder, and what about love?

I step back inside Jana's apartment. It is lime-green and orange; the wood is plastic, and the old phonograph large as an oven. Everything bears the mark of repair, compromise, effort. Imagine if someone hand-constructed a modern dwelling, building everything based on second-hand notes, hearsay, and from scratch – Jana's apartment is a folk song of probable conveniences.

She says nice, melodic things to me from the kitchen. Werfel, bouncing little Tonda on his knee, also says something nice to me, with an incredible grin to boot. My Brazilian friend's big round head is licked by the light being televised onto it by his great-nephew's joy and the TV itself, both suddenly breaking into rapturous applause. Werfel laughs, and claps along. Jana brings me another beer, faces the ovation, bows.

Marketa, Jana's twenty-two-year-old daughter and the mother of little Tonda, is the only person I've spoken English with since the night of the Sound Defenestration Collective some weeks ago. She speaks English poorly, if boldly. She insists that I sometimes do not understand her, and vice versa, because she has been taught only correct BBC English.

In Marketa's old room, beside my cachet of aromatic medieval herbs, I've hung up the one photograph of Kitty I still have – I will not describe it – as well as one of pre-operative, Star Fleet Academy June. I don't expect to get Domenico Ghirlandaio's *Portrait of an Elderly Man with His Son* back from Werfel, and that is for the best. I've also hung up Marie's watercolor Mansion Inn, which Kitty never did get to see.

' "Kitty's Mansion," ' Marketa read, one day, appraising it. 'Burt, in Czech we are famous for artists. This is pig on roof?'

'It's a squirrel.'

'In American English pig is *squirrel*? And pineapple on window?'

'That's my friend, Don.'

'Because this chap is fat, yes?'

Marketa has brought me the books I've spent the last two weeks reading, all of them Prague authors in translation, most of them by 'the very important' Franz Kafka. I began with *The Castle*. Historical fiction, I thought, a fine way to foil oblivion! But it soon became clear that this castle was only some kind of metaphor – what type is it, I kept wondering, when was it built, where, and for which monarch? I promptly closed the book. Yesterday, with an evil augur, I opened *The Trial*.

Jana serves us *smažený sýr* (fried cheese) with fried potatoes and tartar sauce. It's been two weeks of this and even Werfel scans the table in search of a vegetable. Male Goat Beer is poured. The acceptance and downright medieval encouragement of intemperance in Prague is a wonder.

Marketa places her cellular telephone next to her cutlery. She asks me what I've done today and I tell her that I've sat on the balcony drinking beer. Laughing, she translates this into Czech for Jana, who translates it into German for Werfel, by which time it's ceased to be funny and become rather pathetic. Werfel nods his head gravely. 'Is good life here in Prague, no?' says Marketa.

'*Dobrou chut*,' we say.

I slice into the breaded *smažený sýr*. The melted cheese seeps onto the plate. I smile warmly, genuinely at Jana.

Werfel and his half-sister begin to chat. They've become almost like twins. Little Tonda coos and gurgles, happily spitting up whatever Marketa thrusts into his mouth.

The bell rings. Werfel dabs his grin with a napkin. I see in him relief, and I realize for the first time that even he has become tired of taking care of me. It is time for me to go.

My lawyer enters behind a flustered Jana. They'd tussled in the hall, I learn later. Poor Jana trying to explain to Lonna that not only did she have to take her shoes off, but, to prevent disease – and in the Bohemian custom – she had to wear slippers as well. Lonna Katsav did not wear communal slippers.

Little Tonda bawls. Marketa scowls, sliding her cellular telephone where this sophisticated visitor might better appraise it. I do not move. Lonna looks me over as if I were a product she had hoped would be bigger, or cheaper. She is not inebriated. Max Werfel, flushed and giggling, embraces my lawyer and reintroduces his half-sister, who becomes painfully, unnecessarily self-conscious of her home.

But the look on Lonna's face. I can see that she is actually nervous, her eyes skittish. This look I've seen before.

The first time I saw that look, we were standing at Tivona Henry's door.

'Chant now, drink later. That's the deal, old man,' Lonna said. 'Remember why you're here. I want best behavior. You think I'm looking forward to this?'

I knew for a fact that Lonna was looking forward to this. I said so.

To my astonishment, she had jumped at the opportunity of accompanying me on this New York State sanctioned alternative to anger management, the improbable outcome of the suicide attempt a jury of my peers referred to as 'DWI', among other things.

I hadn't known that Lonna could sing. I don't think anyone would have guessed that Lonna Katsav had a beautiful voice, or that for as long as I'd known her, she'd only been waiting for just such an excuse to finally open her big mouth and let it rip. It made me feel better, less lost. If I'd been wrong about my closest friend, then I could be wrong about anything, everyone. I was at a point in my life where that was about as comforting as it got; because if I was wrong about Lonna, then couldn't I be wrong about Tristan? I could be wrong about June. They could be wrong about me. Maybe things weren't as bad as they seemed.

My son had fled to Poland with his grandmother. My daughter, without a goodbye, had returned to California three days after her mother's funeral: neither had spoken more than two words to me during the whole ordeal. I remembered little about those days. Those two words, however, I remembered and will remember for as long as I live. 'Leave us.'

I wore my best sweater and trousers. The same I had worn to court; the very same that I had probably worn to the funeral people assure me I attended. This was parole. Parole wasn't supposed to be fun. Let's start taking things a little more seriously, Burt.

Lonna and I stood before the Second Hand, Third Eye esoteric shop. The chant workshop met somewhere above. Both waiting for the other to open the door, Lonna and I looked at each other and laughed. It was difficult to stop. 'They're going to make me sing,' I said. The autumn breeze was raffish.

'I know,' and Lonna laughed harder. 'Look at you. That outfit.'

'I can't believe they're going to make me sing.'

'I'm so glad they arrested you, darling.'

'They should have arrested me a long time ago.'

Lonna, trying to stop laughing, put her hand on my shoulder. 'Tell me about it,' she said. She wiped her eyes. Leaves rustled about our feet.

They'd known I was coming, of course. The medieval widower, the drunk driver. Nobody, however, knew that Lonna Katsav would be there. Poor Amy Sturk, who'd no doubt already coached the other girls on how to deal with my foibles, and had already planned on ways in which to make me behave, was as thrown and disappointed by Lonna as she was by my clothes. It was clear that she'd thought I would be wearing my tunic, that she had told everyone to expect a tunic.

'Lon,' said Amy. 'That's so nice. To drop Burt off.'

Something almost shy crept into Lonna's face. It occurred to me that I'd never seen Lonna ask for anything, and now she had to ask to join a club, a workshop full of what she'd earlier described as 'frumpy New Age loons'. The room's ceiling billowed with bed sheets and a tangle of Christmas lights sat in the center of the room like a frozen swarm of fireflies; incense, pots of tea, some faces I recognized from the Middle Ages and others I did not. Tivona Henry was meditating in the corner as her chant workshop gathered, practicing vocal warm-up exercises. Most of the women wore soft sweatsuits.

'Thought maybe I'd join too,' Lonna said, shrugging no big deal. Lonna was wearing one of her sexy, short-skirt legal suits. 'You know.'

'Oh.' Amy balked. 'Really? I mean –'

234

'For Burt.'

'Great, sure. Well,' Amy said. Her freckles disappeared, one by one, as her round head grew red. 'But you don't have to. That's really nice but you don't – I'll be here. Didn't you know? Burt didn't say? I mean, no problem. I can drive him and –'

'I can sing,' Lonna blurted, then blushed. 'It's just that I'd like to sing.' How tall and overdressed she looked, and how little her intelligence seemed to echo in this environment. This place was irony-free, sarcasm-free. Lonna was powerless, and it was incredible, touching, and before I knew it I had snapped myself out of whatever despondency I'd crawled in on and said, 'Lonna has a beautiful voice.' I meant it, though I'd certainly never heard it sing.

'I didn't know.' Amy tugged her braids. 'I didn't know you liked Early Music.'

Lonna said, 'I like to sing.' I could see how big of a thing this was to admit.

'Great.' Amy smiled falsely. 'Welcome.' (Three months later, Amy Sturk would stop attending Tivona's chant workshop, opting for private tutorials.)

Lonna backed up against a wall, observing. She monitored her cool. Amy said, 'Burt? Why don't you come over here and meet –'

As I walked over to meet some women, Amy whispered, 'So help me, Burt, after all I've done for you, getting you in here, if you and Lonna try to make fools of us now. If you even dare. If that woman even thinks about getting drunk before –'

'You don't know Lonna.'

'Fine, whatever. Then you. I know you. This could be

so good for you, so important for you. If you let it. This could be exactly what you need. If Lonna thinks she can –'

Tivona stood up, suddenly, her eyes still closed. She began to hum. She was a big head of curly hair on an emaciated child's body. Everyone began to hum, creating a vibration. I tried to laugh, to separate myself from this cultish wave of sound, but I could not. I could hardly move. I looked around me at all those women and found Lonna, my anchor, and she was humming too. Just like that. Not only was she humming, but she was humming seriously, non-ironically, standing seriously beneath a sign that said, 'MYSTICISM IS THE ANNIHILATION OF THE SELF IN ORDER TO MAKE ROOM FOR GOD'. So quickly, I thought. But shouldn't the self put up some kind of fight?

'See?' Lonna said, beaming, on our way back to the Mansion Inn and the celebratory bottle of wine we'd promised ourselves. 'That wasn't so bad. This is going to be fine.'

Later that night, long after Lonna had left, I sat in the corner of the kitchen. On the linoleum. From the other room a record played, one of Kitty's, something by Bob Dylan called *New Morning*. This particular album had a sinister cover.

'You're not in jail?' June asked.

I could barely hold the phone. Red wine everywhere, all over my sweater, the linoleum, my trousers.

'Please, come home,' I said. I repeated myself. The kitchen lights were an icy, silent white. Beyond the kitchen there was only night. Too much of it. There would be a frost, you could feel it.

'You've got to be kidding. What time is it there?'

'I'm alone,' I said. 'I don't know what to do.'

'I heard what you do. You put on a tunic and go out for a drunk drive is what you do. You can't even drive sober, Burt. Seems you've occupied yourself pretty well these days. Bang-up job, as usual. Why do you keep calling me? Stop calling me.'

'I don't know.'

'You're just trying to get Tristan's phone number,' June said. 'You want sympathy? What shit is this?'

'I'm so sorry.'

'For what?'

'Everything.'

'Specifics. Be specific. You don't even know what you're saying.'

'No.'

'Too fucking much.'

'I mean, I know. Please, let me finish.'

'I can't even think about this anymore. I refuse to let this bother me. This is not my responsibility.'

I began to cry.

'You're drinking.'

'Did you know that in AD 1246, June –' I said. 'I only. I – in AD 1246. In the Middle Ages, June, did you know –'

'Oh, my God. You asshole,' June said. 'Stop, stop, stop. Fuck your Middle fucking Ages. I'm hanging up. I will not listen to this. You unbelievable asshole.'

'Please.'

'You're drinking.'

'Listen to me.'

'You're a drunk.'

'June.'

'Drunk.'

I couldn't look up into windows for fear of seeing Kitty's face reflected there. Kitty standing in the kitchen, above me. Kitty outside in that howling black, her bald head shining in the kitchen lights. In the middle of the night I was terrified of going to the bathroom for fear of what I'd see behind me in the mirror. Every corner, behind every closed door. I could not open doors anymore. So I never closed doors. I'd taken to sleeping in the kitchen, on the kitchen floor with the lights on because it seemed the most antiseptic and non-Kitty of rooms; its coldness swallowed misery, absorbed it so much better than warmth and comfort ever could. Soft sofas, cozy beds, blankets, and clean clothing bred misery, compounded it. I tortured myself with Bob Dylan, trying to listen with Kitty's ears. Drunk? June didn't know the half of it.

'Don't do this,' I said.

June began crying. 'You drunk. You child. What have you done?'

'I love you.'

'Go to bed, Daddy.'

'Tell me. Sammy. How is – he was so – and I always wanted to know more about your rocks, about – but you never let me. But you with that look. Everything out of my mouth a mistake. Geology. That time when you were small. You tried to show me your rocks once.'

'Go to bed.'

'It's so lonely here.' I had closed down the Mansion Inn months ago. 'You can't imagine. How big things get when they're empty. Your mother is everywhere, June. Everywhere.'

June said, 'I'm crying. This is too much. What am I crying for? Not you, not you. I don't need this.'

'Did you know Lonna can sing?'

'I'm hanging up.'

'We don't know each other at all, do we? None of us. But you and me, think about it. It's wonderful. That's what I'm calling about. Lonna can sing. Think about it.'

'Dad.'

'We can start again.'

'You've got to go to bed. You've been drinking.'

'But maybe I could visit you? In California. I've never been to California. We could go camping.'

'Camping? Jesus, Burt. Do you want me to call Lonna?'

'That's not the point.'

'The point? *Camping*?' June laughed. 'OK, what is the point?'

'I'm asking you to give me another chance.'

'Stop. Can't you see? Burt? Hello?'

'It's you.'

'I'm hanging up.'

'You who can't see – won't see. Lonna can. I mean. Oh, June, it was so beautiful. Her voice.'

'Enough. You just – over and over. Same thing over and over. What do you want from me?'

'One more chance.'

'I'm going to call Lon, OK?'

'You're not listening. I love you.'

'I'm going to hang up now. Just hold still, I'm going to call Lonna. Burt?'

'Tell her I'm in the kitchen.'

'Tell her what?'

Today, now, one year later, scanning the *paneláky* apartment, Lonna doesn't even say hello. Max, Jana, Marketa, and the baby hush, following Lonna's exhausted eyes to me. I still can't even stand. I'm rooted to this chair, in this Bohemian kitchen. Lonna says, 'This is your last chance.'

XIV

I think about what a kick my Confraternity of Times Lost Regained brethren would get from the taxi that takes us from the *paneláky* back in time to the old, once medieval city. I say, 'It's like a time machine.'

'It's a Skoda, Burt,' Lonna says. 'Welcome to the twentieth century.'

Historic Prague looks much like it is supposed to: the spiked tortoiseshell hump of Prague Castle identical to the one framed and hanging in Jana's kitchen. But I like the one in Jana's kitchen better.

Lonna found me only after Werfel had somehow contacted Tivona with a computer, with an electronic letter. One week before that, Lonna had flown out to Prague, prepared for the worst. The people at the superficially Renaissance hotel I'd been staying at had told her that I'd checked out, mysteriously, in the wee hours of the morning. Then Lonna spoke with my son.

I'd wanted them to worry, I realize, and worse: Lonna knows it. 'Where are you staying?' I ask. 'Isn't it expensive?'

'It's very expensive. Doesn't matter. I'm using your money, after all.' There are black rings around my friend's eyes. She had really thought that I was dead.

She tells me that she'd contacted the vaudevillian Czech police, but they only wanted to keep her busy filling out 'very serious' papers. The US Embassy, for their part, knew only that I had not yet left the Czech Republic in any legal terrestrial manner.

Tristan, of course, had contacted June, and my daughter had promptly telephoned Lonna (a few days before she left the United States) to see if what her brother said could possibly be true. 'What could I say?' Lonna tells me. 'She had everything packed for the big move. She'd been through a lot with the break-up, with that Jack, and she was really looking forward to starting again at the Mansion Inn with you. So of course she went batshit. Good news is she might now hate me worse than she hates you. I helped you. I aided and abetted. Nothing you do would surprise her, but I should've known better, I should have put my high heels down, and maybe she's right, but I think the girl needs to step back and take her own fucking pulse for once, you know? She called another lawyer, who called me. Basically, this other lawyer wants to prove that you're insane. Thinks that way he'll maybe have a chance of getting the Mansion back. Or, at least, wrest control of Kitty's fortune – his actual words. Kitty's fortune. Very L.A. Even if you are insane, there's really nothing they can do but drag it out and hope for some kind of out-of-court settlement, so don't worry. I made you sign over your power of attorney and whatnot to me and I'm not completely insane yet, so things are safe. The Mansion is very much sold. But what I need you to do is don't let on that you're not worried. When you see June. Got it? You might've lost your daughter, but you won't lose your money.'

'That's not funny.'

'Damn right it's not funny.'

'You talked to Tristan?'

'Don't say anything stupid and you might walk out of this with half your family intact. Yup, Tim and I talked. Listen, and don't question anything I do either, OK? I'm maybe going to pay June off, but not right away. Let's see how this goes tonight. The Mansion and everything is gone, but you can afford to set her and your grandson up a bit until you really do decide to die.'

'They can have it all.'

'No.'

'Everything.'

'Oh, no. Stop right there. That kind of bird is not going to fly. That is exactly what you will not be saying tonight, or I will leave you right here right now on the side of the road. She cannot have it all because it's yours, and you need money to live. It is a very simple concept. I don't want any of your medieval munificence tonight. Just please try not to be insane tonight, OK, Burt?'

'I'm sorry, Lonna.'

'Yeah.'

'I don't deserve this. Your kindness.'

'This is business.'

I see my reflection in the taxi window, smiling, ghosting over the facade of a church. I see Lonna smiling too. 'What would I do without you?' I say.

'Yeah, well. Partly my fault anyway. My job tonight is to make sure your kids see they're every bit as selfish and childish as their father. Not that this lets you off the hook.'

'It's going to be bad,' I say.

'You have no idea.'

243

Tristan's building is turn-of-the-century neo-Gothic. It is gray, powerfully aged, and ominous as a boulder set just so on the edge of a cliff. Statues of women covered with tiny pigeon-skewering needles huddle into its ornate corners. One hundred years ago this building would have been more tasteless Austro-Hungarian kitsch; today most tourists probably think it's the real Gothic deal. Fifty years of communist neglect has matured these stones well.

Lonna steps out of the taxi. I collect myself. There is a photograph of a small dog taped to the car's dashboard.

Lenka, Tristan's girlfriend, is waiting in front of the building.

'You must be Lonna from the telephone,' she says. I stand behind Lonna, hiding. 'I am Lenka from Tim. Nice to meet you.' Lenka wears a homemade summer dress with black workman boots. There is a Chinese tattoo on her left shoulder.

'Burt.' She is wary of me. 'Come, good. Let's go.'

The building does not have an elevator. Tristan and Lenka live on the fifth floor, which seems like the tenth floor, what with these overawed ceilings. The tiled, stone stairway is cool as a cathedral. Mistaking my slowness for nerves, Lonna pokes her index finger into the small of my back as if it were a Polish rifle. 'March,' she whispers. I can hardly catch my breath.

'Is a very good place, once very posh. But sorry no lift. Is still state-owned flat, you know, and illegal to rent but we rent anyway for one year and for cheap. Burt, you are staying in Černy Most?'

'Yes,' I huff, gaining the fourth floor. 'In a *panelák*.'

244

'I grow up near to Černy Most. In Hloubětín, also in panel house. Is the real Prague, I think. I don't know. Is real mentality of many people after socialism. You shouldn't have run away.'

'What?'

'Why did you run away?'

'I wasn't exactly made welcome. It was Tristan who ran away.'

'Tim.'

Lonna's rifle becomes a hand. It squeezes my arm in support. 'I think, Lenka, what Burt means to say is that Tim made it pretty clear that he didn't want anything to do with his father.'

'I don't think so,' Lenka says. 'No. I don't think that is true. I know only Tim was so worried.'

My children do not come and greet us as we take off our shoes in the foyer. Nor do they come and greet us when we put on our Bohemian slippers. The ceiling really is very high. The floors are wood. Cardboard boxes lie about everywhere, as well as very old, bloated and mismatched wooden wardrobes. One boasts a poster of a colored man dressed as an Egyptian Pharaoh, balancing a huge golden orb on his head. 'Space Is the Place,' it says. 'Sun Ra & His Astro Intergalactic Infinity Arkestra.' I remember the little boy who was once chased down a United States highway by that sun and I cannot conceive of how we got here, how all those years led to this place. Instead of doors, there are Indian-style beads.

I pass through to the other side.

Candles, incense, Eastern rags, a brass spider of a chandelier, and a few sofas in a huge moth-white room with parquet floors. There are more posters here. Musical instruments line the walls, none medieval, but only a tiny fraction of them Lemko, thank God. There's a stereo and many CDs, a book shelf, no TV. Tristan stands at the furthest reach of this space, backed up against a window which frames the entirety of Prague Castle – his tall body charred by the luminescence, standing there in violent silhouette. He doesn't move. June sits on a sofa, looking at another sofa. Next to Tristan, a wheelchair. Confined to this chair, Anna Bibko stares out the window. This has got to be a joke.

My grandson appears, holding a kitten. He tries to hand it to me, but the animal slips from his hands. Sammy, shrieking, follows it from the room. Lenka follows Sammy. 'I keep Samičko in bedroom together with kitten and me, we watch some video maybe. Some fairy tale,' she says. 'Burt, you like coffee?'

I nod my head yes. I say, 'No.' I stare, shocked at Anna Bibko.

'Fanta?' Lenka asks.

'I'll have what Burt's having,' Lonna murmurs.

'I mean Fanta,' Lenka says. 'To drink. Do you like Fanta?'

'What?' my lawyer and I say in unison.

Anna Bibko in Prague, in a wheelchair.

Lonna, of course, is wondering if my mother-in-law is also a part of the lawsuit and, if so, what that changes.

Lenka hangs there for a moment, confused. 'So no coffee?'

'Mead,' June starts. 'Or anything you got with alcohol. Coffee's way too OOP for Burt.'

'Coffee will be fine,' I say.

'Yes, please,' Lonna agrees.

Tristan turns his grandmother around to face us. I need to sit down. June stands up, but then, thinking better of it, sinks back down into the sofa. She's got some papers in her hand. 'Hey, everyone,' she says.

Tristan marks his sister ambiguously. Their grandmother, that indomitable re-enactor, might as well still be staring out the window: she looks right through me, through everything.

'We were worried, Dad,' Tristan whispers.

June says, 'Speak for yourself, Tim.'

Sleek as a dolphin, my attorney jumps right in, splashing June's rancor and meeting Tristan, warmly shaking my son's hand. Tristan's lips flicker around a smile. Lonna even bends down to Anna Bibko, still in her multihued Lemko costume. The old woman says something in Lemko. Lonna doesn't bother with June. In her face I watch my wife's eyes cloud with pain, again, and I watch them steel in anger. It doesn't have to be this way. I could protect her if only she'd let me.

There's an evil little oxygen machine in the room's corner. Bottles of pills on the coffee table.

Fool. Gorilla. I remember the Anna Bibko who took on the Great War's very own Lieutenant Michniewicz at the last ever meeting of the Queens Falls Historical Society. *You gonna fight communist, huh? Big strong guy, you. So where were you and your big strong USA in 1946? What were you doing when communists come and kill my people with knives, kill my people with fire? Little boys and little girls. Where? I am listening.*

I wonder if she is listening now. I imagine a four-year-old Kitty on her mother's lap, brushing her mother's cheek, mischievously placing pennies on her open eyes.

I sit down on a sofa facing June. Tristan remains standing next to Anna, a hand on his grandmother's shoulder. I imagine failure in her eyes. The last thing those surviving Lemkos probably wanted was a wealthy, costumed American telling them to go off back into the mountains and become shepherds. You could probably rub the skin right off her body.

'Anna,' I whisper. 'Can you hear me?'

My wife's mother doesn't move, nothing. Tristan strokes his grandmother's cheek. 'Grandma,' he says. Then, to me, he says, 'She can hear you.'

'I'm sorry,' I say. 'Anna, I'm so sorry.'

She begins speaking in Lemko, staring full into my face. It is like Halloween. Her hands shake.

'English,' I tell her. I look at Tristan. 'Can you tell her to speak English, please?'

Tristan says something to Anna in Lemko, but his grandmother waves impatiently and continues speaking to me in Lemko, jabbing a finger into the air.

'She won't speak English anymore,' Tristan says.

'Won't or can't?' Lonna asks, as if it were a question of great legal importance. Perhaps it is.

Tristan looks at his sister. June says, 'She's fine.'

'Doesn't look fine,' Lonna says. 'This may be important. Is she taking any medication?'

June says, 'You cold bitch.'

'She's not well,' Tristan says. 'Grandma doesn't know what she's saying. She's ill.'

Anna Bibko keeps speaking.

'What is she saying?' I ask. 'Can you translate, Tristan.'

'Tim,' June says. 'Don't.'

'Tim,' I say.

June rolls her eyes. 'This is ridiculous.'

'She says,' Tristan pauses. 'She says . . .'

Anna Bibko begins to laugh. Tristan steps back.

'Leave Tim alone, Burt,' June says. But she glares at her grandmother. 'It doesn't matter what she says. She's sick. It doesn't matter.'

But it does matter. In the same way that Anna Bibko showed me my future thirty years ago, demonstrating how I could dedicate my life to history, the dying old woman in the Lemko costume is now showing the end results of that dedication, what happens next, what is left: the fury, hopelessness, the rotting present of a life lived perpetually out of period. My heart breaks for both of us.

'I'm so sorry,' I say.

June makes another disgusted noise. 'You spoke with my lawyer, Lonna.'

'June,' I say. 'Please.'

'I did,' Lonna fixes June with her eyes, extending her be-quiet-Burt finger. 'He was charming.'

'So you know why I'm here, Lonna. And you know that –'

'Kiddo. Come on.' Lonna as the benevolent big sister. 'Stop. Let's talk like human beings.'

How whittled-down it looks, my daughter's nose. 'You think I'm not serious? You think this is a joke? That I'm joking?' There are already tears in June's eyes. She won't look at me, only Lonna; and I never did make an effort with my daughter's husband. He was a sullen man with a goatee, Jack. Then I think: but she never let me.

'Tristan,' June suddenly says. 'Tim, hey, don't you want to say something?'

Tristan has distanced himself, as usual. He's further away than his grandmother even, though he tries to say something again. Speak up, I think. I want him to help June destroy me, if only for June's sake. Because Lonna is going to rip her apart. Help her, I think. Somebody help my little girl.

'Jesus Christ. Please, Tim,' June says. 'Sit down, at least.'

Tristan sits down next to his sister. I can't bear his shaved head, or his eyes. From the other room Sammy starts laughing, and Lenka yells, 'Kitty is not toy, Sammy! Put kitty down!'

Breathing stops.

'Sammy, no! Sammy, you kill kitty this way! Please, no!'

Open that door! Open up! Mom, we're here, don't worry! Burt! Dad! What are you doing? You're killing her! She's crying! Stop! Let us in! We know you're in there, open the door or we'll break it down! Open up! Tristan, wait, no! Not yet, no, don't –

'Well, now,' Lonna says, exhaling, brushing the omen aside. The two-year-old echoes of a bedroom door being pounded on. A door collapsing.

Lonna says, 'June, word to the wise. You know me. I will eat you alive. So let's try this as family and see if we can't set things straight, are you all with me?' Lonna smiles, reaches over to touch June's leg. 'June?'

'Family?' June swats at Lonna.

'Your father,' Lonna sighs. 'Please, think about your father for once in your goddamn life.'

'You know what, Lonna?' June says. 'I've had just about enough "father" for one life. Tim and me, we both have. How can we sit here and – and pretend everything's fine after all this?' Then, to me, 'I had everything packed, prepared. Everything, Burt. When were you going to tell me? Did it just slip your mind? When were you going to fill me in? When the fucking moving van pulled up and we got out and –'

250

Tristan puts his arm around his sister's shoulders. I've never been more proud of the boy. I smile at my children, my family.

'Oh, my God, why are you smiling? You're insane! What, how – you've gone too far this time. I only want what's mine, Lonna. What was Mom's. You sold our home. Our home.'

'Don't be ridiculous,' Lonna says, calmly.

'Don't defend him!'

'I'm defending your mother too. Listen to me. I'm defending your family.'

'From me? What? Fuck you.'

'Your father loves you. He loves both of you,' Lonna says. Lonna looks to me: say something. But I cannot.

'Like he loved Mom? Like you loved Mom, huh, Burt? Just like you loved Mom, right? Right?'

'You little girl,' Lonna says. 'You have no idea.'

'I've got some idea, trust me. Better than you I think. I saw what went on in that house, what Mom was driven to. How could I not? Why are you protecting him?'

'You know he doesn't deserve this.'

'It's not like you think,' I begin. 'Let me please try and explain about –'

'It's not like you think, Burt!' June says. 'Nothing's like you think! You've got no idea what was going on right under that nose of yours half the time while you were off having your costume parties, drunk and reading – always reading those stupid books out in the woods in that barn. It's a wonder Tristan didn't burn the place to the fucking ground!'

'Please, let your father speak.'

June laughs, glaring at Lonna. 'You hypocrite. You're a – just like him, you're no different. The two of you. This whole thing, this whole family. It's not normal. Why won't you just say it, why won't anyone just come out and say it? Where am I supposed to go?' Her eyes stamped with the same black rings as Lonna's. June is right. She says, 'This is not normal. Don't tell me that this is normal.'

I stare at Tristan, who stares at the ground, silent and still as his grandmother beside him. Lenka has not returned with our coffees. If only I could hug June, I think. Everything would be fine if she would only let me hug her.

'Normal?' Lonna says. 'Come on. What's that? You look at your father, June. You think he wanted to sell everything, you think he wanted to fly halfway across the globe? Your dad in an airplane!' she laughed. 'Just think about that for a second. Seriously, June. He tried so hard with you, all your life, and got nothing but this selfish woe-is-me shit back, nothing, year after year. Poor you with your nose, and poor you with nobody understanding. You both need to grow up. Normal? Nobody loves you more than he does. He would kill himself for you if he thought it would help.'

'Maybe it would help!'

Lonna slaps June's face.

But Tristan and I recoil more than June. She seems to have expected, even enjoyed it. Anna Bibko is laughing.

'You shut the fuck up,' June turns on the old woman. 'I swear to God. You better just shut your fucking mouth up!'

'June, no,' Tristan whispers. 'Please.' Tristan stands up, almost says something else, thinks better of it, and walks out of the room.

'Tim, I'm sorry,' June calls. 'Tim! Oh, Jesus Christ.'

Taking Tristan's place, Lonna sits down and holds my daughter. June falls into my lawyer, shaking. 'Hey now,' Lonna says.

'How could he do this?'

'How could he not? Tristan moved to Europe, kiddo. Your brother broke his heart and moved away, and you never visited, never even called. Burt couldn't run the place, what was he going to do, box himself up there with all those ghosts in that big old house? Sit out the rest of his life in that prison he made for himself, with you two wonderful wardens not even bothering to pick up the phone and say hello? Take a punishment from his children that he didn't deserve? Think about it. C'mon. Think about him for once, for once only. Of course I helped him sell it. Goddamn happy to.'

'You had no right. It was ours.'

Tristan returns. He sits next to me.

'Wrong,' Lonna says. 'It was his. He has a life too, and it was his. I'm sorry for hitting you. I'm sorry, but it was his, everything bad up there was his to deal with, while you and Tristan ran off to opposite sides of the world. He was the abandoned one.'

Tristan, I notice, has balled his hands into fists, no doubt remembering what Lonna has forgotten: that I abandoned them first. Anna Bibko has fallen asleep.

'It's good to see you,' I say. I look June in the face and she looks back at me. 'I'm so happy to see you, June.'

Rubbing her arms, sobbing, she says, 'This is not normal.'

The room is a big one. It's deep and wide, but we cluster to its center, the five of us. We're all of us around a tiny table, the coffee table. Even Anna Bibko. Two sofas and one wheelchair. Outside, beyond these walls, there is an unknown city. I think of gorillas in a zoo, sitting together, huge and heavy, chewing leaves, occasionally touching with slow strong fingers, staring out at the world with eyes floating in a sadness somehow beyond tears. Tristan has his mother's height and eyes, and now, without the beard, his grandmother's razor-thin lips. June has her grandmother's hair and temper, and her father's nervous stature. Even with Lonna, we somehow coalesce in an animal way: the way June and I move our fingers anxiously, the way Tristan and June breathe and electrically flick their eyebrows. That most indelible, improbable and terrifying thing: a family.

Somehow we make small talk, only occasionally veering into the troubles – those unsolvable messy hiccups that once begun have to finish of their own volition. I even make June laugh. I tell them about Max Werfel plucking dead chickens from the road, speaking as if I was some classical patriarch returned from an adventure. I tell them about Bohemian whores and Sexy Motels. June laughs, Tristan smiles; Lonna eggs me on, happy with the turn of events. I talk of disco dancing and the services of a Bohemian inn. 'Inn' being exactly the wrong word, of course. 'I'm still suing you,' June abruptly amends her laughter, suddenly self-conscious. 'Just so you know, Burt.'

But there is something new in June, something her small fists and her fits of laughter let me see. It is hard to explain, but she is at once more harried and calmer, and, for the first time, I think I see her as others must see her, as her little son sees her. My daughter is a mother. Her strength may only be a sliver of her own mother's, but it's a strong sliver, unbending. Maybe part of her is right, maybe I had not let her become more than the angry little girl, the lonely sad thing with her science fiction and rocks in boxes. She is a woman with thoughts that aren't just a reflection of me, a

254

reaction to me. I see her driving an automobile, buying groceries, thinking alone late at night with the windows drawn, while a TV entertains her family. I see her thinking while preparing complex meals for that family she'd tried for so long to hold together, another family, her own, and I see that new far western life of escape she would turn into sanctuary, even if it killed her. There is failure there now, despair, humor, stubborn hope. I know nothing about her. She has grown up. Previously, I'd always imagined California not as a real place but as someplace other than where I was – an entire state as nothing but a comment and attack on myself. June went west, Tristan east. Maybe that's simply what happens. What did I know?

Tristan hardly speaks. His pain still deep, unacknowledge-able; his confusion and his emotions impossible to gauge. It is hard to not be what you are. June knows herself. She is all surface while her brother – it's impossible, those depths. He doesn't look well, and he won't look at me. He has not yet grown up and it is painful to watch. That pull of what he was, what he is, and what he wants to be. It's understand-able that he wants to be here, alone, in this unknowable city.

Meanwhile, like some Lemko death totem, Anna Bibko sits, watching me, gloating. She's one of June's geologic fault lines, building up pressure. She is a U-boat beneath us all. I know what she must have said to me earlier. I know why Tristan couldn't translate. She is not half as gone as her grand-children think she is.

Reading my mind, perhaps, Tristan tells us what is wrong with his grandmother, and what she's doing with him in Prague. I hardly listen. Because I know what Anna Bibko is really doing; hiding here from her Polish failures, clutching and pulling down the one last thing she has left in this world: my son. I look at his new instruments lined up against the wall. I watch the old city out the window and I remember the last torpedo Anna had launched before she left her Mansion Inn for good. Tristan knows everything now. If she didn't tell him tonight then she told him two years ago, maybe even earlier. How much did it really make a difference? It doesn't make a difference at all. Tristan simply knows – that is all.

Lonna tells a funny story about Kitty too stoned to prepare and serve breakfast at the Mansion Inn. Kitty calling Lonna up and asking her to go to McDonald's and bring over a dozen Egg McMuffins. 'Said they wouldn't know the difference, said she was going to get them started on mimosas. I got there and half of the guests had fallen back asleep and the other half were out on the porch. They had this radio blaring Bob Dylan, of course, and Kitty's got them all plugging their heads into this big bong. I felt like Julius Caesar entering Rome. To this day I've never seen a group of people more excited about Egg McMuffins.'

Then June has one, a Kitty story, albeit filled with occasional stabs at me. Tristan nods, smiling to himself, remembering his own version of his mother. I tell them about the day I met their mother, and June wipes her eyes. She says, 'You never told us.' And so the five of us re-create her, channel her, and even Anna has a say, unwittingly doing her best imitation of dying Kitty. She was so huge, I think, that woman. She had a Kitty for everyone and still enough left over for herself. Too much, she'd told me. So much that she didn't know what to do with it all. It made her crazy, sometimes. She had lovers, well of course she did; and they probably had their own Kitty, and how greedy my thoughts have become lately, wondering at that other Kitty, wishing I could have known her that way too: the indelicate part of her that hungered for the entire world, that needed to take sometimes instead of always giving. Our bed was the center, and I was the calm of her appetites, of Kitty's frenetic hugeness. But how can her children ever understand? Did they understand? She was larger than life, larger than a mother, a wife. But now this – this is what finally happens when someone larger than life dies. Here's the whirlpool we're all trying to swim free of. Here we are clustered in the center of this room in the middle of Europe like bubbles going down the drain. Here we are, finally, having Kitty's funeral.

Lonna, goading us Heckers onwards, forces us to adhere, to see each other today, in a non-historical fashion. I'm prodded into talking about the chant workshop and German nuns. June talks about her separation, her husband. She talks about gardening, taxes, and the weather in California. Schools in California. How much she hates California. She recommends new movies for Tristan to see, she tells Lonna what she reads when she gets a spare second to herself to actually open a book. Tristan, still, says little. He answers questions about his grandmother, he murmurs to his sleeping grandmother. He tells us a little about Lenka. Possibly remembering the instruments he destroyed, and the life we once shared, he doesn't talk about his music. Families are historical things. You have to believe in them for them to be real. They have precedent, they repeat themselves, they have a million points of view and they never stay the same, even after they happen. If you can prove they happened at all. But they're always happening and you'll never understand them: you can dress up, re-enact, but you'll never get to the heart of them, of how they are when they are what they are. It is too terrible to contemplate. The brevity of life, the delusions, all that delusional thinking that adds up to a single, useless, personal reality; and I suddenly crave my tunic, the safety of a medieval re-enactment. The ritual of it. I don't know these people and I never will. Lonna says, smiling, 'Burt, why don't you tell Tim and June about stealing my Saab and almost going to jail?'

Instead, I tell them about that morning at the Hildegard Abbey, the anchorage, letting the girls out of the tent. Halfway through, I start crying. I should never have let them out. They were safer inside.

I don't know what sets June off, perhaps my undeserved, unearned melancholy. I simply do not know. Perhaps the very mention of another re-enactment, remembering the last re-enactment she experienced. In any event, she cuts me off and addresses Lonna.

'You must be able to do something,' June says.

'What?'

'The Mansion Inn.'

'Christ, woman. There's nothing I can do. Nothing. Really, and here I thought that we had moved on.'

'I need that house.'

'June, look at me. Take my advice. You have to move on. This is absurd.'

'Move where, Lonna? Just where the hell are my son and me supposed to move?' And why can't Lonna see what is so obvious: my daughter is scared. She does not know where to go and she wants to go home.

'I have money,' I say. 'June, wait. I have money.'

'Burt,' Lonna warns.

'I don't want your money,' June spits. 'I want my home!'
Lonna shakes her head.

'Don't you patronize me, Lonna. I want my mother's home
back. There must be a way. There's always a way. I don't
care what it takes. I want to raise Sammy with – in that
history, my own history. Stop looking at me like that! Can't
you understand?' She shoves papers into Lonna's hands. 'I
will get my home back, Lonna.'

'You won't,' Lonna says. 'Even if you do, you won't. You're
not stupid, you know that. Sit down.'

'I can try! At least I can try!' and how much like her grandmother she suddenly sounds, how much like her father.

I try to offer June a million dollars, whatever – two million
dollars! – if she would only return to five minutes ago when
anything was possible. Lonna tells me that I don't even
have two million dollars. Tristan says something infuriatingly
unobtrusive.

It is too late. Too quick. June runs from the room and she's
not coming back. Lonna gets up, grins like a huntress, and
follows. They continue arguing in the hall. They remove their
Bohemian slippers, one of which is thrown against a wall.
Sammy starts to cry. The door opens and slams shut. Lonna
shouts, 'OK, I'm going after her! Don't worry, guys! I'll take
care of this and see you tomorrow! This is fixable! Goodnight!'

And so we are left alone with Anna Bibko's snores, her
dreams – and is she dreaming this right now, I wonder? Is
the old Lemko finally dreaming us apart? Tristan will not
look at me. I rub my face with my hands, and I think of
Franz Kafka's castle, knowing exactly what it looks like now.
Exactly what's inside it too.

*   *   *

Tristan and I sit together, awkwardly re-enacting our past. My wife's mother has been wheeled away to another room. Her job is done. I haven't really moved in some time, and neither has Tristan. I've been given a beer and the stereo has been switched on. In this way we work through his mother's death. There's so much we can't ever possibly say, so we sit there and let the silence slowly pluck through those things, strumming out the horrors and misunderstandings, letting them ring and decay, one by one. Blame is a bad ghost, a demon.

'*But I did not see sin,*' Julian of Norwich, another anchorite, wrote in AD 1234. '*I believe it has not substance or real existence. It can only be known by the pain it causes. This pain is something, as I see it, which lasts but a while. It purges us and makes us know ourselves, so that we ask for mercy. It is true that sin is the cause of all this pain, but all shall be well; and all shall be well; and all manner of things shall be well.*'

The beer is good. The music is jazz. *Portrait of an Elderly Man with His Son*, AD 1998. The paint's not dry on whatever we are now. Twenty minutes pass before my son says, 'What do you think of this music?'

My eyes blur. Lonna can sing. Tristan can play the saxophone. No, not Tristan. I wonder if Tim can forgive his father. 'It's ghastly,' I say.

He laughs.

Lenka joins us. She is a mystery, she is new, and with her maybe things can be different. I do not have to trouble her with mistakes if I can help it. Her bare feet pad across the parquet, and she curls up next to my son on the sofa. I've never seen him so comfortable. The girl falls asleep.

It occurs to me that my daughter and I have the same goal; in the end we have the exact same goal. Maybe, with Tristan's help, she and I can meet it, and maybe we can find each other somewhere in the middle where brave failures join forces and face the future. I should hire a new lawyer, one who will let June win.

'It's late,' I say. 'I should go.'

Tristan gets up, gently, so as not to wake Lenka. He doesn't ask me to stay. He walks me to the door.

'Where will you go?' Tristan asks the space above my head.

'Maybe I'll stay here. In Europe.'

He nods neutrally.

'The front door of the building is sometimes locked. If you get down there and it's locked come back up and I'll come down and let you out.'

'Maybe you should come down with me now?'

'It's usually open.'

'Can I see you tomorrow?'

'Not tomorrow.'

'The next day?'

'No. I don't know,' he says. 'Soon.'

'Goodnight, Tim.'

'Goodnight.'

I shake my son's hand. His handshake is a warning and a concession: he will not take care of me. Coiled violence, confusion. I didn't expect his eyes to meet mine but I wanted it, I needed it, and suddenly I can't control myself, because here I am finally holding him, touching him, and when he tries to pull his hand away I squeeze tighter. I clamp down. I will not let him go. He makes a small, shocked noise and there: his eyes finally meet mine. But I do not stop. I find myself crushing his hand with all the power I can muster, as hard as I can, my face and his getting red as he retaliates, squeezing my hand too, both of us, like arm wrestlers, enemies, our bones actually crunching, and his eyes becoming more red along with mine. He groans and I can't control the tears coming down my face. He opens his mouth to speak, to question. But I hold his hand and his fingers even harder, if possible, brutally grinding them, and I don't let go until he finally collapses into my arms. Shaking, weeping, 'I hate you, I hate you,' holding me, hugging me, and I hold him, telling him that everything is going to be all right, finally comforting this boy who is so much taller than me.

The way down is long. The light, which is on some kind of a timer, disappears before I'm halfway down. My footsteps echo more loudly in the dark, and I begin to breathe from my mouth. I cannot feel my right hand.

I'm in a tower. A castle. I'm back at The Abbey, a little boy again, sleepwalking: and it's all been a dream. Tomorrow the nuns will sing their daily offices and then, at breakfast, none of the other children will want to sit with me in case I sneeze and they get germs and their noses grow like mine. But I will come back, I will get married and come back and bring them all ice cream anyway. I reach the ground and walk towards the sound of automobiles. The door is locked.

I've got to go back and get my son to let me out. But I get halfway up the stairs and I stop. From Tim and Lenka's apartment I hear the music of Hildegard von Bingen – at first it's only a CD, our old favorite, *Feather on the Breath of God*. The chant leaks down the stairwell, a delicious fall of voices. I hear Tivona and the others in there. I hear Lonna.

Kitty laughing. June crying. Anna crying. Everyone I've ever known moaning all at once. I do not hum along. I listen and, instead of going up, slowly begin my descent. Step by hesitant step. There is something left for me in this dying century. My family is not history, and I will show them: we are happening now, right now, and will continue to happen all the time, forever, until it all stops.

I'm sitting on the bottom of the stairwell in complete darkness, waiting for what happens next, listening to my son listening to the music. In the blackness the chanting grows. It is quiet, hardly there, but it fills up space, then time. And I feel as though I am little Hildegard, alone in her anchorage, hearing the monks sing their daily offices. I touch the stone walls. I breathe. I remember the clunk of stone upon stone, the monks who sealed me in, their terrible faces, and I remember the family who left me here. Those aren't trams outside. It is a storm of mighty lashings, gnashing and rumble. Outside, the world is fallen, sinful. Here it is safe. Last rites have been said, so in essence I am already dead. I am an anchorite. If I die now I shall live eternally.

But no, there is another choice. Perhaps if I wait long enough they will come. The door cannot remain locked forever. Someone will take care of me, someone will help me. Someone always does. The door will open and I will be led *back into a world of temptations, filth, mistakes, risk. And they do let you out, eventually, and you take your first steps as an adult, away from the anchorage. The rain falls again on your face, and you let the snow melt on your fingers. Sometimes, when you look up, you still expect to see stone; and you laugh. How deep the sky is. How funny the little birds. You will found an Abbey, then another. One on either side of the river. You will be considered wise in the Holy Spirit, strong in the Holy Spirit. Your wisdom will grow, and with it your fame. Your name will be spoken by Popes and Emperors, by peasants, priests, merchants, and children. Hildegard von Bingen, they will call you, and you will travel far from home. But at night, sometimes, you wake and you are back in the anchorage again. You are dead again. You dream that the whole world is but an anchorage attached to heaven; and if you listen closely, you can still hear the music. Those divine sounds falling from above. You yearn with all your heart to go back. But not yet! There are still such miracles left to be performed! You will write down your strange, beautiful visions; and you will write down your music. You will heal the blind.*

Thank You

Joyce and Mike Bala, Lexy Bloom, Alex Bowler, Rob Dinsdale, Dan Franklin, Lucie Frütel, Lolies van Grunsven, Troy Giunipero, Peter Harmon, Jana Wodicka, Jeffrey Wodicka and Neil Castro, Lori Wodicka

And especially
Kevin Conroy Scott

And
Clare Wigfall